THE
LYONS DEN

THE
LYONS DEN

BETH L. BARNETT

PALMETTO
PUBLISHING
Charleston, SC
www.PalmettoPublishing.com

Paperback ISBN: 979-8-8229-4228-8

DEDICATION

TO MECHUL LION, 1811-1855, HIS FAMILY,
AND HIS DECENDANTS

ACKNOWLEDGEMENTS

Eight years ago, my cousin, Senior United States District Judge Howard Sachs, and I had a conversation about our family history that sparked the writer in me. Based on true facts, *The Lyons Den*, which follows the lives of my immediate family, begins in 1847 with the birth of Morris Lion. I'm told burial sites for Lions can be found as far back as 1541 but that was too big a project for me. I've used my imagination to fill in the parts I could not verify.

Andy Barnett, who liked "the business" but wasn't in line to own it, got me started by piquing my interest in M. Lyon & Co. My father, Leslie, passed away, and my brother, Lee, and his son, Mike, who helped me with details, sold the company. Both became well-known artists. Covid was upon us, so travel and libraries were out. The prospects of research didn't look good, but I learned how to use the internet.

So many kind and generous family and friends have helped me. Thanks first to Howard Sachs. He's been an invaluable resource. Also relatives Larry Burgheimer and Jonathon Lyon. Thanks to my son, Tom, a history buff, who encouraged me onward, and daughter, Lynn, who read every word more than once and helped with many revisions. Kudos to my patient husband who emboldened me before his untimely death, and Deborah Shouse, bless her, who struggled through most of my first attempts. Thanks to my writer's groups, the Homers and especially Sally Jadlow, and the Sedulous Writing Group, including Theresa Hupp, Jack Kline, Pemela Eglinski, Katie Arnett, Dane Zeller, excellent writers all, some of whom have been critiquing my work every week or two for the past twelve years.

I'd be remiss if I didn't mention my bridge bunch who understood I could only play one day a week, friends who waited until after five to call, and grands and great-grandchildren who wondered if I'd ever finish this project.

Well, yes! I'm done. It has been a great adventure. My hope is that generations to come will know a little bit more about their ancestors and are able to separate truth from bits of fiction.

IMMEDIATELY FAMILY

Mechul Lion (1811-1866) and his wife, Helena (ne Maier)
    Son: Morris Lion, wife Jetta
        Siblings: Kallmann, David, Karolina, Balbina, Jonas, Maria, Leonard
        Children: Lee, Charles, Eugene, Nell

Lee Lyon: Wife Anna
    Anna's siblings, Gertrude, Lily,
    Son: Leslie

Leslie Lyon: Wife Beth
    Son: Lee
    Daughter: Beth Louise

Theodore Lyon: Brother of Morris, First Wife Bertha
    Son: Bert
    Daughter Helen Jean
        Second wife: Hermine
        Father of Rose
            Mother of Howard Sachs

Bert Lyon: Cousin of Leslie, Husband of Helen
    Son: Theodore
    Jeanne

Second Wife Violet

TABLE OF CONTENTS

PART ONE

Chapter One
ETTENHEIM, GERMANY

1861

At 10 am, on May 24, 1861, the distant bells of the simu-
laneum east of town tolled the hour. The Bar Mitzvah
of thirteen-year-old Morris Lion began. After the lovely
service concluded, a young gentile, Aksel Schmidt, posed
a shocking question. Standing outside the synagogue on
the western slope of the Black Forest in the elfin town
of Ettenheim, Germany, he asked, "Why did the Jews
kill Jesus?"

Herr Schmidt, Aksel's father, cuffed his son harshly.

Until then, the Bar Mitzvah had gone well. Morris read his chosen
part of the holy bible in perfect Hebrew. Not once did he rubbed
his thumb and index finger together, a nervous habit his father abhorred.
Morris's brother, David, and all his younger brothers and sisters sat quietly through the long service. Even though the government forbade Jews
and non-Jews to associate, Morris's best friend, Aksel, and his Catholic
family had come from their farm to attend.

"It takes courage to ask such a question," Morris's father, Mechul,
said, stilling Herr Schmidt's hand. "What makes you think the Jews
killed Jesus?" he asked young Aksel.

"The choir boys say it is true."

Mechul touched the boy's golden hair and looked deep into the child's teary eyes. "I have great respect for your father," he said, and upon his good name would not lie. What you hear is a myth, a made-up story like Hansel and Gretel lost in the Black Forest near where you live. Do you not know Jesus was himself a Jew and very much loved by his people? Some even called him King of the Jews, but the Romans greatly feared him, and a corrupt and malevolent ruler named Pontius Pilate had him killed. That is the truth."

Wiping the tears from his eyes, Aksel stiffened his back and said, "Though they may beat me, I will tell the choir boys they are wrong."

When everyone had gone, Mechul sat on the steps of the synagogue. I should never have allowed Morris to invite the non-Jews, he thought. Had officials noticed, we might all have been thrown in jail.

As Morris's mother, Helena, and his brothers and sisters helped straighten the chairs upon which the attendees had sat, Morris noticed an advertisement under a chair, perhaps dropped from someone's pocket. He reasoned it must belong to one of Mechul's friends.

The next day Morris took it to his father's butcher shop where it might be claimed. There, he found his short, plump, redheaded Uncle Kallmann, five years older than Papa, helping to prepare the kosher beef in Mechul Lion's butcher shop. But today, an argument was in progress.

"You have priced the shoulder so high," Kallmann said to Mechul in Hebrew.

"The time we spend separating the fore-end from the rear and *traibering* the vessels makes the meat more expensive," Kallmann, an expert shochet, explained.

Morris knew that to be considered kosher, Jewish law required not a drop of blood to remain on the parts of the cow to be eaten.

"But," Kallmann exclaimed, kindness pouring from his heart, "The poor Jew cannot afford it, and his family must go meatless for days. I have a solution. I can make the hindquarters look like a shoulder with the banned parts removed."

Morris stood in the doorway, listening.

"Don't be a fool. The Torah forbids it," Mechul said in Hebrew.

"Without reason," Kallmann observed.

Mechul stopped what he was doing and placed his hands on his hips. Glaring at his brother, he spoke in his loud, authoritarian voice. "It is so written. That's the reason."

"But as a gift to a family…"

Morris began nervously rubbing his fingers together.

"First, even I, the best butcher in the territories of Baden, cannot remove all the blood vessels from the hindquarters, and second, it would be a sin against God."

The argument raged on, one crying out for mercy, the other for faith.

Red-faced Mechul slammed his cleaver on his butcher's block. "Have our parents birthed an idiot? Not a grain of sense lodges in your brain. Eating blood is far worse than eating pork. You would bring death upon the doer."

Kallmann's eyes burned into his brother. "Surely God did not mean for his people to starve."

"Who knows what God means?" Mechul roared in German, his face now purple with rage.

"But to never touch meat…" Kallmann pleaded quietly.

"Are you a fool? God commands you do not partake of the blood; for the blood is life, and you must not consume the life with the flesh."

Kallmann's shoulders drooped, and the edges of his mouth turned down. "Where is your heart, my brother?"

As Morris watched in fear and amazement, Kallmann picked up a discarded rear quarter and shook it at Mechul, blood spattering across the room. "I can make this piece of meat almost clean. I can cut it to look like a shoulder. Soak it in salt water. Who would know?"

"God would know!" cried Mechul in Hebrew. "My shop would be unclean. You would break the law of the Torah,". Raising his cleaver, he thundered, "Out! Out of this shop. You are no longer my brother."

Mouth agape, Kallmann dropped the bloody hindquarter and ran for the door.

"We are finished." Mechul yelled, raising a foot to his brother's rear, and slamming the door behind him with such force it rattled the walls.

He turned and looked at Morris, the anger still in his voice. "What are you doing here?"

"I…Nothing-*klum davar*," the boy whispered in Hebrew and ran home with the advertisement still in his pocket. That night, afraid, he hid the flyer in his mattress.

A few days later, Mechul gave Kallmann's Jaeger Flintlock rifle to Morris. "You will find it steady and true, short-barreled, and lightweight," Morris's father said, "and my brother doesn't live here any longer, so he won't be using it."

Morris knew to ask no questions. He took the gun and ran his hand down the stock to the barrel before lifting the weapon gently to his shoulder. It fit him perfectly. He gathered black powder and lead balls and began practicing in the rock range of the town's quarry. When he was able to load and fire effortlessly, Mechul took him to the Schwarzwald to hunt. No one spoke of Kallmann again.

Morris loved wending his way through the spruce and beech tree forest but grew to hate going there with Papa. "Point your gun barrel down. Load quickly, noiselessly. Adjust your sight a smidgen high and to the right. See what a difference that makes? Aim accordingly." His orders shattered Morris's concentration and the hushed silence of the forest.

Still, the boy became an excellent shot because of Papa's constant nagging, usually needing but one bullet to bring down his prey. He could drop a chamois at fifty yards. An apt student, Morris quickly discerned the ways of the animals with the most prized coats—hare, badger, red deer, bushy-tailed foxes, and martins, all of which flourished in the Black Forest. Morris especially coveted the chamois, whose soft, flexible hide was the most prized of the leather industry. His father taught him how to field dress the animals and preserve their fur and hides in a manner that would bring the highest prices, and Papa let him keep a few of the silver vereinstaler coins from the sale.

As Morris grew older—fifteen, sixteen, seventeen—heavier, and as tall as his father, he balked at future instructions. On a day near his eighteenth birthday, when, according to family tradition, he would become a man, he rebelled.

"Lower your shoulder. Relax your thumb, raise your gun slowly with almost no motion," Mechul barked.

Uncontrollably fractious, Morris threw his Jaeger to the ground. The explosion that ensued shook the forest. With horror and dismay, Morris realized how close the bullet had come to his father's head. "Oh my God, Papa. I am sorry," he cried, his heart pounding.

Mechul stiffened his back, turned on his heel, and stalked out of the forest.

"Father! Stop! Please! I said I'm sorry," Morris cried, running after him.

Mechul kept walking, shoulders thrown back, head held proud.

"Father." Morris reached out and touched his father's shoulder. "What more do you want? It won't happen again. It was an accident."

The father shook off his son's hand and continued his march.

Fury replaced Morris's fright. *Damn!* Stubborn old fool. Good riddance. I can go it alone, he murmured to himself. Rubbing his fingers together, he watched his father disappear amongst the stately beech trees. Then he retrieved his gun, reloaded it, and continued his hunt.

At day's end, he had taken a red buck with many points, field-dressed it, and hauled its antlers and choicest parts home. The silvery moon hung high over the woods when he put his bounty in the field house and went to the kitchen. His mother had left out bread and cheese for his dinner. Grateful, he ate and then went to bed. As he slipped into the sweet nothingness of sleep, his anger dissipated, and father's shocked face appeared in his mind's eye. He shuttered and blinked it away as a regrettable blunder.

In the morning, family rumblings awakened him to a new day. "You missed supper," Theodore said in his high, squeaky voice, "and I ate your portion." He was eleven years younger than Morris.

"I ate what little you left," Morris joked, motioning to all his chattering brothers and sisters. "Good morning, Father," he said, his anger slept away. "I got a deer after you left. It is in the field house." Morris smiled proudly. "Perhaps we can prepare it together."

"Today, I go to Haigerloch to visit Silverstein," Papa said. By tradition, the oldest boy in the family often accompanied his father on long journeys to farms and auctions where they procured hides and wool sheered from the sheep. When the farmers needed money or credit, Mechul would become a lender for which he charged a fair rate of interest, never more than the bank. It took a quick mind and mathematical abilities that Morris had inherited.

"David, you will come with me."

Surely, their father spoke in jest. "Papa? Morris said in a teasing voice. "We could take the deer as a gift to Herr Silverstein, and I could brag to his son." Jonas, Maier Silverstein's son, and Morris had grown up together. They were as close as brothers, born days apart in the spring of 1847, and though living in different towns, they often traveled together with their fathers.

The room had gone suddenly quiet. Helena stood stiffly motionless at the kitchen sink. The children's eyes moved silently from one to another. Something was happening, and it had happened before. Father had quit speaking to one of them for some large or small infraction.

"We need to be gone," Papa ordered. "Gather your things, David, while I ready the mule."

"Yes, Vater," David grinned, though his narrowing green eyes looked wary.

Morris understood. Still upset from yesterday's misdeed, the old man was punishing Morris. It was his way of exerting his power and diminishing the victim. Kallmann served as a cruel reminder.

Even though Mechul and Morris brushed by each other in the small kitchen and ate at the same table, the father spoke not a word to his son.

As the days passed, Papa continued to ignore Morris. The other children shot guarded glances but dared not interfere. Even Mama seemed unable to help.

"You should stop this," they heard her whisper to her husband. "Genug iz genug." (Enough is enough.)

But Papa continued the silent treatment, taking one of the other boys on his selling trips while leaving Morris at home.

One night as he lay on his bed nursing bitter frustration, he remembered the little advertisement he had hidden there years before. Was it still there? His mother often plumped up the children's mattresses and refilled them with fresh straw. He found a small hole through which he could stick his hand. With little hope, he felt and found nothing. With one final grab at a tightly woven corner, his fingers touched a crinkled piece of paper. Carefully retrieving it, he stared at the flyer he'd found at his Bar Mitzvah five years before.

New and Elegant Light Draught Passenger Steamer

The picture of the steamboat retained all its color, the blue of the sea, the ocean liner red with blooming white sails.

Bound for St Louis-New Orleans
United States of America
Via: Murphy Shipping Line

The names of the American cities enchanted him and filled him with wonder. He had never heard the names of the cities, but he found them in the dusty copy of the synagogue's encyclopedia. Cities in the United States.

The next time Mechul took David to visit Maier Silverstein, Morris told David to ask Jonas to meet him in the Black Forest.

"My father has not spoken a word to me in over three weeks," Morris told Jonas when they met under the dark green conifers.

"I knew something happened when he appeared with David. Lord be with you. That's harsh punishment," Jonas said. "What did you do?"

Morris told his friend how he'd dropped the gun, and it went off.

"God's blessing you didn't kill him or yourself." Jonas bowed his head. "Did you apologize?"

"Yes, of course, but he wants me to grovel."

"So, grovel," Jonas said.

"No," Morris answered. "But I will try to explain one more time. Perhaps he will forgive me as a birthday gift."

"Ah, yes. We will soon be eighteen."

"It is time we leave this country." How often had they spoken of Jewish conditions in Germany, unable to buy land, poor because their fathers were heavily taxed, taunted by gentile girls, and beaten by Christian boys? They were treated like second-class citizens because they were Jews. In America, no one cared what God you worshiped, or so they had heard.

"I can hardly wait. Have you told your father?"

"Not yet, but I have a plan. Are you still willing?" Morris asked his friend.

"More than ever," the tall sliver of a boy answered with his power in words. Today, he told Morris how a Jew-hating bully had tripped him and held him to the ground unless he promised to write his school paper.

"Did you agree?" Morris asked.

"What else could I do?" Jonas answered.

"I would have killed the bastard," Morris said.

But Jonas shook his head. "'VENGEANCE IS MINE,' sayeth the Lord," and the boy paused to laugh, "even though He sometimes takes His own sweet time about it."

"It may be God's way, but it is not mine," Morris muttered.

Jonas nodded and sat on the stump of an elm tree. "Does your plan include hunting for gold? I've heard there are treasures to be found. And what of your girlfriend, Jette?"

"We will find gold and buy land and own our own business. I will send for and marry Jette, and you will find a beauty to wed. Soon, we will shed this fettered place for the New World." Morris withdrew the wrinkled picture and put it back in his pocket for safekeeping.

Jonas's eyes shone, though his heart trembled with fear.

Chapter Two
ETTENHEIM, GERMANY

1865

Near the end of his route, Morris could see the small, brown, and white Hinterwald cows lazily grazing on the green plateaus. Many years before, the breed had been found to adapt well to the mountainous terrain. They produced good meat, rich milk, and stout, hardy hides. Nearby, the easy-going independent Merinolandschaf sheep nibbled on the grasses, their fine wool used for much-admired clothing.

"Hurry up, Willie," Morris said, giving a tug on the rope tied around his pokey little donkey's neck. Now a wiry boy of eighteen years, five feet six inches tall, muscular, and strong, he hurried the animal along. "I'm going to be hungry as a bear by the time we arrive at the Schmidt farm." The boy clung to his hopes of being invited to share a meal with the family. He had never eaten a non-kosher meal, but he and Jonas had decided keeping kosher in America would be impossible. But Morris wondered if God would strike him dead, for God had decreed Moses write the dietary laws long before the birth of Jesus, and Christians didn't do kashrut.

Aksel's father, Hendrich Schmidt, was a farmer and a longtime customer of Mechul Lion. Neither man had any formal education, but both saw to it that their children, ten in all, attended the school in town.

Today was the Jewish Sabbath, but Morris gave no thought to it as he and his mule transported the hides of the animals his father had slaughtered.

The little creature resisted, for he carried hundreds of pounds of animal skins. But he lowered his head and plodded wearily on as though he understood his place in the world. Together, the donkey and boy emerged from the haunting forest.

They tramped down the grassy knoll to a frame house nestled near the flourishing lower pasture. Morris meant to deliver the hides and collect three cows his father had purchased from Herr Schmidt. He also intended to bid farewell to Aksel. The boys had hunted together, swam in the cold waters of Lake Wilsee, and frolicked in the waterfall fed by the runoff from the hills. But today might be the last time they ever saw one another.

Aksel's mutter asked Morris to share a meal with the family. Fraught with angst and unable to stop rubbing his fingers together, Morris joined Aksel and his family at their table.

He ate the thick, juicy beef, the barley soup, and the dark bread Aksel's mother provided, apprehension bubbling in his veins. Worried each bite would be his last, he washed it down with Herr Schmidt's delicious full-bodied beer. And when later laughter rang round the table, now certain he would survive, Morris's was the loudest.

Breathing a sigh of relief, he thanked God for allowing him to live. With sorrow, he bid a final farewell to his friend. "Jonah and I will leave for America in the morning," Morris told Aksel. "The ship is to sail in five days."

"How I wish I could go with you," Aksel said.

Giving Aksel a final hug, he gathered the three cows, took the rope of his donkey, and headed North to visit Jette.

She lived in Eichstetten, a small village on the Alte Dreisam River near the Schwarzwald. There, her father owned a vegetable and meat market store. Would she wait for him to make his fortune in America? Morris hurried Willy and the cows along.

He arrived at her cottage in the fading light of the evening's soft summer glow. His smile grew wide when he saw her, a slim girl of fifteen years, a dark-haired beauty. She sat on her porch with Ricka, her oldest sister. When Jette saw Morris, she rushed to greet him, hands clasping his. Together, they strolled the banks of the Dreisam to the small lake and the flowing waterfall. As was the custom, Ricka, married to a university professor with children of her own, followed at a discreet distance.

"This will be our last evening before I leave for America," Morris told her, and her sobs tugged at his heart.

Ignoring Ricka's gentle rebukes, Jette flung herself into Morris's arms. "How can I go on living without you?" she asked, tears sliding down her cheeks.

"I will send for you as soon as I can, and then we will marry."

Wiping her tears, Jette sighed. "Mind your manners and your temper," she counseled, for she knew Morris better than his own mother.

"No fraternizing with the seminary boys," he teased as he held her close under the silvery moon.

Their lips touched in a sweet, sad farewell. "Will you wait?" he asked.

"If you don't take too long," she answered in her saucy way and then said, "Wir werden dich vermissen." "I will miss you."

"I will miss you, too, but the truth is, Germany is not a good place for Jews, Jette."

"And in America?" she asked, a canny expression on her face.

"I believe there is a great opportunity, and I will prosper."

"Then I will join you," his sweet fiancé said with a longing farewell kiss.

Morris trusted his mother had prepared a healthy meal. He could imagine her ample figure bustling about the kitchen, a faded blue scarf holding back her graying hair. He hurried Willy along, anxious to feed and release him, tether the cows, and greet Maria, who ran toward him with outstretched arms. She always expected a gift from his travels, and he had one for her this time: a bag of acorns he had gathered in the Black Forest from beneath the towering oak trees. He knew she would plant them, and if not eaten by the squirrels, she would nurse them into growth.

As he entered, he touched his fingers to the bronze mezuzah holding the Sacred Sh'ma prayer and nailed to the doorpost of the house. Then he greeted his brothers and sisters. Karl, the brilliant one, was five years older, studious, a reader, and the best at writing. He worked as a scribe for the rabbi in Stuttgart but had journeyed home for a visit. Then came David, two years younger than Morris but irresponsible and capricious, his brown hair an unruly mass of irrepressible waves that shone red in the sun. He was followed by Karoline, mischievous in thought and behavior. Behind her, Balbina, whose long dark braids reached her waist, set to wed the shopkeeper's son on the Saturday after Yom Kippur. Then, little Maria and Jonas, and finally Theodore, the baby of the family. He appeared to be the most serious of all. Hopefully, he will someday assume his role as a responsible male.

On the Sabbath eve of his eighteenth birthday, Morris sought out his father one last time. Rubbing his fingers together, he said, "Papa, please. Can we talk?"

In the little room Mechul called his study, he turned his eyes to his son. "If I were to agree, what would you say?" he asked.

Gathering his courage, Morris began to speak the words he had rehearsed in the event his father agreed to listen. "Tomorrow," he began, "I shall turn eighteen. Jonas and I have saved enough money to purchase births on a ship leaving Amsterdam for America." He stopped to let the full impact of those words take effect.

Mechul bolted upright. "America?" he said.

"But I don't want to leave you like this. Two grown men should be able to come to an understanding. I bitterly regret what happened in the forest. I could have killed you, and I would have gladly died in your stead. Now I pray for your blessing, and I hope my success in the new world will make you eternally proud."

To Morris's surprise, a smile spread across his father's face, and a laugh erupted from his belly. "So is this the way you choose to tell me you are leaving? What kind of a son have I raised? So big a secret to keep to yourself. For this, I make an exception. I will forgive you for almost killing me and taking the Lord's name in vain. Your bravery in coming here speaks volumes, but this is your only chance. Never disappoint me again."

Morris breathed a sigh of relief and then told Mechul the plans he and Jonas had made.

Mechul grew pensive. "I won't stand in your way but think carefully about your decision. Emancipation for the Jews in Germany appears eminent, so it might behoove you to stay. Things will get better for our people," Mechul said confidently. "I will buy the shop I now rent, and you and your brothers will learn to be shochets. We will sell the meat you butcher for a fair price, and the vegetables your mother and your sisters grow. We might even earn enough to start a vineyard. I will need many reliable pairs of hands."

"I wish you luck," Morris said, but he wanted no part of Germany's antisemitism. How often had he heard the story of Mechul's impoverished Jewish father, Kallmann Senior, and his daily struggle to feed his starving family of eight girls and two boys? How, one by one, he had increased his customer base, herded his animals, pulled a wagon filled with barley and corn, and lent money to his customers—and how he'd died at an early age, exhausted and owning nothing but the clothes on his back?

"When do you plan to leave?"

"Jonas will meet me at the ferry on Monday. Our ship, *Deamonti*, sails from Amsterdam five days later."

"So soon. What's the rush?"

"We are eighteen, father. We are men. We've made plans."

"I see," Mechul murmured in Yiddish. "This then will be our final chat." He brushed at his bushy beard that reached the third button of his shirt. Smiling, he placed his hand on his son's head. "If you love God and pray to Him, He'll take care of you."

Morris realized he was leaving his mother, father, and home forever, and suddenly, tears clouded his eyes.

"Now, follow my instructions carefully. Once you get to America, do not speak Yiddish. Speak only German or French as a Westerner does."

Brushing at his tears, Morris asked, "Why do they hate us, Father? The Christians. Not Aksel, of course. He is my friend."

Mechul gave a great sigh. "Even Aksel thinks of you as different, my son. It's complicated. Christians view Jesus as their savior, whereas we believe the Messiah is yet to come. For many years, Jews have been treated poorly and frequently jailed. Blood Libels, Christ-killers, they call us. All myths. Be prepared. I predict you will find prejudice in the new land, too. It is the gentile way of separating themselves from us."

"But why do they single us out?" Morris persisted. "We look the same as them. Are we a different race, as Aksel's father says?"

"It is our beliefs which separate us. There is only one God. We honor Him by reciting the Sh'ma in the morning upon rising and at night before rest. We circumcise our sons, the covenant between God and the Jews. We observe the laws of kashrut because it is what the Torah tells us."

"I've been thinking about that," Morris said, averting his eyes. "On the Sabbath, Aksel's family and I broke bread together."

Mechul stiffened and glared at his son. "Why would you do such a thing? It is forbidden."

"Tomorrow, Papa, I go into a non-kosher world. If I was meant to die, I wanted to do it at home."

"Now, only your mind will be poisoned," an ugly rebuke. "Keeping kashrut is God's way of reminding you to do good and be a good person." Mechul rose and went to the mantel where the old brown pottery tobacco jar sat. "Lacking the daily hints, you must diligently say the words of God.

Sh'ma Yisrael Adonai Eloheinu Adonai Eḥad:
Hear, O Israel: the LORD is our God, the LORD is One."

Morris had said this prayer twice a day for as long as he could remember so he could be forgiven for letting his mind wander as his father finished the quotation.

"And You shall write them on the doorposts of your house
and on your gates.

*And these words that I command you today shall be in
your heart."*

Mechul withdrew a tiny carving from the tobacco jar, a small mezuzah made of sturdy oak. It contained a parchment upon which sacred words from Deuteronomy, the Sh'ma, were written.

*"Praise to You, Adonai our God, Sovereign of the universe,
who hallows us with mitzvot, commanding us to affix the
mezuzah."*

He handed it to Morris. "When you arrive in America, place this on the doorpost of your home, wherever that may be, and God will be with you," he said. "I have managed to save a little." He dug to the bottom of the tobacco jar. "A few gulden will keep you fed for a while. Guard your money carefully. The world is full of thieves."

On Morris's last night at home, he packed his few belongings and ate the evening meal with his parents, brothers, and sisters. Supper was large for an evening meal but made in honor of his departure. His mother had prepared chopped liver, a fat beef roast his father had brought from his butcher shop, and savory vegetables with dark rye bread. The night brought sadness as they wished their brother well.

In the morning, as the sun began its ascent over the rickety chicken coop, Morris's mother hung a small silver star of David around his neck along with a tightly sewn money pouch she'd made from the skin of a chamois.

David threw his arms around Morris and, sobbing, beseeched, "When can I come?

"As soon as I've saved enough to bring you," Morris said, his brothers' and sisters' forlorn faces burned into his mind.

He hugged his mother, kissed her cheek, and, with gentle fingers, wiped her tears. "I love you," he whispered as he etched each line of her face into his memory.

Chapter Three
AMSTERDAM

MAY 1866

Jonas joined Morris on the short, well-worn trail to the Rhine. Half a head taller but only five pounds heavier, Jonas grinned his crooked smile and adjusted the haversack strapped to his back. The path took them through the rich green valley filled with fertile vineyards, and they playfully called greetings in French and German to the workers trimming the vines. The boys had traveled the dirt road dozens of times herding their fat Hinterwald cows to load on a barge for the trip on the Rhine to the slaughterhouses in Hamburg.

When barge owner Rudolph Eigersteim, a mountain of a man with big arms and short, sturdy legs, caught sight of the boys, he waved and called an affectionate greeting. "I've no room for lazy Jews today. I've got paying customers on board."

The boys laughed. "We've no cows with us because we're off to America," Morris responded in French.

Rudolph's grin was as big as his biceps. "America, is it? Alors qu'allez-vous y faire? So what will you do there?"

"Make our fortunes," Morris boasted.

"Well, come aboard then," Rudolph called with a sweeping gesture. "I've got three mädchens set for shopping. You'll be good company for them when I don't need one or the other of you to steer the boat."

Morris and Jonas took turns – one helped to guide the sixty-meter barge toward Strasburg and Cologne while the other entertained the girls.

Jonas settled comfortably in their midst and told them stories until it was his turn to man the oar. Morris stood at the rail, watching the beautiful river meander between France and Germany through lush fields and vineyards. He told stories of the passing castles and their owners to the cluster of fascinated young females. "Someday, I will be rich enough to own one of those fine castles," he boasted to their swooning.

Though the river was calm, the boys' arms ached from manning the big, long oar. They were glad to jump ashore when the captain steered the barge into the dock at the tiny village of Speyer.

"I have urgent business here," the sailor said, eyeing a riverside brasserie. "Keep an eye out for robbers roaming the Rhine."

"I want to come with you," Morris said. "It will be my first time in a real bistro."

"I'll rest and entertain the ladies while you are gone," Jonas offered, saying he'd enjoy the company of the chattering damsels.

But when Rudy and Morris returned, they found Jonas struggling with three drunk and lascivious hoodlums. The frightened madchens were screaming, and Jonas, unused to defending himself, had tried to protect them but had been knocked unconscious.

Rudy, with his beefy fists, and Morris, lithe and agile, made quick work of the sleazy thieves, tossing them unceremoniously into the Rhine.

Returning to Jonas, Morris began ministrations, but he needn't have bothered. The young ladies pushed him aside and swarmed Jonas, their fallen hero, with hugs and dabs of cold clothes to his battered face, marking the whole nasty affair to high adventure.

With much fanfare and grateful kisses, they coerced Morris into escorting them to Cologne, a colorful place to shop. Jonas, bruised and still aching, didn't make it off the barge until finally docking at the busy port of Amsterdam.

After five days, it was near dusk when Rudy expertly threaded the barge through the jumble of ocean liners, boats, and buoys to a pier and dark before they got the barge unloaded. Morris had seen a few small ports on the Rhine but never anything like Amsterdam. The harbor teamed with all sizes of steam and sailing ships, all shapes of barges, and a variety of private ocean crafts, large and small. "How will we find our ship to America?"

"We'll ask," Jonas said with an easy shrug.

Rudy led them to Der Sigler, a pub on the pier filled with "just off the ship" hungry, thirsty seamen. The captain offered to buy the two boys a good meal before they left for America, saying they'd earned it. Both boys gratefully accepted, their jaws tired from chewing the barge meals of dried meat.

Nudging a place at the bar for the three of them, the captain ordered beer all around. Jonas grabbed the stein set before him. He managed a considerable swallow but, with a startled glare of distress, vomited it back up. Clearly his first taste of beer, "Time ye learned to be a drinking man," the captain said, clapping him on the back.

A bearded sailor with a worn gray coat and weathered cap appeared behind the captain and encircled him with big arms.

"Dutch, ye old bastard," Rudy cried out in joy. "Good to see you. You just off the ship?"

"Aye, and a hard voyage it was. Twenty-one months at sea on a three-master. I'll not sail on another without steam," he said. "And who might you be?" He gave Jonas a poke.

"Meet my young friends from down south," the captain said, introducing them both. "They're off to America on the *Deamonti*."

"A four-masted steamer," the bearded man nodded. "She's docked at Pier Seven, ready to shove off. It's a long, hard voyage you're facing," he said, lifting his eyebrows at the boys. "You're in steerage, I presume."

"We took passage in the tween deck," Morris said. "a good birth and affordable, we're told."

"Indeed," said the seaman with raised eyebrows and a slight shake of his head. "Well then, have a good trip. Now, if you don't mind, I'm dragging your captain, piece of crap that he is, off to a place we can chat? You can join us if you like," Dutch said, "but we'll be boring you with old times, I'm afraid." He held up two fingers to the barkeep and guided Rudy to a nearby wood table.

Jonas tagged along, but loath to intrude, Morris remained at the bar where he listened to the conversation around him.

A small, sly-eyed fellow with a slim, black mustache dressed in business attire leaned an elbow on the bar and said to the sailor on his right, "The ship's steerage is full of them poor emigrants, more than two hundred and fifty in all. That captain had me charge them sixteen gulden a head and four more for rations. Gives me eight gulden for each one I sign up." He smirked.

A shyster, Morris thought, rubbing his thumb and index fingers together. He and Jonas had paid only ten gulden for tween deck passage and meals for the trip.

"I've sailed on one of them emigrant ships," the man on his right said. "Stinks so bad, you can't draw a breath." He wrinkled his face and downed his whiskey.

"The ship is shoving off tomorrow, and for them that lives, it'll be weeks a 'fore they see land again." The salesman reached into his vest pocket and withdrew a coin. Slapping it on the bar, he said, "Headed for New Orleans, she is, and she'll be the last passenger vessel sailing to America for the next two or three months, so I need to watch my pennies."

Aided by the second beer he'd downed, Morris gathered his fortitude and tapped the man on his shoulder, "What's the name of the ship?" he asked.

"That would be the *Deamonti*," the man answered. "You headed for America?"

"I am," he said, feeling gay and chatty. "I'll be aboard when we sail tomorrow."

The salesman turned toward Morris, a smile on his face. "You look like a hardworking lad. Let me buy you another beer," he said.

Morris nodded happily and said, "I heard you talking. Is the ship as bad as you say?"

"Nah," the business-dressed man laughed. "It's just overcrowded. "Trust me. She's a worthy vessel and as safe as can be. Tell me, why are you going to America?"

"To make my fortune," Morris answered his words a bit slurry.

"I can make your trip easier if you've got an extra pfennig or two. I've got one second-class cabin left. Sleeps two."

Morris prided himself on knowing a good thing when he heard it and quickly decided the cabin sounded preferable to the tween deck.

"How much?" Morris asked, jauntily reaching beneath his shirt for his money pouch.

"Only thirty gulden."

"My friend and I already possess third-class tickets," he said. "We'd like to exchange them and the difference for your second-class ticket."

"A wise choice," the salesman said. Morris pulled his purse from beneath his shirt and withdrew enough silver coins to match the amount to pay for a ticket for Jonas and himself and enough left over for another beer in the bargain.

Suddenly, the burly sailor grabbed Morris by the shoulder and yanked the purse from around his neck.

Cursing, Morris went for his pouch, but the burly seaman held it above his head.

Sobering quickly, Morris flung a well-placed knee to the sailor's groin and lunged for his money. The seaman doubled over and came up swinging.

"Fight," someone yelled, and a space opened around them.

Dutch and Rudy rushed to the scene. Morris was no match for the well-muscled seafaring sailor, but in short order, Dutch soon flattened the intruder, retrieved the money pouch, and escorted the slovenly seaman out the door. Morris lay bleeding on the sand-strewn floor.

Jonas knelt and dabbed at his friend's bloody nose.

"Come on, Bube," Rudy said, helping him rise.

"I could have taken him, but he caught me unawares," Morris said, cradling his aching head.

"I'll say this. You've got moxie," Dutch said. "You and your buddy are gonna need it. I've a date with my lovey, and I must be away, but good luck on your trip." He gave Rudy a half salute and disappeared into the crowd.

Morris wiped the blood from his mouth and looked furtively for the agent, but he had disappeared along with the bought and paid for a second-class ticket. He'd been hoodwinked. There probably was no second-class cabin available, but he still had his tween deck ticket, and so did Jonas.

"From now on, hide your money in your shoe," Rudy said as he ruffled the boy's hair. "Tomorrow, you board the *Deamonti*, but tonight, we spend on pleasure."

They dined on crisply fried fish and chunky chips, a treat for boys used to boiled beef and cabbage, and after a refreshing second and third round of beer from the tap, they left the bar together. "We've time for a trip to De Wallen," Rudy said, beckoning them to follow.

"A wall?" a stumbling Jonas asked. "What can there possibly be at a wall?

"Sweet treats for the eyes and other parts," the captain said, eyes twinkling. As they walked next to the busy canal lined with well-lit taverns and distilleries, the boys saw small houses with partly drawn curtains. Morris's eyes lingered on a particular front window, but Jonas quickly turned away, for a scantly clothed woman stood inside. "Did you see that?" he whispered to the captain. "She should draw her drapes."

Rudy laughed. "They have their reasons," he said as they passed another window where a fair girl posed in diaphanous attire. She knocked on the window, beckoning them to join her.

"Where are we?" asked Morris, eyes widening.

"Where sailors take delight following dreary months at sea. For a few gulden, the lovelies will please you in ways you can only imagine. Pick one and have a last fling before you go," he called over his shoulder. "As for me, I have plans of my own," he said and vanished down a narrow alleyway.

Morris had longed for many months to make love to his beautiful Jette, but it was impossible until they were married. Now, with beers in his belly and a swelling in his pants, he yearned for the tender touch of a woman. Imagining himself in Jette's loving arms, he was drawn relentlessly to a beckoning door.

Jonas shied away from those beckoning eyes. With a bit of hesitance and a wobbly turn, he made his way back to the barge, where he gathered his belongings and fell drunk onto a hard bunk.

Chapter Four

THE DEAMONTI

30 MAY 1866

Up before daybreak, Jonas rousted an exhausted Morris out of bed. Together, they rushed to Pier Seven to board the German-staffed *Deamonti*. They slung their packs across their shoulders and bounded aboard, Jonas barely making the transition from land to walkway. A single-stem vessel with two steam funnels and four sail masts, the ship rode low in the water, her gangplank about to be raised.

The first mate greeted them at the rail and hastily took their tickets. He pointed to the hatch that led below. Excited, the boys mingled with the other passengers and watched as the sailors weighed anchor, cast off, and climbed aloft to unfurl the topsails. With creaks and groans, the ship threaded through the harbor and out to sea. It tilted to port as several hundred men, women, and children crowded the rails for a last glimpse of their homeland.

"Fools!" said an odoriferous heavyset man of medium build in his middling years. "Those in steerage will wish they'd never come aboard before this journey is done."

"Why do you say that?" Morris asked, turning to stare at the person who spoke.

"You'll see when you get below deck," the man answered, pointing to the hatch, "but for me, even the tween deck will be far better than that filthy German jail I've just escaped." He sniffed and wiped his runny nose on his wrinkled sleeve.

"And why were you there?" Morris asked.

"My own fault," the man said in German. "Comes from serving poor Jews. Broke the Sunday Law, I did. I stayed open till all hours so the poor souls could get their needs from my store, but time and again, the politicos closed me down and locked me up. Day before yesterday, they caught me yet again, dumb Jew that I am, but this time was different. 'GUNTER SHECHTER,' they yelled, and nearby people turned to stare. 'Obey the rules or next time, we will beat you, throw you into prison, and toss away the key.' They gave me these whacks to prove it." He pointed at his blood-matted gray hair and an ugly, dark bruise beneath his right eye.

"That did it. I decided it was time to leave, even if only on this bloody dreg of a ship."

"Dreg, is it?" Morris said. "We heard she's seaworthy and a luxury liner at that. We paid our hard-earned gulden to obtain passage."

"Someone sold you a bill of goods. She's a leaky, old pile of junk that's been afloat for thirty-some-odd years, but God willing, she'll make it for one more crossing."

"If she's so bad, why did you choose her?"

"Because she's sailing today." Gunter laughed. "If you're in steerage and you expect to get a berth, you'd best get a move on," and he made for the hatch.

"Our tickets say tween deck, Morris said, unsure where that was.

It came as a jolt when Gunter, joining the herd of people, called back, "Same thing as steerage."

That was a word the boys understood.

An edge taken off their excitement, Morris and Jonas made their way down the hatch. The only light came from the open door through which they descended and from between the adjacent outlying boards. Before they'd taken their first step, they heard a cacophony of people sounds, men, women, and children, excited cries of berth acquisitions and belongings stowed. With a hint of dread, Morris led the way.

What met his eyes gave him pause—the ship's hold had been converted from storage to habitation with row upon row of berths. A thin table stretched down the middle with a small space overhead for meager belongings.

Jonas helped a rawboned woman struggling with luggage, and she gave him a toothy smile. Old men hobbled in the aisle, grasping whoever or whatever they could to steady themselves. Husbands with wives and fathers with children strove to get everyone settled and claim berths for their clan, sometimes as many as six or eight bodies in a space meant for four.

As the clamoring crowd carried Jonas and Morris toward the rear, a hand reached out and snagged them—Gunter, his foot on a low bed of straw. "Judging by the mob, we'll be doubling up," he yelled. "Let's grab this berth before others can claim it."

Repelled by the thought of sharing a bed with this foul-smelling lout, Morris shook his head and pushed on, but Jonas stayed. "I don't think we will find anything better."

"It's hardly big enough for one, much less three," Morris cautioned.

"We can sleep head to toe," Gunter said, "and one can stay to guard it when the others leave."

"No," Morris cried. The thought of Gunter's feet in his face disgusted him. He tried to pull away but banged his head on the low-hanging shelf.

"You won't find anything better. You can trust me on that," Gunter said as he blew his nose into his dirty handkerchief.

"Let's take it," Jonas said, tossing his pack on the straw. "We can look for something better later."

Morris acceded and tested the berth for comfort. "Worse than the donkey's stall in my father's barn."

A seaman slid down the hatch and brought a cone-shaped device to his lips. "Listen up," he yelled through the gadget, which amplified his words. "Your captain sends greetings."

The crowd gave a roar.

"Evening meals will be served on the wooden tables in the aisle."

"We can't hear you," someone called.

"You can if you shut up," the seaman yelled, and a hush fell over the throng.

"Line up for your chance at the beef, fish, and potatoes, but lay by what you can," he warned, "for near the end of the trip, supper may well turn to porridge."

Curses and groans met his words.

"Now gimme your ears," he continued. "There are only two heads available, bathrooms to ye landlubbers—one fore and one aft atop deck. Ladies will do well to take someone with them to guard the door when in use, for there will not likely be much privacy." He nodded at a pretty, guileless maiden, her braids wound tightly around her head.

"When on deck, walk close to the rails," the sailor continued, "and don't wander past your destination. If you are swept overboard, no one will turn back to look for you. Captain's orders," he added. "Any questions?"

"What time were meals served?"

"6 bells, 11, and 15."

"Where do we get water, and where can we cook?"

Morris pushed through the mass of humanity to the hatch and scrambled past the seaman up the ladder. Now on deck, he stood a bit wobbly, the ship plowing through the lapping waves.

As a fresh breeze brushed his face, Jonas joined him at the rail. His mouth twisted in a sad little smile. "Not exactly what you expected, I'm guessing."

Morris sighed as he watched the countryside disappear.

Jonas placed an arm over Morris's shoulder. "We'll only be on this Godforsaken ship for a matter of days, and then we'll be in America."

The shapes on the shores faded, the sun high in the sky. When they could no longer see land, they walked aft to the quarterdeck from which they could oversee the entire ship. A gentle breeze puffed up her square sails and propelled her out to sea, alone in the vast ocean.

Below, the gray waters rippled, and the ship forged ahead, driven by the wind in the topsails. Jonas stumbled and caught hold of the foremast. Morris saw him lean against the stout timber and appear to try and steady himself.

"That's Dover to starboard," a young sailor said. He pointed a grimy finger to the shore. Gleaming white cliffs rose from the dark waters as the ship sailed on, carried by the wind in the canvas and the steam-propelled blades. "We'll go through the English Channel and into the Atlantic Ocean. Best you boys get your sea legs afore then." He clapped Morris on the back and went about his duties.

With the sea calm, they made their way past a lounge where a sign on the door announced dining for first-and second-class citizens. Elegantly dressed passengers strolled from their cabins beneath the poop deck, but steerage passengers were turned away by a slender young woman wearing a white waiter's coat buttoned up the middle and a starched white scarf covering her hair.

Morris attempted to pat down his rumpled jacket. With a bit of manufactured confidence, he waved as he strolled by the girl.

Silently, she studied his face and his garb.

"Morris," he whispered, pointing a jaunty finger to his chest.

"Giselle," she answered with a quick little wink.

"Move along before you get her fired," a voice behind him commanded, and he turned to see the handsomely uniformed first mate palming a baton. "Waitresses ain't allowed to talk to the passengers, so stay away from her," he said, "and ye both get below deck where ye belong."

Jonas headed toward the tween deck hatch as instructed. "Let it go," he murmured, tugging at his friend's sleeve.

"Best listen to your friend," the first mate said, brandishing the stick, and grudgingly, Morris swallowed his pride and followed Jonas. As they passed the open salon door, the boys stared at the trays of fare and fresh edibles. "Only boiled meat and potatoes in steerage," the first mate called acerbically. For Morris, it would soon make slight difference.

Having made the rounds of the deck, the boys filled their lungs with fresh sea air and climbed down the steerage ladder. There, they found Gunter dozing on the wedge of straw that would serve as their bed, their packs under his feet. Shoving aside hanging pots, pans, and clothing, Jonas and Morris seized their belongings and stuffed them into what was left of the space in the overhead compartment.

Gunter rose and motioned the boys to sit at the table. Then he straddled a three-legged stool the better to guard their berth. "What brings you two on board this disgusting pile of dung," he asked.

"Our fathers are poor Jewish peddlers," Morris answered. "We're going to America to make our fortunes." Only a slight exaggeration, Morris thought.

"My friend, Sam Gordon, wrote from Illinois," Gunter said, "a place called Quincy where many German Jews live. Told me he'd give me a job selling farm supplies, but I'm not interested. Clothes are my shtick. What's yours?"

At the mention of farm supplies, Morris's ears perked up, but Jonas answered, "We don't know yet. We want to look around. We've heard great opportunity awaits us."

"Have you also heard about the war? The United States has been fighting with itself for five years."

"No," Jonas gasped, and all thoughts of business flew out of Morris's mind.

"Between North and South," Gunter said. He laughed at their worried faces. "Never mind. I hear it's over. It ended a few months ago, and since you are Jews and not schwarzes of African descent, it wouldn't have affected you or any of the others crammed into this hellhole." Then, he pulled a checkers board from his belongings and said, "I'll bet I can beat the two of you every game till we get to New Orleans."

The boys snorted and accepted the challenge.

The women in steerage went cheerfully about chores, caring for children of all ages. Howling infants nursed at loving breasts, and the men read and played games with the older ones to help pass the days. Though loud and rackety, the women kept the hold scrubbed and clean until, full at sea, the storms came, and they became ill.

Morris had never suffered motion sickness on the Rhine, but the rolls of the ocean waves were a far different matter. The farther out to sea the ship sailed, the less well Morris felt. The smell of the boiled beef and cabbage curdled his stomach, and he shoved his helping onto Jonas's plate. To quench his thirst, Morris turned to guzzling water stored in previously used and putrescent wine, vinegar, and turpentine barrels. Though rancid, the smell did not stop him from drinking, which only made him sicker. Vomiting what little remained in his stomach, he curled up, groaning on the minuscule one-third of their berth, but not before Jonas cleaned up the mess and gently placed a wet cloth on Morris's brow.

"Don't worry, my friend," Jonas said. "You'll feel better when the storm abates." Then he downed every morsel of Morris's portion of meat and potatoes.

Morris closed his eyes. He heard Gunter say, "I'm going atop deck and leave this odious-smelling hole," but Jonas shook his head, saying, "I need to tend to my friend."

"Go," Morris urged. "There's little you can do," but Jonas stayed.

Three weeks into the voyage, the storms grew in intensity. Water poured through the hatch and between the boards. The ship's motion jarred bag and baggage in steerage, with people and possessions scattered everywhere.

In desperate need of fresh air, Morris begged Jonas to help him attain the deck. Hindered by the pitches and swells, he grabbed the rail amidship. Thankfully, the captain knew the capabilities of the *Deamonti*. Awash with clamorous waves, the ship twisted and turned. The seaman strove to keep her headed into the storm as the mast groaned and bent and sailors leaned into the gale to keep their footing.

Jonas cried out to the captain, his voice carried by the wind. "Two hundred and fifty people crowded in a space meant for half. Little or no fresh air and conditions not fit for a pig. All sick with loose bowels and revolting stomachs. Naught but two heads for the lot and those inaccessible. Many are ill and some dying."

"Naught we can do about it," the captain yelled back. "Get ye below, and I'll send ye some help when I can."

Driven by the crashing waves, Jonas took Morris to the hatch, followed by the first mate.

"Hurry now. I'll shut 'er behind you, or you all will drown," the mate yelled, and as soon as the two of them clambered down the ladder, the sailor slammed the door closed.

Shivering in the dark, Morris choked on his own vomit. Gunter was nowhere to be seen. All around were sick people cared for by adults, often as sick as they were.

Jonas dipped a cloth into a bucket of brown water, wrung it out, and mopped the sweat from Morris's brow. Then Gunter appeared at his side with something in his hand.

"I've found a bit of ginger," he said as he shaved off a piece. "In the ship's galley," and he placed it under Morris's tongue.

The ginger calmed Morris's churning stomach, and he finally drifted off into a restless sleep.

When Jonas marveled at the results, Gunter laughed and said, "A sideline. "I learned it from my drunken father, a toothpuller whose place I was sometimes required to take."

The storm raged all night, exhausting both passengers and crew. And then the storm abated, and when it finally withered away, the ship cruised smoothly, propelled by its unharmed canvas sails and sturdy twin rudders.

Slowly, Morris regained his equilibrium and his appetite. When the hatch was finally opened, the dreadful stench of waste and illness slowly drifted away. Filth and uncleanliness had exacted their toll. Next, an epidemic of measles took dozens of children. Pulled from their wailing mother's arms, their small dead bodies were wrapped in bits of canvas and dropped overboard. Many continued to suffer from infections and disease and remained incapacitated for the rest of the voyage. Some died and were buried at sea. The captain performed services at night to spare the sensitivities of others aboard.

By the time the ship rounded the panhandle of Florida and sailed into the blue waters of the Gulf of Mexico, Morris had found his sea legs. Calm days saw him strolling the rails, his coat ruffled by the gentle breeze. On one such walk, he saw the young waitress, Giselle. He called to her, but she whirled away, her scarf slipping off her sun-touched braids.

"I only wished to say hello and invite you to join me for a coffee when we land in New Orleans," he called.

"Oh no, sir," she said. "That is quite impossible." She hastened through an open hatch doorway.

"They aren't allowed to talk with passengers or crew," a nearby crew member said.

"So I've been told, and I think that's ridiculous. This is America, isn't it?"

"Not yet, it ain't," came the reply.

Morris returned to the tween deck, where he found Jonas retrieving a shirt he'd kept clean for the landing. Morris put on his one set of fresh clothes, brushed his teeth, and combed his hair. Gunter gathered his belongings and brushed his hand through his dense gray hair.

With its sails neatly stored, the *Deamonti* steamed the final five miles up the Mississippi River and docked at the New Orleans pier. Morris's heart pounded with excitement as the gangplank came down, and he and Jonas disembarked into the unknown.

Chapter Five

NEW ORLEANS

30 JUNE 1866

O n shore, a gathering of colorfully dressed musicians blared lively music from trumpets, saxophones, and all manner of noise-making instruments while shouts and waves from welcomers greeted the sea-weary travelers. Caught up in the music, Morris and Jonas danced their way down to the pier.

There was no containing the bedraggled but joyful moods of steerage passengers who streamed down the gangplank. They walked, hobbled, and limped to shore carrying their children, their sick, their dying, and what belongings they had managed to preserve. Momentarily, Morris caught sight of Gunter's overgrown gray hair in the throng and yelled his name, but the crowd was too great and the din too loud. He wondered if he would ever see him again.

Most lucky souls in the first and second class had already disem-barked, met by relatives and friends. Some departed regally in fancy, fringe-bedecked carriages with prancing horses, their luggage bore atop by liveried servants.

As the boys arrived on shore, strangers greeted them with extended hands and jolly hugs. What kind of a place is this America? Morris wondered.

From out of the lot, Giselle appeared and handed him a cool, ruby-red drink with a stick of juicy pineapple extending through the foam. He took a trusting taste, and she teasingly planted a wanton kiss on his lips. Then, laughing, she slipped away and disappeared like a star in a fog.

As the raucous mob thinned and the music faded away, Morris crushed his empty cup with despair and said, "I'm starving, and I long for the taste of fresh food. Let's find a place to eat. Maybe we'll come across that elusive waitress, too."

With a poke to the ribs, Jonas said, "Have you forgotten your Jette already?"

"Indeed not," Morris responded, "but you must admit that a pretty girl is a welcome distraction." He laughed and returned the poke. "Look. There's a café across the way." He fingered the pouch around his neck. "I don't have much left after Gunter took my money at checkers and disappeared."

"The bastard got most of my funds, too," Jonas said, "but maybe the little we have left will buy us a meal and a bed."

A line had formed outside the restaurant, and as they waited, they heard others speak something that sounded like French. "What a strange dialect," Morris observed.

Jonas agreed.

"Louisiana Creole," said a dark-skinned longshoreman wearing a dirty shirt with rolled sleeves and a hat pushed back on his head. He placed a beefy hand on Morris's shoulder. "What language you speak means little here in New Orleans," he said. "Unlike me and me girl-friend," he pointed to a hefty female standing in front of him, "most everyone is from somewhere else. Even English is foreign, with Creole the preferred choice. Look about you, boys. Some freed Black men speak their own tongue. They're called gens de couleur libres." And indeed, Morris and Jonas overheard Negros using words they could barely understand.

When their turn came to be seated, they joined the dockworker and his gaily dressed, ageless friend, her purple hat tied to her head with a bright orange scarf.

"You off the ship?" the man asked in French, pointing to the docked *Deamonti*.

"Oui," Morris answered. "There was a waitress on board named Giselle. Do you know her?" he asked.

"I do," said the longshoreman's companion, "She works at le Maison des Rois in the square."

"And where might that be?" Morris asked.

"A few blocks from here, but you'd be wise to leave her be. She has a very jealous boyfriend, Damas."

"Sounds like good advice," Morris said, though his interest rose. "Tell me, what is good to eat here?"

"The crawfish is best," the lady said, her accent charming them, and she offered to order for them all.

"Tref," Jonas whispered, meaning unkosher.

"But we must eat," Morris said.

"You boys looking for work?" the Creole asked. "My company's hiring."

"Indeed, we are," Morris said.

The hours are bad, but the pay is good."

"Then that's where we'll head," Morris said, a smile brightening his face.

Belly's full of delicious etouffeé cooked with crayfish, onions, and celery spiced with hot cayenne pepper, Morris and Jonas followed the dockworker's directions to the Royal Cotton Company of Louisiana, where they hired on at the rate of ten cents an hour. "The jobs are yours," the foreman said, "as long as your blood is warm, and you show up on time."

For the next twelve hours, they heaved and hauled heavy bales of cotton in iron-wheeled freight carriers to the hold of a ship and then stacked them one on top of another.

That night, each a dollar and twenty cents richer, muscles aching and bone weary, they wandered down the crescent-shaped streets to find lodgings. On Julia Street, they saw signs hung from lacy iron balconies advertising rooms for a quarter a night. Unlike the ship's noisy, crowded steerage, they thrilled to find a room with two lumpy beds where they collapsed, exhausted. They slept through the noise from the bar below that would have kept less weary men awake.

After a brutal week's work with a bit of cash in his pocket, Morris's musings wandered dreamily to le Maison des Rois. He thought of Jette, missed her fiercely, but reasoned logically a little frivolity wouldn't hurt their relationship. It might be months, even years, before he could send for her.

"First a bath and a shave, then a drink and a little dalliance," he suggested to Jonas, but Jonas said, "You go. I must find a hot tub and a massage, or I'll not survive, and then I'm back to my bed."

Crowds of people and loud music spilled into the streets of Vieux Carréks as the French Quarter had come to be known. Morris found The House of Kings on Bourbon Street. He made his way to the bar, over which was hung a huge golden crown draped in purple velvet and pearl beads. As he entered, a lovely girl in a satiny gown, her creamy shoulders bare, crept up behind him. "A Sazerac with a lemon twist might be just the thing," she whispered in Morris's ear.

"And what might that be?" he asked, his eyes sparkling.

"Rye whiskey with trimmings," she answered, tickling his neck with her tongue.

Spinning around, he gave a whoop of joy. "Is it really you, Giselle?" He threw his arms about her and breathed in the delectable smell of her scented hair. Unable to contain himself, he kissed her full on the mouth and said, "What luck to have found you."

"Come and tell me all about yourself," she said, beckoning him to follow her. "Two of our specials," she called in lilting Cajun to a barmaid as she led the way to a table. "So sorry about the way I behaved aboard ship, but the Master thinks nothing of beating me and locking me away if I so much as glance at a passenger."

"So I heard," Morris said, "and I've also heard you have a boyfriend who does the same thing on shore."

"Oh, Damas." She waved her hand in the air. "Don't worry about him. He's just someone I've known my whole life. He thinks of himself as my protector, but never you mind. He's gone and won't be back for a week. And you? How long do you plan to stay in New Orleans?"

"Forever, if it could be with you," he teased. But then, taken by her doubting look, he said, "My friend and I are traders of furs and hides, but we've heard there's gold to be had in America. Perhaps we'll try that first."

Then it is up the Mississippi, for around here, the only gold is in the pockets of the cotton kings.

They bantered the evening away, talking and dancing. Giselle kept the sugary Sazerac whiskies coming as Morris drank his dock pay, and when the pretty, young maiden plucked what remained in his purse and led him to the stairs, he drunkenly followed, consumed with delight and desire.

Jonas had seen the bathhouse on his way to work each morning, a squat building with chimneys at either end. Across the street from the dock, it beckoned those with tired muscles and sore backs, though the cost, he learned, was two days' pay.

John Robertson, a tall, muscular, free man of color, owned the place along with other valued property he'd acquired at a bargain during the war. His mother and three slave girls, including a beauty named Lucy, kept the bathwater hot and performed magic on aching muscles with strong hands.

As her long fingers soothed the knots from his muscles, Jonas could not help but admire the girl's slender figure, her wide, sloe eyes, and her smooth, ochre skin, and to his chagrin, his soldier jumped to attention. John Robertson offered to sell the girl to Jonas, but the boy humbly declined and hurriedly vacated the premises. He'd not yet been with a girl, and owning another human being was too foreign and abhorrent a thought for the young German.

He spent a bit more of his hard-earned cash on a quick meal from a street vendor and returned to the rented rooms, where he gratefully lowered his body onto the lumpy mattress of his bed and slept.

The next morning, as he rose, he noticed a calendar with a picture of a golden sunset nailed to the door. It reminded him he had forgotten the Sabbath. Aboard ship, that first Friday night, he'd seen a group of Jewish men light a Shabbat candle, say the words, and daven, move their bodies, to connect with the Torah and ignite their souls, but neither he nor Morris had joined them. It became easier and easier to ignore each Friday night after that. The Sabbath became another workday, and like the Christians, Sunday became his day of rest.

Now, guilt overwhelmed him. Before leaving home, he had never missed a Shabbat. Dare he ask for forgiveness? He dressed and went to the window, where he lifted his eyes to the heavens, a Hebrew prayer forming on his lips. But shouting voices from below distracted him.

A small group had gathered. Something was amiss. A man lay half on and half off a green wooden bench beneath the balcony. Was it…? No! It couldn't be…"Oh, my God! Morris!" Jonas cried.

He threw open his door and ran down the stairs to find his friend beaten and bloodied. Aghast, Jonas bent to feel for a pulse, then discerned his friend was alive. "Does anyone know a doctor?" he cried.

"The Touro Infirmary is nearby," said a kind passerby, and some in the group volunteered to help take him there.

The hospital, which had once served as an orphanage and then a home for the Jewish aged, now cared for the city's poor. A nurse helped Jonas place an unconscious Morris in a crowded treatment room. An unpleasant odor of antiseptic and unwashed bodies settled over them, but Jonas was so worried he barely noticed the smell. He left only long enough to get a cup of coffee, and that's when the doctor arrived.

"Someone beat the bloody hell out of your friend," the medical man told Jonas when he returned, "but we were able to save him. He'll need to stay here for a few days. He'll be in ward three. You can visit him there."

Jonas sighed with relief and thanked the doctor and those who'd helped care for Morris. "Who did this?" he asked Morris.

"Giselle's jealous friend, Damas," Morris said, his voice barely audible. "He'd had returned unexpectedly and said he'd kill me next time, but he needn't worry. There won't be a next time," Morris vowed.

"We must find a more hospitable place to live," Jonas said, ignoring the blame for their predicament. "We will travel up the Mississippi, a river that flows a long way north. We'll leave as soon as you are well enough to travel," he said, spooning a bit of soup he'd brought between Morris's swollen lips.

With only a few cents remaining in his pocket, Jonas returned to the docks, but this time, he worked on the wharves where numerous barges and river steamboats moored. As he helped haul a container of hides off a river barge, he noticed the shipping label. Quincy, Ill, it read, and Jonas recalled Gunter mentioning the town.

Three days later, a still weakened Morris left the hospital. Jonas paid what he could, and with only enough left for a night in his rented room, he looked for a way to get them out of the city. Standing on the pier, he saw a uniformed officer on a three-decker steamboat with its engines astern. "Can you use two good seamen?" Jonas called to the mate in German.

"Come tomorrow," the officer answered. Jonas finished his job, collected his pay, and ran to the rented room to fetch his friend.

"You must act like you're fit," he told Morris. "I've got us a berth on a riverboat," he said.

The boat's mate was no fool. The man Jonas dragged on board the next day still had the look of one thrashed within an inch of his life. But the sailor had been in just such a pickle himself a time or two, so he allowed Morris to recuperate on an old cot next to the boiler until he was well enough to work.

On 18 June, the Mississippi River boat, Madelaine Jane, filled with passengers and freight, pulled away from the shore and began its arduous trip north.

Chapter Six

THE MISSISSIPPI

JULY 1866

With great excitement, Jonas helped throw off the heavy lines and weigh anchor. As she hove to, sailors wound the large, greasy ropes into piles. Jonas set about shoveling coal as fast as he could, and the big steam engines spun the twin rudders backward and into the muddy waters of the Mississippi. "Means Big River," the first mate said, "and they're damned right about that. She's huge."

The ten-year-old steamship Madelaine Jane measured two hundred fifty feet from stem to stern. Yet fully loaded, she drew only five feet of water. Internal masts supported a system of hog chains and pulleys that prevented her heavy load from sagging in the middle. Her coal-burning boilers needed constant feeding to make the steam that drove the wheeler.

Below, while convalescing, Morris conversed in French with the senor steam shoveler and wrote his first letter home.

Dear Mutter, Vater, and Kinders,

Thankfully, we arrived safely in America. Violent storms and hardy seas caused me an ugly stretch of seasickness. But Jonas helped me survive. We disembarked in New Orleans, the fourth-busiest seaport on this continent, and immediately found work on the docks to augment our dwindling cash supply.

New Orleans challenges one's beliefs. Endless bales of cotton, millions of pounds of sugar, items too numerous to tell filled the warehouses that line the docks where they await export to worldwide markets. Endless merchandise, shops, and eateries serve the city. Houses of castle proportions border tree-graced boulevards. Cottages that shelter the poor line the streets along canals and waterways.

People of every nationality roam the byways. Creoles, French-speaking people of mixed race, inhabit a section of the city called Vieux Carré. It is a ditzy place filled with bars and restaurants. Beads hang from the trees, and people dress in all manner of colorful apparel. The town celebrates more than four hundred festivals a year. They have a saying—Laissez les bons temps rouler—let the good times roll as they party the nights through. Though I am fluent in French, theirs is a language I find difficult to understand.

White men and people of color walk the streets in harmony. Many slaves are most recently freed. Even those who now own businesses and property are referred to in rude terms such as nigger and boy.

This city shocks our senses, so we do not wish to remain. We have found work on the steamship Madelaine Jane, a vessel that travels up the Mississippi River. There is much of this country to see.

Your son and brother,
Morris
PS: Jonas asks that you share this letter with his family. And, of course, I send love to Jette.

He crossed out the last and wrote her a letter of her own, adding how much he loved and missed her and reminding her of her promise to wait for him, and he would send for her as soon as he earned enough money. And he signed it,

Yours forever,
Morris

Stoking coal was a job he and Jonas performed. In addition, they swept and polished the gilt-edged stairways and ornate passenger areas to a shine, for which they received a dollar a week and two berths in the rear.

Skillfully, the sixty-seven-year-old master, Augustus Anchusa, skirted the numerous sandbars, boulders, and fallen limbs that lurked in the murky waters and finagled her upstream at a speed of five knots per hour. "I've sailed every foot of it without more than a snag on a branch," he'd brag. But that turned out to be a lie. The senior steam shoveler said the boat had run aground numerous times and had even sunk under the captain's command but was raised and refitted to run again.

Canebrakes and forests of Cyprus filled the vast land that grew to the river's edge. From his humble position, Morris could see both coasts lined with cotton fields and bluffs, migrating birds and fish leaping, and splashing in the water, and he envisioned the astonishing wildlife that occupied the shores. He had been told black bear roamed the acreage, and he longed for a chance at a hunt, but that would have to wait.

After traveling two hundred and sixty-five miles northbound with a stop or two to back off an unseen sandbar, the captain directed the boat to the low-lying port of Natchez, a town high on a bluff overlooking the river. It was meant to be a brief stop to pick up fifty bales of cotton bound for St. Louis along with a few upriver bound passengers. By now, Morris was mostly mended and known for his fluency in French. The captain, who spoke only German and English, asked Morris to go ashore and arrange to load the cargo with the cotton bales.

Morris heard the Frenchman spent his time at a bar where murderers, thieves, and prostitutes could be found. With nerves jangling, Morris made his way to the Under the Hill Saloon and there spoke with Allard. "Bonjour, Monsieur. We need your men to load the Madeleine Jane with bales of cotton," he said in French.

"Have a drink, fils," the Frenchman said, beckoning to one of the ladies. "There's no rush, I'm sure."

"Merci, Monsieur," Morris said, "but my captain wishes to get underway."

Laughing, the Frenchman said, "'accord, pas de Cheri," and yelled to the white overlords to have the dock Negros load the bales of cotton.

The Madeline Jane dipped deeper into the water with each bale that came aboard. And Morris watched in horror as vile language and whips cracked over the backs of the sweating Black men. When one of them stumbled and dropped his load, he was severely beaten and driven into the swift-moving waters. Morris grabbed a fallen tree branch and ran after him, extending the limb. The overlords on the dock laughed as the Negro, aided by the stick, frantically struggled ashore and ran away.

Relieved, Morris shook his fist at the white men and yelled a mixture of French and German as they directed their slaves to place the cargo on the already sagging deck of the Madelaine Jane.

With the cotton secure, the passengers began boarding, and Captain Anchusa gave his crew permission for one drink only in the port tavern of Bonne Chance. "But stay away from the slave masters and don't linger," he warned, "as well you know that trouble that will brew."

Loitering outside the buildings, Morris saw men of yet a third color, neither white nor black but burnished bronze, wearing nothing but loincloths covering their manhood.

Upon entering the gloomy tavern filled with men carrying guns in hand or on their hips, Morris ordered what the others of his crew were having: rum in a sweetened mix. Over the bar hung a painting of a voluptuous woman, nude and luscious, lying on her side, her head resting comfortably on her hand and her soft white bottom begging to be caressed.

Morris had ample opportunity to practice his few English words with the friendly deckhands, a bawdy bunch who enjoyed teaching their salty colloquialisms to the eager young German boy.

Against the captain's explicit orders, one drink became many, and a fight ensued, entailing a predictable melee. To help his friends, Morris jumped into the middle of the conflict and defended well until a few solid knocks to his head sent him reeling under a table, his brain in a fog. Men swore in various languages as bottles were broken, heads smashed, and blood from gunshot wounds painted the floor.

At the first opportunity, those who were able returned to the Madelaine Jane dragging their shipmate, Morris, with them. She unmoored at first light, leaving the rest of the injured or drunken crew behind.

Morris's head ached, more from the rum he'd consumed than the fight. For the next few hours, he nursed the throb of his temples and fell into a drunken sleep.

Rousing the remains of his exhausted crew, Captain Anchusa maneuvered the curving bends in the river. He threaded the Madelaine Jane past the numerous pre-sunk boats, eventually guiding her into Vicksburg's beautiful sloping port. There, dock hands loaded hundreds of bushels of freshly harvested wheat.

With glowing sweat and aching muscles, Morris, Jonas, and the others kept the boilers stoked, their labor producing the steam that powered the heavily overloaded boat toward its destination. Dodging rocks and eddies, the captain did not dock his boat again until it reached the largest port in the Midwest and the fourth largest in America—St Louis.

That night, as they sat in the crew's quarter eating leftover passenger fare, Jonas and Morris listened to tall and fanciful tales of hunting and fishing adventures. "The woods are lush with muskrats and beaver if you've a mind, and catfish as big as a whale inhabited these waters. But what's really of interest is the gold they've found."

Morris's eyes jerked open. "Gold?"

"Aye. Gold in the Rockies."

"And where might the Rockies be?" he asked.

"Out west," Makwa, the slim, Ojibwa Indian crew member, told him. "It is only for strong men."

"What of St. Louis?" Jonas asked. "Might one want to start a business here?"

"Perhaps," the mate said.

That night, their work completed, Morris and Jonas went on deck to enjoy the breeze and watch the shores lighted by silver moonbeams. "It's like you hoped," Jonas said, his voice soft and contemplative.

"What do you mean?" Morris asked.

"No one cares that we are Jewish. I've not been asked a single time."

"Nor I," Morris said, astounded. "But we haven't been here very long," he hedged. "Let's wait and see."

When the Madelaine Jane made port in St. Louis on June 30, passengers got ready to disembark. With the captain's permission, Morris and Jonas went ashore to see the roaring town for themselves.

Chapter Seven

ST LOUIS, MISSOURI

30 JUNE 1866

They only had a few hours to see a little of St. Louis. Jonas, hungry for real German food, followed the cook to the Rhineland Diner on Front Street. Morris spent his time at a bar, hoping to learn more about the gold opportunities he'd heard.

"If you must go, try the Rockies—Pikes Peak maybe," an unshaven and bowlegged old-timer told him. "A hundred thousand of us swarmed the mountain in 1859, so by now, it's mostly all been found," he said. "Last time I panned the streams was in '64, and what little placer gold I brung up was only bits and specks. Hardly paid for my groceries. Lode gold what's in the ground has all been claimed."

Discouraged, Morris sipped his beer and spoke with the German prospectors. All agreed with the old timer, but when they started talking about the price of hides, the tune turned different.

"If you got the will to do it, you kin make a living though not what it used to be," a bearded and burly man named Hunter said. "It's a hard life, lonely and dangerous. Indians in the area would as soon scalp you as run you through for what little land they got left after the gold diggers took it all." Hunter took a long drag from his mug. Then wiping the foam from his whiskers and pointing a bent finger at Morris, he said, "But the hide of a beaver or bear still brings damn good money, my boy, more than gold."

"Selling hides is a business I already know," Morris said. Excited and armed with new knowledge, he downed a second beer and went to collect Jonas from the diner. He found his friend gorging on dense, whole-grain bread, boiled meat, and a dark beer chased by bourbon and tap water. "I may have found a way for us to make our fortune," he told Jonas, who waved him off, enjoying the last bites of the best meal he'd had in days.

Back aboard the Madelaine Jane, Jonas, and the cook began to take ill. First one, and then the other doubled up with cramps so severe they screamed in pain. At the start, Morris thought Jonas had a case of the runs common to all sailors upon occasion, but he discovered this was different. When it came time to report to their duties, Jonas lay gasping on the floor of the latrine, unable to determine which end of himself to place over the hole.

As Morris went to tell the captain Jonas was too sick to work, a frantic passenger scrambled on board. "A terrible disease has overtaken the town," he cried.

"I hope it's not the plague like in '49," Captain Anchusa said, "but I'm not taking any chances." He immediately ordered the gangplank weighed, canceled all leaves, and sent the crew hurrying to their stations. "Be away," he yelled in English to the mate on the bridge and ordered the boilers stoked full. He backed the Madelaine Jane from the dock and headed her north at top speed.

With the steamship now safe a midstream, Captain Anchusa listened as Morris told of his friend and the cook's sickness.

"I'll come have a look," the captain said, "but I can guess what it is. Their skin is blue, you say?"

"More like bruised," Morris said.

Captain Anchusa examined the two ill men, nodded, and quickly left the room. "Cholera," he told Morris, "a plague sometimes called the Blue Death. Years before, it ran rampant in the filthy water pipes of St. Louis, and now here it is again. Death usually comes quickly," the captain said.

Frantic, Morris grabbed the captain's arm and screamed, "Do something. You can't just let him die."

Anchusa gently pulled free. "I'm sorry, lad."

The cook passed away that evening.

Jonas lingered on, fighting the dreaded disease. All that day and the following night, Morris hovered nearby, bathing Jonas's brow with a cool cloth. He brought his friend water to quench his thirst and help lower his raging fever. But by the afternoon of the second day, Jonas's agonizing thirst seemed to drive him insane. Before anyone could stop him, he raced to the rail and threw himself into the river, the strong currents sweeping him away.

Morris would have jumped overboard to save him had the captain and the first mate not held him fast. As the Madelaine Jane steamed full bore up the Mississippi, Morris searched the wake behind the ship. All signs of Jonas had vanished. Morris sank to the deck, sobbing. He remained there for hours, miserably messaging thumb to index finger and staring at the swirling water.

When the steamship had gone a good distance beyond St. Louis, the captain called the passengers and the crew together and gave them the devastating news. He paused and surveyed them all. "But we'll do the best we can." He turned and walked to the rear, past a wretched Morris sitting on a passel of rope.

"What if he's still alive? "Morris asked.

"Ist nicht," the captain said.

"He will think I abandoned him."

"He will know you did not."

"But I might have saved him."

"He was all but dead from the plague when he hit the water."

"I have to take him home," Morris said.

"We don't have a chance to find him." The captain spat tobacco juice over the side. "His body's likely halfway to Memphis by now. I know this bloody river. She doesn't give up her dead. She's a dangerous serpent full of fast-running currents and undertows. And snags from fallen trees and the hulls of good ships she's previously claimed."

Numb, Morris stared at the rippling river that had stolen his friend.

That night, under a clear sky lit by a golden moon, the captain conducted a simple prayer service for those passengers and crew who had succumbed to the deadly disease. Christians prayed aloud while Morris bowed his head and whispered the Sh'ma.

The next day, passengers and cargo were offloaded at Alton, a small town on a bluff above the river. There, they'd stored the grain silos until the St. Louis plague passed. Once again, the Madelaine Jane hove to and steamed her way upriver, successfully skirting sandbars, downed vessels, and protruding rocks. Her decks greatly lightened, her fires fully stoked, the ship forged north.

With a sad heart, Morris watched plump geese nibbling tidbits on the shores, ducks and their ducklings bobbing along the banks, and kites nesting on the riversides. There were no castles as on the Rhine and few sloping lawns to the banks, but eagles soared overhead, and beyond the river's bank stretched fields of harvested corn and grain crops lush with ripened heads. Homesick and lonely, Morris knew he had to tell Maier Silverstein and his wife of the death of their son. But how? Should he go home? He had no money to pay for his passage, but a letter would take months to arrive. What difference did that make, he thought. Jonas was gone, his body no doubt snagged and rotting in the deep abysses of the Mississippi. Morris shuttered.

Then, as they rounded a bend, a small town on the east bank came into view, and the captain yelled in his gravelly voice, "There she is. My Bluffs." He pointed to the town settled on the rise. "End of the line," and he guided the Madelaine Jane smoothly alongside the pier.

As passengers went ashore, Morris asked, "Wo sind wir? Where are we?"

"Quincy," a sailor said, "lately named after some president, though the captain still calls it by its original name. Steamships can't go no farther. There's rocks and falls ahead. We'll stay overnight while he visits his wife in the big house he built her."

At a loss as to what to do, Morris sought out the captain, who was busy supervising the offloading of goods and paying his crew. "Are you leaving us here?" he asked the boy in German as he handed him his pay. "Bluff's a fine place to settle."

"I've been wondering how I should tell Jonas's parents what happened," Morris murmured.

"You must write them a letter," the captain said. Then, frowning deeply, he handed Morris four dollars and change. "Your friend earned it. Go buy something nice to remember him by." He patted Morris's shoulder. "Good luck to you, junge. You'll do well in this town." So saying, he moved to the next man in line.

"When I was in New Orleans, a friend mentioned a town named Quincy. What kind of a place is it?" Morris asked a fellow sailor as he gathered his gear.

"Not sure. I ain't never been ashore. A trading post, I reckon. We haul a lot of stuff out of here. Best go see for yourself."

As he walked down the gangplank, Morris noticed lumber and tall bags of wool lining the dock. The shipping labels read, 'Ziskind Wool, Fur, and Hide Co, Quincy, Ill.' Lush green flatlands lay to the west, and birds fluttered in the bushes and chirped overhead.

The main street burgeoned with dry goods stores and hotels. A restaurant called *Der Schwarzwald* caught his eye. Comforted by the seasoned oak, brick decor, and the *Willkommen* sign outside the door, he decided to stop and have a beer.

He seated himself in a booth and read from the mouthwatering menu—familiar dishes like borscht, stuffed goose necks, and sausage with sauerkraut. The waitress, Gretchen, her nametag said, fresh-faced and rosy-cheeked, wore a clean white apron tied around her ample waist. She came to take his order. "Guten tag. Möchtest du ein Bier? Can I bring you a beer?" she inquired, ignoring his youth. "Good German beer made right here in Quincy."

"Ya," Morris answered.

"And what else may I get you?" she asked, continuing to speak German.

He glanced at the prices—10 cents for a beer, 50 cents for the sausage and kraut. "Is the food Kosher?" he asked.

"No, but Deutsch," she answered.

She brought him his beer in a stoneware stein, bold, dark, and stout. The hinged peaked lid reminded Morris of his father's coveted beer stein. He sipped the dark, foaming liquid, hoping the words would come. *Liebe Herr and Frau Silverstein.*

Dinner arrived along with fresh horseradish and pickles, the plate loaded with bits of kraut that flopped over the sides. He ate every bite and drained his stein. Morris wanted to question Gretchen about Quincy. He judged her a longtime resident in her forties, but she had many tables to wait and no time to sit and visit. Now well-fed, he needed a place to sleep. "Is there a house that takes lodgers?" he ventured as he paid.

She shook her head. "So many immigrants coming. There's a hotel. You can try there." Morris thanked her and headed for the door, but as he grabbed the handle, she came running. "Wait," she cried. "Try Mrs. Becker's Boarding House on 2nd Street, not far away. She may have an extra bed, and she speaks German."

The three-story house had gables, a pitched roof, and delicate trim. Edith Becker's welcoming smile and hefty figure reminded him of his mother. "I only just arrived in town, Fräulein," Morris said, "and am low on funds, but I need a place to lay my head."

She had one room left, she replied in his native tongue. "It is in the attic on the third floor and not very big, but it's all I have, I'm afraid."

"How much?" Morris asked, thinking of his thinning pouch. His four dollars had to last him till he could get a job.

"With breakfast and dinner included, my normal fee is $2.50 a week. I have had young men your age who can easily eat me out of house and home, but because you are fresh off the steamer, I will charge you $2.00 a week until you are better situated. Agreed?"

"A small room?" Morris asked.

"Yes. All right, $1.50 because it's in the attic. You drive a hard bargain."

Morris took off his pouch and removed enough to pay her for seven days.

"Do you have work prospects?" she asked.

"I noticed bags of wool on the dock," Morris said. "In Germany, I called on farms with cows and sheep. I know how to trade the hides and wool."

"Ah, then maybe you should go see Isak Lippmann or Herbert Ziskind. They have businesses in town. You can call on them first thing in the morning."

He thanked her. He'd rather hunt for gold, but Jonas would have told him he must make a living first. And thinking of his friend reminded him of the unpleasant letter he must soon write.

A grandfather clock in the hallway chimed four times.

Mrs. Becker fanned her face with her hand. "Oh my. Time slips away, doesn't it? Come. I will show you to your room," she said, leading the way up two flights of oak stairs. "You must keep your room neat, empty your chamber pot, and be at dinner on time—six o'clock sharp."

She plumped up the pillow on the bed, handed Morris a key, and left him to gaze skeptically at his temporary new home. It contained a bed, a tiny desk with a pen and ink, a chest of drawers, and a pine washstand holding a white porcelain pitcher and bowl.

He'd seen worse, he thought, and his mind drifted to a stormy night he and Jonas had spent in the Schwarzwald, huddled together against the cold. *I hogged the blankets then,* he thought, *but I'd be nicer now.* He stared at the street below.

Seated at the desk, he opened the drawer and withdrew a sheet of paper. *Liebe Herr und Frau Silverstein,* he wrote. *It is with deep sadness I must inform you of your son's horrible -* he scratched that out, *ghastly -* he scratched that out, too, *untimely demise.*

He laid down his pen, crumpled the paper, and threw it on the floor. He began a second letter, but the words wouldn't come. Finally, with the third and last piece of paper, he completed his task.

1.July.1866

Liebe Herr and Frau Silverstein,

It is with great sadness and a heavy heart that I write to inform you of your son's sudden demise.

On July 7th, Jonas and I visited St Louis, Missouri, USA. We were there for only a few hours, but long enough for him to drink water poisoned with cholera. I tended to him ardently during his short illness, and his suffering was brief. He died bravely—courageously, I might add.

Deepest sympathy and kindest regards, I will miss him.

Morris Lion

Dolefully, he folded the letter and addressed it. Next, he wrote a brief note to his parents telling them about Jonas's death and assuring them he was fine. He unpacked his few belongings and left the room.

"Where can I mail my letters?" he asked Mrs. Becker.

Smiling, she took them from him. "I'll mail them with mine in the morning," she assured him. She glanced at them and asked, "Letters home?"

"Something like that," he said, leaving to walk off his grief. From the bluffs, he saw the wide river bustling with traffic. The streets hummed with shoppers and children playing in nearby parks. His wanderings took him by busy grocery stores, apparel shops, furniture makers, farm equipment establishments, and even stores where musical instruments were for sale.

At the far end of Second Street stood a non-descript warehouse made of wood and stone. He didn't need a sign to recognize the vile, disgusting smells—Quincy Slaughterhouse.

When he was a twelve-year-old boy being readied for his bar mitzvah, his father had taken him to the shed behind his butcher shop to watch shehitah, the kosher method of ending the life cycle of a cow. It was a scene he would never forget. Mechul first tested the shining, flat butcher knife, running his fingernail the length of the blade to be sure it had no snags. With the animal secured, its head protruding through a slot, Mechul scrubbed the neck and dried it with a soft, clean cloth. Then, he picked up his knife and, with a swift slash, opened the cow's throat. Blood spurted from the arteries like two fountains. The cow groaned as its eyes went dull. Its tongue slid out of its mouth, and the animal sank to the floor.

Morris's stomach rebelled. He did not stay to watch the removal of the animal's skin. With the sight of the dying animal blurring his vision, he vomited and ran out the door.

Over the intervening years, Morris witnessed shehitah numerous times and, under his father's watchful eye, had himself performed the meticulous procedure. Though the smells that emanated from the small building were disgusting, he came to view the procedure as a humane way to end an animal's life—swift, precise, and efficient.

Now standing outside the slaughterhouse near a large pen crowded with cattle, he decided to have a look inside.

Chapter Eight
QUINCY, ILLINOIS

JULY 1866

Morris entered the large, open warehouse with a small office off to the side. Immediately, the foul, mephitic odors overwhelmed him and confirmed his suspicions. Feces lay on the floor, and blood streaked the walls.

Revolted, Morris watched an animal walk down a ramp where a workman brutally hammered a nail into its head. Meant to render the cow unconscious, it failed to do so. Someone stuck a knife in the poor creature's throat more than once, and blood poured from its arteries and veins. With a rope tied around its leg, the animal was hoisted to an overhead bar and moved down a chute where men continued the butchering. In horror, Morris noted the cow was still alive as its head, legs, and hide were removed.

A tall, heavyset man with a bulbous nose approached. "You looking for a job?" he asked, his brows knitting together. He held the wooden handle of a steel blade glistening with the juices. "Sprechen sie Deutsch?"

Morris nodded.

"Ich bin Adolf Landshuth. This packing house is mine. It just opened, and I am looking for strong young men. You need some weight and some muscle, but you might do."

"What does it pay?"

"A dollar a day. Better than most," the owner assured him. "You want the job or not?"

Staring down the line as they talked, Morris couldn't watch the cruelty any longer. "Thank you for your time, Herr Lanshuth," Morris said, struggling not to vomit, "but I am not suited for this job." As he turned to leave, he saw a bloodied young worker with a crop of black hair smirk at him.

"Then quit wasting my time and get the hell out of here." Adolf Landshuth said.

Morris left the building, glad to be gone. He would remember this place and the meat packer who owned it because someday he may supervise the dispersion of cattle, and he sure didn't want it to be there.

Breathing the flower-scented air, he strolled past the town square gardens. He passed a gaunt, bedraggled boy selling homemade candles. "How much?" Morris asked in German. The ragged child held his thin white tapers and a sign that said 1¢ each. "I'll take them all." Morris gently handed the boy Jonas four dollars and change.

Eyes wide, the boy stared at the money and grinned.

With a sad smile, Morris headed home.

"Gentlemen, we have a new boarder," Mrs. Becker said as Morris arrived at the glassed-in porch, which had been turned into a dining area. "For now, he speaks little English, so you must help him learn," she said. She handed Morris a piece of paper with a name and address—Ziskind Wool, Fur, Hides, and Feathers Co. "Try them," she said, beckoning him to an empty chair. She handed a wooden bowl of boiled turnips to one of the six men seated around the table. "Introduce yourselves," she told them.

Everyone turned toward the newcomer. Morris looked round the table and gave his name.

"Frederick," the man at the head of the table said, turning to the person on his left.

"Gernot." They had done this before.

"Karl Rothman," he said, his lips curling in disgust. He looked familiar. Ah, yes. The one who'd made an ugly gesture at the slaughterhouse.

"Leon."

"Hauke."

"And I'm Wolfram," said the muscular giant on Morris's left. "Where are you from?"

"Germany," Morris answered.

"And so are we all," Wolfram answered, but Mrs. Becker insists we speak English at the table."

"I no know," Morris said.

Smiles and chuckles erupted. Frederick served himself and passed the bowl to Gernot as the room filled with the sounds of conversations.

Mrs. Becker brought a platter with meat and potatoes. Thomas, the woman's ten-year-old son, carried a pot of beans, and then they both withdrew and left the boarders to themselves.

Speaking German, Leon, the man on his right, told Morris, "I'm a tailor. What about you?" Neatly dressed, his hair parted fashionably down the middle, he cut his meat into neat pieces.

"Ich bin ein hauthändler," (I am a hide trader) Morris said. "I'm looking for a job. Do you know where I can get one?"

Leon shook his head and forked his food into his mouth.

"I saw you today at the abattoir." Karl's voice boomed across the table. Something in his tone caused the room to grow suddenly still.

"I saw you, too," Morris said. "You wash up well."

The others laughed.

Karl's brows came together, his eyes narrowing into slits. "Is our slaughterhouse not good enough for you?" he asked, and the laughter died away.

Anger rose in Morris's throat, but he swallowed hard. "Shechita, Jewish slaughter, is kinder," he acknowledged.

"Dumb animals. Who cares?"

Leon and Gernot lowered their heads and stared at their plates.

"I do," Morris murmured, turning away.

Karl would have said more, but Fredrick reached across Gernot, tapped his finger on Karl's arm, and shook his head.

After dinner, Leon, the tailor, said to Morris. "You almost got into it tonight.

"He's a schmuck," Morris answered. As he went to his room, he remembered knowing men who dealt with his father. Some thought animals had no feelings and were only meant to be eaten. Karl was like one of them: cruel, brutal, and callous. He vowed they would never be friends.

After breakfast the next morning, Morris took from his pocket the piece of paper Mrs. Becker had given him. He hitched up his pants and hand-pressed his white shirt.

He found Ziskind's at Third and Hampshire. As he entered the flat-top building, he recognized the skunk-like smell, a sure sign of a hide business.

"Mr. Ziskind?" he inquired of a woman seated at the front desk. She wore a prim high-neck white blouse, a full-length black skirt, and her gray hair pulled back in a tight bun.

"He's in the warehouse," the lady answered, pointing the rubber stamp she held to a door in the rear.

Not understanding, he shrugged and shook his head.

With a look of annoyance, she pointed her pen to a door in the rear. Returning to her secretarial duties, she bounced a device on an ink pad to papers on her desk—thump, smack, thump, smack.

Uncertain, he murmured, "Danke Schoen," and walked in the direction she had indicated. Suddenly, the back door flew open, and a round-bellied, clean-shaven man of medium stature came rushing through. He looked startled, eyebrows arching over metal-rimmed glasses. "Oops," he said, sidestepping to avoid a collision.

"Entschuldigung," (Excuse me) Morris said, stepping back.

"Who are you?" the man said in German as he straightened his spectacles gone askew.

"Morris Lion."

"What can I do for you?"

"I'm from Ettenheim, Germany, near the Schwarzwald. I saw bags of wool on the pier with a Ziskind label, so I thought this would be a good place to try and find work."

"I'm Herbert Ziskind," the man said, straightening his glasses. "As it happens, I'm looking for a salesman. Come into my office and give me one good reason why I'd want to hire you." He led the way to a glass-enclosed office beyond the receptionist. Rounding his desk, he motioned Morris to a chair. "You are new in town, I suppose. You say bags of wool on the pier interested you?"

"The men in my family have been peddlers in Germany for generations. We trade in many goods, including hides and wool. I have worked for my father since the age of ten."

"How old are you now?" Mr. Ziskind asked.

"Eighteen."

"The last thing I need is an eighteen-year-old peddler who doesn't speak English," Ziskind said, rising.

"I'm exceptionally good at my trade," Morris said, staying seated.

Ziskind settled back in his chair, deep frown lines crowding his brow. "Now look here, young man. We deal with a wide array of clients. I need an experienced salesman, so why would I hire you?"

Morris turned on his most beguiling smile. "In the old country, I traveled to many farms where I became good friends with my customers. I even stayed at their homes. When it came time to sell their cattle or wool, they trusted me to give them a good deal." He paused. "I will bring much business to your company." He leaned forward, hoping to show he meant what he said.

Herbert Ziskind stared at the boy for a long time. "Jewish?" he asked.

Oh oh. Morris thought Ziskind was a *lantsmann*, a fellow Jew, but he wasn't sure. He nodded, a familiar feeling of apprehension enveloping him.

"Kosher?" Mr. Ziskind continued.

"My father is a shochet, a kosher butcher," he said, rubbing his fingers together.

"Half the people in this town are German, and half the Germans are Jewish. Most belong to B'nai Abraham, an orthodox synagogue. They will welcome you, I'm sure. Some have found orthodoxy too… how shall I say…too difficult for life in America. A rabbi named David

Wise founded a new movement, Reform Judaism, he calls it, to better fit the modern world. Liturgy in English, for example.

Morris sat straight in his chair. "Since the day I boarded the ship to America, I've found keeping kosher impossible. I have no money for a synagogue, but I'm a hard worker. I will serve you well."

"If I hire you," Ziskind said, leaning back in his chair, "and it's a big if, I'd have a few things to consider. I have been looking for the right person to go into the country and drum up trade, but you must be able to communicate. How do you propose to do that?"

"I'm an excellent student. I'll find someone to teach me English."

"I need a salesman to call on farmers, gain their trust, and buy their hides, wool, beeswax, broom corn, tallow, and feathers for Ziskinds. There are several similar hide companies in Quincy, so competition is fierce. You would have to find customers within a fifty-mile radius and procure their products for Ziskind and Company. Does that suit you?"

"Yes, mien Herr. I'm the perfect person. I've been a peddler all my life."

Ziskind smiled at Morris. "You're in America now, and I'm not your Herr. Call me by my name."

"Mr. Ziskind, I'll need some supplies."

"Such as?"

"Needles and thread, scissors, mirrors, picture frames, ribbon, and maybe a wool hat or two. Things people use every day. I'll know more after I've made my first calls."

Ziskind pooched his lips as though thinking. "$5 a week. You buy your products and keep the profits from your sales. I'll provide the mule and the cart. Does that seem fair?"

"Yes," Morris said, his smile fading, "but a mule would require food, and a cart needs a decent road. I'll carry my wares on my back. I keep the profits and $10 for every customer I bring you."

Ziskind's eyebrows knitted together. "You are a shrewd one, aren't you? I like that, but you'll have to speak English. Though many farmers around Quincy are German born, some are not, so speaking English is necessary."

"I'm an excellent student. I will learn quickly," Morris said.

"All right. I'll pay $7.50 for each customer to start and see how you do. And I have a suggestion. Change the spelling of your last name to lYon. More distinguished and distinctive."

Morris squirmed. He didn't want to change his name. It was like giving up his heritage. He looked into the appraising eyes of the owner. "Is that necessary? Lion is a time-honored name."

"It is not a requirement. Just think about it."

Morris sensed a deeper meaning. "I will give it my consideration," Morris said.

When he returned to the boardinghouse, he sought out Mrs. Becker. He found her and her son in the ample kitchen baking delicious-looking apple pies. Ten-year-old Thomas sat on a high stool, carefully slicing apples, which he scooped into a large crockery bowl. Grateful that Mrs. Becker spoke German, Morris said, "He reminds me of my little brothers and sisters," patting the boy's head. "I miss them most of all."

"He's a good lad, and now what about you?"

"I've got a job," he said, "but must quickly learn English."

Hands now busy working the buttery dough, Mrs. Becker said, "You might try St. Francis Solanus College, where Thomas attends school. The teachers are German Franciscans."

"Do they take Jews?" Morris asked.

Mrs. Becker shrugged as she pressed the dough into a waiting pie pan. "I may have a better idea. Thomas is so bored during the hot summer months. Perhaps he could instruct you. He speaks German and English well and would have you conversant in no time." She looked at her son. "Would you like that?" she asked.

Thomas stopped cutting apples and nodded, a broad smile on his lips.

"Would you trust me enough to take him with me into the country to call on the farmers?" Morris asked.

Mrs. Becker stopped what she was doing. "Oh no. He's way too young for that."

"We'd see cows and sheep and chickens," Morris told the boy. "And sleep under the stars at night."

"I don't think…"

"Mother. It sounds like lots of fun."

"I'd take good care of him," Morris promised. "I've a sister the exact same age."

"We'd have to have some rules," Mrs. Becker said.

As the pies baked, they made plans. Morris and Thomas would leave on Mondays and return to spend weekends at home. And Thomas could bring along a book of English he'd used during the school year.

"One other thing," Morris said as Mrs. Becker took the last pie out of the oven. "Mr. Ziskind suggested I change the spelling of my last name from L I o n to L Y o n.. What do you think?"

With a studied expression, Thomas said, "I think it is a good idea. In English, l i o n is an animal."

"It will be hard. You've been an animal for eighteen years," Mrs. Becker laughed.

"Then L y o n will be my American spelling," Morris said.

And so it was settled.

Monday morning, Thomas showed Morris the way to Sam Gordon's dry goods store on Main Street. Hadn't Gunter Shechter, that scoundrel he'd met on the ship, mentioned Sam Gordon's name? A handsome young woman wearing a shirt-like chemisette tucked into her skirt greeted them.

"Sprechen sie Deutsch??" Morris asked.

""We speak English here. Are you a peddler? Is that a list?" she answered, pointing to the paper he held.

He handed the note he'd scribbled in German to Thomas with the necessities he thought he needed. As she listened to the boy read, she asked, "Where does he plan to sell these goods?"

"In the country," Thomas answered. "I'm to go with him and help him learn English."

She smiled and patted the boy's head. "Good. All right. Let's see what we can do."

Morris flashed a grin and pointed to the first items on the list.

"Needles and thread," she said, enunciating clearly. "Those are useful." She led them to the sewing counter. "But if you wish to make a living, you must sell things others do not. These, for example," and she picked up a pair of wirerimmed glasses. "You'd be surprised how many farmers and their wives do not see well. And jewelry for the women. It is the ladies you should concentrate on." She dangled brooches and necklaces before their eyes.

Thomas giggled, and Morris signaled his understanding with raised eyebrows and approving nods.

She collected and wrote down all the items he chose, including those Thomas suggested, a teddy bear sitting on the front desk, and some tiny tin soldiers.

"Anything else?"

Thomas translated, and Morris shook his head.

She handed him a sales slip.

Morris gazed at the numbers. He had almost no money and knew he would need all his charm and persuasive powers, but he had a plan. He began by opening his pouch and showing her the small bits of change tucked into the corners, "but," he spoke in German to Thomas, "Say every word like I say them," he instructed.

"He says to tell you he is employed by Herbert Ziskind of Ziskind Wool, Fur, and Hides, located at Third and Hampshire. He says Mr. Ziskind will vouch for him, and he will pay back every cent with interest," Thomas translated.

Morris intended to pay for the goods from his profits. That was true. As to Ziskind vouching for him, he was not so sure.

The saleslady looked straight at Morris and shook her head. "That will never do. We operate our store on a cash-only basis. Mr. Gordon is adamant about that."

Thomas gazed gloomily at Morris and timidly reported, "She says you have to pay now."

Morris raised his chin in defiance. "Ask her if there is someone else we can talk to?" he said to Thomas.

When the boy asked, she shook her head. "Mr. Gordon is very busy,"
Thomas began to cry.

The lady shook her finger. "That won't do any good."

But Thomas sobbed even louder, and customers in the store began
to stare. With a foolish grin, the saleslady told Thomas to stop crying
and wait here."

She left Morris and the sniffling boy in the tool department with
his sales slip in her hand. When she returned, she said, "Come back this
afternoon at one. You can discuss your business transactions at that time."

With a glint of hope remaining, Morris left to wander the streets
of Quincy. Thomas led him to John's Square, a flower-filled park off
Hampshire. He could see parts of the Mississippi River winding north
from the bluff. Ladies chatted, and Thomas ran to the swings as Morris
observed business establishments surrounding the area—a music store
with a wood and gold colored organ in the window, a three-story brick
hotel, and several beckoning restaurants.

After a penny's worth of ice cream and at the appointed hour, they
returned to Gordon's Dry Goods Store. Morris hailed the saleswoman,
now busy with other customers, and waited impatiently until she motioned him to follow her.

She walked quickly to an office and softly knocked on the door. A
gentleman's voice bid her enter.

"This is the little boy and the man of whom I spoke, Uncle Sam. I
hope they are not disturbing you." She looked at them and said, "Meet
Mister Gordon, the owner."

Morris stepped forward and spoke his name. "Morris Lyon," he said,
extending his hand."

"And I'm his English professor," the little boy said.

Gordon laughed. Balding with a fringe of dark hair hovering above
his collar, the man of middling years rose, reached across his desk, and
shook Morris's hand. "Nice to meet you." He glanced at the woman
hovering nearby. "Thank you, my dear. You may go."

She moved toward the door.

"My niece, Mrs. Feldman. A lovely girl. Her husband was a member of the Eighth Calvary, one of the first of our Jewish boys to die in the war at Gettysburg."

Thomas tried his best to translate.

"Quincy fought on the side of the Union. It was a bloody war ending in Texas a year ago." Mr. Gordan spoke to Thomas as he sat and leaned back in his chair. "Tell Morris I've talked with Herbert Ziskind," he said. "He trusts your friend."

Thomas translated.

Morris said, "Tell Mr. Gordon my father taught me my word is my honor. I would never betray it."

"Good. My niece has your purchases ready. I wish you good luck, Mr. Lyon, and a safe journey." Rising, Mr. Gordon shook Morris's hand, tousled Thomas's hair, and showed them the door.

"I have a surprise for you," Mrs. Feldman told Thomas as she gave Morris his goods. "A friend of mine, Caleb Levy, used to peddle. When he earned enough to start his own business, he gave me his knapsack to pass on to someone in need. It is big and roomy and will hold everything you purchased today. Come see." She took Morris and Thomas to the storage area, and as she stretched to pull the sack off the shelf, Morris could not help but take note of her curvaceous figure and slim ankles.

"You see," she said, pointing to the knapsack straps, "your load will reach from above your head to your knees."

Morris grinned. "Danke, Fräulein Feldman," he said as she showed him how to make everything fit, handing a much smaller backpack to Thomas. "It has a small tear, so it is unsalable but will work perfectly fine."

Pleased, the boy thanked her, prompting her to offer one last gift, a warning.

"You're welcome, Thomas. You and Morris watch your backs. Robbers abound."

After dinner, Morris asked Mrs. Becker if she had scissors he might borrow. She gave him her knitting pair, and he procured a few sheets of Thomas's school paper. These he cut into two by three-inch pieces.

Returning the scissors, he took the pieces of paper to his room and, with pen and ink, wrote ZISKINDS STORE on one side and Morris Lyon on the other.

When he finished his chore, he crawled into bed, recalling the day and Fräulein Feldman's warning. It also occurred to him he should have asked for her first name.

Chapter Nine
THE PEDDLERS

JULY 1866

They rose before dawn. Mrs. Becker fixed Thomas and Morris a hearty breakfast of apple slices, boiled eggs, and Johnny cakes. "Take good care of my son," she told Morris as she packed dried meat, biscuits, pickles, cakes, cups, plates, and utensils into Thomas's bag.

"To lighten his load, only food," Morris exclaimed.

"All right then," she said, removing the items and fussing over Thomas with a nervous but cheerful smile. "Take your English book from St. Francis. It will help you teach properly."

The boy nodded. "Don't worry. I will have him speaking English in no time."

Morris pointed to the door and groaned as he hefted his knapsack onto his back. It felt like a hundred pounds, but he hoped it would be lighter on their return.

Thomas gathered his backpack, mimicking the groan, though his load was much lighter. He kissed his mother and followed Morris out the door, waving goodbye until he could no longer see his home. As the first golden beams of the summer sun pierced the outer edges of Quincy, Morris and Thomas reached the dusty country road. Before them lay fields of half-grown corn with lush green leaves and dancing tassels. "I know a song," Thomas said. "It will be your first English lesson." He began to sing:

"Oh, where have you been,

Billy Boy, Billy Boy?
Oh, where have you been,
Charming Billy?"
"Who Billy?" Morris asked.
"Just a lad," Thomas said. "Now you try."
Morris repeated the words.
"I have been to seek a wife,
She's the joy of my life,
She's a young thing.
And cannot leave her mother."

When he understood the words, Morris wondered silently how Thomas felt about leaving his mother. A picture flashed across his mind—himself as a little boy hurrying after Papa on the dusty paths to distant customers.

"Again," cried Thomas, seeming untroubled.

Thomas insisted Morris learn all seven verses, which the two sang boisterously and off-key. Some fellow travelers smiled and stuck their fingers in their ears. At the first farm, they came to, an old man with baggy pants and a wide-brimmed straw hat pumped water from his well. He greeted them, eager to buy a bag of tobacco, and Morris made his first sale, slipping the little piece of paper with ZISKINDS written on one side and his name on the other into the bag. "To let him know who to contact in the future," he told Thomas.

The farther from town they walked, the fewer people they saw, and the greater the distance between farms grew—a mile, maybe two.

Mid-morning, Morris sold three spools of thread, a package of needles to a farmer's wife, and a knife to an old-timer who sat on his porch carving. Morris had learned the words to "Billy Boy," and Thomas taught him how to use phrases in a sentence, so he tried out some of his new vocabulary on the whittler, and Thomas handed him a Ziskind note.

By now, it was past noon. The humidity from the corn's flat green leaves and the sun's sweltering heat caused both man and boy to drip sweat, so Morris called a halt. He and Thomas dropped their bags and sank to the ground in the shade of a maple tree.

They aired their shirts and drank from the water bottles Mrs. Becker had sent. Refreshed, Thomas suggested a pointing game and later used the words in a sentence. To show Morris what he intended, he aimed his finger at himself. "Me," he said.

Morris pointed to Thomas. "Me."

Thomas shook his head vigorously. "No, No. I'm me. You are you."

Morris seemed confused, but when he understood, he laughed, and the game continued. 'Tree-*tree*. Fence-*fence*. Sky-*sky*,' and Thomas pointed upward and smiled.

Now rested, Morris was anxious to move on. "We seek cattle und sheep," Morris said, using some of his newly learned words. Thomas motioned to a farmhouse near the little town of Ashley. "Perhaps there," he said.

As they drew close, a woman hailed them from the open door. "What have you in your pack?" she asked.

"Whatever you need," Thomas answered in his sweet, youthful voice.

"Do you have any combs in your pack?" She asked Morris.

"Kämme," Thomas whispered.

"Yes, I have comb." Morris dug in his pack and produced a pretty array for the woman to view.

"Come into the shade and show me what else you have, but hurry before my husband returns."

Following along, Morris raised a cautioning eyebrow to Thomas. He took out a few items—hand mirrors, bits of lace, bottles of chamomile and held them up for the woman to see.

As she culled through her choices, under an old elm tree, a man came from the field. "You must go. It's my husband, and he doesn't allow me to buy from peddlers. He hates peddlers." She grabbed a comb, placed a coin from her pocket into Morris's hand, and ran to the house.

"Off my land," yelled the farmer, waving a large stick.

Morris stood his ground. "You sell rinderhäut?" Morris asked.

"He means cattle hides," Thomas quickly translated.

The farmer came closer, eyes narrowing. "Why do you ask?"

"I buy. Big dollar."

"How much?"

Morris knew that farmers had to drive their own herd of cattle to market or pay someone to do it, which cost them time and money.

Morris handed him a paper card. "Ziskind pay good, and I," he pointed at his chest, "come get."

The farmer stroked his short chin beard, mouth twitching. "I've heard of Ziskind. You work for him?"

As Thomas interpreted, Morris nodded and grinned. "I number one salesman," he said.

"Come back in a few weeks. We'll talk," the farmer said as he walked toward his house. "And stay away from my wife," he called.

"He wants you to return on our next trip," Thomas said.

Smiling, Morris picked up his pack and motioned for the boy to do the same. He had accomplished his primary goal. Anxious to find more customers, he picked up the pace. "Hurry," he called to Thomas, who struggled to keep up.

At last, noticing Thomas's distress, Morris stopped to picnic on some of the food Mrs. Becker had sent, and Thomas taught Morris a new song.

> Old Mother Hubbard
> Went to the cupboard,
> To give the poor dog a bone:
> When she came there,
> The cupboard was bare,
> And so the poor dog had none.

That afternoon, they traveled eight miles and made five more stops. It wasn't all honey and roses. At one rundown shack, a crusty old man fired his ancient musket over their heads. Morris and Thomas scrambled hastily up the road.

But farmwives received peddlers with excitement. Morris sold them knickknacks they could buy only if they made a rare trip to town. He made twice what he'd paid for the items at the dry goods store.

At last, Morris said, "One more farm," and pointed ahead where sheep nibbled weeds and thistle in an open field guarded only by a black and white dog.

They found the farmer, a solid young blue-eyed German named Johann, whose grazing ewes had lambs by their sides. "Who shears your sheep?" Morris asked, speaking German.

"I do," the tall, slender youth responded.

"Who buys your wool?" Morris said.

"I sell to the highest bidder," Johann answered, his piercing eyes narrowing.

"That will be me," Morris said. He knew his employer, Herbert Ziskind, would approve. "You have many sheep," he continued. "Next time you shear, I come help."

They shook hands. "My wife is away, so I have no woman to cook, but if you need a place to sleep, you can use my sheep shed." He pointed to a small wooden structure with a weathered peaked roof. "It's not much, but it will provide some shelter. You're welcome to use it if you like."

Morris shook his head. "Danke," he said in German and then switched to English. "We thank, but want see sky," he said, pointing upward as he'd seen Thomas do.

They found a grassy spot off the road under a canopy of maple. Morris leaned his heavy load against a stout trunk and helped Thomas shrug out of his backpack.

Exhausted, the boy listlessly nibbled fruits and cheese, drank from his water bottle, curled on his side, and instantly slept. Exhilarated, Morris stared between the leaves at the glowing stars and dreamt of the future.

He awoke to the sound of a rustle and a click. He peered through the darkness at the tree where he'd leaned his pack. Two men knelt there. They seemed to be releasing its latches. Making sure Thomas was safe, Morris summoned his courage and silently crept forward.

"Look at this," one of them whispered, holding a watch. "It's a beaut," he said as he dug deeper. "One for you and one for me." He tossed the second watch to his accomplice as he continued to rummage through the goods.

With temper rising and longing for his old Flintlock, Morris lunged at the crooks, knocking one to the ground. Hands knotted into fists, he pummeled the other.

"Behind you," yelled an awakened Thomas. Morris turned in time to throw a hard punch at the on-rushing thief. He fell but rose and, with a shake of his head, tried to help his fellow intruder. Morris knew how to fight more than one, having had many brothers to teach him, and Thomas helped by kicking, biting, and throwing water bottles and hard-boiled eggs. The battle ended when the two thieves gave up and ran away.

If not for Thomas, Morris would have gone after them but decided two watches weren't worth the risk. He leaned against the maple tree, assessed his bruised jaw and sore shoulder, and checked on Thomas. Unscathed, the boy helped gather the scattered items. They restored order and laid down to rest.

From then on, Morris accepted offers of sheds or a place to stay in his customers' yards. Sleeping under the stars was too dangerous for an unarmed peddler.

Thomas trekked with Morris all summer. By the time the boy returned to school in the fall, Morris spoke English quite well, except for an accent he couldn't quite conquer.

Traveling alone, he discovered the upland, forested with sugar maple and white pine, undergrown with blueberries, wild lupine, and the innocent-looking but poisonous white flowering dogbane. Longing to hunt as he had in the Schwarzwald, he bought a gun and spent time shooting trophy-size deer, which he butchered to help stock Mrs. Becker's larder.

Ziskind gained new customers, and Morris's savings grew. Once again, he let slide by the high holy days of Rosh Hashanah and Yon Kippur even though his boss had offered him time off with a monetary incentive. Instead, Morris bought a horse and wagon to travel greater distances and carry more oversized items to sell, such as lamps and rocking chairs. Using Ziskind's money, he bought cornfed cattle and herded them to Quincy, for which Ziskind paid Morris his fair share. Barely noticed, a new year came and went.

Morris wrote to Jette and his family once every few months. He told of his state of health and about his job calling on farmers. He noted he missed Mama and her cooking and that he'd learned to speak English from a ten-year-old boy. He told Jette he missed her and would send for her soon, though to brother David he disclosed it might take three years to earn enough money to send for them both. He ended each letter with, "The day will come, so don't give up hope. All my love, Morris."

And then the sad letter from David arrived.

> *Dear Morris,*
>
> *I woke up early and went to the kitchen for tea. I could hear Mama in her garden picking herbs to put in the noon meal. Papa came to the table and asked after her. 'Outside,' I said. Thinking it had been too long, I went to look for her, Papa on my heels. She lay amongst the sweet-smelling basil, hands resting upon her heart. Papa screamed and pushed me away as he knelt and tried to rouse her, but dear Morris, she had left this life. We are all devastated.*
>
> *Her funeral was at the synagogue, and she is buried in the cemetery of Schmieheim. Papa says to tell you not to come home. She's gone. His message to you is to stay and make her proud. And sit shiva. Her death date September 11, 1866.*
>
> *With love from all.*

Tears smudged the words as Morris read them. He touched the small silver star of David that she had hung around his neck, sighed deeply, and felt her near.

When bearded Johann Weber sheered his sheep in the spring, Morris was on hand to help. Johann showed Morris how by placing the sheep against his legs he could place the ewes into the best shearing positions. It was a tricky, backbreaking business, but Johann taught Morris how to remove the wool without injuring the bleating animal. Never as good as his teacher, Morris applied himself and learned to shear fast and clean.

Then they went inside to enjoy a feast prepared by Mary Elizabeth, Johann's beautiful golden-haired wife. As Morris hungrily devoured the pork and beans, he couldn't help but notice her lovely, peaked breasts and rounded bottom.

Johann left after dinner and went to water his sheep. "Are you our new salesman?" Mary Elizabeth asked, gazing thoughtfully at Morris's beardless young face. "How often will you come?" As she picked up his empty bowl, her hand grazed his.

Her touch caused a bolt of lightning to course through his body. He jumped, and she laughed and pulled her hand away.

"I'm not sure, but now and then." he said.

"It's so lonely when Johann's away," she whispered.

"I can only imagine," Morris said.

Ziskind didn't keep track of how often he visited customers, only that he sold them goods and brought them hides and wool to sell. Mentally, Morris began rerouting his schedule. Surely, Johann would be grateful to Morris for keeping his wife safe while he was away.

Wednesday, September 16, 1868, found Morris at the cattle farm of his customer and friend, Bill McIntosh. They had gone hunting for muskrat, a fur more valuable than mink for which Herbert Ziskind paid top dollar.

"You can bring me my share when you come next month," McIntosh said. You're one of the few Jews I trust."

"What?" Had Jew-hating followed him from Europe?

But we are friends. Let's go get a beer."

That night, Morris slept in the farmer's barn, and the next day, he took the muskrat skins to Ziskind's and drove the cattle to the slaughterhouse.

He'd meant to discuss the comment with Mr. Ziskind, but his boss was out of the office.

"Where were you?" Herbert's secretary, Rose Fetterman, asked Morris, her tone accusing. "He wanted you to break the fast with him."

"Ah, yes. Rosh Hashanah," he said.

"It was Tuesday. The office was closed. And next week is Yon Kippur," she said.

He should wear his phylacteries, read the Torah, and ask God to forgive his sins, but he had customers waiting.

Thomas educated Morris about Thanksgiving and the two big Christian holidays, Christmas and Easter. On the Thursday before Easter in April, Morris shot a turkey and brought it to Mrs. Becker to cook for the holiday dinner. It was a hefty twenty-two-pounder and took all day to bake to a delicious golden tenderness. Then, with all the boarders seated, heads bowed, Thomas said a prayer by quoting Abraham Lincoln. "We thank God and commend to his tender care all those who have become widows, orphans, mourners, or sufferers in the lamentable civil strife, and to "heal the wounds of the nation.""

"In Jesus' name, we pray," Mrs. Becker added.

As he looked around the table, Morris noticed Karl Rothman was no longer there. "He caused trouble with other guests," Leon reported, "and he didn't bathe the slaughterhouse smell off himself, so Frau Becker asked him to leave."

"Good," Morris said. "Has anyone taken his place?"

"A young woman." Leon smiled. "She's here on her own, one might say. I understand she will join us for dinner."

That night, Mrs. Becker introduced them to Miss Magda Miriam Szymanski from Poland. "Let's all welcome her and tell her your names."

As usual, Frederick began with a much wider grin than usual, followed by Gernot, then Leon, Hauki, Wolfram, and finally, Morris, who lifted his water glass and made a toast. "From a bunch of oxen to the beautiful lady who now graces our table," he said.

"My, but you are a handsome lot," she said, her English made lilting by her charming accent. She sat in Karl's old place directly across from Morris. He immediately engaged her in conversation.

Where in Poland had she lived?

Krakow.

What did she do?

A teacher of history. "I'll be working with the Franciscans at St. Francis Solanus College," she said.

A Catholic, he thought.

The light-haired beauty captivated him, and she apparently found him attractive as well. He felt her foot rubbing against his and saw her flash a naughty smile. Later that evening, he invited her for a stroll. When she gripped his arm and cuddled close, he could not resist accompanying her to her room. Henceforth, on weekends, he hurried home to enjoy her shameless charms while trying to keep Mrs. Becker unaware.

Chapter Ten
SPRING AND SUMMER

1869

One Saturday, thirteen-year-old Thomas met Morris at the door of the boardinghouse and drew him aside. "After you left for your trip last Monday, I delivered clean towels as usual and smelled Miss Szymanski perfume in your room." He gave Morris a knowing smile. "But if my mother finds out, she'll ask you to leave, and I would hate that," he said.

Morris nodded.

"And by the way, these letters came for you while you were away," Thomas said, handing them to Morris.

"From my father," Morris explained, taking the first one offered.

"Yes, but this one is not," Thomas said, waving a lavender envelope.

"Rascal," Morris cried, all thoughts of the dark-haired Magda Miriam Szymanski disappearing from his head. "And thanks for the warning," he whispered as he grabbed the letters and hurried to his room.

First, he opened the one from his father, three pages of carefully written German telling news of the family. David, now eighteen, hoped to go to America soon and had been studying English at the local school. *The house feels so empty without your dear Mama.* With a pang of homesickness, Morris tried to imagine her kitchen without her. *But Balbina stops by every now and then to help the twins with the cooking and cleaning.* Finally, he wrote, *everyone is well and sends their love.*

Eyes cast down, Morris laid the letter on his desk to read again later.

He picked up the lavender envelope addressed to him with his old name, Morris Lion, studied the beautiful script, ran his fingers across the words, and drew a deep breath, his heart skipping a beat. A letter from his dear Jette.

Morris imagined her writing him as she lounged on a wooden bench near the river that flowed past her father's small vegetable and meat market. Perhaps she sat there and wrote the letter he held in his hand. Carefully, he opened the envelope and, imagining her delicious fragrance, withdrew the papers and read,

> *Juni 10, 1869*
> *Dear Morris,*

Hmm. Not Dearest? How strange. I must tell her I've changed my name to Morris Lyon, but better to inform her in person.

> *I'm now eighteen (my birthday was Dufrene 30. Did you forget?)*

Yes. Damn it! I did.

> *My brother, Fritz, keeps the books in the vineyards north of town, and this spring, he procured a job for me tending the vines. Every day I walk the rows clipping fiendish suckers and any leaf that may cover the burgeoning grapes that deprive them of the warm sun. Though there is a lot of bending and stooping, I love the work, and I am earning my own money.*

Good for you.

> *Have I mentioned Albert?*

No—reading faster—WHO?

*He is a nice Jewish boy from Berlin. Last evening, I went
to a party with him, and we danced together twice.*

What? Morris threw the letter on his desk and stormed around his
small room, yelling, "Jezebel. Traitor." He picked up the letter.

*You haven't written in several months, but your brother
David says you are well.*

"That's because I've been earning money to bring you here," he
fumed, pacing.

*I am sorry this letter is so brief, but I work long hours at the
vineyard to earn money to buy a new gown.*

To wear in Berlin, no doubt.

*And you never know. I might have exciting news next time
I write.*

Oh my God. What are you thinking?

Best as always,

You don't even send *your* love?

Jette

Someone knocked on the door. "Are you all right in there?" Leon
called. "You are making the chandeliers jump."

"I'm fine," Morris said. "Come in and see how I've been betrayed."

Leon entered cautiously, and Morris thrust the letter into his hand.
He sat and slowly read the words Jette had written. "Yes, I can see how

you might be worried," he said, nodding, "but all may not be lost. Tell me about your Jette."

"She's the prettiest girl I know," he said, picturing her shining brown hair tumbling across her lovely shoulders, her large brown eyes encircled with long dark lashes, and her slender body with budding breasts that teased him into craziness. "I've not seen her for three years, but she promised to wait." He stood and tore the letter from Leon's hands. "And now this," he cried, hurling it across the room.

Leon retrieved the letter. Smoothing the pages, he placed it on the desk. "Do calm down, my friend. Tell me, who is Albert?"

Morris sat heavily on the bed, groaning. "Some Jew she met at the vineyard. I wouldn't blame her for marrying him, a wealthy man from Berlin. Far better than the likes of me."

"Come now. She doesn't say she's going to marry him." Leon patted Morris on the shoulder. "I've had some experience with women. I will tell you a secret," he said in hushed tones. "I recently became engaged myself." He frowned. "Here's what I would do. I would write my lady a letter telling her what I have been doing and how hard I have been working."

"It's true," Morris said, "and I've saved quite a lot." He didn't tell Leon he'd planned to open his own business with his earnings. "I have enough to buy her a ticket to New York and one from there to Quincy. "If it were me, I'd get her a birthday gift to send along, something sweet and sentimental. Come with me. We'll get a drink at the bar and talk more."

They walked to the pub, took seats, and ordered beers. "How's the tailor shop going?" Morris asked.

"Pretty good," Leon said. "I've turned it into a clothing store. Both men and women can buy handmade outfits. And I had enough left over to put a down payment on a house. Can't bring Sophie to live in a boardinghouse full of men, can I?" He laughed.

Morris nodded. "So you will be leaving the boardinghouse soon?"

"Yes, but we'll stay in contact. If you can persuade your Jette to come, you must plan dinner with Sophie and me, but for now, you should get to your letter writing."

The two parted, and Morris went back to his room. Instead of reaching for a piece of boardinghouse stationery, he retrieved his bank book and studied the balance at the bottom of the page. His personal funds had grown, and he planned to open his own wool, fur, and hide company, but not in Quincy. With a sense of pride, Morris thought about writing a letter to David, whom he hoped he could soon bring to America to help start a business.

But now, he had a big decision to make. Should he send for David or Jette? Given the circumstances, he saw little choice. If he really loved Jette, he must bring her to Quincy before she did something foolish like marrying a dolt named Albert. As he sat staring at his bankbook, he gave the problem careful consideration.

He had promised David three years ago he would send money as soon as possible to bring him to America. There was no doubt he had accumulated the required funds. David would be useful, but he would need time to acclimate and learn the language.

Yet, Jette was smart, capable, and quick to learn. She would make a good addition to his new business. He'd been in no hurry to marry, content to increase his customer list and seek his own pleasurable diversions. Now he realized he'd risked a fine marriage partner and should move quickly to correct the error. He must fetch Jette as soon as it could be arranged.

Saturday, Morris ignored the Jewish Sabbath and made his way to the offices of the International Shipping Company. Posters of sailing vessels hung on the walls, and a gentleman sat behind a cluttered desk waiting on another customer, a woman with an unruly child on her lap.

Uneasy, Morris stood waiting. The day was warm, and perspiration dampened his shirt. At last, the woman completed her business and left.

The salesman's nameplate said Henry Müller. A fellow of some sixty years sporting a dapper goatee, he motioned Morris to the chair and said, "Phew. It's a hot one, isn't it? So, tell me, what can I do for you?"

"I wish to purchase a ticket from Germany to New York." Morris's voice was firm, but he couldn't help rubbing his fingers together.

The salesman pulled a list from a file behind his desk and thumbed through the manifests. "Well, let's see here. There is a passenger ship sailing the 3rd of July from Bremerhaven."

"No, no. That will never do." Morris figured in his head—sometime in July, she'll receive my letter, and she'll need time to pack and so forth. "I guess she can make it by the end of September."

"I can book her on the *SS Adolophine* to set sail 29 September from Bremerhaven. The vessel *SS Breanna* is scheduled to leave Amsterdam on September 30. Are you interested in first or second class?"

"What is the cost difference?"

"First class on the *Adolophine* is $80 and promises an outside view."

"And second class?" Morris asked.

"Sixty dollars and famously includes meals. Who is it for, may I ask?"

"My future wife," Morris said.

Henry Müller gave a quick little smile. "And her name, sir?"

"Jette Haas," and then Morris had another thought. "I should mention she'll be traveling alone."

"In that case, the *SS Breanna* is the better choice, though a tad more expensive. It provides a matron responsible for the care and safety of single women passengers."

"Is it an old vessel or new?"

Mr. Müller handed Morris the description of the *SS Breanna*. "She's owned by Amsterdam Shipping, which has been transporting immigrants since 1860 and has proved a reliable firm." The salesman peered around Morris at the office where two men in business suits and a fidgety woman sat waiting. "Now, sir, if you're interested, I can reserve her passage today."

The brochure Mr. Müller handed him made the *SS Breanna* appear much finer than the *Deamonti*, that misbegotten pile of junk he'd sailed on. Inside were pictures of the adequate staterooms and the spacious dining areas. "Second class will do nicely," he said. You may reserve a room for her."

"Excellent choice, sir. I will send a letter to my office in Amsterdam. She can pick it up at her convenience. Including the cost of the mail and handling," Müller moved his figures up and down his arithmometer, "the total will be $72.31."

Though it was a considerable sum, Morris had been expecting more. He reached into his wallet, withdrew the required amount, and received a receipt, which he carefully folded and put in his pocket. "May I take this leaflet?" he asked.

"Of course, of course. Thank you, and bon voyage to your bride."

The town carillon rang twelve noon. Morris went down the street to the train depot to check on trains from New York City to Chicago. He'd meet Jette there and take her to Quincy.

"The New York Central Railroad provides such service in a round-about manner," the ticket agent said from his post behind an enclosed counter. He removed his watch from his vest pocket, checked the time, and began to pull down a shade. "I'm closed for lunch. Come back later."

"No, wait," Morris called. "I need to buy a ticket for my lady. She is coming by ship from Germany on October 30th."

The ticket agent sighed. "Maybe," he said.

"What?"

"Her ship may arrive earlier or later than anticipated. Don't buy a ticket here. Send her the money. When she gets to New York, she can go to the train terminal at 27th and 4th Street and get her own ticket." The agent looked at his watch and pulled down the shade.

Morris made a note to write Jette and send her the schedules. Then he went down the street to Heiman's Jewelry Store on 5th, but he found it closed. He'd forgotten today was the Sabbath.

Too late for services at the Synagogue, Morris spent the rest of the day drowning his problems with friends at his local bar and slept off his well-earned hangover on Sunday.

At ten o'clock Monday morning, June 22nd, Morris stood outside Heiman's Jewelry Store waiting for it to open. As the lights came on and the door swung wide, the owner, Hans Heiman, greeted Morris. They'd met at B'nai Abraham, the only synagogue in town where Morris had gone to services. Each of the forty-five members invited promising young Jewish men to observe the New Year with hopes of increasing the size of the congregation. Fredrick from the boardinghouse had persuaded Morris to attend, where he met some of the wealthy Jews in Quincy. But traveling as he did left him no time or interest in joining B'nai Abraham, an orthodox congregation that required frequent attendance and strict observance of Jewish dietary laws.

"Good morning, sir," Morris said to the jeweler, an immaculately groomed, balding gentleman whose blue tie rested smoothly on his rounded stomach. After exchanging pleasantries, the store owner asked, "And what can I show you today?"

"I'm looking for a birthday gift to send my future bride, but it has to be something special." Morris strolled around the shop, gazing through the glass casings at the watches and jewelry displays.

"You must tell me about her," the owner said, his German accent distinct, "so I may suggest an appropriate gift. What kind of jewelry does she like?"

Morris stopped and gazed toward the ceiling. "Well, I don't really know. I haven't seen her for three years.

"After all this time, are you sure she'll still want to marry you?" Heiman asked.

"I hope so," Morris said.

"She sounds like my niece—about the same size, and I know exactly what she would like." He unlocked a case of jewelry and withdrew a gold locket with a dew-drop size rose-cut diamond set in the middle. "One karat," he told the young man.

Morris held the piece in his hand and tried to imagine it around Jette's neck, the diamond sparkling under the store light. "How much is this one?"

"$500."

He quickly set the necklace down. "It is beautiful, but it's out of my price range," he said. "Something smaller and simpler, perhaps."

Mr. Heiman showed him more lockets, gold, silver, and bone, but none came close to matching the beauty of the first one. He glanced toward another glass case with different styles.

The owner appeared deep in thought. Then suddenly, he cried, "Wait, wait. I think I may have the very thing." He went to his workspace and bent to retrieve an item.

When he returned, smoothing his ruffled hair to cover his bald spot, he said, "I've been working on this. It is quite delicate, perfect for a young man to give as a birthday present." With thumb and index fingers, he gently placed in Morris's hand a small, gold heart the size of the cap of an acorn. The entire surface bore tiny seed pearls.

Morris turned it over in his hand, noting the lustrous gold, then to the front, the pearls bluish and softly luminous. "How much?" he asked, thinking it would be the perfect gift for Jette if only he could afford it.

"Because you are of our faith, I will let you have it for $50, including the gold chain. It's a ridiculous price," the plump little man said, cheeks flushed, "but you must promise to join the synagogue and be married there. Is it a deal?"

It was a big expense, and Morris had no interest in joining the temple, but the jewelry had seized his heart. He hoped it would capture Jette's as well. Taking a deep breath, he agreed.

With his prize secured in a soft linen bag, he walked quickly to Ziskind's, where the company's prim receptionist greeted him. He hurried to a desk he used now and then and wrote a letter to Jette explaining how hard he'd been working and how he finally had enough money to send for her. He enclosed the *SS Breanna* pamphlet with instructions on how and where to pick up her ticket.

Taking one of Ziskind's large manilla express mail envelopes used to post by rail to New York and then by ship overseas, he inserted the gift and the *SS Breanna* pamphlet. He enclosed the printed schedule for her train with instructions on how to get to the terminal and what kind of ticket to buy. He encircled a few examples in red. Finally, he wrapped ten ten-dollar bills in a blank piece of paper and placed them next to the *SS Breanna* folder. The letter he withheld long enough to add the date, June 23, 1869, and his final inveiglement.

*I love you with all my heart, the symbol of which is enclosed
as a belated birthday gift.*

You're adoring Morris.

PS I will meet you in Chicago.

He placed the manilla envelope with the appropriate amount of
money for postage in the outgoing mail and left to call on his last customer of the day.

Chapter Eleven
EICHSTETTEN, GERMANY

JULY 1869

Jette's father and her brother had gone to work. Gertrude had fixed the men's breakfast. She then washed Papa's bloody butcher shop shirt and pants, hanging them out to dry. Jette came to the kitchen for tea. As she slathered fresh strawberry jam on her thick piece of bread, she heard the tinkle of the mailman's bell. She jumped up and ran down the path to greet him.

"I have something for you," the postman called and waved a big, brown envelope over his head.

"Oh, Henrich. You are such a tease," Jette said, reaching to retrieve it.

"Express mail," he bantered, his official, red-trimmed postal visor cap slipping over his graying hair.

"Must be something important," he said, giving her the package. Then, straightening his hat and adjusting the brown leather bag, one of two such items he carried, he rearranged his vest so that its large silver buttons aligned. "I have much to deliver today," he said, handing her the rest of her mail before hurrying off.

She recognized the Ziskind name in the upper left-hand corner of the large, brown envelope. Morris had used his employer's stationery before, but what could this be? Rushing home, she called to her sister. "Interesting letters today."

Gertie finished hanging the clothes and came into the kitchen. "What have you there?"

Jette opened the manilla envelope and gently shook out the contents. Ten ten-dollar bills appeared. "Look at this, will you?" she said. "I'm rich." She then retrieved the *SS Breanna* pamphlet. A beautiful ocean-going vessel graced the cover. Inside, she found instructions in Morris's bold handwriting.

This ship will bring you to America. You must pick up your second-class ticket in Amsterdam.

And he'd written more details. But she skipped forward, reading,

The SS Breanna sails on 29 September.

Jette glanced at the calendar hanging on the cupboard door. What was today? 10 Juli. She counted the weeks forward. "That's only eleven weeks from now," she cried, planting a huge kiss on her sister's pink cheek.

Gertie frowned and brushed at her face. "What's all this about?" she asked.

Jette read the letter more carefully. "Morris has sent for me. See?" She waved the ten-dollar bills. "We are going to get married."

"Does he say that?"

"Well, no, but we have an understanding. Before he left, Morris made me promise to wait." She studied her words and said impishly, "The truth is, I got tired of waiting, so I wrote him a letter which, I dare say, got him more than a little worried."

Gertie groaned. "Oh no. What did you write?"

Jette sighed. "Morris's sisters thought he was being unfaithful all alone in America. I wrote him I'd met a man named Albert, fictitious, of course, a silly joke meant to make him jealous."

"Yes, and quite reprehensible."

"Maybe so," Jette said, "dancing around the room, but it worked. "He sent money and bought me a ticket to America."

"And if things change?" Gertie asked, a concerned look on her face. "What if you get there and he won't marry you?"

"Posh," Jette said but saw fear in her sister's eyes. "Oh, dearest Gertie. You are such a worrier. Never mind. I can take care of myself."

Of that, Gertrude had no doubt. Their mother had died of an infection turned septic at age thirty-one. Their father, Liebmann, already 62 years old, was left with four children under twelve. Sixteen-year-old Ricka, the oldest, had cared for the family until she married. Then the task fell to Gertie, twelve, who performed her dead mother's chores as best she could. She tried to keep track of brother Fritz, a lively boy of eleven who took to running the streets, and Jette, a ten-year-old mischief-maker and the apple of our father's eye. Together, they stole their older sister's carefree teenage years.

Gertie's frown disappeared. "All right. Let's see what else he sent." She pointed to the small linen package.

Jette unwrapped a little gold heart encrusted with tiny pearls, clasped it to her breast, and then hung it about her neck. Any doubts Gertie had about Morris's love for her sister fled her mind.

He wrote which train Jette should take from New York to Chicago and where he would meet her. Jette slipped the money he'd enclosed into her pocket. "Well, you'll have to get Papa's blessing," Gertie cautioned, "but I'll try and help you with that," she said, getting back to her chores.

That evening, as Jette walked home from the vineyards with Fritz, she told him of her impending trip to America. When he heard the details of Morris's letter, her brother looked at her and said, "My dear sister, Papa will never let you go."

Jette stopped and gripped his arm. "You and Gertie must help me convince him."

"If it were me or Gertrude off to America, Papa wouldn't give a fig," Fritz said, wistful and sad. "But you're his favorite, his baby girl."

Jette spread her hands. "I know, but we are not children anymore. I am almost nineteen. If Ricka was still here, she could convince him."

Fritz turned and resumed walking. "I'll do what I can," he said, "but don't hold out your hopes."

Gertrude greeted the two at the door. "Supper is ready," she said. "Papa went fishing on the Dreisam and brought home a big salmon. He is washing up, so you must hurry and do the same." Jette noted Gertie had gone to some trouble for the evening meal. She'd set the table with lovely linen only used for special occasions and placed fresh-picked daisies at everyone's place. A pot of soup bubbled on the stove, a succulent rib roast rested in the wood-fired oven, and a big bowl of homegrown vegetable salad sat ready to serve. Papa's fish would have to wait till tomorrow.

He came to the table, rubbing his big hands together. "My favorite matzo ball soup in the middle of summer," he said, peeking under the lid. "And flowers, too? Is it somebody's birthday?"

Gertie laughed. "Of course not. I felt like cooking today."

After slurping their soup and downing the fluffy matzo balls, Papa carved the meat, and Gertie passed the salad. Papa told of his day's events, the ladies who'd graced his establishment, a farmer who brought cows to be butchered, Hans Fienberg's son to be a bar mitzvah.

Fritz complained about his female supervisor. "She's on my behind all the time. 'Keep your mind on the books,' she yells when I talk to the girls."

Jette laughed. "I hear you whistle at the pickers, you naughty boy. The frau is the only one that can keep you in line."

"Well, work at the vineyard brings good money, and the grapes are growing with only a slight insect infestation," he said.

Jette cut the Bundt cake and bragged about the vines she'd tended.

After dinner, Liebmann Dukas Haas rose from the table. His body sagged with fatigue. He grabbed his pipe and, joined by Fritz, made his way to a chair on the stoop for a smoke. Jette cleared the table and washed the dishes. Gertie gathered Papa's clothes from the clothesline and brought them inside to fold. "Now that he's well-fed and content, I'll mention your trip," she said. "Let me handle it."

Jette nodded and pressed Gertie's hand in hers.

The girls joined the men sitting on an old wooden bench that leaned against the stone house. A church bell tower chimed. Daisies danced in the breeze as the golden sun began its downward slide toward the horizon.

Slowly, Gertie drew a breath to speak, but before she could utter a word, Papa said, "I decided to go fishing today and came home for my pole."

Jette stiffened.

"And I found this on the kitchen table." He pointed to the Ziskind envelope.

Heart thumping, Jette said, "Yes. It's from Morris." *Had Papa looked inside?* "A nice long letter," she said with a smile.

"So I see."

"Yes. It's wonderful news," Gertie said. "Jette is going to America."

"No, she isn't," Papa said. "I forbid it."

"And perhaps I'll go with her," Gertie rushed on as though Papa hadn't spoken.

"I have been to Amsterdam many times," Fritz echoed. "I can take them and see them properly on board the ship."

Surprised, Jette clapped her hands, thinking her dear brother and sister had saved the day. "Oh, how lovely. What good times we will have."

"There will be no good times," Papa said, his booming voice filling them with fear. "You are not going. And that is the end of it." He rose and stalked into the house.

Jette rushed after her father. "Wait, Papa," she cried. "Don't you see? Morris and I plan to get married. He sent money and a ticket on a ship with a guardian matron. This flyer explains everything. Gertie and I will share the room. We will be perfectly safe."

"I will not allow it," Papa roared. "If you disobey me, you will no longer be my daughter."

Jette gasped. "Oh, Papa, surely you don't mean that," she whispered. "Perhaps David can take me. He knows about financial matters, and I have money," a spark of hope in her tone.

"This discussion is over." He turned abruptly and went to his bed.

Aghast, Jette stood in the middle of the spotless kitchen, eyes wide, lips parted. As realization dawned, she sank to a chair, her miserable wails filling the pervasive quiet. At last, her breath returned to normal, and her crying stopped. She raised her head from the kitchen table, wiped her tears, clasped the pendant that hung around her neck, and made plans to go to America.

Chapter Twelve
GERMANY

FALL 1869

In the quiet of the room she shared with Gertie, Jette picked up her pen and began a letter to Morris.

August 5, 1869

At long last, you've sent for me. Papa has forbidden me to go, but he cannot stop me. I wear the beautiful necklace you sent close to my heart, and it gives me courage. I will be on my way to you soon.

She had more exciting news to write.

Gertrude may accompany me to America, and Fritz Promises to take us to Amsterdam and see us safely aboard ship.

She didn't disclose how Papa spoke not a word to her and did not acknowledge her presence. If she stood in his way, he walked around her, expressionless, hands at his side.

Nor did she tell Morris that Gertie had abandoned her bold self and crept around the house cleaning and fixing meals often left uneaten or that Fritz stayed away, materializing only twice—once to bring a trunk into which she and Gertie packed their clothes. That left only enough room for a few precious belongings—a favorite tea set and cherished perfume bottles that had once belonged to their mother.

Each day, Jette hoped her father would relent. She greeted him in the morning and blew him a kiss at night, but he was implacable.

On the day of her departure, exhilarated and nervous, Jette presented herself at her father's butchery. Papa stood behind the counter holding up a well-marbled piece of meat for his customer, Frau Grubber, to see.

"Excuse me, Papa," Jette interrupted, unable to control her excitement. "I've come to say goodbye."

"Oh? Where is your daughter going?" Frau Grubber inquired.

"She is not my daughter," Papa said.

Jette hurried to the counter. "It may be a long time before I can come home for a visit."

Papa beckoned Frau Grubber. "Will you please tell this girl if she persists with this nonsense, she will have no home to return to?"

"Leave me out of this," Frau Grubber said.

The butcher threw up his hands and yelled, "Ach! Now, this non-daughter runs off my business."

Tears welled up in Jette's eyes. "I will miss you so, but don't you see? Morris and I plan to marry and have a family of our own." She wiped her eyes. "We'll return someday, or you can visit us in America. Wouldn't that be grand?" She went to kiss him goodbye.

But Liebmann turned his head and pointed toward the door.

Appalled, Frau Grubber followed Jette out. "You poor motherless child," she said. "Sometimes our German men have no *verstand* or understanding. They can be such Dutchmen. He'll miss you when you're gone."

Jette went home to pick up her luggage, but when she arrived, she found Gertie unpacking her half of the trunk. "What are you doing?" Jette asked.

"I've decided not to go," Gertie said, her gaze lowered. "I can't leave Papa alone."

"He won't be alone. He'll have Fritz."

"That boy is so often away. Who will cook Papa's meals and clean his house when he's gone?"

Jette sank to the bed.

"I'm sorry, dear sister. But You'll have Morris to comfort you. "Papa has no one."

"What of the tea set and Mama's perfume bottles?" Jette said.

"You take them. They'll remind you of home." Gertie hugged her sister closely. "I'll miss you."

The sun shone bright on the vineyards that afternoon as Jette and Fritz walked to Rudolph Eigersteim's narrow, flat-bottomed barge on the Rhine. It would take them to Amsterdam. "Only hauling grain today," Rudy said to his passengers. "You're welcome aboard."

"Before you ship off alone to a new country, we must teach you how to take care of yourself," Fritz told Jette, nodding to the captain. "We only have three days, so pay attention."

"What are you talking about, silly? I won't be alone. There are hundreds of people on that ship."

"Did you know that on this very boat, thieves have tried to take advantage of my lady customers?" Rudy said.

Mouth dropping open, Jette looked amazed. She assumed a fighting stance and raised her hands.

"The first lesson is to use your elbows and knees, not these puny things you call fists," Fritz said.

She laughed, but the men were quite serious.

Rudy told her to try hitting his upheld hands, but time and again, she missed. He showed her the right way to throw a punch and how to perform choke holds and clutches. "Wearing a dress makes it harder, but you can do it."

They moved the grain around to make space for her to practice. She had three days to learn, and it took her two to get the hang of it. Rudy showed her choke holds and clutches and taught her how to kick an assailant in the most vulnerable spots. Jette trained with the man not steering the boat every morning and every afternoon.

By the journey's end, she felt ready to face America alone. Rudy gave her this advice. "Avoid risky situations. Trust your instincts. You'll know what to do. Be confident."

She thanked Captain Rudy and hugged Fritz for a long time.

"I wish you would stay," her brother said as he stood on the shore bidding her goodbye.

"Take care of Papa for me," she whispered.

"Gertie and I will do the best we can. And you! Don't forget your lessons."

Jette nodded, threw her shoulders back, and resolutely walked up the gangplank. As a blast from the ship's horn called the stragglers, immigrants crowded the rails of the *SS Breanna*. Climbing to the poop deck for a better view, Jette caught a glimpse of her brother and waved a final goodbye, not knowing when or if she would ever see him again.

Mail to and from Germany took months. Morris had a hard time focusing on his work while he waited to hear from Jette, but finally, her letter arrived. Dismayed that her father had forbidden her to leave, he was dazzled by her spunk to come alone. But then he read further. Her sister, Gertrude, would accompany her. Good Lord. He'd had second thoughts about bringing Jette to Quincy, and now he must reckon with her sister, too. What had he done? He only had until the end of October to figure this out.

Frantic, he went in search of Mrs. Becker. He found her in the yard planting tulips. Calming his ragged nerves, he helped her dig holes for the bulbs and then begged for a moment of her time.

She brushed the dirt from her apron and motioned Morris to the porch swing while she took a seat in the rocker. "Problem?" she asked, gently putting the chair in motion.

"Yes," Morris said. "My girlfriend arrives from Germany at the end of October, and I need a place for her to stay. Perhaps now that Leon has moved…"

"Not here, if that's what you're thinking. It would be highly improper. Do you plan to marry her?" Mrs. Becker asked.

"If she'll have me," he responded, "though I haven't seen Jette in three years."

"That's a long time, but she wouldn't come if she didn't still love you. Let me ask around. Perhaps I could find her a room nearby. My goodness," she said. "You've been here for quite a while. If you go off and get married, Thomas will miss you, and so will I." She patted Morris's shoulder and went back to planting.

The following day, Morris stopped by Leon's store. It no longer looked like a tailor's shop. Handsomely outfitted male and female mannequins stood in the window. Inside, an array of ladies' gowns and menswear hung within easy reach. "Have you time for a drink?" Morris asked.

As they sat at the bar swigging five-cent beer, Morris grumbled to Leon about his problems.

"How do you manage to get yourself into these messes, my friend?" Leon said. "You should have thought of a place for your Jette to stay before you sent for her."

"I know, but what can I do?"

"All right, dummkopf. I will help you. Do you belong to the synagogue?"

"No, and I haven't been observant of traditional laws," Morris said.

"Shame on you. You must ask God to forgive you," Leon said, frowning. "Now's your chance to join B'nai Abraham. Yom Kippur begins Wednesday. Meet me at the synagogue in time for the *Kol Nidre*."

"I will," Morris said, remembering the first words sung of the beautiful, haunting melody absolving Jews of vows they made when forced by anyone to convert to Christianity. It allowed them once again to pray as Jews.

"And don't worry," Leon said. "The rabbi and our members can help in so many ways." He stopped to take a swallow of his beer. "Your father is a shochet, isn't he? I'll introduce you to our butcher. He's a good man."

"I know him already," Morris said. "Ziskind buys his hides."

"So there you are. You already have a connection." Leon finished his beer and rose to leave. "I need to get home to my new bride, but I'll be waiting for you on Wednesday. Don't forget?" he said with a shake of his finger.

Yom Kippur fell on the 16th of September, only a week away. When he got home, Morris went to his room and took down a luggage carrier from the shelf inside his closet. He lay the black velvet pouch his mother embroidered in gold thread with the Hebrew word for *Blessing*. He paused, feeling his mother's love as he touched the word. Since leaving Ettenheim, he had not opened the bag nor felt a need for its contents, but the time had come. He knew he must make a Jewish home for his bride.

He opened the flap and retrieved the kippah, which he placed on the back of his head.

"What's that?" Thomas said, standing in the doorway.

"What are you doing there, you little rascal?" Morris teased.

"Mother sent me to ask when you are leaving. I don't want you to go, Morris. Do you have to?"

A smile crossed Morris's face. "Yes, but don't worry. We will see each other again. I'm not leaving town."

Thomas pointed to the kippah. "Why are you wearing that little hat?" he asked.

"It's a way of showing respect to God."

"The priest at my church wears a similar one," Thomas said. "He says it keeps his head warm."

"Tell your mother it will be another month or two before I leave. I'll let her know in plenty of time to get another border. Now scoot. I have things to do."

Thomas left and closed the door behind him.

Morris reached into the pouch and retrieved his white wool tallit, a shawl with black strips given to him by his father on the day of his bar mitzvah. Though it was meant to be worn at most religious services, his had remained unused until now. Gently, he unfolded it and fingered the fringes, his mind wandering back to the first day he had covered his shoulder with the garment. "The tassels are to remind you of God's commandments and that you must daily perform them," his father had said, and with Mechul's hands upon his head, Morris remembered his words—"You shall be holy unto your God."

Last in the pouch were his tefillin, black boxes with leather straps meant to be worn on his head and his forearm to remind him that God brought the Jews out of Egypt. But the service of Yom Kippur did not require the wearing of tefillin, so he left them untouched.

The next day at work, Morris sought out his boss. Talking with Leon had given him courage, "I have sent for my bride and now must look for a place to live," he told Mr. Ziskind.

"What exciting news. My wife will be thrilled, for it sounds like a party is in the offing." He smiled and stuck out his hand. "Congratulations. When is the event?"

"A party is a very kind offer," Morris said. "She is due to arrive in New York October 29th. I'll be needing the time off then. And, of course, this week for Yom Kippur services."

"Yes, well, there is only B'nai Abraham, and though I'm a member, it is way too traditional for me. A new temple will be built soon, more reform. We set the cornerstone last July at North 9th Street. You might want to keep that in mind."

"Good to know," Morris agreed. "Guess I'll see you at Wednesday evening services," and he returned to his desk to ponder the answer.

Yom Kippur was the longest and holiest day on the Jewish calendar—twenty-five prayer-filled, workless, fasting hours. So many people had come to the synagogue services Morris had trouble finding his friend, Leon. Men and women mingled and conversed out front, but once inside, women sat apart. Only men occupied the ground floor seats, though as time passed, even they got up and wandered around. Morris saw people he already knew: Herbert and Sarah Ziskind, of course, and Alvin Chernick, who owned the tannery and with whom Morris did much business, Isak Lippmann, who owned another big wool fur and hide business in town. Morris waved at Mrs. Swartz from the dry goods store before she disappeared in the crowd, and Hans Heiman, the jeweler, who ended up sitting two rows in front.

The evening service dragged on until nine. People went home to sleep. They returned the next morning after fasting. Morris, whose wavy auburn hair hadn't been trimmed in months, had trouble keeping his kippah on his head, and the tallit dragged on his shoulder. He could sit still only so long, and then he, too, had to get up and wander around.

Tired and hungry, he rejoiced when Leon invited him to his house to break the fast. While snacking on smoked fish, bagels, sweets, and other delights made by Leon's wife, someone caused him to spill his drink. He thought it an accident until he saw Karl Rothman—the slaughterhouse guy. "If it's not the peddler," the man said, his mouth twisting into an ugly grin. "How are you doing, schmuck?"

"You still work at the slaughterhouse?" Morris asked, though he could smell the answer.

"You looking for a job, are you? They don't hire momzers like you."

Rubbing his fingers together, Morris said, "I don't need a job. I work for Ziskind."

"That crook. He won't buy our hides."

"That's because you tear them up at the killing." Morris's temper rose, and he wondered why Leon would entertain this guy.

"You saying we don't do a good job?" Karl said, his voice getting louder.

Leon stepped between them. He stopped a potential brawl with calming words. But Morris knew whatever was between himself and Karl would have to be addressed someday.

Chapter Thirteen
JETTE'S JOURNEY

1869

Amidst the cries and the crush of the other passengers, Jette felt small and very alone without her intended roommate, Gertrude. A steward guided her below deck to the cabin near the dining room and other common areas. Someone had brought her luggage and placed it on a wooden rack. She found a key to her quarters resting on top of the dresser. This would be home for the coming weeks.

Jette sensed the ship's motion taking her away from everything she'd ever known. Gripped with sudden fear, she sat shaking on the bed, a slab of wood with springs and a thin mattress, her breath coming in short gasps, her trembling arms wrapped around her slim body. What had possessed her to leave the secure, loving home of her father and venture upon the seas to an unknown land?

She flung herself on the bed, a flood of tears wetting the hard pillow. After she cried herself out, she fell into a restless slumber, awakened hours later by a knock on her door. "Dinner in ten minutes," a female voice said. Then clicking footsteps receded down the hall.

Jette rose, washed her face, ran a comb through her hair, and smoothed her slim fitting dress. With an approving look in the mirror and a pinch on her cheeks to bring color, she opened her door and walked to an oblong activity area where ten or twelve tables had been set. Hesitantly, she entered the room noting there were no men were about. Women who seemed to speak a variety of languages and looked as confused as herself sat at tables waiting to be served. Taking a breath, Jette entered and chose a seat at a table for ten. "I'm Jette," she said sitting next to an older woman wearing a wool dress with full sleeves and a wide, bell-shaped skirt.

"Hannah," the lady replied. "Sprechen Sie Deutsch?"

"Ja," Jette answered, delighted.

"Jewish?"

Surprised, Jette asked, "Yes. How did you know?"

"Gott sei Dank," Hannah said. "I can always recognize a fellow Jew."

More women arrived at Jette's table until most places were filled with chattering females.

"Have you met the witch?" Hannah whispered.

"Who?" Jette asked, leaning forward.

"The matron."

"Why do you call her a witch?"

Hannah wrinkled her nose. "Because her job is to police us, to spy. My husband, who works in New York City, has finally sent for me, but as I must travel alone, he booked my passage on a ship with a housemother."

"My fiancé, Morris, did the same for me, but I think he meant for her to keep us safe."

"Well, maybe so, but she watches every move we make," Hannah said. "That's her, talking to the waiters."

The pleasant-looking woman seemed to be giving the crew instructions. Then she turned and appeared to welcome the passengers.

"Uh oh," Hannah murmured. "Here she comes."

The matron didn't look like a witch. She appeared to be the mature, middle-aged, nicely styled, with short, gray hair wearing a conservative navy-blue outfit. She seemed perfect for her job.

"Mind if I join you?" she asked, taking the last seat at the table. Then standing, she picked up a spoon and rapped it on a glass for attention. When the room became quiet, she began to speak.

"I am Frau Finkler, your hostess for this voyage. You may have noticed this dining area and lounge is reserved for women traveling unescorted. My job is to keep you safe and comfortable. Welcome aboard. I will be here to help in any way possible."

The room had filled with perhaps forty or more women, some paying rapt attention and others visiting among themselves.

"Excuse me, ladies." The matron fixed her stare directly on those talking. Instantly quiet, they became quite attentive. "Immediately after we dine, I will meet you in the living area to discuss rules and regulations and to supervise our evening activities. I have sewing and knitting goods, if you are so inclined, and reading materials, too. Plenty to keep you entertained until bedtime. Then you must all go to your rooms for the night."

Hannah gave Jette a poke and said, "See? I told you. She wants to keep us cooped up. This will be so boring."

"Now enjoy your first meal aboard the *SS Breanna* and get to know one another. It will be an exciting few weeks." She gave them a warm, welcoming smile and sat to the patter of polite applause. "Now tell me about yourselves," she said to those sitting near her, and the room filled with conversations.

At the meeting following dinner, Frau Finkler laid out the rules.

"Each of you has received a copy of ships regulations." She handed a stack to Jette and said, "Please take one and pass it along. As you will note, breakfast begins at 7:00 each morning. Sunday, however, Christian services will be held here in the salon starting at 9 am, with brunch immediately following at 11."

"What if we don't care to go?" a peppery redhead asked.

"You are free to stay in your room until time to join the rest of us."

That didn't sound very free to Jette.

"Daily activities begin here in the salon at nine each morning. I will post various opportunities for your enjoyment, such as handcrafts, exercises, and games. Lunch will be served at 12 noon and dinner at 6 sharp. You must be on time for meals, or you will not be served."

She stopped speaking, studied her notes, and then said as though she'd remembered, "Fraternizing with sailors or any other males or members of the ship's crew is strictly forbidden. Are there any questions?"

Jette raised her hand. "Will we be allowed to go on deck for fresh air and leisure time?" she asked.

"You are not to go alone. I will lead a group above board, weather permitting. Otherwise, you are advised to stay below."

All went well for the first few days, but as the women became familiar with each other, little cliques began to form. Soon some disagreements turned into arguments refereed by the matron. Frau Finkler also kept busy preserving the chastity of those girls who took an overt interest in the sailors on board. Once, she even found a sunny day to take her charges on the deck naming the parts of the ship and cautioning them to stay away from the rails.

Jette and Hannah stayed to themselves for the most part. They learned to knit, took turns reading books to each other, and played checkers during the long days at sea but Hannah soon felt nauseous and withdrew to her cabin. Frau Finkler and the ship's doctor cared for those like Hannah who suffered seasickness and other infirmities, but with Hannah unavailable, Jette tried to make friends with the other German speaking girls but found them all cliquishly Christian and patronizing.

Suffocating from loneliness, the stifling heat, and poorly ventilated smells below deck, one Sunday morning, desperate to breath clean fresh air, Jette chose to go on deck alone. While most passengers were sleeping or at church services, she found the hatch. Lifting her skirt high to climb the steps, she opened the door. Though the ship plowed through low-hanging clouds, she found her way to the stern deck. There, with her dress whipping about her ankles, she drew a breath and filled her lungs with fresh sea air.

"Watch that you don't fall, Fraulein," a lone sailor said. "The wind can be fierce, and the boards slippery."

"I'm fine," she said, and climbed down the steps to the main deck. Then she made her way through the mist to the prow.

As the steam-powered ship sliced through the water, she saw the rolling waves and felt the ocean spray. She tried to imagine what life would be like in America. In less than two weeks, she would find out.

Lost in thought, she barely heard the sailor approach. "A lovely Jewess like you shouldn't be here alone," he said.

"What?" she gasped.

"Don't worry. I'll give you what you want, Schnuck."

Scared to smithereens, she turned to run, but he grabbed her and whirled her around. Muffling her cries with his mouth on hers, he tore at her dress and groped her chemise-covered breasts. All at once, she heard Captain Rudy's voice in her head. *"Avoid risky situations. Trust your instincts. You'll know what to do. Be confident."*

To her regret she'd forgotten his first advice, but the rest came rushing back. She reared back, hand-chopped his throat, and drove her knee hard to his groin. He fell to the deck howling, his cries blowing unheard off the starboard bow. Jette gave a mighty kick to his doubled-over form and bolted to the passageway hatch and raced to her quarters. Safe inside her cabin, she locked her door and fell, shaking to the bed.

After her heart quit racing, she bathed, and scrubbed her mouth clean. She washed and mended her blouse as best she could and silently thanked Fritz and Rudy for saving her life. That night at dinner, she heard a sailor had fallen overboard. H*er* sailor? she wondered.

The next day the matron gathered her charges together and introduced them to a handsomely dressed woman. "Frau Braddock is a friend of our captain. She is American-born and has kindly consented to teach you a few words of English to help you get along during your first few weeks in the New World."

"Praise the Lord," Jette whispered to the recovering Hannah.

"Who needs English?" Hannah replied, still pale from her seasickness.

"Guten Morgen," the captain's wife said. "Good morning."

"Good morning," Jette repeated the phrase, the words feeling strange in her mouth.

"My name is Roberta Braddock," the composed woman said.

"My name is Roberta Braddock," the immigrants answered.

"No, no, no," the captain's wife said as she laughed and shook her head. "That is MY name."

One by one, the students understood their mistakes and retried the phrase.

"My name is Jette Haas," Jette announced, understanding the power the new language would give her. She was eager to learn more. Frau Braddock came for only an hour a day except on Sundays, and the few sessions were too short to learn more than a little English. As the time to land in New York City approached, Frau Braddock gathered the women around her and gave them instructions for disembarking. "My dear ladies," she said, "If you've friends or family at the dock to welcome you, you may leave the ship when we land. Otherwise, stay on board and you will be taken to Castle Rock Processing Center."

"What is a processing center?" Jette asked Hannah.

"I don't know but because you have been a good friend, I will tell you a secret. My husband told me to be sure not to go there. They register your name and count your money and sometimes make you bathe. You must get off the boat where we dock."

The day the *Breanna* arrived in New York Harbor, its horn gave three loud blasts and Jette, filled with excitement, caught her first glimpse of America. She tried to disembark with Hannah, but her friend rushed off the ship and Jette had to waited her turn. "Oh, yes," she lied when asked, "Is someone meeting you here?" As other passengers disembarked, she followed along.

In the middle of the melee, Jette stood alone on the busy New York wharf, her trunk by her side. Horse-drawn buggies circled the waterfront. Taking a deep breath, Jette held up a finger.

One pulled up beside her, and the roughly dressed cabby with a jaunty red cap on his head called out cheerfully, "Aye, and where might ye be goin', milady?"

What little English she'd learned flew out of her head. "I must get to the train station," she said in German.

"What's that you say?"

"Hauptbahnhof," she yelled as though he was deaf.

He shrugged, shook his head, and urged his horse forward.

Frustrated, she fished in her handbag for Morris's letter of instructions. Railroad station at 27th and 4th, he had written.

As the crowd on the waterfront thinned out, a horse-driven carriage with big wheels appeared. Its driver sat above the conveyance wearing a black coat and a top hat. Frantically, she waved at him, and to her great relief, he pulled over.

"Bahn," she said. "Train."

"Which train station?" he asked.

"27 and 4," she said, holding the letter for him to see.

He came down off his seat and looked at the writing. "Twenty-seventh and fourth. New York Central Station," He smiled kindly at her. "I been in your shoes," he mumbled to himself. I'll take you where you're going." He opened the door to the carriage and motioned her in.

It was two steps up, and her dress brushed the dirt from the rim of the wheel, but she ducked low to protect her hat and gratefully collapsed into a seat inside. The driver closed the door and climbed up top. "It ain't far," he called to her through a small door atop the carriage.

Though Jette didn't understand, his voice sounded cherry, and she allowed herself the pleasure of settling back and enjoying the ride. The wharves disappeared, and the streets became a tumult of people and conveyances surrounded by buildings so tall they blocked the sun. She noted women wearing layered skirts, the top one pulled up to shockingly show the petticoat beneath. Long sleeves, high necks, and small hats appeared to be in style. Everyone seemed in a hurry.

Her carriage pulled to a stop in front of the terminal. The driver removed her trunk and helped her step down. Brushing at her dress, she thanked him and paid him with coins that appeared to be adequate. Then with a *danke* to the driver and a gentle pat on the neck of the carriage horse, Jette clasped the handle of her trunk. Dragging it behind her, she entered the train station walking right past the newspaper on the stand near the door. It read October 28, 1869, a day earlier than Morris expected.

For Morris, the closer October 29th came, the more excited he got. Jette and Gert would have traveled by train from New York to Chicago on Tuesday. They should arrive at the Canton Terminal, where filled with eager anticipation, he'd pick them up. He got to the terminal, but they weren't there. He tapped on the lady's room door. "Jette?" he called and even looked inside but there was no one there. Morris found the ticket agent in his office, "My fiancé and her sister are traveling on the train from New York to Chicago. Is it late?" he inquired.

"No. That train arrived on time," the ticket agent said. "Maybe your party missed their connection. There will be another tomorrow. Come," he said. "We'll check on the board outside."

Morris scanned all the bulletins. "Oh No!" he cried. The *SS Breanna* docked 10-28. Pier 57 10 am EST. Royal Dutch Shipping. A day before I expected." He wrang his hands. "They speak not a word of English, two German girls, alone in the city," he moaned to the ticket agent.

"Try the depot at Wells Street," the ticket master told him.

Morris raced to the depot, but the sisters weren't there either. Oh God! Where were they?

Frantic, Morris made his way to the Miriam Depot on West Kinzie and Canal Street. Maybe their train took them there, but the building stood empty of passengers. As a last resort, he went to the police station on State Street. A fat sergeant with brass buttons straining to stay latched, manned the desk. Morris related his story.

Though sympathetic, the policeman offered little help. "We'll check on the stations, but that's all we can do. Don't worry. They'll show up. They always do."

Morris turned away, fraught with despair. Loath to give up, he tried one more location, the Chicago branch of the Chicago, Burlington, and Quincy Railroad at Webster and Van Buren. Had anyone seen two women traveling alone? No one matched Morris's description.

At the police station, Morris left word where he could be reached. Not knowing what else to do, he bought a train ticket back to Quincy. Upon arriving, he went to Ziskinds and slumped into the chair at his desk.

"Boss wants to see you," someone said.

Morris nodded, knowing he was in trouble. He got up and knocked on Mr. Ziskind's door.

"Come in."

He opened the door, and there stood Jette, lovely beyond words. "Oh, my God. Is it really you?"

She laughed and ran into his arms. "They hugged and kissed. Then remembering where they were, Morris took her hand and led her to a chair. "How did you get here?"

Scowling, she said, "I thought you were going to meet me."

"Lord knows, I tried," he said.

"You have much to explain," she said in a stern voice.

"As do you and your sister."

"She couldn't come."

Eyebrows raised, Morris gave her a questioning look.

Mr. Ziskind smiled and said, "Get out of my office, you two. Morris, take the rest of the day off, but you must keep your appointment in Chicago tomorrow. And you, my dear," he said, addressing Jette, "must take him firmly in hand."

She nodded, unmistakably up to the task.

Chapter Fourteen
QUINCY, ILLINOIS

1871

As they stepped out of the office into the descending sun of late afternoon, she waved her hand in front of her nose. "What is that awful smell?"

"It's probably skunk skins, but Mr. Ziskind says it's the smell of money—furs and hides. He stopped walking and solemnly took her gloved hand in his. "Can you ever forgive me for not meeting you? Your ship arrived a day earlier than I expected. I went to Chicago, but you weren't there."

So that's what happened. You came but on the wrong day." She burst out laughing.

He shook his head. "How did you manage, and where is Gertrude?"

"It's a long story, and I'm starving."

"Of course you are. Let's leave your belongings here, and I'll take you to one of my favorite places to dine. There's a nice German restaurant down the street. Would you like to give it a try?"

Jette nodded vigorously and allowed him to guide her through the bustling streets to Der Schwarzwald. Inside, flickering lanterns gave the paneled restaurant a woodsy, comfortable feel. The hostess came to greet him. "Good evening, Mr. Lyon," she said with a beautiful smile. "Table for two?"

"Yes, my favorite by the window, if you please." He switched to German. "This is my Liebchen, all the way from Eichstetten. She only arrived today and is hungry for some good Saxon food." Turning to Jette, he said, "Meet Gretchen, the first person to speak to me in Quincy."

Morris laughed and gave her a warm look when Gretchen responded, "Yes, and he's been a good customer ever since. He dines here often. Follow me."

She led them to a pine table in the center of which sat a chunky clay pot filled with fresh yellow chrysanthemums. "What may I get you, my dear? And you, Mr. Lyon? Your usual black beer?"

Yes, and tea for the lady?"

Jette held up her hand. "I'll have what he's having," she announced.

"Good choice," Morris said.

Bowing, Gretchen left and returned with two frothy steins of beer, a bowl of German cheddar cheese spread, and finger-sized pretzels.

When she'd gone, Morris leaned forward and raised his stein. "A toast to my beautiful Liebchen, here at last. I have something exciting to tell you."

"I can hardly wait to hear," she said, a curious smile appearing on her lips.

"I've changed my name."

"What," she cried. The smile disappeared.

"Only the i in Lion to a y, instead. Here in this country, the name Lion means a fierce animal. Some friends and customers teased me about it, so my boss suggested I change the spelling to L Y o n." "Do you mind?" I hope not because someday soon, it will be your name, too."

As she frowned, considering the change, Morris gazed at her. "You know, I remember you as a pretty fifteen-year-old girl, but here you are three years later, a young woman of beauty and grace."

Her smile returned.

"When I couldn't find you at the Chicago railroad station," Morris said, "I almost went crazy. I looked for you and Gertrude everywhere. I even wondered if I would recognize you."

"I am so sorry," Jette said. "I followed your directions, but fates turned against me. And no one I encountered spoke German."

Morris nodded, silent.

"Gertie decided she couldn't leave father, so the extra money you sent came in handy. The only tickets left on the train were in first class." She laughed. "Using my non-existent English and my stupidity, I took all the money from my purse and laid it on the counter in front of the ticket agent, hoping it would be enough."

Morris stared at her. "What if he'd simply picked it up and walked away?"

"But he didn't. Instead, he licked his fingers and carefully peeled off a few bills. He shoved the rest back to me."

She dipped a pretzel into the cheese, took a bite, and followed it with a swallow of beer. "Next, I had a porter help me find a plush seat on the luxurious Erie Canal Train to Chicago. In the dining car, no one spoke German. The schwartzes in spotless white coats and white cotton gloves helped me order from a menu I couldn't read."

Morris burst out laughing. "How did you manage to get from Chicago to Quincy?"

"You must have just missed me. I showed people your letter. A nice couple walked me to the right station. When I arrived here in Quincy, I had only to mention Herbert Ziskind's name," she said nonchalantly, "and here I am."

"It's a miracle," Morris grinned. "A testament to your ingenuity."

Jette glanced at the menu. "Well, at least I understand this," she said, pointing to sauerbraten, "one of my favorites."

"Sounds good to me," Morris said. He motioned to Gretchen, who came and took their orders.

While they waited, they snacked on the pretzels and cheese. "So tell me, "Jette said, "about your life in America. Your work? Your friends? Your activities? What may I expect?"

He described how he'd peddled items to farmers in the country, "At first, I sold shoes, scarves, mirrors, notions of one kind or another, needles and thread."

"Farmers buy needles and thread?" she asked, eyebrows raised.

"No. Of course not. Their wives do."

"So you called on the wives?"

"No, no. Well, yes. It was a long time ago. Now I buy and sell many things, such as wool, fur, hides, feathers, tallow, beeswax, and even broom corn for Ziskind. I don't call on the women anymore."

"Because they have enough needles and thread?" she teased.

"No, because the money comes from the farmer's wool and hides."

Gretchen brought their dinner, soup first, salad, and the ginger-spiced roast topped with lush brown gravy.

"Yum," Jette said. "The ship's cooks lacked imagination. I've been so hungry for good German food."

They ate and chatted affably. Gretchen returned and suggested they try the specialty of the house.

"Don't tell me—Black Forest Cake," Jette cried.

"Ja—chocolate cake filled with fresh cream and cherries soaked in Kirschwasser."

"Who could resist? Perhaps Morris and I can share." She placed her hand on Morris's arm possessively.

"Oh, no. I want one of my own."

Gretchen returned carrying two slices covered with creamy chocolate and cherry-coated icing. "On the house," she said. "Guten appetit, Frauline."

Jette ate a few bites. She moaned with delight, wiped bits of cream from the edge of her mouth, and took a final sip of beer. "Delicious," she said. "Thank you for a lovely meal. But now, dear Morris, you must help me find a place to stay."

He noticed she placed her hand to her mouth and delicately yawned. "I bet you are tired," he said.

"It has been a very long day."

"I've found a cottage I think will be most suitable," he told her.

"A cottage?"

"It needs work and furnishings."

"And then?" Jette prompted, but Gretchen came to ask if they needed anything more.

Morris declined and requested the check. "Well, I…ah….think we should do what we planned before I left home."

"Yes, and what was that? It's so long ago I scarcely remember."

He stared at her, trying to read her thoughts. He took her hand and firmly said, "We should marry."

"Perhaps," she said, a slight curl to her lips, "but suddenly, I feel like we barely know each other, Morris."

"I'm still the same me."

"Are you? And am I the same?" she asked. "Maybe we should take some time and find out."

He withdrew his hand. "If that's what you want."

They left the restaurant, Morris feeling the strain between them. They walked to a lovely hotel at 3rd and Main, The Quincy House. He escorted her through the female entrance that bypassed the bar and the billiards tables and engaged a room for her. She offered to pay with the money she had left over, but he gave the clerk enough for a week's stay.

"I'll fetch your bags here from Ziskind's and have them sent up to your room," he said. "Will you be all right?"

"I'll be fine," she said.

"Tomorrow is Friday," he told her. "I have an appointment in Chicago at the stockyards and won't be back until late Saturday night. I've been staying with my friends, Leon and Sophie Stern, while I get the cottage ready. Why don't I bring them with me on Sunday morning? We'll have brunch together and go see the house."

"Gut," she said, "Until then." She gathered her skirt and began the two-story climb to her hotel room.

Jette unlocked the door to her room, flung it open, and threw herself on the bed. Things hadn't gone as planned. He didn't meet her in Chicago and left her to find her own way. He'd changed his name. She groaned. After years of thinking of herself as Frau Lion, though it sounded the same, she'd have to be somebody else. She rolled over and stared at the ceiling. Did he act too friendly with Gretchen at the restaurant? Was he different than the boy she remembered?

Worn out, she removed her clothes, washed herself as best she could, and crawled into bed.

That night, Morris walked back to Ziskind's to retrieve Jette's belongings, wondering what she was thinking. Didn't they grow up together? Of course, he was the same. Why not marry right away and save the cost of a hotel room? Hadn't he already given her his heart, the gold one she wore around her neck? He shook his head in disbelief.

As he reached the door to Ziskind's, he stopped and gazed in the direction of the hotel. She had looked so small and beguiling. He had very much wanted to kiss her, to take her to her hotel room, but the time and the circumstances prevented that. He would have to convince her to marry him if he still wanted that.

Feeling fully refreshed the following day, Jette decided to familiarize herself with her new surroundings. First, she treated herself to tea and biscuits in the hotel's dining room, the cloth-covered table set with silver utensils and crystal glassware. She'd thought the language might be a frustrating problem, but her server spoke German, as it seemed many people living in Quincy did.

To get the feel of the land, she walked to the bluff overlooking the river. Though the size of the Mississippi dwarfed the little Dreisam in Eichstetten, the sight of the river reminded her of home. She sat on a bench, fighting tears, fear, and longing. What have I done? she asked herself.

Breathing deeply, she turned her back on the sadness and brushed away her tears. She walked aimlessly back to town, looking at the shops and their decorated windows. In doing so, she stumbled upon a name she recognized—Heiman's Jewelry Store. Wasn't that the place Morris purchased her necklace? Yes. Of course. She remembered the packaging. Unable to resist, she went inside and asked to see the owner.

"Sprechen sie Deutsch?" she asked.

"Ja," he answered in her language. "How can I help you?"

"I'm Jette Haas. I believe you made this necklace for me," and she took the little gold heart from beneath her blouse.

Hans Heiman lit up. "I did indeed. I remember making it for Morris Lyon. He's a lovely young man."

"I arrived only yesterday, but his boss, Mr. Ziskind, sent him to Chicago to work today. He won't be back until Sunday."

"Business is business," Heiman said, "but you, my dear, must join me and my wife, Tillie, for early Friday dinner and Shabbat services. She will be delighted, and you'll get a chance to meet our friends. You must come with us."

"I would love that," Jette said, delighted."

That evening, when she arrived back at her hotel, she found a note pinned to her door. It was from Morris, and he'd written in German,

Jette,

Looked but couldn't find you. Have arranged for brunch tomorrow with Leon and Sophie Stern. Please meet me in the lobby at ten.

Morris

The sun shone bright through the hotel windows. People gazed at Jette as she walked down the stairs wearing a dress of powder blue with cream-colored collar and cuffs. She'd slept well, and some of her doubts about Morris had dimmed.

He kissed her lightly on the cheek and introduced her to Leon and Sophie Stern.

In English, Jette smiled and said, "Hello. Nice to meet."

Leon and Morris laughed, and Sophie said, "Nice to meet you, too. Where did you learn that?"

"At services Friday evening. I go with Heiman's."

Brown-haired Sophie, a few years older and a little heavier than Jette, she took the young girl's arm, and they walked together, chatting in German.

"We know a nice little diner down the street where we can eat and become acquainted."

After omelets, coffee, and talking, Morris took them to the cottage he'd bought. Though empty, Jette said she loved its little front porch, the living room, kitchen, and bedroom on the first floor. But the two tiny rooms upstairs were marred by the view of an ugly, old privy in back. Swallowing her distaste, she and Sophie chattered in German about furnishings and common interests while Morris pulled Leon into the garden for a private talk.

"She says she wants to get to know me," he said. "She's known me since childhood."

"How long has it been since she's seen you? Years, no? Give her time."

"I thought we'd be married right away, but I guess you're right. She wants us to date—no chaperones—everything else the same."

"Hmm. Could be fun," Leon said, a sly grin creeping around his mustache and upper lip. "What did you tell her?"

"I'll do as she wants for a while. But we'll see."

Upstairs, looking down at the garden, Jette said to Sophie, "I feel like I barely know him."

"I think you are wise to wait and be sure. Why don't you come to stay with us for a while? Morris can sleep at the cottage until you decide."

"That's a wonderful idea. Are you sure you don't mind?"

"Of course not," Sophie said. "I'd love it, especially now." She glanced at her waist and patted her belly.

Jette squealed.

"Shh. Leon doesn't yet know," Sophie whispered.

Jette stayed with the Sterns long enough to decide whether to marry Morris. For now, she had doubts. If need be, she could get a job as a German-speaking nursemaid and earn enough to go back home.

Morris continued to work long hours, though once he'd asked Jette to join him for an evening of dancing in Chicago, which she refused. There'd be no train home until morning. "It would be improper," she said.

When fall arrived, Morris had two reasons to visit the Weber farm. The sheep needed shearing, but more than that, he wished to discuss his problems with Mary Elizabeth. He timed his trip so that Johann would be gone gathering his herd. "You are a woman of experience. What shall I do?" he asked the lovely farmer's wife. As she rubbed his neck and patted his hand, she advised Morris on ways to woo his Jette. They spent the rest of the evening entertaining each other.

Following Mary Elizabeth's advice, Morris sought Jette out on the weekends for dinner and consulted her about changes at the cottage. He took her for walks in the parks or picnics by the river. Young and inexperienced, she sought ways to keep him off balance with girlish questions and tricks to assure herself he truly cared.

The end to her foolishness came quickly. They had gone to their cottage, where Morris said he wished to make final repairs. As he opened the front door, Jette noted a look of pride on his face. "What is it?" she asked.

He led her into the backyard, saying, "A little surprise."

She squeezed his hand and eagerly scanned the area but saw nothing new. "What is it?"

"I know the sight of that privy upset you. Don't you see it? There's a new shrub in front of it now."

"That's my surprise? A new privy would have been nice, but a shrub to hide it? Is this a joke?"

He turned and walked away.

"Wait," she called, but shaking his head, he went inside and closed the door.

She sat on the back stoop and stared at the healthy little laurel he'd placed in front of the privy and realized what she had done. The thought of losing him made her tears flow. The only thing she wanted—to marry Morris—may now be lost.

She stood, brushed her skirt, and straightened her silk blouse. Not if she could help it. She would not lose him to imagined sins. Not without a fight. She found him in the kitchen, a paintbrush in his hand, touching up the kitchen cabinets he had repaired. He took note of her with a sideways glance and went back to his painting.

"I've come to apologize," she said gently, "not only for what I said in our backyard but for how I have behaved since I arrived in Quincy. How can I explain it? Fear? Lack of trust? Stupidity? Can you ever forgive me?"

She came from behind and lightly placed her arms around his waist. "I've been horrible, a bitch," she said in German, laying her head on his back.

He placed his paintbrush on a piece of paper, wiped his hands on a cloth, turned, and held her at arm's length. "There is nothing to forgive." He shrugged, lightly rubbing his fingers together. "It was too much to expect we could still be in love after so long a time, but don't worry. It's not too late. I shall sell this cottage and use the money to send you back to Germany where you can be with your family and find a man of means. You deserve a successful husband; thus far, I am nothing."

She reached up and touched his cheek. "Stop, Morris. Morris. Give me a chance to make up for my mistakes. I've been stubborn about many things, using your new name for one. From now on, you will be Morris Lyon to me, my dearest. I've been childish," she said, embarrassed and looking away, "insisting on so long a time to get to know one another again. I've known and loved you almost all my life. Against my father's wishes, I came here to Quincy to marry you, and if you'll still have me, that's what I intend to do. Ich liebe dich, Morris, my darling. Will you marry me?" Jette knelt before him.

Laughing, he raised her into his arms, his lips brushing her cheek, her hair, and the little gold heart she wore around her neck. "I accept, my dearest one," he whispered, kissing her the way he'd wanted at the Quincy Hotel.

Faint with joy, she returned his caress. "Soon, I hope."

Morris reached for his old purple coat hanging on the brass door-knob. Silently, he withdrew the small oak box his father had given him, took out the mezuzah, and nailed it to the front door post. This was now their home.

But where to get married? That was the next question. Morris remembered something Mr. Ziskind had mentioned. He made it a point to go ask him. "I'm glad you kept it in mind," Ziskind said, seated in his office desk chair. "We're building a new temple, more reform. We set the cornerstone last July at North 9th Street."

"You say reform. I've heard the word, but what does it mean?"

Ziskind drew a deep breath, and his eyes grew large and then returned to normal. "That's a BIG question requiring a long and thoughtful answer, which I'm not fully qualified to give. I like a mixture of Hebrew and English in my religious services. I want my wife sitting by my side, and I believe the words of the Hebrew Bible were inspired by God, not written by Him. There you have it in a nutshell. For more, you'll have to go ask the rabbi."

That suited Morris's idea of a temple in which to marry. Though Jette frowned, she didn't object if it's what Morris wanted, so they joined the new B'nai Sholom the very next day.

At sundown on the 17th of December, Hanukkah Eve, 1870, the nervous groom, thumb and first finger rubbing together, awaited his bride in the rabbi's study at the reform temple.

Where is she? He wondered as the window light began to fade. Wiping his brow, he paced.

"Sit," Rabbi Wise commanded.

Morris sat, then stood. "What if she's changed her mind?"

Best man, Leon, adjusted his friend's tie. "She'll be here in her own good time."

Attended by Sophie, Jette finally arrived. Gowned in soft blue taffeta with a high bodice and lace trim, her loveliness left Morris breathless.

Together, they went to the rabbi's desk where they, Sophie, Leon, and the rabbi, signed the ketubah, a formal marriage contract that would protect Jette in case of divorce or, God forbid, Morris's death. Then, standing beneath the simple canopy of cloth held by Leon and Sophie, Rabbi Wise performed the service. The nervous young couple exchanged vows and gold wedding bands, hers engraved Morris to Jette and his engraved Jette to Morris. Finally, the rabbi pronounced the blessing. With his heel, Morris shattered the towel-wrapped glass goblet, reminding all to mourn the loss of the temple in Jerusalem and to emphasize the fragileness of marriage. After a brief celebration, they went home to their cottage, and finally, Morris tenderly claimed his bride.

Chapter. Fifteen
WELBORN, ILLINOIS

1871

O
n their weekend honeymoon in Chicago, Morris spent an extrava-
gant amount of money—$7.50 for a night at the fine Palmer House
Hotel, including meals—but he wanted to treat Jette to something special. That evening, they dined on caviar and champagne, steak, and
cherries jubilee.

As Morris toasted his bride, he spied an old acquaintance enter the
restaurant—Gunter Shechter. Morris hardly recognized him. Though
they'd met in steerage, Gunter looked now like he belonged in first
class. He glowed with good health, his opulent hair neatly groomed.
He wore a custom-fitted tweed suit with a vest and tie that perfectly fit
his filled-out body. "That scalawag saved my life," Morris explained to
Jette as he hailed him. "Had he not found some curative ginger in the
galley, I would have died."

The two men greeted each other with handshakes and broad smiles.
"Meet my beautiful wife, Jette," Morris boasted. "We've only just got
married."

Gunter made an elegant bow. "Proud to make your acquaintance,"
he said. "Your husband caused me nightmares of worry." He turned to
Morris. "It's good to see you, old friend. How's your companion? His
name slips my memory."

"You mean Jonas," Morris said, the joy gone from his voice. "He
passed away—in a tragic accident."

"Good Lord. So sorry to hear that." Bold as ever, Gunter pulled out a chair. "May I join you?"

"Yes, do," Jette said graciously.

"You're looking prosperous," Morris said. "What brings you to Chicago?"

"Customers. What else?" Gunter answered, speaking German. "I've founded a woolen mill in a nice little town in the middle of farming country. And I, too, have a loving companion. She's a doozy of a girl named Juliette, whom I met in the New Orleans square. You remember the French Quarter, I'd wager. Plenty of gaiety there." His broad wink included Jette.

Morris nodded, though his New Orleans memories were dimmed by the liquor he'd consumed.

"You seem to be faring rather well yourself," he said to Morris. "What is it you do?"

"I work for a hide dealer in Quincy, a fine man teaching me the business, though we must scrimp and save for trips such as this." Morris took Jette's hand and smiled. "But tell me more about your woolen mill. My company, Ziskinds, also deals in wool."

Gunter happily complied. The topic took over their dinner conversation and continued long after. Finally, Jette said the discussion was fascinating, "but I'm tired from sightseeing all day. Time for bed. Don't you agree?" she asked.

"You go along," Morris said. "I'll be there soon."

"If you don't mind, but don't be long."

It was past one in the morning before Morris came to bed. Dressed in her diaphanous silk wedding nightgown, Jette had lain down to wait for him. She blinked open her eyes and frowned when he kissed her awake. "What time is it? What did you talk about?"

"Our conversation lasted far too long," he said. "I've had much more important things in mind." He tucked her into his arms. "I am the luckiest man alive, and I've been ignoring my beautiful wife. Well, no more and never again."

That night, he made ardent love to her—passionate, tender, and filled with the joie de vivre. The next day, he took her shopping, spending his small reserve on trivial items she admired: a pretty parasol to twirl, a perfume container, and a compact for her purse with a tiny mirror inside. They lunched at Adolphus and took the train back home.

Morris resumed his work and travels. The talk with Gunter remained firmly implanted in his mind. And alone, except for Saturday nights and Sundays, Jette went about becoming an American house frau.

Morris's country trips allowed him to procure wool from the sheep growers, hides from the cattle raisers, and annual grasses used to make brooms. He also bought beef tallow and beeswax made by the farmer's wives and their lonely daughters.

In his bachelor days, he had warmed the beds of many charming young things. Now, he graciously declined those little trysts without losing business, but Johann Weber's wife, Mary Elizabeth, presented a more complex problem.

Though Johann's wife had been fun to schtup, Morris could no longer continue doing so. He had plighted his troth to Jette and intended to keep his promise. As April shearing time drew near, Morris worried about how to handle Mary Elizabeth.

Johann Weber was Morris's most significant wool account, and to deny Mary Elizabeth Weber would be risking his income and his job.

Soon after they were married, Jette missed her monthly bleed. Then, in January, her breasts began to ache, and morning sickness caused long periods of discomfort. Coupled with another missed period, she proudly announced, "We're to have an heir."

Morris tried to share her delight even though he could barely support Jette and himself, let alone a baby. He longed to send for his brother, David, and start a business of his own, but those dreams would have to wait. He hated leaving Jette alone for days at a time. If only her sister, Gertrude, had come, life would have been much simpler.

Yet Jette seemed more than able to cope. She proclaimed her love of the cottage, fixing it up, refurbishing other people's forsaken furniture, and not complaining about the nights alone.

Then, one cold Sunday morning, after a loving frolic in their bed, Morris noticed blood on the sheets.

"Did I hurt you?" he asked in alarm.

"No. Nothing to worry about," Jette assured him. "Sophie says it is not unusual to spot in the first few weeks of pregnancy.

"Perhaps I should stay home and care for you. You can rest while I take a few days off and do the cooking." He figured if he couldn't go to the Weber farm for the April shearing, he wouldn't have to contend with Mary Elizabeth.

She laughed. "No, thank you. You're a terrible cook. Make your rounds in the country. I'll be fine."

Uncomfortable with the circumstances, he left the next day. When he returned the following Saturday, Jette threw herself into his arms. "Something awful happened," she sobbed. "Sophie came, but we couldn't stop the bleeding, and now our little one is gone." Weeping, she hid her face in his shoulder and cried. "There will be no heir."

Holding her close, Morris raised her face to his and kissed away the tears. "It's you I care about," he said. "Have you seen the doctor?"

"Sophie insisted. He says it's a common occurrence."

"How are you feeling?"

"Awful. I so wanted this baby."

Tears rose to his eyes, and with sweet tenderness, he said, "Don't worry. There will be others. God willing, we'll have lots of children."

He did his best to comfort her with dinners out and visits with friends, but she remained quiet and withdrawn. And he was becoming taciturn as well since each day brought him closer to sheep shearing time at the Webers.

Then, Morris came up with a solution. He'd take Jette with him to the Weber farm. Morris laughed at the simplicity of the plan. When he suggested the trip to Jette, she said she'd love to see her new country.

Morris drew money from his expense account at Ziskind's and rented a horse and buggy. With Jette comfortably seated next to him, he set out for Welborn and the Weber farm. He wanted her to see the land as he'd first seen it with Thomas.

Greeted by greening fields and a few new calves frolicking in the pastures, Jette took deep breaths of the sweet, clean spring air. "I'm feeling better already," she told Morris.

They stopped at the first farm. "This is where I almost got thrown off the property," he explained. "Remember, I spoke little English, and my interpreter was a ten-year-old."

The old farmer, dressed in faded pants and a worn coat, told Jette, "I thought your husband and his little boy had come to rob us. But then the child explained, your husband would drive my cattle to market for me in exchange for the hides. We soon became friends." He winked at Morris, and they had a good laugh.

Morris stopped again soon and introduced Jette to the farmer and his wife. "It's a long way to town for me with eight children and a husband to care for," the comely woman of indeterminate age said. "But your Morris has brought me everything I need for the past three years, even the rocking chair upon which you sit."

While Morris talked business with the farmer, Jette observed the wife feeding chickens, nursing sick calves, and caring for the children. It seemed a difficult life, one Jette told Morris she did not envy, but much like she'd seen in Germany.

As dusk approached, they left Morris's last farm account of the day and drove across a small rivulet of the Mississippi. The horse splashed through knee-deep water, and the buggy wheels rumbled over the rocky riverbed. On the far side sat the little Missouri village of Welborn.

Morris stopped the buggy in front of the small hotel, handed down his bride, and paid the stable boy a dime to care for the horse and the rig. Then, with much fanfare, he escorted Jette through the front door.

A short, round-bellied, middle-aged man with a big, bushy mustache stood behind the front desk. "Morris," he called. "It's been too long. No festivals to attend?"

"Meet my wife, Jette," Morris said, hoping for no more mention of the festivals where he'd brought many young women seeking entertainment. "This is Chet Wigley, the proprietor of the hotel."

Wigley straightened his face and tugged at his vest. "Wife, is it?" He smiled at the girl. "I'm amazed this rascal could corral such a lovely young woman. It's indeed a pleasure to meet you, Madam." He made an exaggerated bow and then turned to Morris with a sly grin. "Congratulations. You want your old room at the top of the stairs?"

"That will be fine," Morris said. "Do you still serve those damnably good steak dinners?"

"Of course. They're my specialty."

When they got to their room, Jette untied her straw hat and threw it on the chair. "He's an odd little man. Known him long?"

"Since I began peddling this route. The summer festivals are parties held by the river."

"And you came to them?"

"Sometimes with customers," he answered, remembering he'd brought Mary Elizabeth to gamble in a wild strip poker game in Welborn on the Fourth of July.

"Sounds like fun." Jette yawned. "It has been a long day, hasn't it? I'm exhausted."

"We'll rest, have a steak dinner, and get a good night's sleep. We need to get an early start to Ashley and Weber's farm, but it's a beautiful drive, one reason I brought you this way."

"What's the other reason?" she asked.

He laughed and gave her a hug. "I needed a nice place for you to stay. Thomas and I slept on the ground."

She snickered and asked, "What do you sell to the Weber's?"

"I buy his sheep and sell his wool. In the spring and the fall, I help shear his sheep. The wool, hundreds of pounds of it, is coveted by Ziskind buyers. I think you will enjoy seeing the process."

Early the following day, Chet Wigley had their horse and buggy sitting out front. Coffee and sweet rolls awaited them in the lobby. After they ate, Jette and Morris set out for Johann Weber's sheep farm.

They rode by the slender tributary of the Mississippi in the gray mist of dawn. Silver maple trees and river birch had already leafed out. Morris pointed to mallards and ducklings pecking on the bank. Greening cattails poked their heads out of the water.

"Look," Jette exclaimed, pointing to the primrose and bluebells in the meadows near the shore. "Just like home." She called hello to the bald eagles swooping across the water. The orange sun painted the crests of the ripples, and the air filled with the sounds of mating songbirds.

Johann greeted them at his barn door, waving a foot-long pair of shears. "So happy you're here," he called. "I've got these all sharpened and ready for you. And who might this be?" he asked, stroking his long, black beard and pointing the shears at the girl by Morris's side.

"My wife, Jette, from Eichstetten, Germany."

"Ah, where Merino sheep thrive. I started my herd with a few of that breed." He reached for her hand. "Let me help you down, my dear. You must come meet my wife. She will be glad for the company. Put your horse and buggy up, Morris," Johann said. "We've a good day's work ahead of us."

Before Morris could intervene, Johann hustled Jette to the two-story white house. Morris worried what Mary Elizabeth would say when she met Jette. But then she appeared at the door, buxom, blond, and very pregnant. This problem, too, seemed solved.

He took a grateful breath as he put the rented horse out to pasture and the buggy in the barn.

Johann's herd numbered close to forty, mostly ewes and a few rams, each weighing over two hundred pounds. Whereas the farmer had mastered sheep shearing years ago and could easily shear three or more in an hour, it took Morris much longer.

The two women seemed to have struck up a nice friendship. They brought lunch to the men at midday, and Jette watched the shearing with awe.

Johann and Morris finished the job before dark. They brushed at the wool on their clothing and washed the lanolin from their hands. Tired and dirty, they went to the house where the women had prepared an evening meal—mutton and noodles.

"As soon as we eat, Jette and I must get on the road," Morris said. "Luckily, it's not far, and a bright moon will guide our way."

"You're welcome to stay the night," Mary Elizabeth offered, "in the new baby's room. Come see." She beckoned to Morris.

"It's lovely. You should go look," Jette said, a deep sadness filling her voice. "We've recently lost one of our own," she explained to Johann.

Morris's heart ached for her at the telling.

"Oh my. I'm so sorry," Johann said.

"When is yours due to arrive?" Jette asked as Morris rose.

"Any time now," Johann said.

Mary Elizabeth led Morris up the stairs. Out of earshot, she pointed to her belly and whispered, "It's yours, you know."

"Impossible," Morris said. "There is no way it can be mine."

"Oh yes. It is quite possible. In fact, it happened exactly as I planned when you came last September to help shear the sheep. Johann has been unable to give me the child I longed for. Then you came along—a healthy young German buck."

Morris's mind swirled. "Even so, it could still be Johann's."

"Not likely."

He sank into the rocking chair. "What is it you want? Money? I have none."

"Only your promise to care for the child if we can't."

He thought for a moment. "I'm Jewish."

"She laughed softly and said, "I know, but believe me, one's education determines one's faith, not one's body. My baby will be raised a Christian."

"But the child will have Jewish blood," he said.

"Only you and I will know," she whispered, taking his arm, and leading him back down the stairs.

Chapter sixteen

QUINCY, ILLINOIS

1874

Green sprouts of flowers began to emerge one sunny afternoon in Eichstetten, Germany. It was a perfect day for fishing. Liebmann Haas, Jette's father, took his fishing pole from the closet and closed his butcher shop. He made his way to the rickety Dreisam bridge, baited his hook, and threw it into the fast-moving stream. What happened next is a mystery. It was supposed a fish took his line and pulled him over the railing to the sandy beach below. He was found dead there, his neck broken.

Shocked and saddened, Gertrude and Fritz made the proper arrangements. Ricka and her family traveled the dusty road from Heidelberg for the funeral.

Jette sat shiva in Quincy for seven days of mourning and prayers. She lit the yahrzeit candle and covered the mirrors so that she and her husband might contemplate their inner selves, not their images. She placed a basin of water and a towel by the front door. Mourners ritualistically washed their hands before entering, and for whom Jette prepared a nosh tray of nuts and fruit.

Morris refused to sit shiva. "I will honor your father's passing in my heart," he told her. "But seven days not working we can't afford." So Jette visited with those who came, recalled the good times with her father, and read from her prayer book until finally, the time arrived to snuff the seven-day candle.

To Jette's delight, Morris offered to send for Fritz and Gertie. That kindness, however, turned out to be unnecessary. Brother Fritz picked out a few items for he and Gertrude to keep, sent their mother's cherished little dresser and dining room furniture to Jette, and sold the house on the river. Then, with Morris's help, he and Gertrude made their way to Quincy.

When they stepped off the train from Chicago, April had arrived, and the smells of spring filled the air. Jette ran to greet her brother and sister, calling to them in German. Fritz yelled a lusty hallo. Gertie threw her arms around Jette and dissolved into tears of sadness and relief.

It took a few days to get everyone settled. Mrs. Becker had an opening for Fritz, and Jette fixed up the bedroom next to Morris and hers for Gertrude. They reminisced for the first few days, and then Morris found Fritz a job. Gertrude's mood didn't' improve, though Jette took her shopping and to meet new friends.

"We must practice English here at home," Jette suggested, but her sister resisted, seeming quiet and withdrawn.

"Give her time," Sophie said. "It's all so new and strange for her."

Not long after, Morris realized his dream of bringing twenty-five-year-old David to Quincy. Darkly handsome but quirky and unpredictable, he'd become not the best but the most popular peddler at Ziskind's. Now, with two family members involved in buying and selling wool, fur, and hides, a business of their own seemed a distinct possibility.

In late May of 1873, Jette found herself once again pregnant. Having miscarried before, she told no one except Morris. But this time, she had no problem. With great excitement, she confided in Gertrude, who had, at times, practiced mid-wafery in Germany. But even this didn't improve Gertie's mood, though Fritz seemed thrilled at the prospect of being an uncle.

Jette grew bigger and bigger, even borrowing her friend Sophie's maternity clothes. On the last day of December, she felt the first pangs of childbirth. Morris called the doctor, but the man had gone to Chicago for the holidays, leaving the orthodox synagogue's midwife in charge.

Morris panicked. "I must find another doctor," he cried.

"Ask Gertrude," Jette countered, but Gertie shook her head sadly. "I've forgotten all I knew."

Morris called Leon. "What must I do?"

"Stop worrying," Leon said. "I know the perfect person. She delivered my dear wife, Sophie."

Mauvine was a buxom, bossy woman in her fifties who arrived wearing a blue canvas apron with a scarf to match. She sent Morris to the kitchen to wait. "Don't worry," she told him kindheartedly. "These things take time."

While Gertrude and Fritz waited in the kitchen, Morris paced the hall outside their closed bedroom door. Jette's cries tore at his heart. "Can't you do something?" he yelled once, exploding into the room.

"Leave and don't come back till I call you, "Mauvine said.

At last, lying in bed exhausted, Jette sobbed, "I can't do this anymore."

"Hush now," the midwife told her. "You've done all the hard work."

A breath of chloroform dulled Jette's brain, and forceps guided the baby into the world. On the first day of 1874, Jette gave birth to a healthy eight-pound, ten-ounce boy.

At last, Morris was allowed to go to his wife, who lay sleeping, their new son nestled in her arms. Placing his hands gently on either side of his newborn's face, he blessed the child with a prayer as he'd seen his father do. Then, with a kiss on Jette's lips, he sat by her side until she awoke. "I've been thinking about what we should call him," Morris said, taking her hand in his. "I like the name Lee, brave and stalwart like his mother, but strong as well. Do you agree?"

She smiled and suggested Liebmann Lee. "My father would be pleased."

"A fine name," Morris said, picking up his son. "And we shall call him Lee."

Morris arranged for the synagogue mohel, a specially trained man, to perform the ritual covenant between God and his people. Lee's circumcision would take place eight days hence with his family in attendance.

On that day, holding his son on his lap, Morris placed his finger, coated with whiskey and sugar water, into Lee's mouth. As the baby fitfully sucked, the mohel performed his duty. Ritual prayers ended the service as the mohel placed the crying baby into his mother's comforting arms.

Six months later, Jette asked Gertrude to help her dust and clean the cottage. Over the past few months, Gertrude's mood and English had noticeably improved. She helped wash their mother's tea set, polish the dining room table, and plump the sofa cushions. Jette invited the growing family for Sunday noon dinner. She and Morris had a much greater purpose than sharing a meal. They had something important to discuss.

Serena Guttenheim, the foxie, curvaceous daughter of a wealthy Quincy grocer, met and set her cap for David only months after he arrived. She introduced him to all her friends, country club life, and high living. Once she had him in her clutches, she allowed him to sweep her off her feet. Not long after, they were married in a fashionable wedding at B'nai Shalom.

Jette vowed to get along with her new sister-in-law, though she thought Serena a spoiled, rich man's daughter and a bit of a kvetch, especially now that she carried her first child.

Sweet, whimsical David swelled with joy, as did his wife's father. Thrilled at the coming of a new heir, the grocer provided much-needed financial support to the young family.

Gertrude helped Jette prepare sauerbraten for the family get-together. She marinated the beef in red wine, vinegar, onions, bay leaves, sugar, peppercorns, and other special ingredients for a full week before baking. "Time is the secret," she told Jette.

Fritz arrived early, proclaiming he could hardly wait for a traditional, family-cooked dinner.

"Where are Serena and David? They are always late," he said.

"They'll be here soon," Jette assured him, though she, too, wasn't certain.

An hour went by, and then another half-hour. Jette had turned off the heat under the sauerbraten, worried that even the slow-cooked meal would be ruined. "I wonder if they forgot?" Morris said, and just after that, they arrived.

"You must excuse us," David said. "My poor darling couldn't find anything that fit her," and laughing patted her pregnant belly.

Jette offered them drinks, but Fritz said, "Let's eat," so the growing family finally sat down at the dining room table. Fritz and Jette agreed Gertrude's delicious sauerbraten tasted as good as ever. Jette felt a yearning for her homeland, for the crystal-clear air, the clean, fast-running Dreisam River, the red brick buildings, and the cobblestone streets of Eichstetten. Even Serena and her fussy tastes seemed to enjoy every bite.

Finally, with a sigh, Jette cleared her throat and said, "While we are all together, Morris and I have an important matter to discuss."

Everyone grew quiet except for Serena, who rose and headed for the bathroom. "Wait. I'll be right back. This baby makes me pee." When she returned, she said, "All right, now. What's so important?"

"As you know," Jette said, "Quincy has been our home since we arrived in America. I love it here, but Morris and David believe circumstances make it time for us to move."

"What?" cried Serena, taking a poke at her seated husband. "You never said anything to me about moving."

"Hush, Liebchen," David said, patting his wife's hand. "Just be quiet and listen."

Morris picked up the conversation. "My employer, Herbert Ziskind, owns the largest wool, fur, and hide company in the United States with business branches in Nebraska, Wisconsin, St. Louis, and more. This year, he plans to move his main office to Chicago. He offered David and me jobs there. But we think it's time to open a store of our own. The question is, where?"

"We can't stay here," David said to Serena. "Isak Lippmann is already competing with Ziskind in Quincy."

"We need someplace smaller than Chicago," Morris said, "but with certain requirements."

"Well, since no one asked my opinion, I'll give you mine right now. I'M NOT MOVING." Serena pierced the air with her look at David.

"You and I will talk about this later," he told her.

Morris nodded and continued his commentary. "For one thing, we need to be near transportation, a railroad to be sure. I've heard of a place that might be perfect, a lovely town called Carthage. It's surrounded by sheep and cattle farms, and it already has a woolen factory, a leather goods establishment, and a slaughterhouse. Tracks for the Missouri, Kansas, Texas Railroad are being laid right now."

"Where is this place?" Gertrude asked.

"In Southwest Missouri. We chose Carthage because of its proximity to Oklahoma and Texas ranchers. They drive their herds past the town to markets farther north. We'll get their cows fat and sassy, not trail weary and thin. The cattlemen are eager to sell. We can buy what we want, judge pricing and futures, and ship our hides via the railroad to the best markets. Make a nice profit for everyone."

"Missouri?" Serena groaned. "All our friends are here. We have a new temple and good schools for later." She touched her protruding stomach.

"Carthage will be a fine place to raise a family," Morris said.

David nodded.

"You go!" Serena said. "I'm staying here. David! Get my coat."

"Don't leave," Jette pleaded. "We need to talk. Surely, we can work this out. Morris! Do something."

With an apologetic smile, David did as he was ordered. "Don't worry," he said. "She'll come around."

The door closed behind them, and Gertrude quietly said, "No, she won't change her mind, and I'm staying here, too."

"I hoped you'd come to Carthage with me. Why would you stay here?" Jette cried.

Gertie turned away. "I love helping you care for the baby, but I have other plans. I'll tell you later," she whispered. She turned to Fritz. "Tell us what you think?" She asked her brother.

"I'll go. I can learn to speak Missouri English." He laughed. "David can come later."

Morris smiled. "We need a good bookkeeper, and he will be perfect for the job."

Jette excused herself and went to nurse the baby. She wished he'd cuddle sometimes, but when she held him, he strained to stand, his little legs getting strong. He'll be running around in no time, she thought. When he quit nursing, he fell asleep, and she put him back in his crib.

By the time Jette returned to the kitchen, Fritz and Morris had gone for a walk, and Gertie had begun doing dishes. Jette took the tea towel from her sister and said, "Come tell me your plans."

They settled on the sofa, and Gertrude said in German, "I have a secret."

"Ich liebe Geheimnisse. I love secrets," Jette said.

"I've met a man."

"Really?" Jette shrieked. "Do I know him? What's his name?"

"Karl," she said. "He is the foreman at the slaughterhouse."

"Where did you meet?"

"At the temple. Sophie introduced me. We've been seeing each other since the Hannukah dance." She giggled, eyes raised, hands crossed on her breast self-consciously.

"So tell me about him, you minx. What's he like?"

"He's from Stuttgart, a little younger than me," she said, blushing, "and has been here for ten years. He speaks very good English and gets quite annoyed when I make stupid mistakes. He has plenty of money and buys me trinkets like this." She held out her arm and showed Jette the ivory bracelet she wore.

"I noticed that tonight and wondered if it was new."

"He has invited me to dinner next Saturday night at Der Schwarzwald. Why don't you and Morris join us? You can meet him then."

"Gertie has a boyfriend," Jette told Morris that night as they lay in bed. He's from Stuttgart, speaks good English, and has been in Quincy for ten years."

"That's nice," Morris mumbled as his eyes closed.

Chapter Seventeen
QUINCY, ILLINOIS

1874

Morris and Jette dropped Lee off at Sophie and Leon's and arrived at Der Schwarzwald right on time. "There they are," Jette said, nodding at a table.

Gertrude sat holding hands with her sharp-nosed, plaid-coated companion, her eyes sparkling.

Morris froze. "Don't tell me that's the man Gertie is dating."

"Do you know him?"

"Yes. He's a snake in the grass."

"Oh my goodness," Jette said out of the corner of her mouth. "Gertie's expecting us. Let's try to have a nice dinner." She took Morris's arm and steered him to the table.

"Here you are," Gertie chattered as she took Jette's hand. "I'd like you to meet Karl Rothman. We've been dating for quite a while." She turned to Morris. "By the way, he says he knows you."

"We've met," Morris said. He kissed Gertie's cheek, pulled out a chair for Jette, and sat down. Addressing Karl, he said, "So, Rothman, you've been seeing my wife's sister, have you? Tell me, where did you meet?"

Gertie answered the question for him. "At the Hannukah party last December. He was the first gentleman to approach me."

"The only one, actually," he said.

Gertie winced.

"Your friend, Leon, pointed her out, so I asked her to dance," Karl continued offhanded. "We've been together ever since, haven't we, love."

Morris looked ill.

"How nice. Tell us about yourself," Jette said. "What is it you do?"

"I'm in hides," he answered, "a business similar to your husband's." With an eyebrow raised, he gave her a lascivious look. "How about you? What do you do?"

"Now see here, Rothman," Morris said, but Jette ignored the boorish question, and Morris looked away, brow furrowed.

Gertie filled the awkward silence. "Remember, I couldn't speak a word of English when I got here," she chattered, "but Karl's been teaching me. He takes me to plays in the park and carnivals down by the river. Last week we even went to see a ventriloquist playing in the town square."

Karl patted Gertie's hand. "And she's doing a great job. Don't you agree?"

Laughing, Jette nodded. "She's kept you a deep secret. All this time, I thought it was me doing the teaching and bringing joy to my sister's life."

Gertie looked lovingly at Karl. "I've been afraid I'd lose him," she said. "Who would want an old woman like me?"

"I do," Karl said. "And now that you mention it, I'd like to propose a toast. Oh, but you don't have your drinks yet, do you?" He yelled at a woman taking orders. "Waitress!"

With looks of surprise, people at other tables raised their heads to stare.

"Yes, you," Karl motioned to the startled server.

She lifted her eyebrows and nodded.

Morris looked embarrassed and commented that the restaurant seemed unusually busy.

When the drinks arrived, Karl raised his glass of whiskey and said, "It's time I tell you the good news. Gert and I are getting married." He raised the drink to his lips.

Morris cringed, and Jette's face lit up with surprise. "Oh, my goodness. Why didn't you tell me?" she asked her sister.

"Because it just happened," Gertie said, beaming. "He asked me right before you arrived."

"And?"

"I said yes," she said, blushing.

Karl stuck out his chest. "See how smart your sister is? She knows a good thing when she sees it." He put his arm around Gertie and gave her a squeeze.

"She's a wonderful woman, and you're a lucky man," Morris said to Karl. "But since she has no father to look out for her, I feel it my duty to ask. Have you the financial means to care for my wife's sister?"

"My job is secure, and they've offered to sell the slaughterhouse to me, but I don't want to be tied down in case something better comes along." He paused. "Like Gert here. She's a prize, don't you think?"

"I do," Morris agreed.

Jette picked up the conversation and valiantly carried it through to the end of the meal.

Morris called for the check.

"What a nice time we've had," Gertie said, hugging her sister.

"Thanks, old friend," Karl said, his voice tinged with sarcasm. He and Gertrude left, leaving Morris with the sizeable bill. Silent, he and Jette retrieved Lee and returned home.

"I don't approve of this marriage either," Jette finally said, but what can I do?"

"You'd better talk her out of it. She's making the biggest mistake of her life. He's heartless and cruel. I can assure you, he'll make her life miserable."

"Perhaps you could speak with her."

"She won't listen to me. You must try."

But there was no talking Gertie out of her decision. "Morris doesn't know Karl like I do. He's smart and successful, kind, and generous." She held up her hand. "I wanted a simple gold band, but look at the engagement ring he bought me." She jiggled her finger, showing off a diamond the size of a plump green pea.

"Besides," she said, "he's the only man who's ever asked me to marry him, not counting Hans, the boy who dug turnips for Papa." She grinned, but then her smile faded. "But Papa's gone now, and I'm not getting any younger. I want a husband and a family, like you have, not spinsterhood."

"I understand, but money doesn't buy happiness. Perhaps you should take a little more time and be sure. Come with us to Carthage. We can explore the new town together, and Lee would love it, too. Then, after a while, if you still feel the same about Karl, Morris and I will give you a wedding."

Gertie twisted her ring round and round on her finger. "He told me you might disagree, but we've already made other plans." She looked at Jette, a plea in her eyes. "Please try to understand. It's not like you need me. Serena has asked for my help with her new baby, and I want to be with Karl. He's talking to the rabbi. We'll marry much the way you did in a simple ceremony in the rabbi's study."

Jette sat on the sofa and took her sister's hand. "I am only thinking of what's best for you. When do you plan to get married?"

"Before you leave for Carthage, I hope. I want you to be there. You and Fritz are all the family I've got here." Tears flooded her eyes, and she collapsed into Jette's arms.

As Jette rubbed her sister's back, she, too, began to cry. "And Ricka," she sobbed. "Even though she is in Heidelberg, you will always have her."

So it was arranged. Although Morris made known his dissent, Jette convinced him to stand up for the man he despised, and on the 3rd of May 1874, Gertrude and Karl were wed.

Morris told Herbert Ziskind the news of his move. "You've been a fine teacher, but I want a business of my own."

"The older man had closed his eyes and frowned. "I've wondered when you would come to that conclusion. You're a good salesman, and you know the business, though I don't relish the competition."

"I won't stay here in Quincy."

"Well, that's a relief."

Grinning, Morris continued. "I have a friend, Gunter Shechter, in Carthage, Missouri. "He says a fine building has come on the market. He thinks it will be perfect for my business. I'd appreciate your opinion."

Ziskind stood, his brow lines growing deeper. He went to the window and looked out, hesitating before he answered. "Why would you go to an unproven territory? It's a bad idea. Small town. Too far south." He turned and faced Morris. "If you stay with me, I'll send you to St. Louis or perhaps even New York. I need men like you."

"I appreciate the offer, sir, but I wish to try it on my own."

"Well, I hate to lose you," Ziskind said.

"I won't go until I have all my accounts in order, and you've found someone to replace me, but I'd like to aim for July or August. That would give me time to acquire some sheep and cattle customers and get to know the lay of the land. My friend in Carthage will help me with that. But I have one small problem—David. His wife is bent on staying here, at least until their baby arrives."

"Yes, well, that is a problem. David is very likable, I agree, but he needs strict supervision. I won't keep him unless he changes his ways."

"I quite understand," Morris said. "I'll speak with him before I leave."

The next day, Morris investigated the only bank in Carthage. He found it had opened its doors in 1868 and had built an enviable reputation. Without David, it would be hard, but taking a deep breath, Morris made his decision. He wrote to the Bank of Carthage to arrange for a loan on the building. The officer, a man named Deutsch, wrote back his chances were slim without collateral. "When you get to town, come see me. We'll talk." That was not reassuring, but Morris decided to give it a try.

With David in tow, Morris went to call on each of his customers and tell them goodbye. David would be their salesman now. "You're on thin ice with Ziskind," Morris told his brother. "If you plan to stay in Quincy, you need to party less and take this job seriously."

"Don't you worry, *Morris*," David teased. "I'll be fine."

Last on his list of people to see was the Webers. Mary Elizabeth waved at them from the doorway. Motherhood obviously agreed with her. She looked healthy, rosy-cheeked, and happy. Three years before, shortly after his and Jette's visit, baby Susie had been born. Though still unsure of the truth, Morris went each spring and each fall to help shear the sheep. Susie grew bigger and prettier each time he saw her, and he wondered many times if she was his.

When she saw him coming, she ran to him, arms open wide, red highlights bouncing in her auburn curls, and green eyes dancing. "Uncle Morris." That's what her mother instructed her to call him.

Susie flew into Morris's arms. "Did you bring Susie a lollypop?" she cried, rummaging through his pockets.

David watched the display with amusement.

"My godchild," Morris explained, putting her down and patting her auburn locks.

"Is she Jewish?" David asked, nodding at the blond and buxom Mary Elizabeth.

"No, but it's an honor she and her husband wished to bestow upon me. How could I refuse?"

"Didn't you have to promise to raise the child Christian?" David asked.

"It's not like that. I'll explain later."

Such a pretty child," David said. "She seems to have taken quite a shine to you."

"That's because I bring her sweets."

They went to the barn to collect Johann's sheepskins.

"Susie knew you were coming," Johann said, giving his little girl a hug. "She's been waiting all day."

"This is my brother, David," Morris said. "He'll be your salesman now, though I regret he has no sheep shearing experience."

David doffed his cap. "A pleasure," he said. "Perhaps I can learn."

There's no need. "Thanks to Morris, our merino wool brings such good prices I can afford to hire a shearer, but we will miss your brother."

"I'll do the best I can to make up for your loss," he said, "with his usual, engaging smile."

They stayed long enough to discuss pricing and futures, but the day grew short. The light began fading to gray, and long shadows stretched across the fields. With the sheepskins loaded into their wagon, the brothers made ready to leave.

"I'll say goodbye to your wife," Morris said, and as the others trailed along, he walked to the house.

"I'll miss your visits," Mary Elizabeth said, and with a quick hug and a nod to Susie, she said, "We'll forever be grateful."

PART TWO

Chapter Eighteen
CARTHAGE, MISSOURI

1874

Morris discovered the house on Maple Street by accident. The railroad had not yet begun to run, so he took the stagecoach from Springfield, Missouri, to Carthage. On the trip, he had started a conversation with a well-dressed, heavily mustached man of middling years. "Business in Carthage?" Morris asked in his friendly manner.

"I live there, but not for much longer," he said. "Name's John Ingram. I'm in insurance. I've found a great opportunity in St. Louis and now must sell my house in Carthage. What about you?"

"I'm starting a business in Carthage and need a house large enough for my growing family," he said.

"I may have exactly what you're looking for."

In Carthage, Morris went with John Ingram to inspect the house. He found it in a most desirable location in a nice neighborhood within walking distance of town. It was an eight-room house that included a bathroom with a clawfoot bathtub and a hanging wall sink. He thought the clapboard and stone house would please Jette. It needed some repairs, though he feared the expenditure might be well beyond his means.

Having made his living as a peddler, he knew how to barter, so he decided to give it a try.

"Look as much as you like," Ingram said, "and then come by my office on Elm Street, and we'll discuss it."

Morris followed Mrs. Ingram and her four children around the house, taking note of cracks in the walls and missing tiles on the kitchen floor. The indoor plumbing seemed to work, and that would delight Jette. But when asked about the heating, Mrs. Ingram said they'd intended to get it fixed but had neglected to do so.

Morris went to the office on Elm Street, where he found the insurance salesman busy packing books and equipment. "Sorry for the mess in here, "Ingram said. "We can go across the street and talk in the park."

They sat at a picnic table. A warm breeze stirred the leaves of the tall, old elm trees. "Good fishing?" Morris asked, noting the meandering stream.

"Crappie and perch," Ingram answered. "The kids love it. Do you have any children?"

"One, but we hope for more," Morris answered. "Tell me a bit about life here in Carthage."

"It's a fine Christian town," Ingram began. The word Christian caught Morris's attention, causing him to wonder about antisemitism. He remembered what Jonas had said, and so far, he'd still encountered very little or none.

"Honest, God-fearing people live here with adequate shopping and new businesses cropping up all the time," Ingram continued, his words reassuring. "It's a good place to raise a family."

Morris saw children playing nearby. "I like your house, but it appears to require repairs."

"Agreed, but for $3000, it's a bargain. I'll grant there are newer places, but they cost much more."

"I'm short of cash, and what with starting a new business…" Morris shrugged.

"My job in St. Louis starts next week. I'm in a hurry to sell, so maybe I can come down a little. Say 500 dollars."

"In that case, I can come up a little, say, 500 dollars."

They settled on $1800, a hefty sum Morris hoped to borrow from the bank.

They shook hands, deciding to make final arrangements the next day. But first, Morris needed to find Gunter Shechter. "Where," he asked John Ingram as they parted, "might I find the woolen mill?"

"Down Central on the left. You can't miss it. An old building made of limestone."

Morris found the place easily. On his way, he noted a general store advertising clothing, a millinery shop, and a dry goods establishment with woven blankets hanging on a rack outside the front door. A tiny Italian restaurant named Marios seemed to do a thriving business. The town appeared in good shape and growing.

The hum of grinding wheels came from inside the woolen mill. When Morris entered, he saw his friend, Gunter, cranking the handle of a big machine.

"H e l l o," Morris yelled.

Gunter stopped cranking and rushed to greet his friend as the clatter of wheels ground to a halt. "So you've made it," he said, grasping Morris's hand. "You've come at a perfect time."

Morris smiled, rubbing grease from his fingers.

"Sorry, lanolin," Gunter said, handing Morris a cloth.

"What are you doing?"

"I'm carding," Gunter explained. "This remarkable machine disentangles, cleans, and straightens the wool into threads for the making of blankets and cloth. Come take a look."

"Be careful you don't get yourself caught in that thing," Morris said.

Gunter shook his head and laughed. "Let me show you how it works." He wiped his hands on a towel and, cranking the machine, pointed to two large, rough-covered boards. "They rub the wool fibers together," he yelled over the noise. "That's called carding," He pointed to the strands of wool coming out at the other end. When he stopped cranking, the wheels stopped turning, and the machine went quiet.

"Wonderful, but how do you stand the roar?"

"You get used to it," Gunter said. He put his hands on his hips, stretched his back, and took Morris by the arm. "But what am I thinking? I bet you're anxious to see what I've found for you. Come. I'll take you to the warehouse I have in mind."

He opened the door and guided Morris to the building on Maple Street. "It was built by a man named Scofield," Gunter said, "a confederate who the Yankees ran out of town in '65. It's been empty ever since. Now, the bank owns it. When I heard it was for sale, I immediately thought of you. For one thing, the bank president is Jewish," he said.

Morris nodded. "Now I know why I trusted your judgment. Let's go see what you spent my money on."

A large brick building, it backed up to the rails of the Missouri Western Railroad. The Spring River ran beyond the tracks and under a long, narrow footbridge. "If you wished," Gunter commented, "you could float bags of wool and containers of hides from outlying farms right to your warehouse."

"That might work," Morris agreed, "but I want to inspect the building from top to bottom."

"I need to get back to work, but let's have dinner with my girlfriend, Juliette. She's a great cook, and I think you will like her."

"Later, after Jette arrives," Morris suggested.

The warehouse was a perfect place to cure hides and store wool, feathers, and beeswax before shipping. Plenty of space for an office up front with a desk or two and a place for his files. Morris inspected every square foot. Could it hold the immense weight of the hides? There were places on the floor that would need reinforcement.

He found the door that led to the basement. As he descended, he noted the wood steps needed replacing. The interior was completely dark. He slipped on the greasy, wet floor. He decided he'd seen enough, but as he remounted the stairs, he heard a skittering sound. Rats, no doubt, but there it was again, a muffled noise he couldn't identify. Though pressed for time, he gingerly walked back downstairs. Reaching into his vest pocket, he retrieved a wooden match and struck its phosphorus head on the wall. The flare lit a portion of the large, empty room. At the outer edges, he saw something lying on the floor. "Aha," he said and walked forward, fingers about to be burned. On the third match, he found clothes and a makeshift bed. It appeared someone was sleeping in the warehouse basement.

As he lit his last match, he heard the thwacking of running feet and saw a dark shadow of a being hurrying to the door.

"Stop," he cried, but the figure bolted up the rickety stairs two at a time. Morris gave chase. Dashing across the warehouse floor, he yelled, "Stop, or I'll shoot," though he had no gun.

A tall, gangly Negro, wearing ill-fitting clothes and a cloth on his head, came to an immediate halt and raised his big hands high in the air, "Don't shoot me. Please, sir, don't shoot," he begged. "I jest leavin'."

Morris had seen Black men before, first in New Orleans and then in Quincy—people who had ridden the so-called freedom train in Missouri and then crossed the Mississippi River into Illinois. "Who are you?" he called.

"Ira, sir. Ira Henderson. I was one of Massa Scofield's slaves."

"Turn around so I can see you. But do it slow," Morris warned, "and don't try anything stupid. What are you doing here?"

As the Negro turned and lowered his hands, Morris observed the bulging muscles of his shoulders and forearms. "Since Massa Scofield left, I ain't got nowhere to go."

"Can't you work?"

"Yes, sir. I used to haul rock marble from the Massa's farm."

"Are you honest?"

"Oh yes, sir."

Morris took his hand from his pocket as though releasing a gun. "I must say you look good and strong."

"I am, sir."

"Don't call me that. My name is Morris Lyon. I'm going to be the owner of this building." He paused to think and came to a quick decision. "I will need a warehouseman. Someone to tote hides and bags of wool. And to watch the place when I'm gone. You think you can do that?"

"Yes, sir. That'd be easy, sir. I surely can."

Morris gave a little laugh. "You'll find out different, I'm afraid, but all right then. You're hired," Morris said. "One dollar a week to start, and you can sleep in the basement until you find a better place to stay. And don't call me sir."

"Yes sir, boss," Ira said.

Morris looked at his watch. He would have to hurry to get to the appointment he'd made with banker Deutsch. "I have to go," he told Ira. "Close the door when you leave, and be ready for work Monday morning." Morris hustled to the street. He stopped short, feeling good, and took a long, deep breath. He'd just hired his first employee, a man he knew nothing about, but it would all be irrelevant if his next undertaking proved unsuccessful.

He walked to the bank, a two-story brick building on Main Street. He opened the heavy wood door, entered, and noted a gold-plated sign.

Office of Albert Deutsch

President

The Bank of Carthage.

He knocked lightly on the door and heard someone say, "Come in."

A gentleman sat behind his mahogany desk. He presented an awe-inspiring figure in an exquisitely pressed dark suit, an impeccably knotted bow tie, a perfectly trimmed beard, mustache, and thinning graying hair with not a single strand out of place.

"Can I help you?"

"Are you Mr. Deutsch?" asked Morris.

The man nodded.

"Good afternoon, Mr. Deutsch. I'm Morris Lyon," Morris said, exhibiting confidence he did not feel, "most recently a trader at Ziskind's Company in Quincy, Illinois."

"I've been expecting you," the banker said, rising to shake Morris's hand. "My dear friend, Herbert Ziskind, wrote you'd be calling. Come in. Have a seat."

With surprise, Morris did so, and the banker continued. "I've known your former employer for a good many years." He sat and leaned back in his chair as though recollecting. "We two Jewish boys met when we were your age, I expect; he's a poor young peddler, and I'm a fresh out of college bank teller in Chicago. We became good friends over the years."

Mr. Deutsch stopped talking as though remembering some unspoken time. Then he tilted his chair forward and said, "Herbert asked me to help you get started. So tell me, what can I do for you, young man?"

Pleased, Morris said, "Well, sir, Mr. Ziskind has a big business in Quincy, and I've been able to save a little money. I have a friend here in Carthage who advised me to purchase the Scofield warehouse."

"Yes. I have your paperwork here in front of me. Gunter Shechter. He stopped by to discuss the Scofield building. It's been a real drag on the market, so I was delighted to hear of your interest, though I believe you put a down payment on it, sight unseen. Not a wise move, which I hope you won't regret."

Trying not to be rattled, Morris settled in his chair and took a small breath. "Actually, I have just come from there, and the building, though not perfect, seems adequate for my purposes," he said.

"Let's hope so. At any rate, how else can the Bank of Carthage help you?"

"As you are no doubt aware, Mr. Ziskind's business operates on astute trading. To thrive, the company needs ready cash. Here in Carthage, in order to run my own business successfully, I estimate I'll need a loan of $50,000."

Mr. Deutsch's face remained placid. "A day? A week? A month? What are you asking, Mr. Lyon?"

Morris rubbed his fingers together and blushed deeply, embarrassed. It was a huge amount of money, and he meant for the year.

He was ill-prepared for this kind of discussion. He was making a botch of it, and he knew it. "Ahem." He coughed. "Annually, sir. You see, Like Ziskind's in Quincy, my kind of business needs operating capital. I hope to borrow $50,000, which I will repay exactly one year later, every penny."

"You have collateral, I suppose," Mr. Deutsch said.

Morris's hopes plummeted, but he in no way meant to give up. "Only my good name and abilities," he answered, "and the house I've recently purchased on Elm Street, with a loan from your bank, I'm hoping. And, of course, the Scofield building."

"Upon which you've made only one down payment. I don't think so, young man."

Morris's mind whirled. He needed a substantial bank loan, but if this, the only bank in Carthage, was unwilling, where else could he go? Maybe Joplin, a thriving Midwest town but inconveniently twelve miles away. And what if they, too, turned him down. Springfield is a distant third choice. He couldn't suppress a soft sigh.

Deutsch pressed his lips together and sat wordless. At last, he picked up his gold-tipped pen and said, "What say we start this conversation over?"

Grateful, Morris nodded.

"First, let's remember this is a bank. We are in business to make money. The requests you made are ridiculous. You already owe the bank a considerable amount on the warehouse payment, which is due monthly."

Morris sat frozen, wondering where Mr. Deutch was going with this.

"So let's see what we can come up with, shall we? Suppose you tell me about your business."

A glimmer of hope appeared. Eagerly, Morris explained how he planned to make customers of every farmer within a fifty-mile radius, especially those raising sheep and cattle, how he would purchase their goods at excellent prices, send wagons to collect the products for M. Lyon to sell to merchandisers, tanners, and woolen manufacturers. He described how he planned to cure hides for distant customers in Lyon transport wagons so they wouldn't spoil. The rest would be salted in his warehouse before shipping by rail to brokers he knew in Chicago and St. Louis.

They spoke for the rest of the afternoon. Mr. Deutsch listened carefully to each detail. Occasionally, he scribbled something on the pad of paper. Eventually, he laid down his pen and said, "I think we can work something out."

"What do you have in mind, sir?" Morris said, elation flooding his exhausted brain.

"First, you must go home and write a prospectus. It will be your guide going forward. If I approve, I can show it to my board of directors. The Bank of Carthage may be willing to loan you $10,000 a year to get you started. We charge 1.9% interest monthly on all loans. Is that something you can agree to?"

"Yes, sir," Morris said, nodding. "It sounds most reasonable. You won't regret it."

He rose, and the banker came around his desk to shake hands on the agreement. "Let's hope you are right. As you assimilate into the community, I'm sure we shall have a long and profitable relationship," Mr. Deutsch said to the much-placated young man.

Jette had a hard time keeping track of seven-month-old Lee. He could already get around, hitching along on his stomach using a bent leg and his foot to propel himself forward. Jette had her hands full, trying to pack their belongings. She couldn't take everything, so she gave away, sold, or tossed what she thought they wouldn't use. Morris had arranged for a few cherished pieces of furniture to be shipped: Jette's dresser that had belonged to her mother and the dining room table and chairs.

On July 15, she removed the little oak box containing the mezuzah from the doorpost. Wrapping it in a soft hanky, she slipped it into a pocket of her purse. Then, with the baby in tow, she and Fritz left Quincy for Carthage. Gertie went to the train station with Leon and Sophie to see them off. Karl was too busy to come.

"I will write as soon as we arrive," Jette promised. And she did.

August 1, 1874

Dearest Gertie,

After a long and arduous train trip, we arrived safely in Carthage. Luckily, Fritz was great with Lee, helping to keep him entertained. But riding in the rail car with only a door cracked open at the end through which hot air blew left us quite uncomfortable and thirsty. Lee nursed me dry, but Fritz made friends with a porter who kept us supplied with water.

We changed trains in St. Louis, a bustling hive of activity. I did so want to explore the city, but our train schedule didn't allow it. We had tickets on the Northwestern Railroad to carry us to Pierce City, Missouri. We would disembark and take a horse-drawn wagon twenty-four miles to Carthage, but we heard exciting news. New track had been laid from Pierce City to Carthage, and we would be one of the first to ride on it.

As our train finally pulled to a stop, my Morris stood there on the platform, arms open wide to greet us. Never was I so glad to see anybody. He took us home to the house he'd bought. More about that in my next letter.

Hope you are well. Give my best to Karl, and don't forget to write.

Alles Liebe, Jette

Chapter Nineteen
CARTHAGE, MISSOURI

1974

Jette's heart quickened when the train stopped next to the wooden platform. She handed the wiggling baby to Fritz and rushed into Morris's arms.

With joyful hugs, he lifted her off her feet, whirled her around, and gave her a zealous kiss. "Thank goodness you're here safe and sound," he whispered. "I've missed you so."

Morris greeted Fritz with a slap on the back. "Good to see you, old man." He plucked Lee from his brother-in-law's grasp and held the baby high overhead. "Would you look at that, young sir? You've grown so big. Wait till you see your new home. There are so many places to play."

Lee squealed and kicked his chubby legs. Fritz stowed the bags in the rear of the horse-drawn wagon Morris indicated and crawled in back with them.

With wife and child on the wagon seat, Morris grasped the reins and giddy-upped the rented horse for a guided tour home. "Look there," he said as they entered the town square, "at those fine brick buildings. You'll find the mercantile full of things you may need. There's the bank next door and the Two Sisters dress shop, a dandy-looking place to browse."

He turned to speak to Fritz. "If you look past the bank toward the river, you'll see our warehouse. I've already hired a warehouseman, a big Black fellow able to handle our goods. Get rested. We must soon head into the country to find customers."

"Look there," he said, pointing across the street. "I've been to that grocery store. It's owned by a Pole named Olek and his wife, Katarzyna. Right next door is Heist's meat market. I've offered to supply him with beef."

"Kosher?" asked Fritz.

"Naw. I don't think they've heard of such a thing in Carthage. He's Lutheran, I expect." He tapped the reins. Over there is a park and the…" Morris continued, but Jette interrupted.

"Where's the synagogue?"

"I don't believe there is one," he answered.

"No Synagogue?"

"Maybe Joplin or Springfield." Morris spurred the horse to a brisk gait. "But folks here seem quite friendly. Wait till you see your new home."

They arrived at a tree-shaded residential street. Morris stopped the wagon in front of a two-story cottage. Gunter waved and yelled hello from the front porch. Alongside him stood a young woman of light color half his age. "Welcome," he cried, holding a picnic basket for them to see. "Juliette and I've come to welcome you to your new home."

Dressed in sunny bright colors, with smiling pink lips, glossy black hair, and dancing amber eyes, the girl rushed to the wagon and reached for the baby in Jette's arms.

Juliette grew up poor and hungry in the New Orleans Square, born to a Frenchman who abandoned her at birth and a Haitian mother. The Catholic priests in town taught the little girl to share the word of God and the work of Jesus Christ on Earth. Her mother, a devout Catholic turned Mambo voodoo priestess, kept them from starving by selling charms and magical powers. "God won't interfere in your daily living, but the spirits can," she told her daughter.

Befuddled, Juliette determined to wait and see. Then, at barely sixteen, she fell under the spell of the exuberant, wily, and lustfully persuasive Gunter Shechter.

Her light-skinned beauty, raven hair, and raucous gay spirit captured the decades-older German Jew. He took to him this lovely maiden with nary a thought of marriage.

While Gunter made his way in the business world, Juliette sang French ditties in boisterous saloons. When he finally settled on the woolen mill, she willingly went with him to Carthage, Missouri…tiny, white, and protestant.

"Here, let me take him," Juliette said to Jette. "You must be exhausted."

Gratefully, Jette handed Lee to Juliette and graciously accepted Gunter's hand to climb down. Startled, Lee opened his mouth with the threat of a screech, but when he looked at the young woman, his imminent shriek became a symphony of boisterous coos.

Fritz also stared at Juliette until Jette called for him to take the luggage inside.

"No worries," Juliette told her. "We'll care for your little one and arrange a picnic here."

Jette thanked her, ran up the porch steps, and burst through the front door. She gazed at the rooms, dining on the left, living on the right, empty but inviting. She could see herself cooking in the kitchen where the previous owners had abandoned a long oak table and benches. She squealed with joy when she turned on the faucet over the sink, and water ran out. Most exciting was a small, private room with a vanity, water basin, bathing tub, and a boxy commode. Upstairs, Jette found three rooms with windows overlooking the yard. Tears of happiness filled her eyes.

"Well? What do you think?" Morris asked, standing behind her.

She threw herself into his arms, her face brimming with smiles. "It's perfect," she said, "exactly what I wanted. I know we will be so happy here."

He took her hand and let her downstairs. Juliette had arranged lunch on the porch. Wait until you see what Guenter's basket contains."

Jette marveled at the rosemary-scented baguettes. "Baked fresh this morning," Juliette said, "plus we brought the jambon, crispy cornichons, and three kinds of cheese. The vegetables are straight from my garden."

Gunter added the coup de grâce, a bottle of lovely French red wine, which they leisurely sipped while Juliette fed bits of brie to little Lee. And then, to everyone's surprise, she placed the rim of her wine glass to his lips, and he began to drink.

"No more nursing for you," Jette said, astonished.

"And he'll sleep well tonight," Juliette said.

It took a month or two for Jette to acclimate to her new environment. Finally, the furniture arrived. Jette placed chairs on the porch where she and the baby could sit and enjoy the nice weather. Fritz found rooms at a boardinghouse near the center of town, and both men left for weeks at a time to work the new territory.

But for Jette, the nights were endless and lonely. In Germany, she'd had many friends she'd grown up with, and in Quincy, she'd gotten to know people at the numerous temple functions she attended. Here, she found it strange not to have a synagogue in which to pray or friends with whom to kvetch. Of course, there was Gunter, a strange one, and Juliette, exciting and sometimes troubling to be around.

Whereas Morris had been in America for ten years and had grown used to a mix of Jews and Christians, she had lived only in Eichstetten and Quincy, surrounded by Jewish family and friends.

One day, shortly after Morris and Fritz left town, two women knocked on the door. I'm Elisha Janes, and this is Mary Woodson. We've come to pay a call."

Delighted, Jette invited them in for tea.

They asked about Jette and her family and told her about theirs. "Have you joined a church yet?" Elisha asked. "We're Baptists, but there are other Christian religions in town."

"Is there a synagogue?' Jette asked. "I'm Jewish."

"Synagogue?" Mary said with disdain.

"After that, no one came to call. A week passed, and the heat of September drove Jette and baby Lee to the porch, but not a soul stopped by. Jette wished Gertrude had come to live with them.

She took to reading by lamplight, for she had a love of words. First came the Torah because she missed attending Synagogue. She realized she would have to provide services for special Jewish days. She loved Victor Hugo's Les Misérables and the poetry of Christina Rossetti, especially Goblin Market, parts of which she memorized and told Lee.

The next afternoon, a heavy-set woman with jowly features and the girth of a wagon wheel knocked on the door. "I'm Ruth Hamilton," she announced, handing Jette a plate of ginger cookies. "I've been in Carthage since before the war. Know everyone in town, so you need anything, just ask. Me and my husband Rupert live in the white house across the street. I've come to welcome you to our neighborhood."

Jette invited her inside, but Ruth said, "Better out here, hot as it is, where we can see and be seen."

"Have a seat then. I'll bring you a glass of lemonade."

"Tea is my preference, but I'll drink what you have."

The woman cajoled her considerable body into a big porch chair, and the sound of a creak caused Jette's heart to skip a beat. She hurried to get the lemonade, replaced the cookie plate with one of her own, and returned with Lee toddling by her side. "How old is your baby?" Ruth asked as she waved to a woman passing by.

"Nine months on September first," Jette said, corralling Lee as he headed toward the steps.

"Too young to be walking," Ruth Hamilton said. "Left untethered, he'll grow bowlegged."

"No way to stop him, I'm afraid," Jette said, proud he'd walk so early.

"Best you tie him down for another few months, or you'll have a difficult child."

"Oh, Mrs. Hamilton, I don't think..."

"Call me Ruth," the woman said. "And you best listen to me. My husband Rupert...he's a professor. Says children who walk early have problems when they get older."

"What kind of problems?"

"Headstrong. Unruly. See that woman across the street waving at me? That's Missus Thompson. Yahoo. Hello," she hollered. "They live down the street. Take her son, for example. Walked when he was less than a year. Did you hear about him? Got in a fight again. They kicked him out of school. Now he's working for Olek, the grocer."

"My husband says that's a good place to shop."

"I noticed your mister's gone a lot. Rupert's a volunteer safety officer, and he says to tell you there's thieves about."

"Tell Rupert I thank him," Jette said.

"Can't be too careful these days. There are still some confederates in town. I'm a Yankee, myself. You?"

"Oh, yes. We're from Illinois. Yankees, for sure."

"Some folks are still fighting the war hereabouts."

"Who's that?"

"Christians who don't know no better. We still got Black folks in town."

"Will they cause harm?" Jette asked.

"Who knows. They used to be slaves and they don't have much learning."

"Morris hired one. Morris says he's nice and intelligent. More tea?"

Ruth shook her head. "Got to be getting home. Rupert will be back anytime now. You need anything, you can give him a holler."

"That's very kind. It's been so nice meeting you, and thanks for the cookies. They are much appreciated," Jette said, returning the plate.

After that, ladies from the neighborhood came calling with welcome casseroles of stews and puddings. Jette made it a point to learn everyone's name. Some were younger women with small children, like Kathleen O'Donoghue, who became a good friend. On warm days, the women invited Jette to join them at the park by the river. It provided benches, swings for their little ones, and places to play and enjoy a cool breeze.

When Morris came home, she told him about the two ladies who came to call. "I wondered if we'd find Jewish prejudices here in Carthage. I'm afraid there is, but we must learn to ignore it," he said. "In the meantime, we'll work hard on the business."

For the first few months, his spirits were high. "Business is good, and I'm finding lots of customers." But then, he seemed to be overwhelmed with money problems.

"Can Gunter help?" Jette asked, but Morris shook his head.

"What I need is a bookkeeper, but we've no money for that," he told Jette.

"How about Fritz?" she asked.

"No. I need him to learn the business. I was thinking of you. I'm sure you can do simple numbers."

"What? You know I'm not good at ciphering."

"It wouldn't be for long," Morris said, a pleading note in his voice. "I've made an office at the front of the building with a desk and a few filing cabinets. That's where you will work."

She looked at him, astonished. "And what do you propose I do with Lee? He needs fresh air and sunshine. Surely, you don't think I'd take him to a drafty old warehouse."

"Of course not," Morris protested, though a deep frown betrayed his guilt. "Perhaps you could ask Juliette. She seems to get along well with him."

"You ask her," Jette shot back as she walked to the front door.

"Where are you going?"

"Out," Jette said, so angry she could no longer talk. And she let the door bang shut behind her.

The following day, however, she agreed to stroll with Lee and Morris by Spring River. "Perhaps we can run by the warehouse. I can explain what your duties will be. It's an easy job."

With the temperature inside the building hovering in the nineties, Morris spread a blanket on the office floor and sat the baby down. "Now, here's what you must do." Morris explained her duties.

Jette tried to listen but couldn't help watching Lee as he toddled around. Then he stooped, picked up something wiggly and black, and popped it in his mouth. She gasped and made a grab, but it was too late.

It was gone. "Oh, God. What was that?" she cried on the verge of tears. "If he dies, it will be your fault."

"Aw, honey. He'll be alright," Morris said, patting her shoulder. "Babies eat dirt all the time. Now, pay attention. You must record the transactions, pay the bills, and keep the receipts. Fritz and I will be out on the road, so you will be in charge."

Jette picked up Lee and hugged him. She didn't remember agreeing to do this. "All right. What are my hours."

"Eight till five."

"So long?" she choked.

"Someone should be here, so people know we are open for business. It won't be bad. I'm already mostly organized."

"I know nothing about running a business, Morris."

"I've already ordered the supplies you'll need to pay invoices and deposit incoming checks. And keep records of our new accounts. Maybe a few other things. Nothing to it. You'll gain experience as we get more customers." Morris put his arms around Jette and Lee. "You can do this, sweetheart."

Lee wiggled to get down.

"You won't be completely alone. "Ira, the new warehouseman, will be in the building." He handed her a key.

"Isn't that just like a man?" Juliette said the next day when the two women met over tea. "Go about doing what they like and leaving us women to figure out how."

Jette adjusted the sleeping Lee in his carriage and took a sip of tea. "I can't take him to that old warehouse. It's so hot and dirty. There's no place for him to play." She groaned and shook her head in disgust. "Would you be willing to care for my baby all day? He's very active and quite a chore. And I'll pay you as much as I can."

"I'll do it, but only for a little while."

"Six months," Jette said. "After that, Morris must find someone else."

When Morris arrived home, she informed him of her plans and time allotment. That night, she put Lee to bed, made Morris a nice dinner, and succumbed to his endearing charms.

Jette's dilemma upset Juliette's plans. Sometimes in the evening, she was used to going with Gunter to a bar where they'd made friends with the jolly, fleshy Angelina and the ladies who ran the saloon. Gunter enjoyed his dark German beer, and Juliette sang with the easy-going, loose-jointed, tall, skinny, and sometimes drunk piano player, Happen Stance. Altogether, they charmed the saloon's customers with their merriment and the slightly off-color songs she'd learned in New Orleans.

Now, each nice day, she took the rambunctious Lee to Spring River Park, where he played with other children. She cautiously sat apart, the only person of color. One day, a young woman with a swollen black eye sat next to Juliette and struck up a conversation. "You aren't from Carthage, are you?" the woman said.

"No. I'm of Haitian descent," Juliette said. "I'm here watching my friend's little boy." To her surprise, the next day, she was joined by more women. "My husband beats me," a young wife whispered. "Do you have a cure for that?"

"Why would you think such a thing?" Juliette asked.

"We've heard Haitian women have secret knowledge and powers," one of them said. "Your looks and calm demeanor lead us to believe you might be one," she said.

Remembering her mother's gift of voodoo and witchcraft, Juliette answered craftily, "Perhaps." The young mothers included her in their conversations about childcare, cooking, and troubles with husbands.

As the men sat on the banks of the stream fishing for crappie and bass and while casting an eye on her own young charge, Juliette saw financial possibilities. By the end of six months, she found herself with a booming business.

When a child in Eichstetten, Jette attended the traveling circus with her siblings. There she watched in terror as a half-naked man the color of coal bent iron bars with his bare hands. Her memories came flooding back when she first glimpsed the hired warehouseman. Black and brutish with hands the size of dinner platters, Jette knew he could snap her in two on a whim. Hiding her fears, she approached him with caution. "I'm Mrs. Lyon," she said, "the owner's wife, and you must be Ira."

"Yes'm," he responded. "The Boss, he told me bout you."

"Where were you born?" Jette asked in a kind manner.

"In Mississippi."

"That's a long way from here."

"Yes'm, but Massa Schofield, he brung me. The Boss say I's to do what you say."

Jette knew no more than Ira, but she suppressed a smile. "The first deliveries will be arriving soon. You must sweep out the warehouse and keep it clean."

"Yes'm," he said and went about his chores.

What was Morris thinking, Jette asked herself, leaving that poor fellow and me to figure out where everything was to go? Finding the Black man gentle of manner and respectful, she unlocked the door from the warehouse office. She dispersed the hundred-pound hides to the basement and the giant sacks of wool to the second floor, with the more fragile beeswax and candles assigned to the main floor where she could keep an eye on them.

More and more merchandise arrived. Jette was kept busy finding a place for it all. Another warehouseman was required. With Morris gone, his little wife dispatched Ira to find another good worker, perhaps a freedman like himself. When Otis joined M. Lyon and Company, the two former slaves and the little woman tried to run the bustling, brand-new store.

The basement ran red with blood from the dripping hides, and the second floor groaned under the weight of huge sacks of wool. M. Lyon and Company teetered on the brink of bankruptcy as invoices went unpaid, checks were credited to wrong accounts, and bank payments went into arrears. No matter how hard she tried, Jette couldn't keep up with it all.

Sobbing, she watched in a panic as Morris's plans went awry. He had to rush home to salvage his business. She fretted as he spent precious dollars on an experienced accountant from Springfield. Secretly, she was glad he had to stay off the road to repair the second-story floor and realign the goods.

Finally, with advice from Mr. Deutsch, the banker, Jette rejoiced as Morris saved his business, though it was a long struggle. She forgave him, and as soon as Fritz's knowledge and English were good enough, her brother took over the front office.

Chapter Twenty

CARTHAGE, MISSOURI

1876

R elieved of her bookkeeping responsibilities, Jette gratefully resumed her household duties. By October, she recovered her confidence and, to her delight, found she was pregnant again.

One afternoon in October, she and little Lee accompanied Juliette to the park. Surprised, Jette noted several people appeared to be waiting for the Haitian girl. First, one and then another approached Juliette, slipped coins in her pocket, and whispered in her ear.

"What is it they want?" Jette asked.

"Gris-gris," Juliette answered with a smile. "Charms and amulets. Those silly souls have decided I am a voodoo queen. I amused them with card readings and voodoo prognostications."

Jette's eyes opened wide. "Really?"

"Yes. The first suffered the effects of a summer cold, and I suggested a magical amulet, really only a mint. The woman recovered and soon told a friend. That one suffered heavy monthly periods and eagerly tried one of my made-up charms. When I let slip I could conjure the sex of the babies they carried, my value rose. Now, my list of clients and their problems continues to grow."

"They believed you?" Jette asked.

"It seems so. After all, I have a fifty-fifty chance of being right, and my mother taught me midwifery and her fanciful, conjuring skills. My successes, though few, have become well known, and more women than ever request my services." She showed Jette the coins the woman had given her. "They believe I can grant their wishes. Voodoo preaches that beliefs and faith are half of getting well." She pointed to a man coming toward her. "See that fellow? He comes for my help. Stay here while I speak a few words."

Jette saw Juliette speak to the man, and then he slipped money into her hand. When she returned, Juliette showed Jette the bills he'd given her.

"You must stop this immediately, my dear friend. It's far too dangerous."

"I'm earning spending money, and it's all in fun," Juliette replied, smiling.

"I, too, can incantate," she said. "I predict you are getting yourself in a slew of trouble." She grabbed the bills from Juliette's hand and ran after the man. "Take back your money, kind sir," she called out. "It was all in jest." But he hurried away.

Gunter Shechter's business boomed. He no longer needed to go out into the country to collect wool for his mill. Morris did that for him. After paying Morris a middleman's fee, Gunter produced and sold so much cloth he soon needed another carding machine. And Juliette often found people waiting in the park to see her. She, too, ran a thriving business.

But when Jette's time came to give birth, Juliette attended her. She asked Gunter to stay with Morris while Fritz collected hides in the country. Jette's labor was intense, but only four hours in all. Charles was born on December 20, 1876. Juliette reported mother and baby both doing well.

"You men take Lee and go for coffee while we get cleaned up here," she instructed.

"She didn't say where," Gunter whispered as Morris wrestled two-year-old Lee into a coat. "Follow me," and he headed for the Red Roof Saloon.

"I don't think this is what she had in mind," Morris said as they entered the noisy bar.

"Not to worry," Gunter said, taking Lee from his father's arm. "Order us a couple of drinks while this little rascal and I go find my friends."

Morris lost sight of his son while ordering, and when Gunter returned, Lee wasn't with him. "Happen Stance and Angelina will entertain him while we celebrate. They love little ones and will take good care of him." He waved at a heavily rouged woman dressed in an abbreviated and frivolous outfit. After she held up Lee and waved back, Gunter clinked glasses with Morris and said, "Congratulations. A second son." He swallowed and promptly ordered another.

Morris hailed the bartender as he scooped up Gunter's money. "Do you know anyone who can do a bris?" he asked the barkeep.

"A what?" the busy man asked.

"A bris," Morris said, annoyed.

Gunter gave Morris a poke. "Did you forget? We're in Christian Carthage, Missouri."

"We must have the boy circumcised, and I can't do it. Can you?"

"Lord, no, but you won't find a mohel here."

"What about Joplin?"

"Nope. Not enough Jews for a minion there, either. Why don't you ask Albert Deutsch? Maybe he knows ten other male Jews."

"I can't. I barely know him."

"Well, here's another idea. There's a new doctor in town, Webster by name. Got himself an office over the liquor store. Seems like a nice enough fellow. You should talk to him."

Happen Stance banged songs on the piano as they finished their drinks and watched the round, scantily dressed barmaid dance Lee around. Then they collected the child and headed for home.

"A doctor?" Jette exclaimed when Morris suggested it. "What of the religious part, the Brit Milah?"

"We'll figure something out."

Morris met with Doctor Hugh Webster, who had recently graduated from Harvard Medical School. A tall young man, appropriately dressed in a suit and tie with neatly combed hair and polished shoes, he confessed he had recently begun his practice in the reconstructed space above his father's place of business. "Would you be willing to circumcise my son?" Morris asked.

"I've not done one, but it's a simple procedure," Doctor Webster said. "I don't see why not."

"And would you be willing to do it in our home?"

"I've heard it's a religious custom. I'm Christian, you know."

"Makes no difference if none other is available," Morris said.

The doctor nodded his agreement. Morris offered a reasonable recompense, and arrangements for the service were completed. Noon at the Lyon house seven days hence.

In her letter to Gertrude, Jette wrote:

> *It was supposed to be only Fritz, Lee, Morris, and me. And baby Charles, of course. But then Morris invited Gunter and Juliette. Wishing to be helpful whilst I first nursed little Charles, Juliette took Lee to the park, and that's where things got out of hand. Lee babbled to the mothers present about the new baby, and Juliette, kind as she is, invited them to come to the bris.*

> *Imagine my surprise when on the arranged day, the ladies began to appear. Twelve of us gathered around as the doctor performed the deed. Morris, pale as death, held poor, screaming Charlie on his lap. Not until it was over did he remember to put his bourbon and sugar-laden finger between Charlie's lips to help dull the pain. Gunter didn't know the proper Hebrew prayers, so he used one said over something good to eat. When the doctor finished, I grabbed Charlie and tried to comfort him, hoping fervently he hadn't been mentally scarred for life.*

> *Having never seen anything like it, the Christian ladies covered their mouths in horror. One or two sobbed at the cruelty, but some sympathetically patted my back. Ruth*

Hamilton from across the street said she thought the act wicked and evil. I'll no doubt hear more from that lively old gal.

The ladies and I went into the living room where Juliette, bless her soul, had prepared the Brit Milah. She understands nothing Jewish happens without the serving of good food. She had prepared a fine celebratory repast.

Charles finally quieted down. Morris, the doctor, and Gunter joined us in the living room, and we all enjoyed Juliette's feast.

You asked how I'm doing. The answer is well, though I'm lonely when Morris is away. As far as I can tell, Carthage is Jewless. There may be a few of us living in Joplin, but it is half a day's buggy ride away. Still, I've managed to make a few friends here. Sometimes, they invite the children and me to their church doings, festivals, and the like.

This year I learned more about Christmas. I know you've heard of Kris Kringle, the magical fairy who brings gifts to children. Kathleen O'Donoghue next door has seven little ones and another on the way. Each child gets a present. Lee wants to be a O'Donoghue. Maybe next year, Santa can stop here on his way west.

Kathleen, who's Catholic, invited our family to attend Christmas Midnight Mass. I accepted, not knowing there was no Catholic Church in Carthage. The service was held in our small, windowless city hall meeting room, yet I must say it glowed with candles, and the burning incense smelled nice. The congregants, all twenty of them, touched their fingers in holy water, crossed themselves, and knelt before sitting in rickety chairs. The traveling priest, a young man sent from Springfield, wore a splendid white robe embroidered with gold thread. I didn't understand a word of what he said because he spoke Latin, but Kathleen explained the communion to me. She said the priest placed a thin wafer on the congregants' tongues, which to them was the body of Christ. Up till then, I thought it must be nice to be Catholic, but that gave me pause. Oh well. Kathleen and I remain good friends.

Have I told you about Juliette? She is great company. Fritz has eyes for her, but she keeps him at bay. Her voodoo spells and mystical tales save me from feeling depressed and lonely. I stay busy raising my family, with more to come, I expect. I bet you are hoping for a boy, and I'm bent on having a girl.

Please write more often. I miss you.
Alles Liebe, Jette

For months, Jette heard nothing from Gertrude. Then a letter arrived at last, but it had devastating news. David's wife, Serena, was ill. "She has breast cancer, and David and her father are searching for the best doctor to treat her," Gertie wrote.

I myself am pregnant with another but am having problems of my own. It's Karl. He has little interest in me or the children. He promises to give me grocery money but then spends it on trifles or liquor. When drunk, he demands favors but otherwise stays away for days at a time.

Thank God for David, she wrote. *With all his troubles, he pays me to help with his children, though hardly enough to feed my growing brood.*

Morris cursed aloud when he read Gertrude's letter. "Karl! That misbegotten cur. I knew she shouldn't marry him. I'll send her what I can, but she must promise to leave him. Write her and tell her she should come to Carthage to live."

"I wish Gertrude would move here," Jette said one afternoon as she and Juliette sat at the long kitchen table drinking tea.

"I could try to cast a spell," Juliette offered, winking, "though, at such a distance, it might not work."

Jette frowned. "This is nothing to joke about."

"I shouldn't tease, but my clients believe in my spirits and gris-gris. I'm beginning to believe in them myself." She exploded with laughter, tea spurting from between her lips.

"Maybe you could magically make Karl disappear," Jette said, wiping the table with a napkin.

"Afraid not. My spirits do no evil."

Jette nodded. "I'm so tired of worrying about my family. Is there nothing else to discuss?"

"Well, I may know something of interest, but it's a secret. You mustn't tell."

Even better, Jette thought as she nodded her agreement.

"Well then, last August," Juliette said, lowering her voice, "a limestone miner named Averie sought me out in the park while his pregnant wife tended their eight little girls nearby. Lean and flat-bellied with his miners' hat set back on his head, he nodded at them and said, 'As you can see, I've been cursed with only daughters. If you could conjure a boy, I'd show my gratitude in a most rewarding way.'

"I asked what reward he had in mind. He replied that he didn't have much to give, but he had one item of great value. He'd be willing to trade for a son."

"What?" Jette asked, captivated.

"He said, 'Many years ago the Spanish inhabited this territory. We ran them out in '46. In their rush to leave, they were said to have buried wagons of gold and silver, but no one ever knew where. The Spaniards never came back to claim the treasure, though many have searched far and wide. Then, one day, near the marble mine where I labor,' he told me, 'I took a break to relieve myself. I saw drawings of an unusual nature. I found it displayed a map with signs and symbols of wagons filled with gold and silver. I made a rubbing of it, but I worried someone else would find the map, so I crushed the stone with my tools. Many caves in this area contain marble, zinc, and iron. Now I'm sorry I destroyed the rock with the map, for I'm sure it tells where to find the treasure, but this is all that remains,' he said waving the paper in the air, 'and it is yours if you conjure me a son.'

"I laughed, but I felt empathy for him and decided it would be a kindness to all if my spirits could prognosticate a boy."

Juliette took the pot from the kitchen fire. She poured each of them another cup of tea.

Jette took little Charlie from his cradle. "So.. .?" she asked, baring her breast and placing her nipple into Charlie's searching mouth.

"I had first to consult with my spirits and then manufacture a potion for the man's wife to consume. The baby is due any day now."

"And the map?"

"I convinced him to give me a quick look, and it was as I thought, lines and squiggles. He retains it, but I should have it in my hands soon for a closer inspection."

"Sounds like a trick," Jette said with a wink.

"Not if my spirits are willing, Juliette said, rising to leave, "and if Averie happens to get a boy. I must be going. Your brother, Fritz, is expecting me at the Red Roof Saloon."

Jette blinked. "Be forewarned. He fancies himself in love with you."

"I know, the silly fool, but having a drink with him is his reward for bringing Gunter a load of wool," she said, hugging Jette and Harry before heading out the door.

"Where have you been?" David asked as she seated herself in the booth.

"Oh, my darling. You are such a pest. Have you been waiting long?"

"A lifetime, you minx, since the moment I laid eyes upon you," he said. "Let me fetch Angelina."

But the waitress was busy serving drinks to a horde of celebrators gathered around none other than Juliette's miner friend, Averie. He spied Juliette, and grinning wide, he yelled, "It's her whose spirits brought me a son." He pushed his way to her table. She rose to congratulate him, and while bestowing upon her a huge hug, he palmed the treasure map into her hand. "God Bless," he whispered. "Ya earned this but be forewarned. There are others about who would kill to get their hands on it."

Juliette quickly pocketed the wrinkled paper. Then she, too, joined the celebration.

That night, she crept from the bed she shared with Gunter and found her way to the kitchen. There, she lit a lamp and examined the map she laid on the table. Was it her imagination, or could she see the outline of a wagon with bags atop? This squiggly line—is it a river or a lake, perhaps? Spring River or Center Creek? And the dot—a tiny blotch—or could it be the entrance to a cave? She studied the map till her eyes burned, taunted by the quest for abandoned gold.

Though Gunter laughed when she told him about the map, he went with her to the Office of Claims and Deeds in Carthage, where they learned that caves in Missouri are ubiquitous. Undeterred by Jette or Gunter, Juliette picked a free graph and sectioned it off to provide order to scout the territory. Upon occasion, she'd enter a cave, hoping it might be the one, but she'd had no luck. Some days, she thought she felt eyes upon her, but when she'd look, no one would be there.

After weeks of finding nothing, she stopped. Jette said, 'I told you so,' and Gunter breathed easy when, at long last, she put the map in the heel of an old shoe. "Good," he told her. "We can get our lives back."

Chapter Twenty-One
CARTHAGE, MISSOURI

1878-80

In the following years, Jette and Morris found themselves in a maelstrom of joy and misery. On January 14, 1878, Eugene arrived. "All third babies are easy," said Kathleen O'Donoghue, now the mother of eight. And she proved to be right. Unlike his older brothers, chubby, blue-eyed, fair-skinned Eugene never complained. He didn't get colic like Charles, and unlike Lee, he kept his sunny disposition from the moment he woke in the morning until put to bed at night. A pure joy he was, and though Mrs. Hamilton from across the street advised Jette to quit while she was ahead, Jette still had set her heart on a girl.

Ricka wrote with news. Her husband, Helmut Rosenblum, had been offered the long sought-after professorship at the University of Illinois. Ricka and her family moved from Heidelberg to Chicago. Daughter Hermine, now eighteen, would start school as a college freshman at the University in the fall. Both sons hoped to find work in Chicago.

M. Lyon & Co. began to grow. Farmers in Southwest and Middle Missouri sold their hides to Morris. The skins were rushed to Carthage for salting to keep them from spoiling. They cured for thirty-four days before being sent to tanneries, some as far away as St. Louis and Chicago. Lyon sold sheep's wool to local woolen factories, tallow to soap manufacturers and high fashion designers. Every product had multiple buyers, most especially broom corn and honey sold to small-town merchants.

Saturday Sabbath became a distant memory. In Carthage, Missouri, Sunday meant church for some and everyone's day of rest.

On the first of October, Morris received a brief letter from his brother, David. That night, after he'd helped settle the children in their beds, he showed the note to Jette.

Morris,

I write to inform you that Serena's father, Hans, and I have found a doctor we believe can successfully treat Serena's invasive cancer. Unfortunately, he resides in Heidelberg, so we must return to Germany.

We leave soon. Could you and Jette come for one last visit?

Yours in despair,
David

Jette shook her head. "It's too arduous a trip for me and the children," she said, "but you must go. It's you he needs."

Morris scowled, deep worry lines creasing his brow. "How will you manage without me?"

"I'll be fine," she said, "and Fritz can handle the business while you're gone."

"But…"

"Not as well as you, "she acknowledged. "However, we will survive."

"Someone has to keep Fritz's brains on the business. He's our numbers man, and sometimes his mind wanders. Two weeks will do it. I'll tell Fritz to stay here with you and the boys while I'm gone."

"Will you look in on Gertrude while you're there? I haven't heard from her in weeks."

"Yes," he answered, "and her ne'er do well husband, too."

Lee had kicked off his covers as usual, Charlie slept sucking his thumb, and two-year-old Eugene snored softly in his crib. After readjusting Lee's blankets and gently taking Charlie's thumb from his mouth, Jette kissed each of the boys. Morris watched from the doorway and then followed her to bed.

"Maybe this one's a girl," he said, placing his hand lightly on her belly.

She rolled toward him, nuzzling her nose in his neck. "Maybe, but if not, we can always try again."

He laughed and wrapped her in his arms. A light fall breeze came through the open window, and she cuddled close, his warmth comforting.

"I wish I could go with you," she said. "You must promise to tell me all about it."

"This is no pleasure trip," he reminded her.

"Even more reason to remember every detail," she said.

Jette loved having Fritz stay with her. They'd always been close, and now they would have an opportunity for long talks and shared memories. Plus, the children adored her brother. Each evening, as Jette busied herself in the kitchen, he'd play with them and read them stories. It was he who answered the door the day the police came, holding Lee by the collar.

"What's this?" he asked, eyes wide with surprise.

"You his father?" the officer said, loosening his grip.

"No, his uncle. His father's away. What's he done?"

Lee wiggled loose and straightened his shirt with a hangdog look.

"Him and his buddies been at the railroad tracks climbing in and out of the rolling boxcars. It's the third time we caught 'em, and it's gotta stop. They're trespassing, and it's a fact one of them's gonna get killed."

Fritz stiffened. "Are you sure you have the right kid? He's only seven."

"Eight soon," Lee mumbled.

"It's him, alright. He'll likely get hurt running around with them older boys like he does. Best you keep him at home."

"Thank you, officer." Fritz grabbed Lee by the shoulders, pulled him inside, and closed the door. "You're supposed to be taking care of Charlie. What were you doing at the railroad tracks?"

"We play hide and seek in the boxcars. I can climb clear to the top if I try."

"Not anymore. You are not to go there again. Understand?"

Lee squeezed his eyes narrow, puckered his mouth, and said, "You're not my father."

"I am while he's gone. Now go tell your mother what you did."

Jette stood at the table, mopping up Eugene, who had smashed his potatoes into his dark red hair. "You went where?" she said. "To the railroad tracks? My God. You could have been killed. I thought you were outside minding Charlie. You know better than to leave him alone. Who are these older boys?"

"Billie O'Donoghue and his friends," Lee said.

"Neighborhood kids," Jette explained, with a glance toward Fritz. "I want you to stop playing with them. Understand? Stay with Charles and boys your own age. I'm going to need your help around here. We have a new baby coming soon."

"We do?" he said, wiping his weeping eyes. "A boy or a girl?"

Jette tousled his hair. "We won't know till it gets here, but we'll love it no matter what, won't we?"

Lee gave a skeptical nod.

Jette placed her hands on his shoulders and drew him to her. "Now, for leaving Charlie alone and going to the railroad tracks without permission, you must be punished. No dessert for dinner, and you have to go to bed with no story tonight," she said.

"I swear," Jette told Fritz later. "I don't know what gets into that boy. He gets harder and harder for me to keep in tow. I'm glad you were here. Morris will have to take him in hand when he gets home."

"Have you thought what it will be like with four?" Fritz asked.

"No worse than three, I expect, but a day off now and then is nice. Juliette has asked me to go walking in the country on Sunday. Would you mind staying home with the big boys? I'll take Eugene with me."

He raised an eyebrow. "I'd rather walk with you and Juliette. Why don't we all go?"

"You scoundrel," Jette teased. "You just want to be with Juliette. She's taken, you know."

"They're together in appearance only," he said. "If Gunter cared, he'd marry her."

"Maybe it's her who doesn't want to get married. Did you ever think of that?" Jette said.

"There. You see? She doesn't want to marry him. She's waiting to marry me."

"Oh, Fritz. You are such a fool. All right. You can come along on Sunday if you promise to take care of Charlie and Lee. I'll push Eugene in the buggy."

For five years, Juliette had not once looked at the map hidden in her shoe. She'd spent her time at the Red Roof Saloon divining spirits for clients or catering to customers' needs. By now, she decided if someone had been following her, they would have given up. So when she suggested Jette needed a day out, Juliette's thoughts were on the map. A walk in the country would be perfect.

On Sunday, Juliette found her friend in the kitchen making a large picnic lunch. "Fritz insisted on coming along," Jette declared. "He's so infatuated with you."

"It's all right," Juliette said. "Hopefully, the boys will keep him busy. I think we can make a day of it at the river."

Lee and Charlie ran ahead, and Fritz, as promised, followed close behind. "Over here," called Juliette to them. "Let's follow the Spring to the bluffs."

Juliette said she loved the month of October, a slight chill in the air. The river waters rippled over rocky shoals. Sparrows flitted in and out of the switchgrass, and the pungent sumac glowed red in the sun. A snapping turtle basked on a floating log. The boys and Fritz wandered along the shoreline, collecting things they found.

Juliette and Jette meandered along an old wagon trail beneath the bluffs on the curve of the river. Before long, the town faded from view.

Glancing about and judging them to be alone, Juliette reached into her pocket and withdrew the wrinkled map.

"Do you still have that silly old thing?" Jette asked. "I thought you'd given up long ago."

"I've tried, but it haunts me. See that bluff ahead? There may be a cave hidden there. We could stop for lunch and then take a look. Maybe find a hidden treasure."

Jette pursed her lips, her hands encircling her stomach. "To tell the truth, I feel more like napping than caving."

"If you're not up to it, we can wait for another day," Juliette said.

"Why don't you and Fritz go?" Jette said in a teasing way. "The boys can stay here with me."

"You know the last thing I want is to be alone in a cave with Fritz," Juliette grinned. "I'm on to your tricks. But we can take Lee if you think he is old enough to come along."

Jette agreed. "But you'll have to keep an eye on him. He can be trouble."

In the quiet of the day, the little party ate lunch and drank cold water from the brook. Then, while Jette, Charlie, and baby Eugene napped at river's edge, the rest headed up the rocky bluff., Small and sure-footed Lee scampered up the incline covered with saplings, red-berried bushes, and possum haws.

Fritz helped Juliette climb, her skirt a hindrance. Halfway to the top, she stopped. "Up there," she said, pointing at a gap in the rocks. What's that black hole under the leaf-covered ledge?"

Fritz stood straight and stretched his back. "I think it's a cave," he said. Lee whizzed around them like a jackrabbit and headed straight for the inky opening.

"Come back here," Juliette cried. "Heaven knows what's in there," but Lee ran under the shelf and disappeared.

"Don't worry. I'll get him," Fritz called, huffing up the hill.

Juliette struggled to the mouth of the cave. "Fritz? Lee?" she called.

No one answered. Gripped with fear, Juliette stepped further into the darkness, rocks sliding under her feet. In the fading light, the passageway narrowed.

"Fritz?" Her voice echoed back at her. "Lee? Where are you?" Through the darkness, she saw the flicker of a lighted match. "I'm coming to help."

"Don't come any farther, Juliette," Fritz hollered. "I can hear the sound of water close by."

"Where's Lee?"

"I'm trying to find him. *Lee?*" he yelled. "Answer me, son."

"I'm here," came back a small but frightened voice.

Fritz struck another match. "Don't move, Lee. I'm coming to get you."

Juliette held her breath and waited. What was that small, black, round object she saw lying on the ground? Too worried about Lee, she disregarded it.

"I see you. "Don't move," Fritz called. "I've got you." They came out of the darkness, Lee tucked firmly in his uncle's arms.

Flooded with relief, Juliette followed them to the cave opening.

"Darn kid," Fritz said, setting the boy on his feet. "There's a lake in that cavern. Lord knows how deep it is. We'd have lost him for good if he'd fallen in."

"I could have swum," Lee said.

"Or you might have drowned. So much for hidden treasure," Juliette said. "I'm done caving for today. Let's get out of here."

Fritz and Lee went ahead, but curious, she returned to where she had seen the circular object. Moving the dirt with her foot, she picked up what looked like a coin. She took it to the mouth of the cave. The beat of her heart grew faster. In her hand, she held what looked to be a gold piece struck with an ancient cross. Was it part of the fleeing Spanish loot? Had she found the treasure cave? Breathing deeply, she tied the coin in her hanky, placed it firmly in her pocket, and followed Fritz and Lee.

Morris arrived home on the Monday afternoon train. From his seat by the window, he gazed at the autumn browning of the rolling Missouri landscape while wondering how many cattle and sheep grazed those opulent fields.

His thoughts drifted back to the last time he'd seen Jette's sister, Ricka. Many years ago, she and Gertrude had been tasked with watching him and their little sister, Jette, as they strolled together in Eichstetten, Germany. He hadn't seen Ricka again until now. She and her husband lived in Chicago with their eighteen-year-old daughter, Hermine. Sharp of mind and wit, Hermine would make a perfect mate for Jette's brother, Fritz. Puckering his lips, Morris wondered how he could arrange it. The train pulled into Carthage, and Morris felt a flood of affection when he saw his wife and children waiting to greet him.

"Mama's made beef brisket and noodle kugel with raisins," Lee said, "and she set the table with our best party dishes."

"Yes, and she said if we spill on the tablecloth, we'd get a whippin'," chimed in Charlie.

Everyone laughed. They all knew Mama and Papa didn't believe in whippings.

That night at dinner, Jette asked Morris, "Did Ricka say anything about Gertrude?"

"Ricka asked Gertrude to come live in Chicago with them," Morris said as he carved the meat, "but she refused. She wants to stay in Quincy, to be there when Karl returns." Morris shook his head with a look of disgust. "She's a mess, alone in that house with two babies and a third on the way."

Jette glanced at her own swelling stomach. "I didn't know she was expecting. Where is Karl?"

"Prospecting in Montana. Left her penniless and without any resources. I doubt he'll ever return. She's been selling her jewelry and her furniture to buy food."

"Oh, Morris," Jette whispered behind her fingers, tears filling her eyes. "That's so sad."

He passed his handkerchief to Lee to give to his mother, but Lee rose and pressed the kerchief tenderly to Jette's cheek.

"I took her shopping," Morris continued, "and stocked her up on groceries while I tried to figure out how to help. The next evening, I had dinner with Leon and Sophie. Leon owns a big clothing store in Quincy and another in Chicago. His wife designs an expensive line of clothing called Sophies. She sent you a sample."

"Oh, good," Jette exclaimed.

"I think they came up with a solution about Gertrude. It was Sophie's idea. When she heard of Gertrude's circumstances, she, too, broke down and cried. She and Leon have recently built a new house and are desperate for a housekeeper and someone to take care of their kint when they are away. Gertie could be the answer to their prayers."

"What did my sister say to that?"

"She said she'd never take charity."

"Sophie told her it wasn't a handout. Gertrude would have to work hard, but there's room for her and her children. Before I left Quincy, arrangements were being made."

Jette looked again at her budging middle and spoke softly to the baby inside. "Your daddy is a miracle worker."

"Not quite," Morris laughed, "but maybe. There's more to tell, but it can wait until we finish dinner."

That night, after putting the boys to bed, Morris and Jette curled up by the living room fire. She tickled his chin and, in a devilish manner, said, "We had a little excitement here. Nothing big, you understand. Just that Lee got himself arrested and then got lost in a cave." Morris's shocked expression made her laugh.

She went on to tell him of Lee's misadventures and the punishment she'd administered. "Don't worry. It won't happen again."

"You were way too easy on the boy," Morris said. "I'd have whomped his behind—both times."

"We don't 'whomp' our children," Jette reminded him.

"Maybe we should. But don't worry. I'll have words with him in the morning."

Jette nodded and then said, "Tell me more about your trip."

Morris yawned, stretched, and extended his legs. "Serena has been seen by numerous doctors, but no one has given them much hope. Her father found one at the Heidelberg University Hospital who appears to have some success in treating breast cancer by removing both breasts. They plan on leaving Quincy and moving to Heidelberg soon.

"David is selling the house. It's in a quiet neighborhood not far from the center of town. The day I visited, a colored maid came to the door and said Mrs. Lyon was upstairs packing. David was in the library.

"I found him, thin as a rail, sitting before the cold fireplace, simply staring. The worry over Serena and the strain of work had gotten to him. He broke down and sobbed in my arms."

Jette groaned. "Oh, sweetheart."

"We reminisced and talked about his wife, the kids, and his future. For now, he must toughen up and be there for his family. I told him Ziskind has a connection in Heidelberg. Maybe there's a job for David there.

"The next day, I had business in Chicago. It's been almost five years since we left Quincy," Morris continued thoughtfully, "and I wanted to drop by and see my old boss. He's gone bald and grown stouter, but he's as nice as ever. I asked him about my brother. Mr. Ziskind said he would discuss David's employment with a wool dealer he knew in Heidelberg. Though I knew Mr. Ziskind wasn't sorry to lose David, I thought him very charitable and said so.

"Mr. Ziskind told me he had offices now in Chicago, St. Louis, and New Jersey. They are the largest traders in the country. That's going to be me someday." Morris's gaze drifted off.

David suggested I send for our little brother, Theodore. You remember him, don't you?"

Jette wrinkled her brow. "Not really. He was a child when I last saw him, but I think that's a great idea."

"I've given it some thought. If Theodore's willing, I'd love for him to come. Fritz shows up less and less often and disdains travel in the field. Maybe Theodore can take both Fritz and David's place in my business."

Chapter Twenty-Two
CARTHAGE, MISSOURI

1881

Finally, at the beginning of 1881, Jette got her wish. They named the new baby Nell, but everyone called her Nellie. The whole family doted on her, especially Lee. With the older boys now in school, Jette had time to play with little Eugene and make adorable clothes for the baby girl.

One early morning at the beginning of summer, a knock came on the door. "Who can it be at this hour?" she said to Eugene, safe in his highchair, his little spoon dipped in his gruel. With Nellie on her hip and the older boys out playing, she went to answer. To her surprise, she found Lee's teacher, Earnest Halsey. "Oh, oh," she thought. "Lee's in trouble again."

He was a tall, thin young man, neatly dressed, his vest buttoned, light-colored hair parted in the middle and cut carefully just below his ears. And he said he had news to report.

"Come in and have a cup of coffee with me," she said, motioning him toward the kitchen, but he politely refused.

"As you are no doubt aware," he began, standing stiff as a board, "Lee causes me no end of trouble," Mr. Halsey reported. "No matter which class I teach, be it first grade or sixth, if Lee isn't staring out the window, he's interfering by calling out questions. 'Mister Halsey,'" the teacher imitated, 'What's this mean? What's that mean?' It's really quite annoying."

""Oh, dear. I certainly understand," Jette sympathized. "What can we do?"

"I'm happy to report I may have solved the problem." Mr. Halsey puffed out his chest. "I've bought your son a dictionary. Though I'm only paid $37 a month for my teaching, I have willingly parted with my money to stop the constant interruptions. Now, I merely need to point to it when he starts to ask a question, and he flips through the pages and finds the word."

"Ingenious," Jette said, clapping Nellie's hands with hers. "I've noticed his vocabulary is improving. But you must allow us to reimburse you for the dictionary. How's he doing otherwise?"

Mr. Halsey's smile faded, and his expression became quite serious. "Lee is an unusually bright young fellow. He picks things up so quickly and is easily bored, which, I believe, is the cause of his behavior problems, though heaven knows he has the devil in him as well." The teacher grinned. "I'm having him teach the younger ones when I'm busy. He's a good reader, and your Lee is a big help."

"I'm glad to hear that."

Mr. Halsey quickly held up his hand. "That doesn't mean there's no room for improvement. He has a temper and is quick to fight." The teacher paused, and Jette shifted baby Nellie's chubby body on her hip.

"Actually," Mr. Halsey continued, "that's why I have come to see you. This school year is almost over. I'll be going back to help my father on his farm. I have some books I thought Lee might enjoy reading. I've brought *Gulliver's Travels* and *Tom Sawyer*, a boy like himself. I can bring more tomorrow if you agree. And then there's the library. You and your family might find it useful. Our school has over a thousand books."

Jette wanted to hug Mr. Halsey. "How very kind of you," she told the teacher. "And he will take very good care of your books, I assure you."

Morris came home from his buying trip that evening, and Jette gave an accounting of Mr. Halsey's visit. "He makes Lee sound like my oldest brother, Karl," Morris said.

"I've never heard you speak of him."

"I barely knew him. They say he was brilliant at reading Torah before the age of five. Left home early to become a scribe for the rabbi in Stuttgart but died of the lung disease while still young." Morris wrinkled his brow. "Lee may be smart, but he needs to know how to work. I've been thinking of taking him with me. How would you feel about that?"

"Maybe next year," Jette said, absently folding clean clothes from a basket.

"I'm going to Sarcoxie on my next trip. I'd take him along. Harry, too, if you want. That should give you some respite."

"No. Harry is too young. Lee's the hard one to keep track of. Take him if you like."

Juliette had grown tired of Carthage. The intrigue of the treasure had dimmed. She'd returned to the cave more than once, always careful not to be followed, but found nothing other than the rock walls of the deep cavern with the lake at the bottom.

Life with Gunter had become boring. No longer the frisky, merrymaking lover she'd followed to Carthage, he spent hours at work or reading before the fire. She yearned for the fun and nightlife of New Orleans. "I must go home," she told Gunter. "There are things I want to do before I grow old, people to meet, parties to attend. Come with me or not as you will."

The next day, she plucked the map and the blackened coin from the shoe where they lingered and laid them on the kitchen table. What to do with them? Perhaps give them to Fritz. The coin might be worth something. It could be a gift for his fruitless devotion, and the treasure would be his reward.

Juliette laid her plans carefully.

She rested naked in Gunter's arms, cradled in the soft-sheeted bed, a June breeze ruffling their filmy curtains.

He stirred and brushed his hand over her curls as he murmured, "You were but a child when we began this journey, and I a gay blade."

She tickled the gray hair on his chest and brushed his shoulder with her lips.

"We've had fifteen splendid years," he said, caressing her, "but I choose to stay in Carthage. My business produces a fine income. My old legs can no longer frolic, though there are parts of me that still function rather well."

She laughed, thinking of the others whose beds he had probably occupied. "I'm sure you'll have no trouble meeting those needs."

"For you," he whispered, "much life lays ahead." He touched the places he would miss. "But fear not. I shall see to it you never want."

Filled with grateful passion, she teased him one last time into a night filled with ardent love.

Fritz proved a particular problem. "You're leaving?" he wailed as they stood at the bar of the Red Roof Saloon? "Where will you go?"

"Home, my dearest tormentor. I will miss you."

"When will you return?"

"Never. I'm done with this sad little town."

"I don't blame you for leaving that old man."

"It's not only him I'm leaving, my idiot fool."

"I understand," Fritz rushed on. "You've just been waiting for the right time to marry me." He grabbed her hand. "We can go now and find the justice of the peace. Oh, how I've longed to make you mine. I'm coming with you," he exclaimed.

Gently, she pulled her hand away. "I must do this alone, my gigantic nuisance, but I have something for you far more valuable than me."

"No such thing exists," he said.

"There's where you're wrong. Come with me to the river."

Captivated, he followed her. Once seated under the umbrella of old cottonwood trees, she gazed at the rippling waters and began to speak. "My dear Fritz."

She had never before called him by his given name, only silly ones like sweet dolt and precious dimwit. "We are on different paths. You must stay here and find your way. I have to leave and seek mine. It is time I go home to New Orleans to a different life."

"I will find you."

"You must not look. She placed the map and the coin in his hand. "Do with the coin what you want. I trust you now to find the treasure. When you do, you can share it with a new true love. That's your task."

Fritz gaped at his hand and then threw its contents to the ground. "You are my true love. I don't want these without you," he said. "Stay here. We can marry and search together."

"It's settled," Juliette said. "You must accept things the way they are." She rose, kissed his cheek, and walked away. He gave chase, but she shook him off, and at last, he gave up. To him, she was gone.

Jette and Juliette sat in the Lyon's warm kitchen, remembering times past. "I wish you weren't leaving, but I do understand," Jette said with an aching heart, tea finally gone cold. "There is so much life left for you."

"And you, my dearest friend. "I conjure only goodness for you."

"With warm hugs and glistening eyes, their last precious moments slipped bye. They hugged, then waved farewell until each faded from view.

Juliette had said goodbye to Gunter at home. But there he was, dressed in his finery to bid her adieu. As the train whistle blew, she mounted the steps and found a seat. The locomotive lurched forward once, twice, and a third time before beginning its smooth run toward the east. From her window, Juliette waved farewell to the little crowd and to Lee, who ran alongside to the end of the platform. As the train rounded the rippling Spring River, there stood sad-faced Fritz, hand raised in parting. Silently she bid him adieu.

Chapter Twenty-Three
CARTHAGE, MISSOURI

SUMMER 1881

Eight year old Lee could hardly believe his ears. His father told him to gather a few things and get ready to travel. "Just me?" the boy asked.

"Yes. I am going on a buying trip to Sarcoxie. You are old enough to come along."

"Oh boy," Lee said, feeling special, though a little on edge when his father said, "You and I need to have a man-to-man talk."

Kissing his mother goodbye, Lee waved to his brothers and sister and, acting quite grown up, sat beside his father on the horse-drawn wagon.

The dirt road followed the railroad tracks, and when Morris halted the wagon next to a line of empty freight cars, Lee's nerves began to rattle. "I hear you got in trouble with the police," his father said.

"I didn't do anything bad," Lee said. "We play hide and seek on them. That's all."

With his eyes on the horse's swishing tail, Morris snapped the reins, and a cloud of black flies burst into the air. "You trespassed," he said.

"What's trespassed mean?"

"It means setting foot on property that doesn't belong to you."

"We didn't hurt anything."

"You broke the law and disappointed me greatly."

Nothing worse than that could happen. Lee felt sick to his stomach and hung his head, choking back tears. "I only…"

"No excuse is acceptable. Now, about the cave."

Lee realized his mother had told his father everything. "Running into an unknown place was downright stupid. I thought you were smarter than that."

The painful words hurt his feelings, and Lee hid his face in his hands.

For five hours, they rode along the railroad tracks in utter silence.

The morning train chugged toward Carthage, gray smoke swirling from its engine. Lee wanted to wave at the engineer, but his eyes focused on his shoes. The horse was a slow walker, the trip long. He needed to stop, and finally, he said urgently. "Papa, I have to pee."

Morris halted the horse.

Lee jumped down and ran into the field. He could hear the twitter of birds and, glad to be out of the wagon, ran through the grasses until he found a place to relieve himself. A rabbit jumped out of the purple flowering weeds and raced toward the timberline.

A gunshot rang out, and Lee felt the bullet wiz by his head. He couldn't stop what he was about, but he saw a rabbit fall.

"Haven't lost my skill," his father called, lowering his rifle. "When you're done, bring him here. We'll skin him and have him for lunch."

Lee stared in horror at the rabbit.

"Is he dead?" his father asked.

"I think so."

"Well, walk over and pick him up."

Wrinkling his nose, Lee did as told. But first, he kicked at the furry, brown animal with his foot. When it didn't move, he plucked one of the critter's long ears with his thumb and index finger and carried it back to the wagon.

"We'll have this fine fellow for lunch," his father said. He pulled a knife from his pocket and flipped it open. "Here's how you do it," and he showed Lee how to skin and gut the rabbit.

They gathered a few branches, built a fire, then threaded portions of the flesh onto sticks and roasted the meat. Lulled by the warm breezes and serenaded by the songs of buzzing insects, Lee's image of the dead rabbit disappeared as a mouthwatering smell took its place. In jovial comradeship, he and his father enjoyed their impromptu repast, the boy's lesson well learned.

At the mercantile in Sarcoxie, a young boy of about fifteen years ran to greet them. "Hi, Mr. Lyon," he called. "I'll take your horse and wagon for you."

"Thank you, Hiram," Morris said, flipping a coin to the boy. "Come along, Lee, and meet our customers. There's a barrel of pickles near the door. Snag one, and you'll blend right in." He ruffled his son's hair.

The store owner, bald on top with a fringe of gray, his salt and pepper beard neatly trimmed, adjusted his glasses and greeted them. "Glad you're here. We've been waiting." He motioned to a table surrounded by men, young and old. "Have a swig," and he handed over a pottery jug. "You can quench your thirst with our homemade apple cider, though it may have a bit of a bite."

Morris looped his finger into the vessel's handle and raised the spout to his lips. One swig left him blinking and smacking his lips. "I need to take some of this home."

Laughter circled the table.

"Sorry, we're late. We stopped for lunch on the way," Morris explained, wiping his mouth on his sleeve.

Lee, too, ran his mouth over his shirt sleeve and said, "Rabbit. Tasty little critter he was."

"The boy did a good job skinning him," Morris said. "Teach 'em young, is my opinion."

Heads nodded.

"Have a look about while we talk," Morris said, so Lee took a spin around the store. He saw brooms and buckets, a counter full of hats, bottles full of mysterious fluids, bags of seeds, and more. Boldly, he snatched a pickle from the barrel by the door.

"How much you givin' for pelts," a serious young man inquired of Morris, his thumbs hitched loosely in his suspenders.

Lee saw Morris sit straight. He sounded different, more business-like when he said, "That's what I like, a fella who gets right down to it. What kind of pelt are you talking about?"

"Say coon," the young hunter said.

"My competition is buying raccoon for a dollar fifty a prime pelt. Lyon will pay you a quarter more per skin. $1.75," Morris answered.

"Say I bring you fifty a week? What's it come to?"

Morris hesitated.

"Eighty-seven fifty," Lee called from his place by the pickle barrel, mopping juice from his chin.

Morris gave Lee a surprised look and said, "Yep. That's right." "$87.50. That's twelve dollars a week better than our competition."

"That ain't counting my time to haul 'em to Carthage," the hunter said.

"Hauling's on you, but you bring me fifty pelts or more, I'll give you an extra buck. Agreed?" Morris glanced at his son.

"$87.50 for fifty," the seller said, "plus a dollar for hauling. Agreed."

Lee saw his dad rise, slap the young man on the back, and turn to the others. "Bring me all you got, boys. Furs are higher this year than ever before. Hundreds of good, steady hunters bring us their skins. We stand ready to pay the highest prices on record."

"How much for mink?" a young man called out.

"We're still paying four dollars, but the market is slipping, so bring 'em soon. Skunk and muskrat, a dollar. If they're green but salted and in good condition, I'll pay more."

Standing in the back, a man pointed to an ad taped to a bulletin board. Taking it down, he said, "Once, I sent a shipment to this here house." He adjusted his broad-brimmed hat. "See there? The ad quotes higher prices, but I learned it don't pay to play a dark horse. Lyons got a reputation for being honest. They get my furs."

Morris nodded his thanks. "Trappers shipping to Lyons know we pay the highest prices, give liberal grades, and prompt returns. I'd be proud if you folks here in Sarcoxie would give us a try."

"Count me in," said the old hunter.

"Me too," called a boy from the rear. "I shot seven rabbits just today."

Morris reached into his pocket, pulled out a roll of bills, peeled off a few, and handed them to the lad. "You got yourself a deal. Take 'em to Carthage tomorrow." He grabbed the apple cider jug and passed it around to cheers and applause. "Now, someone tell me where's the best place to eat in Sarcoxie," he asked. "My boy Lee and I are buying.

Good, Lee thought, the sour pickle teasing his appetite. I'm starving.

Later, after Morris had treated the hunters to dinner, he and Lee got a room at the hotel. "When'd you get so good at numbers?" he asked Lee at bedtime.

"What do you mean?" the boy asked, barely able to keep his eyes open.

"Back there at the mercantile. You figured faster than I could."

"Comes natural, I guess," Lee said and flopped on the bed, exhausted.

When he awoke, he found himself alone in the strange room. Yawning, he rose and went to the window. Barely light outside, the street was already humming with people, horses, and wagons, the rattle of traffic loud to his ear. The door to the room flew open, and in walked his dad, shirtless and freshly shaved. "Good morning, sleepy head. Get dressed. We need to get a move on."

They spent the rest of the trip calling on established customers—sheep farmers who sent their wool to Lyons for shipment to mill outlets, honey producers who trusted Lyons to get the best price at town mercantile stores, and cattlemen whose cowhides Lyon sold to top-paying tanners as far as St. Louis.

As they headed home from their last customer, a farmer in Cherokee County, Kansas, a distant roar grew louder and louder. "What is that?" Lee asked his father.

"I expect it's a cattle drive, son. If the cattle growers sell their cows in Texas, they maybe get a few dollars a head, but if they can get their herd to Chicago, they can get $60 or more. So they collect a bunch and drive 'em north on the Chisholm Trail to places like Wichita or Quincy, where their stock can be shipped to the east."

Lee nodded as the first cows appeared on the horizon. "Why don't we ship 'em from Carthage? We got a railroad there."

With a broad smile, his father said, "You're right. We do, but there's hundreds of longhorns in that herd, and Carthage is way too small to handle them all."

"We could ship fifty, couldn't we?"

"Maybe. Your uncle David once mentioned the thought to me. Why don't we give it a try?" He talked to the trail boss and arranged to buy the steer at ten dollars a head. Morris hired cowboys to help get the animals to Carthage, where he housed them in the stockyard. He needed to find and commission boxcars to get the cows to St. Louis, where he sold them for fifty dollars a head.

But there was a hitch. Some died along the way. The cowboys, the railroad, and the owners of the stockyards all had to get paid. Though Morris's business made a few bucks, what sounded like a good idea had turned into a big headache. They would never do it again.

All that summer, Lee traveled with his father. He learned to be honest in all his dealings. Tough though fair, he found Morris's customers trusted him and looked forward to his coming. He amused them with stories of his adventures, some true and some embellished.

There were times when they'd travel from dawn till dusk in silence. Morris seemed lost in thought and paid little attention to the boy by his side. Lee missed his mother and his brothers but read the books Earnest Halsey had sent along. Some he read to himself—Hawthorne's Wonder Book, causing Lee's mind to overflow with Greek myths.

One day, he began to read *The Golden Touch* out loud. To his delight, his father made a game of turning everything into gold—the wagon wheels, the horse, and even each other. But the thought of being forever made of gold, their eyes, their hands, their whole unmovable bodies, turned out to be so alarming they ended their play, and once again, silence reigned.

Sometimes, Lee would get rid of excess energy by running next to the wagon or wandering into a grove of trees. They would stop to rest the horse at the creek crossings, and all would drink the sweet, clear water. Upon occasion, Morris reached into the wagon for the fishing poles he'd taught Lee to make from green sapling branches, string, and pins. If lucky, they might catch a few sunfish or bass and make a meal.

Lee learned sheep smelled sweet and grassy from the lanolin. Too many cattle hovering together gave off the odor of rotten eggs. Pig farms were the worst, so disgusting they never went there at all.

He learned terms used in his father's hide business. Hundredweight or CWT meant every hundred pounds a steer weighed could be worth $100.00. Thus, by doing some simple math, he could calculate the expected value of the cattle his father bought on a given day.

By the time 1882 rolled around, Lee thought his father's business might one day be M. Lyon and Son.

Chapter Twenty-Four
KANSAS CITY, MISSOURI

1882

On January 15, 1882, Jette bundled all the boys into their coats and scarves, tucked twelve-month-old Nellie into her pram, and headed toward town. On the way, she and the children crossed the street to Ruth Hamilton's house. "Can I ring the bell?" four-year-old Eugene cried.

"You can't reach it," Charlie taunted. He'd recently turned six and had already caught up in height to Lee, the oldest of them all.

"Yes, I can," Eugene lisped. He jumped, caught hold of the cord, and gave it a yank.

The bell clattered, and soon Mrs. Hamilton opened the door. She wore a worn, woolen housecoat buttoned up to the neck, her bony feet in squashed stained slippers, faded netting covering her hair rolled in knots of cloth. "Land of mercy," she fussed. "It's too early to come calling. What do you want?"

"We're going to the post office and thought maybe you'd like us to pick up your mail," Jette called from the curb.

"I ain't in a rush," the woman grumbled and shut the door.

"Old cootie," Lee murmured.

"No name-calling here," Jette said.

The mail contained a letter addressed to Morris from his brother, Theodore. Jette placed it unopened on the hall table, where it taunted her the rest of the day. Once, she even reached for it, tempted to steam it open, but breathing deeply, she shook her head and went about her chores.

The boys were playing games in the living room when Morris arrived home that evening. Charlie jumped up and raced Eugene to open the door. Father's home," he cried.

Morris removed his shoes on the porch. It was Charlie's turn to scrub off the skunk smell, which clung to the soles from the animal gore that collected on the warehouse floor. He picked up Nellie and swung her over his head. Jette came with a welcoming kiss and announced that dinner would be ready soon.

Later, with the dishes done and the children snug in their beds, Jette gave the letter to her husband.

Dear Morris,

Bertha and I have discussed going to America and decided it is the right thing for us to do. Bertha is my intended, and I know you will love her, but more about her later.

Being the baby of the family has not always been easy. Popa is reluctant to see me leave, but David has returned to Germany with his family, so I feel comfortable accepting your offer to join you in business. You won't regret it. Father has been a good teacher. I know my trade.

Bertha suggests I go ahead to Carthage and get settled. She has a good job teaching and wishes to fulfill her responsibilities. I will send for her when it is feasible.

I have booked passage on a ship due to arrive in New Orleans in April. From there, I will take a train to Carthage. Look for me in May. Details later.

Best,
Theodore

"With Theodore on board, I can enlarge the business. Albert Deutsch has invited me to lunch on Monday," he told Jette. "He said he had something important to discuss. I'll tell him about Theodore joining my business."

"Isn't it a little early, Morris? You haven't seen Theodore since he was a boy."

"You're right. But he's been working for our father. That has to say something about his good nature." Morris laughed.

Monday noon, Morris and Albert Deutsch met for a delicious Italian lunch at Marios on the square. Over whiskey, the two talked of everyday matters, the weather, and the health of their wives and children. "I rode over to Joplin this weekend. Have you noticed what's happening southwest of town?" Albert asked Morris. "There are mines everywhere—limestone, zinc, and lead. A smart man might want to get involved."

"I've got my hands full of wool, fur, and hides," Morris said. "My youngest brother is coming from Germany to join me in business." I have in mind to make him a partner when the time is right."

"That's good news considering the growth of your business, which brings me to why I invited you to join me today." The banker leaned back in his chair, adjusted his tie, and twirled his glass in his hand. "I have friends in and around the Town of Kansas. They tell me that the area is growing fast. I don't want you to leave Carthage, but as a fellow landsman, I believe the time has come for you to move."

"Why now?"

"Three things all having to do with its location—a new stockyard, the railroads, and the Hannible Bridge over the Missouri River. It is making the Town of Kansas the gateway to the East and the West. If you decide to go take a look, I'll put you in touch with my friend who controls the railroads."

"I would appreciate that," Morris said. "I've heard the stockyard recently added forty acres with loading docks on both rails. They say it's second only to the Chicago stockyards in size. Knowing someone in charge would be very helpful."

"There are few Jews in Carthage, and I'll miss you," Albert Deutsch said, "but if you stay, I'd advise you to invest in mining. Otherwise, you should go."

"Mining is not for me," Morris said, "though I'm sure there is money to be made."

Albert nodded. "I understand, and you'll find more Jews in the Town of Kansas, many of German descent.

Morris frowned, wondering why Albert mentioned this. Was it kindness or a warning?

"With Theodore to help," he continued, "I'll have more time to pay attention to growing my business."

Today's lunch featured wild mushroom fettuccine, and as they feasted, Morris said, "If all you say is true, I should make arrangements to visit the Town of Kansas soon."

Leaving Fritz in charge during the slow January week, Morris hopped aboard the train bound for the Town of Kansas. An early morning haze spread over the vast grasslands. Tiny towns dotted the landscape and valleys, punctuated by rolling tree-covered hills. Morris's heartbeat quickened as the train pulled into the Union Depot. With a mixture of excitement and trepidation, he left the quiet comfort of his passenger car and entered the tumult of city life. Saloons and brothels, gambling establishments, and tattoo parlors covered with black soot from the coal-fired train engines surrounded the depot for blocks.

He was tempted to stop for a drink, but instead, boarded the horse-drawn cable car and made his way up the Ninth Street incline to Union Street and the office of George Nettleton. It was a series of stops and starts for the old horse and bone-cracking jolts for the passengers. Yet along the way, Morris couldn't help but notice the location had the advantage of being close to the stockyards and the Union Depot, ideal for meatpackers and shipping, surrounded by rails.

The building on Union Street was a beehive of activity, with men dressed in business and work clothes. "Where can I find Mr. Nettleton?" he asked, and a gent in shirtsleeves thumbed toward the rear.

Tall, well-dressed, broad-shouldered, and middle-aged, Nettleton had a head of well-barbered white hair. Morris summoned his courage and approached with grave aplomb. He thrust out his hand. "Morris Lyon," he said. "Albert Deutsch sent me."

Nettleton glanced at his watch, and with a hearty harrumph, shook Morris's hand. "Yes, yes. Of course. I remember, but young man, as you can see, you've come at a difficult time. My old friends from the Wabash Railroad have only just arrived." He surveyed the group and then said, "Tell you what. We're about to go have lunch at the Missouri Tavern. Get yourself a room at the Gillis House and meet us at the tavern next door at noon. I'd love to hear about Carthage and my old friend, Albert."

Morris couldn't believe his luck. "Noon it is, sir," he said, grabbing his bag. "And where might the Gillis House be?"

Nettleton had turned back to his railroad friends but called over his shoulder, "Down by the river." Morris once more climbed aboard the slow but serviceable cable car and asked the driver about the hotel.

"It's on my route on Front Street. Used to be the Eldridge House."

"Been here long?" Morris asked as the driver tapped the horse and the cable car got underway.

"Since the war," the old man said, "the town's growin' and movin'. See them buildings over there?" He pointed south. "They wasn't even here a few years ago. Now there's places you can buy your pants ready-made, garment stores, they call them. And right where we're headed, on Fourth Street, shops, and stores with all kinds of goods popping up everywhere. You should have yourself a good look around. But be forewarned. A man ain't safe in the market after dark. There's pickpockets and thieves everywhere."

Morris thanked the driver and got out in front of the Gillis House, an imposing, four-story brick building overlooking the Missouri River. What must have once been a fine place some years ago had now seen better days. Run down and gloomy, the rooms were fair-sized though dark, with tall, narrow windows that allowed little light that kept out heat and cold. Lit by lanterns, the cost fit Morris's purpose—a dollar a night. He had little time to freshen up and do a bit of exploring before meeting Mr. Nettleton and his friends. He walked up the hill to Third and Walnut Street. To the north lay the river. To the west, he saw brick buildings three or four stories high. Behind them ran multitudes of railroad tracks. He decided to investigate more after lunch, but for now, he went next door to the tavern.

Mr. Nettleton sat at a table with three others. "All I could drag away," he said. "Meet John Hanaway, James Jones, and Bob Simon. They work for the Kansas Pacific Railroad. They've been responsible for the rail transportation of cattle from Texas and Western Kansas."

"It's a pleasure to meet you, gentlemen. I'm familiar with the operation," Morris said. "Not so long ago, my son and I bought cattle off the trail and shipped them to St. Louis via your line." He laughed. "But we're not drovers, and we won't do that again."

"Whatever possessed you?" Hanaway questioned.

"It was a whim, I suppose."

George Nettleton ordered beer all around. "What brings you to my fair town?"

"I'm a trader of wool, fur, and hides, and I'm thinking about moving my business here. I need access to the rails and the river. I'd be happy for any advice you care to give."

Jones said, "My friend Charlie Hopkinz might be able to help find a building. He's got land near the river for sale."

Morris picked up his beer. "I'd be most grateful," he said, toasting his host. The others raised their beer steins and drank.

"Excuse me, but I'm a stickler for names," Bob Simon said. "I've heard yours before. Lion, is it?"

"I know a couple of Lions," John Hanaway chimed in.

"I spell mine with a Y," Morris informed them.

"The one I know is a butcher in Wichita." Bob Simon said, and Morris thought fleetingly of Kallmann but shrugged.

"Jewish," Simon persisted.

"Could be my father's brother," Morris said cautiously, studying his beer, but when he looked up, he saw four pairs of eyes staring back at him. "He left Germany years ago," he hurried on, "and I haven't seen him since I was a boy."

"So you're Jewish?" Simon asked, lips curling.

"Does it matter?" Morris asked.

Nettleton shook his head. "Not to me, it doesn't. Business is business. Let's order. The steak here is pretty good." He motioned to the server.

With the conversation faltering, Morris looked worried, and Nettleton reached over and patted his shoulder. "Let it go," he murmured and casually sipped his beer.

Morris nodded. Though he'd hoped otherwise, it seemed antisemitism had a toehold in the Town of Kansas.

When Morris returned to Carthage, Jette said, "I don't think Fritz paid attention to M. Lyon & Co. while you have been gone. His mind seems to be elsewhere. He and a crazy friend are talking about a hidden treasure he thinks lies at the bottom of the lake he and Juliette found. I tried to dissuade him, but he wouldn't listen."

"Damn that boy! I haven't seen him since my return, and I found things in complete disarray," Morris said. "It's my own fault. I should not have left him in charge."

Fritz didn't come to work the next day either. Morris went to look for him at his apartment, but he wasn't there. Morris decided to try the Red Roof Saloon. It was afternoon, and only a few drifters sat drinking or playing pool. "How you doing?" Angelina said." Happen Stance nodded and banged a few welcoming chords.

"I'm looking for Fritz."

"Juliette gave him her treasure map, and he and Riley went to check it out. I haven't seen him since then," Angelina said.

"How about his friend?" Morris asked.

Happen Stance lifted his hands off the piano keys.

Angelina shrugged and pointed to a man sitting alone at a corner table. "That's him over there," she said, fingering the beads on her dress.

Morris pulled up a chair at Riley's table and sat. "Buy you another?"

Riley nodded. Angelina brought him a fresh drink and lingered.

"Did you and Fritz go treasure hunting?" Morris asked.

Riley nodded.

"Find anything?"

Riley shook his head.

"Do you know where he is?"

"In the cave," Riley murmured, his unshaven chin trembling. "He said he'd been there before. He said a Spanish treasure was buried in the lake. As soon as we walked into that God-forsaken place, I got the shivers." Riley's voice dropped to a whisper. "I told Fritz I don't know how to swim. But he said not to worry—he did."

"And then?" Morris asked.

Riley gulped his whiskey, coughed, and wiped the spit from his lips. Happen Stance, and the others had joined Angelina listening.

"A bat came into the cave and flew at me. I ducked, and it swerved toward Fritz. He dodged and fell into the water."

"Didn't you pull him out?" Morris asked.

"I never seen him come up," Riley moaned. "I called and called…but he didn't answer. I held the torch over the lake as far as I could reach. Then I saw him floating in that still, black water. 'Grab the rope,' I yelled, throwing it to him, but he just floated face down. I shouted and threw it again and again till I couldn't see him no more."

Angelina and the others had gone still. "You left him?" Morris said. "Why didn't you go for help?"

"I did, but I couldn't find anybody. I went back to help Fritz, but I figured he'd gotten out by hisself cause there weren't no sigh of him, and the lake was still as death."

"You stupid bastard." Morris cried, raising his fist.

Angelina stayed his hand. "No need for that. The zinc miners will find him," she whispered.

But they didn't. Fritz's body had sunk out of sight.

"Juliette should be told," Gunter said when he heard the news, but bless me, I've no idea where she went. Nothing she could do, anyway. Best we leave it at that."

Heartbroken, Jette penned the awful news to her sisters. She wrote,

Dearest Gertrude and Ricka,

Our adored brother Fritz has left this life.

He so loved his Juliette, he told me he knew she'd marry him if he found the treasure.

Though I tried to dissuade him, he searched the depths of the murky black lake in a God -forsaken cave he, Lee, and Juliette had once discovered.

Sadly, the dark waters claimed him. Though the zinc miners used every means known to them, they never found his body.

With all our dear children present and tears in my eyes, I said Kaddish.

Fritz will remain in our hearts forever.

Lovingly,
Jette

After a small service, she asked Morris to take her to visit the site of the lake.

"Was that the day Lee ran alone into a cave?" he asked.

Jette nodded. "Lee would have drowned had Fritz not found him. Though we didn't realize it at the time, my brother saved our son's life." Tears slid down her cheeks as she laid her head on Morris's shoulder. As he held her close, her pain clutched his heart. "The Town of Kansas beckons," he said. "It's time to move."

"I'd like that," she said, raising her sadden eyes to him. "Carthage will forever hold bitter memories."

The month of May brought summer's warmth and promise. Theodore's boat arrived in New Orleans, and Morris and Jette met the train that brought him to Carthage.

"That can't possibly be him," Jette said as she noticed the six-foot, slim, clean-shaven youth disembark from the train. On closer inspection, his neatly trimmed brown hair showed traces of auburn, "but it must be," Jette whispered. "He's the only man on the platform."

Morris took a tentative step forward. The young man glanced in their direction and then ran to them. He embraced his much shorter brother with a robust hug. "Morris. You look just like Papa."

Jette laughed. "And you look nothing like the scrawny little kid we last saw. I'm Jette, in case you don't remember." She presented her cheek for a kiss.

"Scrawny? What's scrawny?" he asked. "I learn English in school, but not the word scrawny."

"Dürr," she laughed, translating the word into German.

Morris slapped his brother on the back. "C'mon. Let's collect your luggage and head home. You've a lot to learn and not much time to do it."

"And then?" Theodore asked.

"We are moving to the Town of Kansas."

Morris spent time getting to know his youngest brother. Loath to leave Jette for long, he took the young man on a brief horse and buggy trip. He found Theodore bright and easygoing, far more adaptable to country life than David had been. He already understood and spoke good English, his accent quickly fading.

"Tell me about the family," Morris asked as they drove by small creeks and rivers running clear and cows growing fat.

"Not much different than when you left, I'd wager. The Gentiles still think the Jews are dangerous, so they treat us like human excrement. Only the well-educated and wealthy are tolerated, and even at times they too are disrespected."

"Why do Father and the others stay?" Morris asked.

"It's like always," Theodore answered. "One gets used to where one lives and can't imagine living elsewhere. Bertha and I decided long ago to leave. It was just a matter of when."

Morris gazed at a passing stand of oaks and sycamores. Then he said, "The future weighs heavily on my shoulders. Due to the arrival of the railroad, Carthage is booming. But my banker, Albert Deutsch, believes if my business is to grow, we must move to the Town of Kansas. There is a new railroad bridge over the Missouri River. I've met a man who will help me. He manages the railroads and the stockyards."

"Good," Theodore said.

Morris's mood suddenly lightened. He motioned to the green pastures with a broad sweep of his arm. "What you see is but a fraction of the territory we could cover. Miles of fertile land where cattle, sheep, and multitudes of products are grown." He slapped his brother on the back. "You must hurry and learn about our customers. Jette is anxious to leave."

Theodore brushed at a buzzing fly and uncurled his legs. "I'll be ready whenever you say."

PART THREE

Chapter Twenty-Five
KANSAS CITY, MISSOURI

1883

LEE

I was nine when my father, Morris, moved his business and our family to the Town of Kansas, and he bought the property between Second and Third Street on Delaware. Not counting the basement, the sturdy brick building had two stories with a flat ramp on rollers in between. When loaded with hundred-pound sacks of wool, it took two strong men to hoist the sack to the second floor. I rode the elevator for fun till my father found out and forbade it.

Father's brother, Theodore, sent for his girlfriend, Bertha, who lived in Germany. I liked her right off, not pretty but handsome in an easygoing sort of way. She had thick, brown hair pulled back in a no-nonsense bun and intelligent, brown eyes framed with a sweetness that invited me to be her friend.

They were married at Temple B'nai Jehudah, near where we lived. Our house had three bedrooms, a bathroom, and a dining room big enough to seat the whole family. Bertha and Theodore moved right down the street. Mother and Bertha spent a lot of time together shopping and visiting. They grew herbs in their gardens and shared recipes and gossip.

I'd never been to the temple before, but my mother said we had to go and learn about our religion. She made me and my two younger brothers and Nellie take baths and put on our good clothes. My father said he didn't have time, so he didn't attend very often, but Mother insisted we all go on two days—Rosh Hashanah, the Jewish New Year, and Yom Kippur, the day of atonement.

We children didn't understand Hebrew. All we knew were a few German words our parents used in jest, like *schmalz gesicht,* which means fat face, a term my father jokingly called Nellie.

My mother and father enjoyed entertaining the rabbi for dinner, and he told us about Jewish communities back East.

"Since coming to this country, you and many of your young Jewish friends have been so intent on opening businesses, I notice you've stopped performing some important Jewish religious practices," he chastised my dad, "like going to Friday night services and closing on the Sabbath."

Aiming to end the conversation, my father said, "I think we can still be Jewish. As you can see, we are doing fine."

"Be careful," he cautioned, "or you'll lose your identity."

Eventually, that rabbi left, and another one came, but he, too, would soon be gone. Before long, the busy, young B'nai Jehudah population quit going to temple except for an occasional Friday night or Rosh Hashanah and Yom Kippur high holy day services.

The new rabbi and his sweet wife became good friends with my parents. Mother liked that men and women sat together in this rabbi's congregation. Services were in English with only a little Hebrew, and keeping kosher was optional.

My mother became president of the Temple Sisterhood. I remember because her job kept her attention off me.

Two boys my own age lived near me. Both were named Henry. I called them Henry One and Henry Two. Henry One reminded me of a giraffe. He had a long, skinny neck, spindly legs, and big ears that stuck out of his head. Henry Two was short and nimble, the smartest. We went to the same grade school in the Linwood district and became best friends.

As we got older, the Henrys and I found ways to ditch school since the only thing we liked was recess. We'd spend the days carousing in the West Bottoms and hitching free rides to the stockyards on the horse-drawn cable cars.

Sometimes, the men who bought and sold the cattle needed an errand boy. For a few pennies, Henry One, Two, and I did whatever they needed. In no time, we got to know the cowboys, Slim, Bucky, and Geronimo, to name a few. They wore out the horses they rode in half a day, herding cattle from one pen to another or into waiting boxcars. Then they'd give us each a nickel to rub down their mounts and water and feed them fresh hay.

I quit school at sixteen, or rather, they kicked me out the same year my Uncle Theodore's wife, Bertha, almost died having a baby, a girl they named Helen. Papa said I either had to go to school or work for him. I had no interest in doing either, but it didn't matter. My mother and father were both so worried about Aunt Bertha they didn't bother with me.

The Henrys and I got full-time jobs at the stockyards. It didn't pay much, sometimes only a quarter a day, but it was enough for us to go down the street to the billiards hall and shoot a game or two. Henry One was tall and rangy, appearing old enough to get a drink at Jim's Saloon or a come-hither look from the brothel ladies, but Henry Two was small like me. We stuck to gambling parlors. He got a cross tattooed on his shoulder. I wanted one too, not a cross, but a rose maybe, though if I'd shown up with one, my mother would have murdered me.

The Henrys and I thought working at the stockyards was a lot of fun, even though it was dangerous work. There'd been a huge influx of cattle, as many as a thousand a day. One and Two were working on deck three, and I could see them from where I stood below, manning the gates. Opening and closing the gates was a very important job. If you didn't do it right, the herds could get mixed up, or too many cows would go into one pen and trample each other—or you—to death.

On one particular day, the Henrys were steering incoming cattle to the third deck holding pens. I didn't see it happen, but tough little Henry Two got pushed over the fence. When I looked up, he was dangling over the longhorns while clinging one-handed to the rail. I flung open the gate to the pen and rushed in to flag the steers away. As Two let go, I broke his fall and checked him over to be sure he was alright. Too late, I remembered the gate. I raced to shut it, but by then, thousand-pound animals with lethal horns brushed me aside like a fleck of dust. Crushed against the fence, I could only watch as they stampeded down the long, center aisle. The cowboys wheeled their horses around and raced after them. Geronimo, the grizzly old Indian, stopped long enough to yank me over the fence. He paid little attention to my screams of pain as he hauled my body onto his horse and took me to the rail booth, where workers stood open-mouthed in shock and dismay. They took me from Geronimo and assessed my wounds, broken ribs, battered body, and banged-up head, while the thundering herd of cattle swarmed onto the city streets and scattered in every direction.

Once I halfway recovered, I staggered out to help collect the animals. But without a horse, I was of little use. Weak-kneed and aching, I inveigled one and then another back to the yards. I reeled up one street and down another, broken ribs making it hard for me to breathe. I could hear the whiz of cowboy ropes and whistles as they nudged the frightened cows back to the stockyard. It was midnight before we could corral the last of them into their pens. Unperturbed, the cows mooed and mingled while I, exhausted and lucky to be alive, sat on the curb, my head in my hands, until a stockyard guard escorted me off the premises for good.

My mother found me in the morning, collapsed on the kitchen floor. Though she was used to my shenanigans, she called for Dad to help get me to Doctor Finkelstein, who said I'd live, youth being in my favor. He taped my fractured ribs and advised bed rest. My mother took me home, put me on the living room sofa with a copy of _The Last of the Mohicans_, and fed me matzoh ball soup. My father said as soon as my ribs healed, I'd go to work for him at M. Lyon and Co.

A few weeks later, I began my life at "the store." That's what Dad called the building. He started me in the hide cellar under the tutelage of Ira. "Teach him well," my father instructed him.

"I surely will, Mr. Morris, sir," he said, grinning. "I'll teach Mr. Lee all I know."

"No need to 'Mister' him. Just treat him like one of the boys."

Ira handed me a pair of boots four sizes too big, a heavy apron, and leather gloves that would have been loose on Hercules. Dark and dank, the hide cellar smelled grossly sweet and metallic. Though someone mopped now and then, blood from the cowhides soused the floor, making it slick and slimy. Muscular, sinewy, sweat-glistened Black men salted raw hides, each skin weighing up to a hundred pounds. When they saw me, they laughed. Standing in front of a stack of hides, one of them yelled at Ira, "We 'posed to salt wid him?"

"Put his skinny little butt to work," my overseer ordered. I watched as they evenly distributed about a quarter of a bucket of salt per hide, then folded the skin, tossed it into a different pile, and repeated the task. They handed me a bucket of salt and told me to get busy, but I could barely lift the bucket, much less a salted hide.

Some of the hides needed fleshing. Big Mo was in charge of that operation. He carried a razor-sharp knife in a sheaf on his belt, which he used to remove big chunks of meat that still clung to the hide.

I did my share of floor mopping and took their unmerciful teasing without complaint. Now and again, they'd grab me and toss me on top of a stack of offal, laughing as I clambered off, covered with cowhide stink. Even though they called me names, "white ass" and "pussy boy" being their favorites, I'd made up my mind not to care.

But eventually, I had enough. The next time the salters decided to use me as their whipping boy, I lunged for Big Mo's knife. I grabbed it from its sheath and, crouching, waved its glistening sharp blade in their direction.

"Who's first?" I cried, lunging at the worst offender. "You come near me again, I'll cut your balls off."

"Whoa," someone whooped. All stopped dead in their tracks, hands raised, slowly backing away.

Big Mo made a move. "Think twice," I said, tossing his knife from one hand to the other.

He stood stark still. Then he broke into a grin and started to chuckle. Everyone in the room joined in. Pretty soon, they were hee-hawing and doubled over laughing, their big bodies leaning on each other while I stood there stupefied.

"Ya done it, Lee," Big Mo said, stifling his roar. He put his big black hand on my shoulder while easing the knife from my hand. "You win." The gang converged on me, the men reaching to shake my hand.

It wasn't until later I realized I could have ended it a whole lot sooner if only I'd not been so pigheaded. They'd toughened me up and taught me a lesson I'd not soon forget.

In the next few months, I learned a lot about hides—size, color markings, texture, feel, what made a usable hide, why some got tossed aside, and how to properly cure them to prevent bacterial growth.

At night, exhausted, I'd come home smelling so bad my mother made me wash before I went inside. Sometimes, too tired to eat, I'd hose off and crawl naked into bed to sleep until my alarm woke me, barely rested, at four-thirty AM.

My father never asked about my job. I figured Ira kept him informed about my doings. I didn't grouse about the treatment—I didn't want to give him the satisfaction. By the time I'd been down there for six months, yelled at, pissed on, and accepted, I guess he finally figured I was ready for the second floor.

That's where the hundred-pound sacks of sheep wool were stored. I was no help when it came to lifting those bags, but I could work the desk, and that's where my real training began.

Ross Cartwright had been with Lyons since the business moved to Kansas City. He became my teacher and, as it turned out, a good friend. He was a few inches taller than me, smart and meticulous with non-descript brown hair, cut short and seldom out of place. He wore trim, khaki-colored pants, a clean shirt, and his ubiquitous leather jacket.

Among other things, he ran the scales and determined where the wool was to go. "This is where you learn how to grade wool," he told me. "Go grab a couple of handfuls out of that bag and bring it here. Now tell me what you see."

I wasn't sure what he meant. "Well...it's curly and dirty and greasy," I said, biting my lip and wiping my hands on my pants.

"Right. It's full of grass and dung and suint, which is sheep's sweat. We call it the yolk," Ross said. "The grease you dirtied your pants with is from lanolin made by the sheep's glands. What else do you see?"

"The hairs are strong and wavy," I said, beginning to understand what he was driving at. "When I crunch a handful together, it springs back."

"Yes. Those are fundamental traits of grease wool or unwashed fleece. We assess those qualities and grade the wool from very fine to very coarse. Starting today, you will learn all seven grades and weigh every bag of wool that comes in or goes out of the store. It's one way we pay the bills."

I spent the next two years on the second floor. My father often sent me to sheep farms with Uncle Theodore, his best-traveling salesman, so I could lay hands on the animals. I would sink my fingers into the wool of Merino and non-Merino sheep and feel the difference in fiber and strength, elasticity quality, and grade. I learned how to assess the shrinkage caused by dirt-heavy wool, which could decrease our profits by as much as 75%.

My mother, who loved to read, stumbled on a James Howell proverb—*All work and no play makes Jack a dull boy*. She applied that to me, now eighteen years old, and convinced my father to give me Sundays off. On Saturday night, the Henrys and I would go to town looking for something to do. I didn't drink...well, a beer now and then, but that's all...and with no time to date, my knowledge of the opposite sex was limited to my mother and my sister.

On the Fourth of July 1890, we took the streetcar to Troost Park, where people picnicked and rented boats on the lake. The Henrys, who were much more worldly than I, had brought a flask and a bottle of whiskey along. They sat next to a bunch of giggly girls and soon offered them shots of bourbon for kisses.

When my turn with the bottle came, a floozie blonde settled onto the blanket and cuddled beside me. She took the bottle from my hands and put it to her mouth. And then, her mouth on mine, I felt her lips open and liquor trickle pleasantly down my throat. I found this manner of drinking most enjoyable. Using this method, she and I downed more than half the bottle until the Henrys intervened. The girl got mad and grabbed the bottle, much of which spilled on my shirt. So then, drunk and smelling like a brewery, I climbed on top of our homebound streetcar and, for some unimaginable reason, yanked the rail from the overhead electric wire.

"Hey," the gripman yelled when the streetcar ground to a halt. "What the hell are you doing up there?"

I jumped down and ran, drunk and unsteady, but the angry passengers caught me. And that's how I ended up spending my first night in jail.

My father bailed me out but quit speaking to me again and confined me to my room on Sundays with no books to read and nothing to do. Mother stayed out of it, and fearing retribution, so did Charlie and Eugene. But not Nellie. She earned my adoration by bringing me the mostly unused and unnoticed book that sat on the living room table, _Samuel Johnson's Dictionary_.

I made a sour face and groaned the day she snuck it to me, but it turned out to be my salvation. Beginning with the fascinating word Aardvark, it kept me enthralled until my reprieve. I found Johnson's way of illustrating a meaning particularly entertaining. For the word fart, he quoted a Jonathan Swift poem.

> As when we a gun discharge,
> Although the bore be ne'er so large,
> Before the fame from muzzle burst,
> Just at the breech it flashes first,
> So from my lord his passion broke,
> He farted first, and then he spoke.

My father heard my roar of laughter and, believing me alone without diversion, must have thought me on the brink of mental collapse, so set me free.

On my birthday, Mother surprised me with a dinner party. She invited the Henrys, a few other people I knew, and Anna, the daughter of her friend Josephine Rothgeisser. My life was about to take on a new dimension. I'd had little time for girls other than an occasional assignation with one of my farm customer's daughters, who lured me into her father's barn and enthusiastically taught me the basics. Nor had I experienced parties or party games.

After dinner, we played charades. With people's names as the topic, Henry One began acting out a lengthy, wordless attempt. Anna sat beside me. I paid little attention to the game, overcome by her enchanting scent.

Henry One madly gestured to his mouth.

"Dr. Horowitz, our dentist," Two yelled.

One shook his head disgustedly and jiggled the circle of his thumb and middle finger.

"Bell," Anna cried. "I've got it. Alexander Graham Bell."

"Right," One yelled and, pretending exhaustion, fell to the floor.

We cheered and laughed. Then my mother called, "Time for cake and ice cream," and we moved to the dining room. Nineteen candles and one to grow on glowed brightly on the cake's chocolate icing. Nellie, who loved ice cream and cake more than life, grabbed my hand and pulled me to the table.

But I hung back, and Anna joined me. "Did you know Bell's wife was deaf? His mother, too," she noted. "He gestured so they'd understand him. I've often wondered if that's how the game came about."

Finally, it came time to open my gifts—only trinkets the invitation had instructed. Roars of laughter and approval followed—a bar of shaving soap for my straggly mustache, homemade jellies, and jams to fatten my skinny bones. One and Two gave me a whiskey-filled metal flask, which they hoped would discourage me from nipping at theirs. When all the gifts appeared to be opened, Anna slipped a tiny package into my hand. Unwrapping it carefully, I found a small gold key. "What's it to?"

"It's for me to know and you to find out," she answered, reaching into my watch pocket and slipping it on my keychain.

Chapter Twenty-Six
KANSAS CITY, MISSOURI

1893

Clearly intrigued, Lee began a romance his mother encouraged. Jette pled her son's case, begging Morris to at least keep the boy in town long enough to court the girl.

Donning the pajamas he hated but which Jette insisted he wear since daughter Nellie was born, Morris grumbled, "He's old enough to choose his own girlfriends without your interference."

"A little nudging never hurts. After all, your father introduced you to me. Remember?" She soothed his cheek and helped him button his cotton tops.

Morris got into bed. Confined by the sheets, he kicked his feet free. "All right, so…" he muttered.

"She comes from a nice German family," Jette said as she curled up next to him. "I met her mother at the temple's Relief Society luncheon. She brought her three daughters from Leavenworth, where her husband owns a dry goods store. The oldest, Gertrude, married a doctor. It would be good to have one of those in the family."

Always plotting, aren't you?" Morris said, the beginning of a smile on his lips.

"I believe the next oldest, Lily, married a salesman," Jette said, ignoring the comment, "and the one you met tonight, Anna, is the youngest. You must admit, Lee does appear taken with her."

"As much as any eighteen-year-old fella, but all right. I'll put him on the order desk for a while. He has to start there sometime anyway."

Jette hid her grin. "You're a dear," she whispered. "Maybe one of our other boys can begin to travel with Theodore and learn the business. How about Charlie? He's sixteen now."

"Neither Charlie nor Eugene has an ounce of interest in wool or hides, and that's good. "Only one son should inherit a business," Morris contended. "That prevents arguments. No. Theodore can handle the sales calls for now. He'll have to stay close to home anyway. Their baby is due in late February."

"I hope it goes easier for her this time," Jette said, concern in her voice, "but in any case, I know Bertha is thrilled."

"Yes…well after the birth, if it's all right with you, I'll send Lee back out on the road. We can't do without salesmen, you know."

"Yes, dear. Let's hope for good things by then," she said. Pleased, she kissed him a tender goodnight. Moments later, he reached for her in the darkness and warmly pressed his lips to hers. "I love you, Jette."

"I know," she said.

Throughout January and into the next month, Jette noticed Lee's increasing friendship with Anna. "He goes to Leavenworth to see her," she told Bertha. "Takes her out to eat, and on nice days, they stroll by the river."

"How do you know what they do?" Bertha asked, resting her head on her hand.

"Because he confides in me and asks my advice," Jette said.

"Oh? And what do you tell him?" Bertha asked while stroking her budging belly.

"Lee is such a serious boy. He doesn't have much of a sense of humor, but Anna makes him laugh. She's a smart one and clever, too. She uses her quick wit to charm him. She brought deviled eggs with smiling red-hot pepper faces to our New Year's Eve party. That tickled his funny bone and our guests."

"They do seem to make a good match," Bertha agreed.

"Let's hope she can settle him down. But tell me, how are you feeling?"

"I'm fine except for these nagging headaches." Bertha rubbed her temples.

"Have you talked to Dr. Finkelstein? What does he say?"

"Only that headaches are normal and to cut out the salt in my diet. To tell the truth, this time has been harder than Helen. But I'm not as young as I used to be. I do hope it's a boy. Theodore so wants a son. Thank goodness, there are only a few weeks left to go."

"Well, I'm right down the street if you need me."

"I know, my dear friend. You are a treasure."

For Jette, the days flew by. She cooked and kept the house clean, made Nellie's costume for her school play, and attended The Relief Society and Sisterhood meetings. One evening in late February, just as the family sat down to dinner, Theodore burst through the door, out of breath and distraught. "Bertha has gone into labor," he cried. "I'm on my way to fetch the Doctor, and Helen is sleeping. Can one of you stay with them until I return?"

"Of course," Morris answered. "I'll bring Helen back here to stay with Nell until the baby is born."

"Thank you. I'll be back as soon as I can," Theodore said as he rushed away.

Leaving Lee in charge, Jette and Morris flung on their coats and ran the few doors to Bertha and Theodore's house. Jette roused the sleeping four-year-old Helen and placed her in Morris's waiting arms. Then she went to sit with her friend.

Bertha lay on her bed sobbing, her hands pressing her temples. "I don't know which hurts worse, my head or the labor."

"Maybe I can help with the headache," Jette said. She wet a cloth with cool water from the pitcher. Wringing it out, she placed it on Bertha's forehead.

Bertha sighed but flung it aside. "It does no good."

By the time Theodore returned with Doctor Finkelstein and a nurse, Bertha's contractions had become frequent. Clutching her head, she cried, "Doctor. Please. Can't you do something to take away this agony?"

"Soon, my dear girl. Pain is normal when having a baby."

Bertha screamed, "No! I mean the throbbing in my head!" Her hands mashed her temples. "It's killing me."

"Your head?" he exclaimed. "I didn't realize." He rushed to grab instruments from his bag, "Hurry," he yelled at the nurse. "Help me get her into position. We must deliver this baby right away."

"What is it?" Jette cried.

"You! Leave! Wait outside," Dr. Finkelstein ordered. "We'll do what we must. Go stay with Theodore."

It was past midnight when they heard the lusty cries of the baby, one o'clock before the Doctor, sober and pale-faced, appeared with the infant in his arms. "Come have a look at your fine, healthy son," he said softly to Theodore.

Bursting into a smile, the proud father peered at the sleeping infant. My wife?" he asked, touching the tiny child's hand. "How's she doing?"

Eyes closed, Dr. Finkelstein lowered his head.

Theodore's smile faded. "What's happened?"

"You must understand. I tried everything I could, but we weren't able to save her. I'm afraid you're dear Bertha has left us."

"What do you mean?" Theodore pushed the doctor aside and raced to his wife's bedside.

"Eclampsia," Dr. Finkelstein told Jette and Morris, his voice sounding old and weary. "Even if we'd known, there is no cure."

"Bertha! Bertha!" They could hear Theodore wailing. "Did you hear? We have a son." They saw him lean down, kiss her bloodless lips, and grasp her hand. "Don't leave me," he sobbed. "I wanted a boy, but not without you."

Jette drew a sharp breath and fell into her husband's arms. He led her to a chair and knelt by her side as she covered her face and sobbed.

"I've arranged for the nurse to care for the baby until tomorrow," the Doctor said, "and called for the undertaker as well."

Jette thanked him and went to comfort Theodore. She found him sitting beside his dead wife, staring at the wall.

"Go home," he told her listlessly. "I wish to be alone."

Eyes filled with tears, she beckoned to Morris, and the two of them slipped quietly from the house.

The next morning, Jette woke to find Nellie and little Helen standing by her bed. "I want my mommy," Helen said.

Eight-year-old Nellie shrugged. "Sorry, Mother. I tried to make her wait until you woke, but she keeps saying she wants to go home."

Jette yawned and then rose, flooded by memories of the previous night. "Of course you do," she told Helen. "But first, sit." She patted the bed. "I have some good news. Your mother has brought you a beautiful new baby brother."

"A boy?" Helen cried.

Nell audibly groaned. She'd hoped for another girl.

"When can I see Mommy and the new baby?" Helen asked.

"You can see the baby as soon as you like. But sadly, you won't be able to see your mommy anymore. She passed away."

Nellie gasped and covered her mouth.

Staring at Nell in a daze, Helen said, "Can you take me home, please? I want my mommy."

Jette took the child in her arms and drew her close. "She's not there, Liebchen."

Helen burst into tears. "Where is she?" she whimpered. "I want my mommy."

"I know, darling. She'll always be here in your heart. Someday, you'll understand."

Nell and Helen stayed home with the nurse and the baby while family and friends rode in silence to Elmwood Cemetery, forty-three acres of peaceful solitude at the southeast edge of Kansas City.

Standing by the open grave, the rabbi performed the ritual funeral service. As he read the 23rd Psalm on that cold, bleak February day, his vibrant voice blanketed the sobs of those in mourning.

Morris had not spoken Hebrew since leaving Germany, but today he stood beside his grief-stricken brother and softly whispered the Kaddish. Yis-gadal, v'yis-kadash sh'may rabö. And then, beneath a sturdy young maple tree, Bertha was laid to rest.

Returning to Theodore's home, Jette dipped her hands in a bowl of water set by the door, a reminder of the value of life. She greeted Helen with a hug. While the others gathered in the living room, Jette found the nurse in Bertha's rocking chair humming to the baby. "He's just finished his four o'clock bottle," the woman said. "Would you like to hold him?"

"Later," Jette said, looking at the crib. Anticipating a boy, Bertha had stitched a new blanket in brown and gold threads with giraffes, lions, and deer. Tiny bells hung on ribbons above the cradle, and a teddy bear sat at the head.

Who will take care of Helen and this child? Jette wondered. A nurse for now, but then what? A new thought began to take shape in her head.

That evening at dinner, with the family seated around the dining room table picking at food their friends and neighbors had prepared, Jette said to Theodore, "Does the baby have a name?"

"Bert," he said, tears welling up in his eyes. "After his mother. She would have liked that."

"How lovely," she said. "I've been thinking. You need someone to care for him and Helen." You can't do this alone." Jette lowered her fork. "I have an idea," she said. "My oldest sister, Ricka, lives in Chicago. She and her husband have a daughter named Hermine.

"Hermine graduated from the University of Illinois, where her father teaches. Several years ago, she met and married a student from Baltimore, but Ricka recently wrote he passed away."

"What are you suggesting?" Theodore asked, head raised, eyes narrowed.

"Perhaps she might come to help with your children. We know her. She's family, and it would be far better than hiring a stranger."

"Hum…family, you say," Theodore stammered.

"The perfect solution," Morris boomed, hands raised in the air. "She's a lovely person."

Theodore's shoulders sagged. "I'll think about it," he answered.

Even with the nurse's help, nights with the newborn baby convinced Theodore to give Jette's idea a try.

"If Hermine is willing," Jette said. "I'll write her and see."

Jette's niece, Hermine, and her husband, Abraham, had been married only a few years. He worked at a law firm, and she trained in the sciences and found work at the new Johns Hopkins Hospital in the lab. They both loved children, so they bought a house with a picket fence and addressed the task of making babies, but none had come.

One day, while mending the fences, Abraham caught his hand on a rusty nail. He developed blood poisoning, and Hermine took him to see the doctors at Johns Hopkins. They applied leeches and advised bloodletting. "We don't do that here," they said. "For bloodletting, go see your barber."

Hermine searched the streets until she found a shop with a red and white sign advertising a barber who bled patients. She rushed home and took the feverish Abraham to the shop, where the bloodletting began by slicing the blue veins in the sick man's arms. As the dark red fluid flowed into a pan, Hermine prayed it carried away the infection. But no amount of bleeding saved Abraham from the deadly sepsis. Helpless, Hermine watched the life drain from his body, a painful and wretched death. Bereft and alone, the young woman had only enough energy to go to work in the lab and take the trolley home.

Jette's letter to Hermine came as a godsend. She was needed in Kansas City to care for two orphaned children and their widowed father.

Hermine remembered Morris from Quincy. Not handsome like her father but smart and kind. Why not go? she thought. It will take my mind off my troubles. If I don't like Kansas City, I can always leave.

Morris thought it best for Theodore to at least spend parttime on the order desk. The nurse looked after baby Bert and young Helen during the day. At night, Jette included them in her family's dinner, after which Theodore went home to care for his often-fussy son and sad little girl. By the time Hermine arrived, he was exhausted.

With Hermine there to cook, clean, and look after the children, life returned to normal. Jette went back to her volunteer duties at the Temple Relief Society. Theodore returned to his regular job at M. Lyon and Co., and Lee continued courting Anna. Hermine fit right in. She fussed over the baby, kept him well-fed and content, and brought Helen out of the doldrums.

At Jette and Morris's Thanksgiving dinner, everyone saw Theodore and Hermine's affection for each other. After the feast, Theodore rose with the girl by his side. "Hermine and I want to make a toast," he said. "We wish you all good health and happiness and hope you wish us well in return." He paused and then, with an impish grin, said, 'Hermine and I have decided to marry."

Open-mouthed silence reigned, even amongst the youngest children, and then came shouts of joy.

"Marry?' cried Jette. "How wonderful."

"Congratulations." Morris raised his glass.

Helen clapped her hands and ran into her new mother's extended arms.

"A great idea," yelled Lee. "I hope someday to get married."

Eyes lowered as if in prayer, Anna thought, *I hope to me.*

Chapter Twenty-Seven
KANSAS CITY, MISSOURI

1896

LEE

My father's business was growing fast. Theodore and Hermine's daughter, Rose, had just been born, so Theodore stayed in the office to take and process orders, and Dad sent me out on the road. That meant little time to spend with Anna, though her little gold key on my watch fob chain kept reminding me of her.

Gone for months at a time, I saw little of Anna, but when home, I took her to dinner or strolling along the Three Mile Creek alive in spring with fragrant lavender flowers and redbud trees. At times, she'd read to me from her diary funny little excerpts of things we had done. But when I'd ask to see more, she would snatch it away, telling me laughingly it kept private her secret thoughts. Yet, as time went by, I began to think of us as a couple. I told her about the farms I visited and brought her honey from my customers and beautiful peacock feathers for her hats. She taught school in Leavenworth and made me laugh at her antics to get the children to learn. Occasionally, I'd ask about the gold key, but she'd wink impishly and look away.

I saw the Henrys now and then, but they were growing up, too. Henry One worked in construction, and Henry Two, who'd gone to Yale, came home to work in his father's bank.

Anna became my best friend, yet in truth, I found myself far too busy to dwell on matters of the heart. When I turned twenty-one at the beginning of the year, my father asked me to accompany him to a meeting of the wool buyers in Chicago. Time you met some of our best customers," he told me. "But you can't go in khakis. Go buy yourself a new suit. We at Lyon's must present a prosperous appearance."

I contacted Anna. "He says I have to look good," I told her. After much cogitation at the Woolf Brothers clothing store, Anna settled on a dark, three-piece affair: coat, trousers, and waistcoat. Next came several white shirts and black leather shoes. "And you have to get rid of the suspenders," she said. "They look hokey and countryfied."

I made arrangements to pick up my altered clothing and invited a friend, Samuel Kander, and his sister, Mathilda, to join us for dinner. He suggested we dine at the Savoy on 9th Street, a restaurant with handsomely uniformed Negro servers, white tablecloths, and candles flickering in silver holders. Now and then, other acquaintances stopped by to greet us as well. When I was by myself, I didn't meet many people, but with Anna along, making new friends became easy.

The following Thursday, my father and I boarded the train to Chicago. I stared out the large windows at the leafed-out trees and the herds of cattle grazing on the greening fields, but my father's mind was on business. "Watch what you say," he cautioned me, drawing my attention away from the view. He mentioned the names of a few brokers we'd meet. "Don't argue politics. You are there to make friends. Pay attention to the negotiating I do. I'm taking you along to listen and learn."

We disembarked at Union Station and made our way to the Tremont Hotel. I'd never seen anything like it, hundreds of rooms with private bathrooms costing a whopping $3.50, including meals. The large lobby overwhelmed me with its grand staircase, multiple dining and meeting rooms, cafes, and a barbershop. We went to our room, washed up, and changed into clean shirts. The meeting planners had arranged a five o'clock cocktail hour. We'd have dinner later, on our own.

My father seemed to know everyone. Relaxed and confident, he introduced me to customers and competitors alike. Drink in hand, he greeted each man warmly and asked after their wives and children. It was a side of my father I'd never seen. He smiled and made easy conversation, often introducing me and pointing out that I was his son. I felt proud to be there with him while holding a glass of whiskey, a rarity, and enjoying the plentiful hors d'oeuvres.

Dad asked Raymond Hicks, a broker, and his wife, Violet, to join us for dinner. Hicks, it turned out, was one of M. Lyon & Company's best customers. We went to one of the luxurious hotel dining rooms to eat and relax. We had ordered drinks when I saw a look of startled surprise followed by one of recognition on my father's face. He jumped up and motioned for two people to join us: an older man with a girl my age.

The man wearing tan slacks and a black jacket hurried to shake my father's hand. "Morris Lyon," he cried. It's been years. I barely recognized you. Where's your hair?"

My father brushed at his bald spot, and both men laughed. "Johann Weber. Who could ever forget those quizzical, blue eyes?"

Mr. Weber turned to his daughter. "Susie, you remember Uncle Morris, don't you? He used to bring you lollypops."

She broke into a fetching grin. "So it was you who addicted me to sweets. Of course, I remember," and she gave him a big hug.

"Lee," my father said, addressing me over her shoulder. "It's been over twenty years since this girl's papa taught me how to shear sheep."

I stuck out my hand. "Pleased to meet you, sir."

"And these are my friends, the Hicks," my father continued, introducing our table companions.

"You must join us," Raymond Hicks insisted. "Anyone who had the patience to teach Morris to shear wool is a friend of mine."

"I'm afraid that's an exaggeration," the farmer said graciously as he seated the girl. "He," Johann said, pointing at me, "must be your son."

"Our oldest," my father said.

Susie and I smiled at each other, but I had trouble relaxing my gaze. Something about her drew my attention.

Once we were all seated and the conversation proceeding, I looked more closely at the girl. It felt like I'd met her before. She had a full, sweet face, almost beautiful, and round rosy cheeks. But her dark hair, touched with glints of auburn, drew my attention—the same, I thought, as Uncle Theodore. I noticed my father also staring at Mr. Weber's daughter. "How's your mother?" he asked her.

"She died of scarlet fever in '85, I'm afraid. It's been just my dad and me ever since."

Visibly saddened, my father expressed his condolences, and the dinner continued. I couldn't keep my eyes off Susie. Her soft voice and smiling face enchanted me and kept me wondering if I'd met her somewhere before. "Perhaps we can have breakfast together," I whispered to her as we broke up for the evening."

"I'd love that," she said. "I'll ask my father." She spoke to him, and he nodded with enthusiasm.

But when I mentioned the date to my father, he shook his head. "I'm sorry," he said to Weber and his daughter, "but I'll need Lee the rest of the trip. This is a learning experience for him, and sadly, there'll be no time for…"

"But surely, one breakfast?" I interrupted.

"It's late, and we must retire. Let's say good night," he instructed me. He paid the bill and, taking my arm, moved me toward the elevator. I muttered my apology, and brushing by her, I noticed the depth in her dark brown eyes. And then I knew. She reminded me of him.

Susie looked disappointed, but she told the Hicks good night and thanked my father for a pleasant evening.

He bid everyone a profitable weekend, and I followed my father to our rooms, wordless and perturbed. Inside, with the door closed and the lights turned on, he faced me and said, "You are never to see that girl again."

"Why?" I asked.

"Because I said so."

"But why?"

"That's the end of it." He removed his suit coat and flung it on a chair. "Go to bed," he ordered me. "We have a big weekend ahead."

I did as he said, resentful and full of unanswered questions.

The next day was filled with meetings and a banquet on Saturday night, where we sat at a table near the Hicks. We didn't see Johann Weber or Susie again.

The meeting in Chicago was a great success. When we got home, I looked for the Weber account in the office files but found none. I asked my mother about the incident with Susie Weber. Her advice, "Let it go. Trust your father to know best. And by the way," she said as she continued to wind the skein of yarn I held between my hands. "It's time you and Anna married."

"We're just good friends," I said, untangling the threads.

"Yes, and so much more. I can tell. You've been a couple for two years. Besides, I long for a grandbaby, and so far, you are my only hope."

I gaped at her. "I have never thought of such a thing," I murmured.

"I bet Anna has," she said. "Ask her."

That conversation made me think about Susie in a different light. Though her cute, curvy figure had put thoughts in my head, I realized I loved Anna. We knew and liked the same things and people. My mother was right.

The next day, I stopped by the school where Anna taught before heading out of town on a hide-buying trip. I asked the principal if I could see her telling him I intended to ask for her hand in marriage. He gave me an encouraging pat and suggested I take her outside for lunch.

We sat on the playground steps, sharing peanut butter and jelly sandwiches. I took the keychain from my pocket and fingered the gold key thoughtfully. "I think I've figured out what this is," I told her, "But first, I have a question."

Her eyebrows danced. "Good. I love guessing games."

"This isn't a game," I said.

A kickball rolled in our direction, and she picked it up and tossed it back into play. "All right then. What's the question?"

I felt my heart pounding. "Will you marry me?"

"If you know what the key unlocks, you know the answer," she said.

"I must admit I thought it the key to your diary, but you've not let me read it, so that makes no sense."

Anna laughed. "For the smartest man I know, you're the dumbest. It's the key to my heart, dearest, and yes, I will marry you," she cried joyously.

Thrilled, I gathered her into my arms and kissed her right there on the playground steps. The little boys hooted, and the little girls squealed behind their cupped hands, but we didn't care.

"I will always love and care for you," I told her and kissed her again.

"And I—you," she said.

We married the following August. Leslie was born nine months later, in May. His grandmother had been right about it being a good thing having a doctor in the family. Her sister's husband, Bruno, had attended Leslie's complicated birthing and saved his and his mother's life. Leslie would be our only child.

When I met Morris Ripley years later, he told me that five hundred miles from Kansas City, he, a Russian immigrant, had journeyed from his dry goods store in Richmond, Texas, to the mountainous village of Ruby Hill, Nevada. Young and adventurous, he'd heard there was silver to be found and planned to claim his share. Unfortunately, he'd come too late. By the time he arrived at Ruby Hill, where only a few hovels stood, most of the precious metal had already been dug. Disappointed, he browsed the stores lining the stone streets nearby Eureka Springs. At Franz Stelar's large dry goods store, he met the owner's attractive, twenty-four-year-old daughter, a teacher named Rose. She was the youngest of five children, four girls and a boy cruelly crippled by a badly curved spine.

A fine-figured maiden with a glowing complexion, Rose fit her name. She had dark, softly waved chestnut hair and penetrating brown eyes circled by thin, frameless glasses. Sharp-witted and well-read, she quickly captured Morris's fancy. He couldn't believe his luck. Why, he wondered, had no other fellow snatched up this fine-looking, engaging schoolteacher? In no time, he found he genuinely loved her. Sensing she returned his feelings, the clean-shaven and slender-built fellow proposed marriage. "I will cherish you forever if you come with me to Richmond,

Texas," he begged, "where my own dry goods store provides me with a decent living."

She laughed and said yes if he'd do her a favor.

"Anything," he cried.

"Change your last name. I don't wish to be known as Rose Ripinski.

He bristled in consternation. "My name is who I am," he said and related all his objections, chief among them his heritage and the name of his store."

Her brow wrinkled in thoughtful contemplation. "Perhaps a tiny change would be acceptable."

He eyed her critically. "To what?"

"Ripley. Keep the RIP and change the last five letters to L E Y."

Morris rolled the word around on his tongue. "That is preposterous—Ripinski to Ripley." He frowned.

"Hardly anyone will notice," she reasoned, "and it sounds less Jewish and more American."

"And if I say no?"

She shrugged and sadly shook her head. "Then I won't marry you."

Morris went to consult the girl's father in the sweltering back room of the Stelar Dry Goods Store. "She wants me to change my name," Morris said, swatting at the flies buzzing about his head.

"It would be a worthwhile sacrifice for the reward of an otherwise fine young woman," Franz counseled, fly swatter in motion.

So the last Stelar daughter married Morris Ripley, and they moved to Richmond, Texas, and the newly named Ripley Dry Goods Store. Two years later, Rose and Morris moved Ripley's Dry Good Store to Denver, where they bought a bungalow and settled for good.

At the age of twenty-six, Rose gave birth to a daughter she named Beth, a beauty destined to become Leslie's wife.

Chapter Twenty-Eight
KANSAS CITY

1899-1910

Though M. Lyon & Co. had great possibilities, it had one severe problem. Lee and his father talked about it endlessly but could find no real solution. Morris told Lee about his visit with Albert Deutsch in Carthage, but this was a far different situation. Finally, Morris suggested the one thing Lee found hard to do: call his friend Henry Two.

Now the chief financial officer at the First National Bank, Lee made a special appointment to see him. "I need your help," he said. "I have a cash flow problem. I'd like to borrow a hundred thousand dollars on the first day of each January and repay it on the last business day of each year."

Henry's mouth fell open. "Are you crazy?" he gasped.

"No. Can we talk about this? It just makes sense," Lee said. "We pay our customers in cash, so we have a constant need, but we find it difficult to keep an adequate supply of money on hand.

"You can always borrow more," Henry answered.

"That keeps us guessing, and if we don't have the money in the bank, we won't bet against the come."

Lee watched as Henry Two crunched his lips and stared out the window. Finally, he said, "I remember the day at the stockyard many years ago when you saved my life. Maybe now I can return the favor." He leaned forward. "It will take some time and effort, but I think I can figure out how we can do it, and with appropriate interest," he winked, "I believe the bank can handle the loan."

Lee saw his "Henry" friends at the Chamber of Commerce meetings, and sometimes they'd meet at Jim's Saloon in the crumbling West bottoms, where they'd have great laughs together over their youthful stockyard antics.

Occasionally, they'd have lunch at the plush Kansas City Club, where both Henrys belonged. Lee had entertained thoughts of requesting a membership years later after he and his family were listed in the Social Registry, until an embarrassed and shame-faced Henry told him the club didn't take Jews. That's when he felt the full sting of antisemitism.

Lee mentioned the fact to Lester Ginsberg, a skinny, young Jewish attorney. "Nodding knowingly, Lester asked, "Have you ever been asked to join the University Club?"

"No, but that's different. I didn't even graduate from high school," Lee told him.

"Wouldn't have mattered," Lester sneered. "Jews are verboten. Why do you think only Jews are members of the Prospect Club on Quality Hill? It's because there's nowhere else for them to belong.

The Chamber of Commerce made no such distinction, but Lee realized the friends he made there were daytime friends only. After that, the meetings became less enjoyable. Though he continued to support the institution financially, his clients were stockyard traders and cattlemen from out of town.

Wool, furs, and hides had become the most important part of the business. In late April, Morris called him into his office. "I think it's time you checked up on our customers in Kansas," he said.

"I agree. I'll tell Anna I'm leaving next Monday. I'll be gone a couple of weeks, so if you need anything, you just ask her," he told his father. They smoked a pipeful together and discussed plans and where Lee should go.

It was late spring of '03 when Lee hitched up his horse and buggy and began his annual trip to call on the Lyon cattle and sheep customers in Kansas, a trip he enjoyed. Farms near Topeka, Vermillion, Salina, Mulvane, and Eureka were on his list; the farthest, Abilene, one hundred and sixty miles from home.

The day he reached Emporia, it began to rain. Good, Lee thought, gazing at the green fields of Turkey Red wheat Eastern Europeans had brought to Kansas. He rented a room in nearby Wichita, sleeping restlessly through the stormy night. A heavy mist greeted him the next morning, the day's travel made worse by the constant rain.

Hoping for sunny weather, Lee headed west, but the rain kept coming. Daily storms drenched sprouting corn and soy fields. Hail flattened crops. Tornados downed barns. Lightning ripped trees in half. Customers offered Lee refuge. Peering at his flattened crops, one said he'd lived here fifty years and never seen anything like it.

By the third week in May, overflowing Kansas creeks and streams were draining into the Kaw River, which ran by the busy Kansas capital of Topeka on its way to Kansas City. With farms and towns under water and bridges over roads collapsed, Lee turned his wet horse and buggy toward home. Tired of slipping and sliding over muddy trails, he left them with a farmer he knew and caught the train to Kansas City's Union Depot.

As the engine chugged through soggy Kansas, water lapped at the rails. Disembarking at the West Bottom's train station, he found the depot closed. The railroads had discontinued their services. Water covered his shoes and appeared to be rising. Across the street were thousands of cattle in the stockyards, cowboys huddled anywhere they could find cover. "The Missouri and Kaw are flooding," he yelled at them. "Get out while you can."

Lee ran to Jim's Saloon. You've gotta leave, or you'll drown," he told the old man.

"The paper says it's just another spell of bad weather," Jim said. "A little rain never hurt nobody."

"This isn't just a little water," Lee told him, grabbing the handles of Jim's chair on wheels. "The Kaw has jumped its banks, and the Missouri continues to rise. Looks to me like the rivers have merged. Everyone needs to get out," and he hurried his friends to the door.

Lee knew some of the poor immigrants who had found affordable housing in the West Bottoms. As he pushed Jim up the 9th Street Hill, he yelled, "Take your kids and leave." They shrugged and shook their heads.

"They ain't got no place to go," Jim said.

From the top of the hill, they could see homes, restaurants, cafes, packing plants, warehouses, factories, and the stockyard submerged under seven feet of river water or more. The roads were impassable, and streetcars stopped running. Thousands of cattle had drowned and were lying in the streets: their stinking carcasses left bloated and rotting. The Kaw looked like a lake, with water stretching miles in every direction.

When Lee finally made it back to Kansas City, he found the town without gas, water, and electricity. Police and fire services were in short supply. Exhausted, he joined firefighters trying to put out blazes caused by lime igniting in rail sidecars. Boats arrived to rescue people from rooftops.

The newspaper said forty-seven people died, and it cost Kansas City sixteen million dollars to repair the damage. M Lyon and Co. helped politicians raise enough money to build dikes to hold back the rivers. A new railway depot was planned; everyone knew most of the West Bottoms was gone for good. Jim's Saloon closed, as did other small stores, but the houses of the poor remained open. A New York paper said it was the worst storm ever to hit Kansas.

President Roosevelt appointed Oscar Straus Secretary of Commerce and Labor, the first Jew to hold a cabinet position. That simple act had a positive effect in Kansas City, where Jews were elected to public office, one in commerce and one as an administrator in the mayor's office. Lee received a hero's award. "Jews are finally being recognized," he told his friend, Lester Ginsberg.

"But not for long," came the doubting reply.

Formal dinner parties became the favorite way to entertain their acquaintances. Anna would prepare for days, getting everything ready, and then hire a cook, kitchen help, and maids to do the final preps and serving. Lee became an expert at hosting such affairs dressed in the finery Anna bought him—black tie, tails, and stiff white collared shirts.

Of course, every woman in their social circle reciprocated, the point being to outdo one another. One night, Lee and Anna had been invited to the home of Freddy and Hannah Stern. "Frederick," the host corrected Lee. The Sterns had come to Kansas City from Germany, their small Bavarian village near Ettenheim. Freddy created a highly successful financial concern, but Lee thought he'd become impossibly pompous and vain.

Right before time to go, Anna went to Lee, sobbing. "You must go along without me. I've come down with a case of the grippe." She brought her kerchief to her nose and blew.

He thought she did look flushed, and when he felt her brow, she seemed warm. "I'll tell them we can't come," Lee said as he began to remove his formal waistcoat.

"Oh no, no," Anna said. "We both can't decline at the last moment. Besides, I'm sure dinner will be wonderful. Hannah loves to show off."

Lee gritted his teeth and held out a dangling shirtsleeve. He hated attending any social function without Anna.

Lee arrived at the Sterns' sumptuous two-storied house in time for drinks and hors d'oeuvres and to mingle with the ten other guests—a prominent lawyer, the mayor's Jewish assistant administrator, a merchant, two doctors, and their elegantly gowned wives. At seven sharp, the butler announced dinner, and they strolled past the curving staircase to the beautifully appointed dining room table. Hannah Stern made an announcement. 'My maid, Maddie,' she said, 'took ill today, so won't be with us, nor sadly, as you know, will Anna Lyon. Apparently, both suffer the same malady, but Anna was kind enough to tell our cook about her woman who could take Maddie's place.'"

Something niggled Lee's brain when Hannah said, 'her woman.' They didn't have a woman other than Ruby, a young, pigtailed Negro girl who helped with the cleaning and laundry on Wednesdays. He could hardly imagine Ruby serving a party at the Sterns."

"The hostess rang a little silver bell, and the service began.

Lee noticed the Black woman's thumb plop deep into Frederick Stern's bowl of soup, and so, I suspect did his wife, Hannah. Her look of annoyance made Lee hide a smile behind his hand.

Bits and pieces of salad slid off the plates as the maid elbowed her way between them to set down the dishes. Lee watched Hannah grow increasingly exasperated.

At last, the main event, a rib roast, was placed on the buffet and expertly carved and distributed by the butler, followed by the new maid carrying a silver gravy boat. Frederick was the last to be served. It was then the unthinkable happened. With a devil may care look, the maid poured the gravy right down Frederick's neck."

Freddy leaped from his chair with a thunderous howl, tore at his waistcoat, and sprang for the stairs. The maid fled to the kitchen. Hannah Stern roared through the swinging door like one of Teddy Roosevelt's rough riders. Lee and the rest of the guests sat wide-eyed, in open-mouthed stupefaction."

Hannah yell, "Where did this woman come from? Whoever hired her is fired." And then, to shrieks of laughter, she loudly cried, "Why it's you, Anna Lyon!"

The erring Black maid turned out to be Lee's wife. Hannah Stern and Anna burst through the door, convulsed with laughter. Sighing with relief, Lee joined in the merriment and enjoyed the rest of the party.

Chapter Twenty-Nine
KANSAS CITY, MISSOURI

1911-1918

LEE

Unfortunately, Fredrick's friend, the mayor's Jewish assistant administrator, got caught dipping into government funds. Disgraced and facing prison, he put a bullet into his head.

My father had recently purchased a black Packard touring car and, with some hesitancy, let me borrow it to take Anna to the graveside service in Leavenworth. I loved driving it, and the shiny brass lanterns and black leather seats caused quite a stir.

We saw sprinkles of early June flowers dotting the roadside grass as I lowered the windows, eager to inhale the fresh, pure air. We would have loved the day if it hadn't been for the funeral. Apparently, others felt the same since cars lined the road around the cemetery, and a crowd stood near the gravesite, one behind the other. The rabbi took advantage of the numbers and the weather and spoke much longer than necessary to plant the poor man in his grave.

At last, the coffin was lowered into the ground near a mound of freshly dug dirt. I watched as first one man and then the next picked up the shovel, placed a small amount on its edge, and dumped it into the grave. A custom meant to help speed the deceased person's return to earth, I did it hoping death wasn't contagious.

Anna and I strolled with friends back to my father's Packard. Ahead of us were people I knew, and I heard one ask the other, "Did you know the heeb well?"

"Hey!" I said, stepping up to face him.

"Sorry, Lee," the man said.

My wife flashed me her look, but all the rest of the day, I felt the slow, steady drip of antisemitism.

Anna invited my father to dinner that night, and it was over the chicken I told him of the day's events.

"What's a heeb?" Leslie asked.

"Not now." Anna shook her head.

"I hear it at school," Les said.

My father spoke up. "It's short for Hebrew, not a nice way to refer to a Jew." I believe it reminded him of the relative we might have living in Wichita, a butcher, or perhaps someone in the meat packing business. "I've never cared to investigate, but if you're traveling that way this summer, you could try to find him," Anna suggested it might be good for Les to go along.

That's how I came to take my thirteen-year-old son, Leslie, who weighed less than a hundred pounds, on a wool and hide buying trip in Kansas.

A friend had fixed up a broken Pierce-Arrow Roadster, and he offered to let me use it. He said it could go more than thirty miles an hour, much more efficient than a horse and buggy. He brought it to our house one day and showed us how to crank it to start. It wasn't easy, but both Les and I could manage the task.

Sturdy canvas top, rubber tires, black body, black fenders that Les polished to a brilliant shine, Anna didn't know whether to laugh or cry as she watched us pull away from the house on our first noisy venture. We drove down the street, Les yelling at friends.

On this trip, I thought I got to know my son, and he got to know me.

We spent the first few nights near Wichita. Les learned how to fill the car with gas, and I learned how to use the pedals. He could barely see over the steering wheel, but I decided he needed to know how to drive in case anything happened to me.

My customers lived on surrounding farms, where, after making calls, we summoned the courage to look under the hood but not touch anything for fear of shutting her down. Everyone admired our mode of transportation, though neither of us had any idea how it worked.

We tried to find a meat company named Lion, but none existed though we discovered two meatpacking companies in town. The first we visited had only recently opened, so the owner could tell us little or nothing about earlier days. But he entertained Les with stories of the old Chisholm Trail and told him he'd been one of Teddy Roosevelt's Rough Riders in Cuba. Les's eyes popped open. He'd read about them in his history class.

"Did you know," the meatpacker told Leslie, "Old Teddy Roosevelt favors the Jews? The first lad killed in our fight with the Cubans was a sixteen-year-old Jewish boy. To look at Roosevelt now, you'd never guess it, but he'd been a sickly kid. He told us when he saw the local Jewish merchants exercising indoors, he did the same and made himself strong."

I saw a look of interest come into Leslie's eyes. "How did the meatpacker know we were Jews?" he later asked. I didn't know, but I thought maybe it was because we inquired about one.

At the second company, a wood building with a front porch, we found an old man stoop-shouldered and bent, slaughtering chickens for the day's sales.

"Do you happen to know Kallmann Lion?" I asked.

The butcher looked up and nodded. "He's no longer among the living, but he left me his shechita knife and taught me Kashrut, so I can help you if that's what you want."

"He was my grandfather's brother," I told the man. "He came from Germany many years ago, and we never knew what became of him."

"I will tell you what I know," he said.

He led us to chairs on the porch. Les settled on the steps, and the butcher said, "A sweet little man, your uncle. We butchered together all these years since the war. I'm Catholic, so Kallmann kept our Jewish customers happy. One day, a Cherokee Indian came into our place. He had feathers in his hair, black circles around his eyes, and a bow strung with an arrow. Scared the liver outta both of us. 'Shalom Aleichem,' he says in a loud, gruff voice. I thought he was talking Injun and went for my gun, but Kallmann got all excited and said to the Indian, 'Are you Jewish?'"

Leslie's eyes widened. "Why would he think that?" he asked.

"He's speaking Hebrew," I told my boy. "Shalom Aleichem means Peace Be with You."

The butcher, Jebadiah, said, "That's right. Wohali, the Injun, wasn't Jewish. He and his tribe had come to Oklahoma and Kansas to escape the southern Baptists who wanted the Indians dead. He just wanted to trade his tribe's pottery for beef. He and Kallmann got along well."

"What does Wohali mean in English?" Leslie interrupted.

"It means Eagle—strong, brave, fearless. And he was that. After a while, Kallmann would go spend thirty or forty days at a time in the Cherokee village. They'd hunt and fish together. Kallmann told me Wohali's people worshiped one God, Yehowah. They knew many words of Hebrew and had customs and ceremonies like those of the Jews. My friend would come home anxious for beef. He said the Indians made him eat eggs because their meat wasn't kosher."

"What happened to them?" I asked.

"Wohali died some years back," Jebadiah said. "Kallmann married a Cherokee woman. Far as I know, they had no children." He retrieved a long, silver knife with a worn wooden handle. "Here's his shechita. It's yours if you want it. Mind you, it's sharp as a razor."

I held up my hands, my fingers spread. "No. It's yours. He meant you to have it."

A customer came up the path. Jebadiah rose, our meeting over. His last words to us were, "Cherokee and Jews are survivors, not victims. They and their people live on."

We bid him farewell and went to our car. "Are you hungry?" I asked Les as I started the engine and drove away.

"Starving," he answered.

"We should eat before heading to Emporia," I answered. "It's eighty miles and will take us a few hours, but I have customers to see along the way."

After lunch, we filled our extra gas tank, got back into the car, and hit the road. Les slept, and before long, it started to rain. The heavens opened, and unable to see the road, I pulled over.

"Where are we?" Les asked, wakened by rainwater coming in on his side of the car. "Somewhere in Kansas," I said, gazing at the muddy road and the matted green fields.

The rain didn't stop, but it lightened, so I decided we'd better get going. I put on my hat, got out of the car, and grabbed the crankshaft. I tried it over and over again, but stiff and hard to turn, the car wouldn't start.

"Let me try," Les said.

"You're not strong enough, and you'll get drenched," I said. "Stay in the car."

"Someone has to fix the engine," he said, jumping out and jerking up the hood. We both looked inside, puzzled and finally, Les said, "Dad, why don't you get back in the car? Then, if I get the thing started, you can rev her up."

With little or no hope of any success, I did as he asked. I saw him jiggle some wires, first one and then another, swat at something, and then crank the shaft with all his might.

It started.

Les jumped back inside. I hit the gas pedal and didn't stop driving until we reached Emporia, sixty miles and hours away. We drove around town until we found a mechanic.

I laughed when I told Anna what happened.

Until the trip to Wichita, I'd paid little attention to my son's education, but now I realized I'd one day want him in the business. I needed to get him started and where best but in Ira's hide cellar? He was way too slim to do the heavy work, but under Ira's gentle tutelage, he could exercise muscles and brain.

The rest of the summer, Les and I drove to work in the morning and home together at night. He didn't complain about the blood and guts of the cellar and often had funny stories to tell. But that changed in September when school began. Les started school at Westport High, and I, leaving Theodore in charge, went to New York to see my broker.

Upon my return, Anna proudly told me of Les's latest endeavors, Latin and Greek and the Irving Club, a literary society.

Disgusted, I suggested football and told Les to clean the warehouse skunk smell off my shoes, reminding him we were in the practical business of wool, fur, and hides.

That evening at dinner, Les asked, "Where is Serbia?"

"In Europe," I answered. "Why?"

"I read in the paper I used to clean your shoes that Austria declared war on Serbia and that the United States will likely get into it."

"That's ridiculous. There's not going to be a war, and if there is, we'll have nothing to do with it."

Les got good grades in school, and I made it a point to converse with my son and even take him to work with me on Saturdays once in a while. I found him to be good company. One evening, he said, "Dad, I ran into an old friend named Charley Ditzman. He goes to Yale and is studying aviation. Boy! I wish I could fly."

I lit a Camel cigarette and offered him one. He was sixteen now— old enough to learn how to smoke. "Yale," I said. I hadn't finished high school, but I'd always hoped he'd go to Harvard, where my friend Lester Ginsberg went.

"Charley says most of his friends are men studying aviation. This summer, he's going to help his roommate, Trubee Davison, and the others build a real flying machine. Wouldn't I love to help, though he says I'm too young?"

But that conversation sent Yale to the top of Les's college list, and I finally agreed to let him go if he was admitted. I'd heard that German balloons and zeppelins were already finding ground artillery. "It's crazy," I said. "Those things will never be able to sustain flight in the air."

In 1915, *The Kansas City Star* wrote about a marauding German submarine that sank a British ocean liner named the *Lusitania*. Though more than a thousand people died, and the Germans sank American ships when they found them, President Wilson and the politicians in the United States ignored the fighting in Europe. I continued to tell Leslie there would be no war.

On a sunny day in June 1917, with clear and welcoming skies, Les and the other graduating Westport seniors sat on the high school playing field, the legs of their chairs digging holes in the fresh summer grass. The girls donned white dresses with purple bows, and the boys, ill at ease and itchy, wore new suits and purple ties. The principal stood on the platform with the teachers who had shepherded the kids through their tender teen years.

When the principal called my son's name to issue his diploma, he stopped and smiled. "Leslie Morris Lyon," he said loud enough for everyone to hear. "Les had the highest grades in his class." Anna and I beamed. The principal plowed on. "Leslie is president of the prestigious Irving Club, belongs to the German, Radio, and the Westport High School Clubs, and is a debate team member."

The principal stopped to allow for polite applause. "And," he said, with a congratulatory grin, "Leslie has not missed a day of school in all four years." His classmates erupted with cheers, jeers, and wild catcalls. Everyone laughed, even Les.

All that spring and summer, we read articles in *The Kansas City Star* about battles in Germany and France, but President Wilson kept us out of the war until April 1917, when he sent troops to help France and England fight Germany. Les had little interest. He had friends who'd enlisted, but he was too young and had his heart set on going to Yale.

One Sunday in July 1917, I picked up the newspaper, read the headline, and threw the whole thing on the dining room table. "So much for your flying machines," I angrily told Les, pointing to the front page.

There was a picture of an aircraft floating in the Atlantic. YALE STU-
DENT CRASHED PLANE INTO SEA, read the headline.

Anna picked up the paper and read aloud, "'The plane broke in two,
leaving the young Yale pilot alive but seriously injured.' That does it,"
she said. "I'm withdrawing your application to Yale and filling out one
for Harvard instead."

"No," Les cried. "The crash doesn't change a thing."

"Yes, it does," I said. "Your mother worries you will take up flying."

"But you promised I could go to Yale."

"Well, your mother has changed her mind." I stood and walked into
the living room.

"She can't do that," Les yelled from the kitchen.

"Of course, she can. And for your information, I agree, and I pay
the bills around here."

Les jumped up, his chair clattering backward, and bolted to his room.

"Get back down here and apologize," I shouted, but he ignored me. I
stormed up the stairs and burst into his room, feeling flushed with anger.
He lay on his bed, sobbing. "You can't treat your mother that way," I
said. "Quit acting like a baby. Go down and apologize."

He shook his head, wiping tears away with his shirtsleeves.

"Do it NOW!" I roared.

I'm sure I scared the daylights out of him, but he mouthed a big,
round, silent "no."

"All right. I'm done with you," I said and left his room.

I went downstairs to calm Anna, who was also crying and quite
upset. I hugged her and told her I agreed entirely. Not to worry.

Leslie didn't answer when I called him for dinner. He must have
slipped down the stairs unheard and left. We decided to eat without
him. But upset, neither of us had much of an appetite.

Before long, he returned, likely driven home by hunger. He sat sul-
len in his chair. As usual, I carved the meat. He held out his plate, but,
angry, I paid him no mind.

"Dad?" he said.

I didn't answer.

"May I please have a piece of roast?"

I acted like he wasn't there.

He looked at his mother. "I'm sorry," he said. "It's just that I had my heart set on Yale."

"I know," she answered.

His eyes returned to me. "May I please have some dinner?"

I ignored him for a few days, and the next thing I knew, he turned eighteen and joined the Army.

Chapter Thirty
KANSAS CITY, MISSOURI

1917-1921

Leslie arrived at Camp Funston, four miles east of Fort Riley near Junction City, Kansas, on a jouncing, crowded Army bus with fifty other nervous recruits. Those who lived in Missouri expected a desolate wasteland. Instead, they found a thriving city on the banks of the Kaw, complete with stores, coffee houses, bars with dance floors, and other entertainment places. A sergeant directed them to a nearby building where they were ordered to strip. Naked, they huddled, hands modestly covering their private parts, and checked for visible signs of disease. By the time they'd been poked and punched, eyes, ears, and noses evaluated and ordered to spread their cheeks, all signs of dignity had disappeared. Brushing at their newly shorn heads, they donned ill-fitting uniforms and were ordered to a two-story barracks, their home for the next three months. Housing Les's whole company infantry, the building contained 150 beds, so crowded together they got to know each other by the sound of their snores and farts. In addition to sleeping quarters, the building had a well-stocked kitchen, a huge mess hall, supply rooms, and the forbidding company commander's office.

Since he'd salted and lifted hides, Leslie thought he'd be fine with the basic training, but he hadn't reckoned with ruthless drill sergeants. Unrelenting, they kept the new recruits marching or engaged in excruciating exercises from dawn till nightfall. Exhausted and drained by the merciless Kansas sun, they fell into their bunks each night, a blaring bugle rousting them out at reveille. The drill masters resumed training them for war as soon as they were dressed, inspected, and breakfasted, with never enough time to eat.

As a part of the 89th division, now deployed to France, Les's bunk-mates and he thrilled at hearing about the exploits of their overseas Sunflower Brigade. Rumor had it they'd soon be shipped to the Argonne Forest to replace the dead and wounded, so they trained even harder on the flat, blazing-hot Kansas prairies.

One day, Les and three other soldiers were assigned to load a large cannon onto a caisson, a heavy artillery cart drawn by two horses. The wagon's large wheels, made of wood and steel, were punctuated with round metal ground-gripping lugs. As they lifted the heavy cannon onto the carrier, the horses moved, and one of the caisson wheels fell on Les's foot. At first, he didn't realize what had happened. He tried to walk, but his boot wouldn't follow. Then came realization and searing pain. Gasping, he tried to lift the wheel. "Hey! I need some help here," he cried. Then, more frantic, "Can someone get this thing off me?"

The three soldiers rushed to help, but the wheel wouldn't budge. Frank Sampson, the smallest, got the horses to pull the caisson forward. As the wheel turned, Les felt the bones in his foot crunch. "Thanks," he whispered and fainted.

At Camp Funston Hospital, they realigned Les's bones and encased his foot in a heavy plaster cast. Crutches became his new artillery. The doctor, a civilian with a son overseas, sent Les home to recuperate. His friends came to the train station to see him off and vowed to keep in touch. Les hugged Frank thanked him with a fiver and promised to return soon.

He and the rest of Les's friends returned to Camp Funston unaware of a more dangerous situation than the war—the arrival of the Spanish flu. First reported in Spain, the virulent strain made people sick with high fever, aches and pains, and extreme exhaustion. Made worse by the war that caused people to be in close contact, half a million sickened, and fifty million died.

Anna cried with joy when she saw her boy. Lee greeted Les with open arms. They fixed a bed for him in the living room until he could manage the stairs, and his mother set an ashtray on the coffee table. Together, Les's parents kept him safe and well-fed, his new trim figure soon gone.

On the morning of November 11, 1918, Les's father bought a newspaper on his way to work. To Anna and Les's surprise, he came roaring back home waving *The Kansas City Star*. "The war is over," he cried, grabbing his wife by the waist and whirling her around.

Les took the paper from his father's hand. "An armistice has been signed at 6 a.m. central time," he read out loud. "The greatest war in history has come to an end."

There was cheering in the streets and celebrations all over town. Les and his parents hugged each other and ate dinner that night at the fancy Savoy Grill.

Leslie heard his friend, Frank Sampson, died of the Spanish flu. Those who survived at Camp Funston were mustered out and scattered to the winds.

His foot healed. His discharge papers arrived late in December. Altogether, he'd spent eighteen weeks in the army, all but seven of them at home, away from Camp Funston, the war, and the flu.

Soon after the war ended, Leslie applied to Harvard. A congratulatory letter from the school notified him he'd been accepted into the freshman class. With enrollment down forty percent, the school honored those who had served with a full year of college credits. For some unknown reason, that included Leslie, which meant he could graduate in three years instead of four.

He arrived in Cambridge on January 14, 1919, a week before classes began, along with forty other Harvard neophytes. He found his freshman dormitory, Grays Hall, situated on the immaculate Harvard Yard, a large park surrounded by many other brick buildings.

His roommate, Hardy Murphy, had already arrived and begun unpacking. Tall and muscular, dark facial hair growing, his hair was buzzcut army style. He looked up, announced his name, and pointed at the army duffle Les carried. "Been in the war?" he asked.

"Artillery, but I never got overseas. You? Been in the army long?" Les asked.

"Five years. Career army sergeant. Heard about Harvard and decided to get some free education, but before I got out, I killed my share of dirty krauts in France."

"Krauts? Germans?" Les said.

Hardy wrinkled his nose and said, "Yah, mien Herr. Where you from?"

"Missouri," Les answered.

"Hardy laughed. "Way out West. You an Indian?"

"No. A Jew," Les vacuously replied.

Hardy stopped unpacking. "I didn't know kikes lived west of the Mississippi."

Shocked, Leslie slowly lowered his duffle bag to the floor. He had already begun not to like this fellow. "You got a problem?"

"Absolutely. I won't room with a dirty heeb." You gotta go." He opened the door. Picking up Les's duffle, he tossed it out of the room. "Now you," he said, pointing to the hall.

Leslie knotted his fists and lunged at Murphy. It's you who's leaving," he said as he flipped the former sergeant around and sent him flying through the door.

Murphy rose, ducked his head, and stalked back into the room. He was twenty pounds heavier and trained in hand-to-hand combat. Poor Les never had a chance.

After a few of their classmates stopped the fight, a Harvard official sent Hardy Murphy to get reassigned to a different dorm and Leslie to the hospital to treat his cut upper lip and broken nose. Hardy moved to off-campus housing. Les heard he left Harvard at mid-term, deciding college life wasn't for him.

Eric Herzl, Leslie's new roommate, arrived at Harvard the day after Hardy Murphy moved out. The committee that assigned dormitory rooms at Harvard decided the son of a Jewish Austrian professor from Vienna provided the perfect solution. Eric spoke fluent German, French, and English, came from well-to-do parents, and conveniently filled the quota of Jews in Gray's Hall.

It didn't take long before Les and Eric became good friends. Eric's father, who taught philosophy at the University of Austria, had kept his family in Vienna during the Great War. Though the city suffered mightily from embargoes on food and clothing, no battles were fought on the city streets.

Les and Eric studied and partied together. They had long midnight discussions for the next three years. The subjects included American baseball, about which Les knew much, world conditions, where Eric excelled, and women, which baffled them both.

One night, Leslie asked, "What was it like in Vienna during the war?"

Eric stretched and brushed his dark hair off his forehead. "I wanted to go fight, but I wasn't old enough. My father insisted the war would be over soon. But my city changed. Many men joined the army, so women took their jobs. I remember thinking it strange to see ladies repairing broken pipes and cleaning the streets. My sister and I became student volunteers collecting and delivering clothes and food to the poor. My mother complained about the cost of groceries."

Eric went to the coffee pot on Leslie's dresser. He refilled his cup and returned to his desk. "Jewish refugees from Russia and Poland, victims of antisemitism, poured into Vienna. My father struggled to help them find jobs and relief, in particular his uncle, a lawyer named Theodor."

Intrigued, Leslie said, "Tell me about him."

"He thought Jews should have a state of their own. It's an interesting idea, don't you think?"

"I'll need time to digest it. Off the top of my head, I'd say it's absurd." Leslie closed his books. "I've got an exam tomorrow, and tomorrow night there's the social. I'm going. Wanna go with me?"

Eric smiled. "Yes. I always enjoy those get-togethers. But if I'm going to be a doctor, I need to study. Exams are soon for the Medical University School of Vienna. That's where I want to go."

Leslie met Beth the next night at the Harvard-Smith spring college party. She said she had only recently recovered from chickenpox, but intrigued, Les wanted to see more of what was behind the delicate gossamer veil she wore. He thought her a mysterious figure, noting she floated gracefully from one Harvard man to another, her melodious voice engaging each in conversation. He decided he wanted to get to know her better.

Beth thought Leslie handsome in his tan slacks and brown leather jacket. Though some of her friends said he didn't look Jewish, she knew he was. How to meet him, her scheming mind wondered. When he turned his green eyes on her, the veil became a problem. She lowered it only long enough for him to quickly glimpse her pretty face.

Approaching, he said, "I'm Leslie Lyon. I don't believe we've met."

"Beth Ripley." She gave him her hand.

"As in *Believe it or Not?*" he asked with a sly grin.

She'd heard that line before and, acting somewhat offended, shook her head.

"Is that why you're wearing a veil?" he inquired.

Unamused, she answered truthfully, "No. I've been cooped up with the chickenpox, but I'm over it now except for a few unsightly places."

"Oh. I . . sorry," he stammered. "I mean, I'm glad you've recovered. Where are you from?"

"Denver," she answered, forgiving his oft-heard joke, "but I'm a student at Smith. What about you?"

"Harvard now, of course, but originally Kansas City, Missouri."

"We're you in the war?" she asked.

"Yes," he said, "briefly, but I'd rather hear what you study and what you find fun."

"I'm an English major and enjoy traveling and shopping. What about you?"

"Economics and swimming are my latest interests," he said, and they spent the rest of the evening getting to know each other.

Before they parted, Leslie asked, "Will you lower your veil so I may sneak a peek at your beautiful face? That way, I will recognize you the next time we meet."

"No," she whispered, whirling away. "Tonight, I will remain Mysterious Beth."

"Wait," he called. "Where can I find you?"

"Chapin House at Smith College," Beth Ripley said and was gone.

Beth arrived at Smith, an unsophisticated seventeen-year-old girl who had been thoroughly protected at home by Rose, her ever-vigilant mother. She was smart, a good student but wide-eyed and naive—a girl who knew nothing about men. Though she saw Les now and then, she decided to see others as well. She accepted a date with Mitch Aronson, a Harvard man. He took her to dinner and, in return for a few kisses, promised to take her to see the New York shows. But he had buck teeth, bad breath, and a penchant for the mundane, and after a few dates, she stopped seeing him.

Next, she met Rodger Brunstein at a college friend's house. He had easy manners and a fancy car. She dated him more than once until the night he asked her to come home with him to see if they were sexually compatible. Dismayed, she declined and bid him adieu.

Macy Gordon had a horse he let her ride, but she sensed he had ulterior motives.

She was learning and felt in control, and it all seemed like harmless fun until she accepted a date with a young doctor named Louis. Older and studious, he smelled like shaving cream and wore thick, metal-framed glasses. He picked her up in his blue automobile with the top removed and took her out for an evening of drinking and dancing. She drank more than she should have.

Time flew by. Her dorm closed at ten, so she would have to slip in without the proctor knowing. Louis parked his car, top-down, across the playing field from the dorm to avoid being seen.

Intoxicated by too much liquor and the sweet smells of spring, Beth yawned and stretched her hands upward toward the star-filled sky. Louis reached for her slim body. He took her in his arms and sought her lips for what she perceived as harmless kissing.

But then, he removed his glasses, and things got out of hand. Maneuvering his fingers up Beth's shirt, he caressed her breasts, moaning.

"Wait a minute," she cried. He scared her, and she tried pushing him away. How had things gone so far? She reached for the door handle.

"Aw, come on," he whispered. His hands roamed under her skirt. "I'm a doctor, and doctors know how to treat their patients." He began to unzip his pants.

"I'm not your patient," Beth cried, jumping out of the car, "and you're not my doctor."

"I thought this is what you wanted," he called as she ran across the field to her dorm without looking back. Rumpled with her seventeen-year-old innocence shattered, she made it to her room undetected. The next day, head aching but still intact, she decided to see only Les. They dated, she exclusively, for the rest of her college years. They fell deeply in love, and when he proposed, she immediately accepted.

Rose saw to it that her lovely daughter was married in style. Hadn't Morris said, "spare no expense," though he thoughtfully added, "within reason. I'll take care of everything."

Beth's trousseau contained silk undergarments, top-quality towels and linens, and table settings for twelve. It took every cent Rose and Morris had and then some to provide their daughter with an unforgettable evening. Wedding guests came from Kansas City and mixed with Denver friends. They were married on June 29, 1921, by Rabbi Ishakoff from Temple Emanuel in the grand ballroom of the Brown Palace Hotel. Beth looked exquisite in her beaded ivory silk Gatsby gown, her father stately in white tie and tails. Rose saw Morris hand the rabbi a hundred-dollar bill for performing the ceremony, but as she later put it, "We only have one daughter."

Chapter Thirty-One
KANSAS CITY, MISSOURI

1921

The Town of Kansas had grown to more than 300,000 people. Now called Kansas City, it thrived just as Albert Deutsch had predicted it would. The rebuilt stockyard flourished between the thick limestone bluffs of the fast-flowing Missouri and Kaw Rivers. The second largest stockyard in the world, it processed thousands of animals each day.

Sitting at his office desk, Morris Lyon gazed wearily but with pride and satisfaction through his glass window at his two competent secretaries, his brother Theodore and Theodore's son, Bert. He could hear Lee in his own enclosure clicking away on his new adding machine and Leslie talking into the black telephone receiver. The family business was doing well.

Morris heard the clanging switch engines behind the building as they picked up box cars loaded with salted hides headed to Chicago or New York. To the east sat the farmers market where lush produce from fertile fields had been brought to trade. South of M. Lyon & Co. sat many brick buildings housing the thriving garment industry. Hundreds of women operating industrial sewing machines sewed cloth into clothes for pennies a day. And beyond those brick and limestone buildings came the sounds of the growing city. In terms of business, coming to the Town of Kansas had been the right decision.

Sweating, Morris flipped the switch to the little fan sitting on his desk. He took his white linen handkerchief from his pocket and wiped the perspiration as it rolled into his side whiskers. Summer had simmered into August, and the last few days had left him tired and loath to work.

The week before, he had attended Leslie's wedding in Denver. Oh, how Morris missed his Jette. She would have loved the lavish dinners Rose and Morris Ripley hosted. Dear Jette, gone now for three years. Kidney and bladder cancer had seized her vitality and then her life. She'd been like glue holding them all together, and he still felt lost without her. They'd buried her at Elmwood Cemetery, a gravesite for him waiting beside her.

Morris didn't let his flagging age and energy keep him from attending his grandson's wedding. Theodore and Bert ran the business while he and Lee were away. Denver's cool June days and chilly evenings felt like heaven compared to Kansas City's oppressive, hot, humid summers. The distant snowcapped mountains reminded him of the days he and Jonas had dreamed of hunting for gold in the Rockies. If Jonas had lived, would they have gone to Colorado?

The trip had tired him. His thoughts rambled to the day before the wedding. Morris Ripley left his busy dry goods store and showed Morris the flourishing tree and brush-covered land bordering a long, low-lying valley near the wide South Platte River. "It's for sale, and I'm sorely tempted," he told his guest. "If they dam the river, the property surrounding a proposed lake will be worth a fortune, but there are so many "ifs," and I'm not sure it's worth the price they're asking. What would you do?" he asked.

"Do you know when a dam will be built?" Morris inquired.

"Not for years, I think."

"Then I wouldn't buy property now," Morris said. "Wait. Sounds like there'll be plenty of time to speculate later and accumulate the money needed."

Morris nodded in agreement.

Now, mopping his face again, Morris tried to resume processing a wool order, but even that simple task exhausted him. Miss Johnson came into his office with a glass of water. She had been one of his first hires, a small, prim woman with her hair worn in a tight little bun. In the beginning, he'd been impressed by her modest dress, proper demeanor, and a pencil at the ready tucked neatly behind her right ear. They'd gotten on well. After eighteen years, hair gone gray, she still wore her hair in a tight little bun, the pencil behind her ear.

"I bet you could use this," she said, handing him the glass of water. "It's a very warm day." She adjusted his fan to recirculate more air around him.

But he lifted his hand and motioned her away. "Never mind. I think I'll go home. Ask my son if he'll take me."

Morris saw Miss Johnson enter Lee's office and point in his direction. Lee nodded and, within minutes, came to get him. "Come on, Dad. We've been so busy since the wedding. It will be a good time to chat." He waved to his secretary, Miss Evans. "Back in an hour," he said.

Morris hobbled out to Lee's big, black Packard using his ebony cane with the polished gold nob. "Nice car," he said, patting the shining side lantern.

"I like it," Lee said, starting the engine. "We almost bought a Ford."

"What stopped you?"

"Anna. She picked up a copy of Henry Ford's <u>Dearborn Independent.</u>"

"I've heard of him," Morris said. "When Jonas and I left Germany, we thought we left that kind of hatred behind." He wiped his brow and rolled down his window. "Jew-hating," he sighed. "It's like a contagious disease passed down from one generation to another. We have our own Henry Ford right here in Kansas City, except he's in real estate."

"Lester Ginsberg says the same thing, but I hope you're both wrong," Lee argued as he pulled up to Morris's house and helped his father get out of the car.

"We're not wrong," Morris said, his ebony cane tap-tapping on the sidewalk and up the front steps. "You want to come in for a while?" he asked, ringing the doorbell.

"I'd better not. We've got a lot going on at the office," Lee said. The maid opened the door. "Here's Magnolia. She'll get you some tea. I'll drop by later."

"Hot day," Morris said to the Negro woman, who looked nothing like the dainty flower her name implied. A substantial person wearing a crisp, white uniform, she grasped her employer's arm and guided him toward the kitchen. "I've made your favorite soup today," she said in her high, lively voice. "I put in plenty of meat and vegetables like Miss Jette used to say and marrow to soothe aching bones. Come have some. It'll cool you off."

"Soup? On a hot day like this? That's insane," he said, smiling. "But bring me a bowl. I'll give it a try. I remember when Jette made enough marrow bone soup to feed the family for a week. The kids liked it best with matzo balls, and it kept us all strong and healthy." He sat at the kitchen table where Magnolia served him. "Almost as good as my wife's," he said, teasing the maid as usual.

"Now, Mister Morris. You stop that, or I won't give you anymore later," the maid grinned. "But for now, how about a nap." She helped Morris into the living room, the coolest part of the house. Miss Jette had kept the heavy, satin drapes drawn shut because of the sun's heat and its penchant for fading the colors on her needlepoint chairs.

"You jest stretch out on this here sofa," the maid suggested. With strong, experienced hands, Magnolia plumped the pillows and helped Morris sit and lay back. She adjusted the little fan on the leather top table next to the green Dalton lamp and left the room.

Nell arrived at dinnertime. "Where's Daddy?" she asked Magnolia.

"Been sleeping like a baby all afternoon. The heat must a wore him out."

Nell went into the living room and turned on the lamp. "Time to rise and shine, Daddy," she said, touching his shoulder. But in an instant, she knew. Sleeping peacefully on that hot summer's day, her father had passed away.

He was buried at Elmwood, next to his beloved Jette, just as he wanted. Lee's family purchased a large marble headstone engraved with the name Lyon to mark the graves of their parents forever. The cemetery was filling up fast. Would there be room for him, he wondered.

PART FOUR

Chapter Thirty-Two
KANSAS CITY, MISSOURI

1920'S

Anna and Nellie sat shiva, but Lee refused, at least in the traditional way. He wore his regular leather shoes, shaved as usual, and avoided his living room, where relatives and friends had gathered to mourn Morris together. He sat alone on the back porch, watching one rabbit chase another. It brought back the pain he'd felt the time he'd seen his father kill a rabbit, the horror of skinning and roasting it, and the guilt of enjoying eating it. He remembered his shock at meeting his father's secret daughter and the fervor with which Morris competed for government bids. Anna called him to dinner, but he had no appetite and instead walked down the street wishing he'd stayed on the day Morris died for that one last visit.

Knowing his father would understand, he went back to work the day after the funeral. He was about to go into Morris's office when he saw Miss Johnson sitting at her desk, hands neatly folded. "Come join me," he said, sitting in his father's black leather chair.

"It won't be the same without him," Miss Johnson said. "I will stay for as long as you need me, but the truth is, I wish to retire."

"How many years has it been?" Lee said, a catch in his voice.

"Too many to count," she answered softly.

"I'll miss you both. The fact of the matter is there would be no business without you."

She patted his hand and hurried away.

Morris's brother, Theodore, came from his next-door office and knocked on the metal frame. "We should talk," he said.

Lee motioned his uncle to a chair.

"Bert insisted I speak with you," Theodore said. "He believes this should be my office now. Though your father was eleven years older than I, this is a family business. Since I'm now the oldest member, I should be president."

Lee raised his eyebrows. It was a foregone conclusion. Les would inherit M. Lyon & Co. For as long as he could remember, Lee's uncle had been at Lyons, assuming various roles. Sometimes, he worked in the warehouse, sometimes in the inner office at his desk. But Morris ran the business. "I'm afraid I don't look at it that way," he said, "and neither did Dad. Perhaps you've forgotten. My father brought you from Germany and gave you a job. Thanks to him, you've been able to make a nice living for yourself and your family. And thanks to him, your son has a good-paying job."

Theodore sighed. "I thought you might feel that way," he said placidly, "and to tell you the truth, I'm glad. I was afraid you'd want me to take over. He reached into his shirt pocket and took out a package of Lucky Strikes. "To be honest, I wouldn't want the job if you gave it to me." He tapped out a cigarette. "I have in mind to work for a few more years and then retire. I've joined Oakwood Country Club, and I'm learning to play golf. You don't have to worry about me, but my son may be a different matter." He ground out his cigarette in an ashtray and rose to leave.

"What do you mean?"

"I'm sure he'll want my part of the business," Theodore answered.

"You are an employee, not an owner," Lee said, his face growing red.

"Well, fine. You're the boss. You can straighten him out. "I'll be gone, so that will be your job."

"That's fine," Lee smiled. "Now get the hell out of my office. Oh, and send Miss Evans in."

While he waited, Lee thought about Theodore. He'd always liked his uncle and would be sorry to see him go. But Theodore's twenty-eight-year-old son, Bert, was a different matter. He'd come to work at Lyons after only a year in college. Though his mother had passed away giving birth to him, he'd inherited her quick mind as well as his father's gift for figuring numbers. He could be charming and, though easily riled, a willing employee. But now, he would bear watching.

Virginia Evans had been Lee's secretary for the past ten years. She was an unimposing young woman with a perpetual smile. She seemed to love her job and do it well. "I'm so sorry about Mister Morris," she said. "He'll be sorely missed."

"Thank you. You are very kind, and you're right about that," Lee said, chewing on his cigar. "He'd hate to see us dilly-dallying around."

Miss Evans waited patiently without comment.

Finally, Lee announced, "Well, we'd better get down to business. I need to write a few letters, so later on, make time to take some dictation. First, though, I'd like to speak to our employees. Gather the office help, and then come get me."

Miss Evans nodded. Knowing her boss well, she had already bought donuts and made coffee.

For Lee, the business with Theodore had been a little unsettling. Outside of work, he saw little of Theodore and his family. Anna and Theodore's wife, Hermine, kept in touch because Thanksgiving and Christmas dinners occurred on a regular basis. But Lee still thought of Hermine as Theodore's new wife even though his first wife, Bertha, had died so long ago.

Miss Evans interrupted his thoughts. "They're ready, Mr. Lee."

Biting his lip, Lee thought, God! How I hate these situations. He rose and followed Miss Evans. Eight people, including Theodore, Bert, and Leslie, stood waiting, solemn, heads bowed. Miss Evans had not included the warehousemen. She'd correctly assumed he'd wish to address them later.

Lee stared at the office personnel in silence—Miss Johnson, Miss Evans, Ross from the wool floor, who still came in now and then, and other more recently hired people. He cleared his throat. "I wanted to take a few minutes to thank you."

And then suddenly, he teared up. What was happening? He never cried, hadn't cried, not once, since his father died. And now here. The tears flowed. He struggled not to sob aloud.

Turning away, he pulled his handkerchief from his pocket, wiped his eyes, and loudly blew his nose. "Sorry. This has been a difficult time for us all," he finally managed. "You've kept the place running, for which I am very grateful." He paused and glanced at their faces. Standing in the back by the warehouse door, he recognized a retired employee he hadn't seen for years. "Ira?" he called. "Is that you?"

"Yessir."

"How long has it been?"

"A while, now, Mistah Lee. I'm nearin' ninety."

"My father thought very highly of you. He considered you family, and I do too."

Ira brushed a tear.

"We've all worked hard," Lee said to everyone, "and helped the business grow. My father would want you to know how much he cared about you. To each, I extend my gratitude." He glanced at the table his secretary had prepared. Relieved, he said, "I see Miss Evans has coffee and pastries available. Please help yourselves."

When he returned to his office, Leslie followed him and took a seat. He lit a Camel cigarette he pulled from his shirt pocket. "That was nice, Dad. You said all the right things."

Lee shrugged.

"It feels so strange in here without Grandpa."

"We're all going to miss him. Don't get me started."

"All right. Sorry." Les's expression brightened. "Let me get your opinion about something else. Bert and his wife are going to Fitzpatrick's Saloon on Broadway a week from Saturday night. He's asked Beth and me to come along. Do you think it's too soon after the funeral?"

"No, but have you heard of prohibition? Lee asked.

"Yes, of course, but everybody's doing it."

"Tom Pendergast has seen to that," Lee said. "I knew his brother, Jim. Did I ever tell you about their saloon in the West Bottoms?"

Les's eyes sought the ceiling. "A hundred times," he said, which made his father laugh.

"But I won't go if you think it's too soon after…"

"Go. Go. Just don't get caught." Lee sat up straight and slapped his desk. "Listen. I've been thinking about something. During the war, your grandfather sent me to Washington to bid on wool the government made into uniforms. We got some of that business, but I believe it's a huge, untapped market."

Leslie brightened. "Absolutely. Why haven't I thought of that? I bet some of my Harvard friends could be very helpful."

"Well, think about it, and we'll talk again after things calm down."

In the past few months, Les had been too busy getting married and learning the business to do much carousing, so when Bert suggested a place called Fitzpatrick's, he wanted to go. Flattered that Bert had asked him, Les saw it as fun and an opportunity to get to know his older cousin. Bert was already married with two children. Though they worked in the same office, he and Les had never been close. Bert had different friends and acquaintances, and Beth barely knew Helen, Bert's wife.

Beth bought a sparkly, new mid-calf length dress. The couple met with Helen and Bert outside the saloon. They could hear the band before they opened the painted green door and walked through an underground tunnel into the basement speakeasy. A noisy, crowded room greeted them. Bert hailed Jasper and held up four fingers. The well-dressed host guided them to a table in the smoke-filled room.

The band played so loud it kept conversation to a minimum, but Jasper heard well enough to take their drink orders of bootlegged scotch and bourbon whiskey.

Lights focused on the musicians obscuring the brick walls, the low, tin-tiled ceiling, and the concrete floor, but the improvisational jazz made up for it all. "Do you know who is playing the trumpet?" Les asked his cousin.

Bert laughed. "It's a coronet, and he's good, isn't he? His name is Lamar Wright."

"Marvelous," Leslie cried. "Come on, Beth. Let's dance."

She jumped up, and they hit the dance floor and didn't quit until the band took a break.

When they returned to their table, Bert ordered another round of drinks. Beth whispered something to Helen, who softly announced, "Excuse us, boys. We girls need to freshen up." The women picked up their purses and left.

Three businessmen dressed in rumpled suits and led by Jasper passed by. The fourth, a short, stocky fellow wearing a fedora, glanced toward Bert and nodded as they made their way to an empty table.

"You know those guys?" Leslie asked.

"One of them. Hey, TJ," Bert called out.

"Golly," Les said, impressed. "You know everybody."

"I get around." He gave Les a gentle poke in the ribs and grinned. "Who is he?"

"Name's Tom Pendergast. Nice guy."

"What's he do?"

"He's in the concrete business. Builds roads and bridges. But he also helps feed starving kids. That's how I got to know him. I help hand out the food now and then."

Pendergast left his group and headed up the stairs. "He's got an office here. You want to meet him?" Bert asked.

"Not tonight," Les said, "but another time, perhaps." He reached into his pocket for a cigarette.

Beth and Helen returned. The band came back, and the two couples spent the rest of the evening enjoying each other's company, eating, drinking, and dancing. When they got home, Beth said, "We ought to see more of Bert and Helen. They're a lot of fun."

But too much got in the way of the friendship. Lee kept the boys on the road, drumming up business. Bert covered the farmers in Kansas, Missouri, and Colorado. Leslie went east to cultivate middlemen, associates, and friends he made in college, sons of prominent men who worked in New York and Washington, D.C.

All through the twenties, M. Lyon & Co. grew and prospered. Beth had a baby on June 2, 1924, a boy they named Lee Ripley. The same month, Les's Harvard roommate, Eric Herzl, graduated from medical school in Vienna. He sent a formal invitation and enclosed a handwritten note.

> *Please try and make it. My new wife, Trudi, and I shall show you and Beth a wonderful time. Vienna is hopping.*

Les wrote,

> *Bad timing, I'm afraid. Our first heir just arrived, a boy we named Lee, after my father. Beth joins me in sending hearty congratulations.*

> *Your wedding gift, a silver tea set, is on its way, and we expect to join you in the future for a fine repast.*

But the time never seemed right. In 1926, Eric wrote,

> *Dear Les,*

> *I'm here in Palestine, treating sick Jews who can't afford doctors or medications. Chaim Weismann and Albert Einstein have founded a university at Mt. Scopus outside Jerusalem and asked me to teach there. I'm flattered but dubious.*

> *Remember our discussion about Jewish assimilation? Uncle Theodor Herzl didn't believe in it. Although Trudi and I have integrated into Vienna's social life, assimilation here in Palestine hasn't gone well. I'm hoping someday, Jews and Arabs can live peacefully together, though that's not the case now. Carving out a Jewish State might be the answer, so I've decided to buy a small property in Tel Aviv. I can hear*

you scream NO but don't worry. I can only afford a little. I'll write more about this later.

Eric

Les responded to Eric's letter as Eric predicted he would.

I'm glad you are helping sick Jews and have found a place in Tel Aviv, but don't buy any property in Palestine. It's a poor and infertile land. Just ask the impoverished Arabs who live there.

Teaching sounds interesting, but you should go home and take care of your family and your Austrian practice.

Here in the United States, business is booming, and I'm working hard for my father. Beth and I have a four-year-old son and another baby on the way.

Stay safe, my friend, and best as always,

Les

Coming home one evening, Leslie drove by the Country Club Plaza, J C Nichols property with Negro and Jewish covenants, and beautiful Loose Park. "I think it is time we got a bigger house," Les told his pregnant wife, pointing to a beautiful acre.

"I love this neighborhood," Beth said. "It's close to everything I need—shopping, and schools, and the park. Can we buy it?"

Les agreed and made the arrangements.

Aunt Gertie's doctor husband was playing golf the day Beth went into labor. He rushed to the hospital in time to deliver a healthy baby girl they named Beth Louise after an aunt she might never meet and called her Betty Lou. In June of 1929, Leslie moved his young family from the bungalow on Broadway into a much larger house he had built on the lovely, tree-shaded lot near the Plaza.

"And you should hire help," he told his lovely wife, which she gradually did. When Beth volunteered at the Benjamin Dispensary and the National Council of Jewish Women, she hired a black cook, Neosha, a big, jolly, round woman with a hearty laugh. Les paid her $5 a week with half a day off on Thursdays.

Monica came next, a young, pretty, white girl who became the governess for the children, for which she was paid $6 a week. She slept in baby Betty Lou's room and had Sundays off.

And then came Della, Black, middle-aged, thin, and often unseen as she bustled about cleaning or doing the family laundry in the basement on the modern ringer washing machine.

Les paid Monica more than Neosha because she cared for the children. Yet everyone knew it was Neosha who ran the household help.

But it was Monica who stayed when the horrible thing happened.

On the afternoon of October 29, 1929, Les sat in the small office of the Undersecretary of Commerce in Washington D.C., negotiating the price of Lyon wool. Through the open window, he could hear the rumble of traffic and the construction of the government's new commerce building. "I think half a dollar a pound is reasonable," he said as he lit a cigarette. "It's going for a dollar a pound in Utah."

The paunchy, balding Franklin Oberly leaned back in his leather office chair. "Even a quarter a pound is reasonable, but on today's market, it's unrealistic, what with wool on a downward turn. Now tell me, how much do you have?"

Before Les could answer, a clerk burst through the door. "Sorry to interrupt, sir, but you need to take this call." He picked up the phone on the desk and handed it to his boss.

"Oberly here," the Undersecretary said. "Down forty percent? My God. Keep me informed." He replaced the receiver and turned to Les. "There'll be no deal today, Mr. Lyon. The stocks have slumped, and no one knows where it will end."

With the market crashing, Les wired his father. "What do you want me to do?"

"Catch the first train home," Lee responded.

By the time he arrived two days later, his father, gray with fatigue, had assessed the situation and placed M. Lyon & Co. under firm, steady control. No one could afford a fur coat any longer, so that market went into the ditch. The wool market, already in decline, continued to fall, though, with careful domestic and overseas marketing, there was still money to be made. Hides did better because people still needed shoes, at least those who could afford them. But could M. Lyon and Co. survive the bitter depression?

Both Leslie and his father worked hard, spending long hours at the office. With careful management, they retained their customers and provided them with much-needed services. For four years, the men barely saw their wives or friends, but at last, the business stabilized.

One day, Lee told Les he hadn't seen the Henrys in ages.

"Why not give them a call?" Les asked.

Lee and the Henrys made a date for lunch on the first Wednesday in January 1933, just a quick get-together—beer, a sandwich, and a little time to talk at the Prospect Club. Henry Two called and said, "I need to be back at the bank for a meeting by two. Let's meet at Wolferman's instead." So the date was set.

The major topic of conversation was the crash and the state of the economy and then they turned to the measles epidemic. "Both my grandchildren have it," Two said. "High temperatures and sore throats. Poor kids. They are miserable."

"Leslie tells me it's a dreadful disease," Lee agreed. "I hear a lot of people are dying. Little Lee caught it over the holidays, but so far, I think Betty Lou has escaped." He sipped his beer.

Henry One stared out the window at the low clouds hanging over gray, icy Walnut Street. A chilling drizzle had begun to fall.

"What we all need is a good game of golf," Lee said with a laugh, "though given the weather, I'd like playing gin rummy better."

Henry Two picked up the menu and put on his frameless glasses. "Plenty of golf clubs in town to choose from."

"Not for Jews," Lee said.

"Don't start," Two said. "Let's have a nice, peaceful first-of-the-year luncheon."

Henry One continued to stare out the window and, in a listless voice, said, "I've got other things to worry about."

Two agreed. "With Franklin Roosevelt president, things will pick up. The New Deal will take some time to implement, but it should help the economy recover."

"Too late," One sighed.

"Never too late," Two counseled. "I will never forget. The rush on the bank nearly overwhelmed us. Fortunately, we had enough resources to see us through."

Lee crinkled his eyes as he shook his head. "I don't think my father ever bought a stock or a bond. He didn't trust the market. Too busy selling wool, furs, and hides."

Looking sallow and wan, Henry One muttered. "My father made a fortune in the stock market, but it's all gone now. He died five years ago, so maybe he's the lucky one."

No one spoke. Two picked up the wine list and waved it about. "Let's drink to a brighter future," he said. "What's everyone having?"

The next morning, Lee found *The Journal Post* folded on the breakfast room table. He opened it and saw the headline halfway down.

"Oh my God," he gasped.

Henry Forrester Found Dead.

Henry Forrester of Forrester Grain and Milling Company fell from the top floor of his building last night. A suspected suicide, he is the second Kansas City businessman to die in this manner since the crash of '29. Forrester leaves his

*wife, Madeleine, a son, Gordon, and his fourteen-year-old
daughter, Lillian. Obituary to follow.*

He picked up the phone. "Have you seen the paper?" he asked Henry
Two. "Why didn't he say something?"

"I think he did," the banker moaned, "but I guess we weren't listening."

Chapter Thirty-Three
KANSAS CITY, MISSOURI

1932-1933

By November, the demand for wool and hides began a slow, steady increase. Bad weather kept Bert in town, and he and his wife, Helen, had gone to dinner a time or two with Beth and Leslie.

The week before Thanksgiving, Les was sitting at his desk writing orders when Bert stopped off and said, "I'll be back in an hour."

At that moment, Lee came from his office waving a check in Bert's face. "Did you send a donation to Tom Pendergast from M. Lyon and Company?" he asked.

"Yes," Bert said. "I thought you'd approve. It's to feed starving kids."

"M. Lyon Company's reputation is built on honesty and integrity. We don't do business with crooks."

"It was only a few hundred dollars," Bert said, heading for the door. "Can we talk about this when I get back? I'm late. I'm helping Pendergast at a charity event."

Face turning red, Lee grabbed Bert's arm and barked, "I won't allow it."

Bert pulled away. "Uncle Lee," he said. "You own me twelve hours a day. What I do with my time off shouldn't concern you."

"As a member of this family and its business, what you do reflects on all of us," Lee said, eyes blazing. "Tom Pendergast is a thug."

"Who gives to indigent children," Bert replied.

"With money, he gets through rigged elections won by fraud and manipulation. If you think he's the leader of the Democratic party, you're wrong. He has never been elected."

"That may be, but he provides jobs for thousands of people and puts food in the mouths of the poor."

"Good Lord. Don't you know he's the head of a political machine of pimps and whores, with hundreds of racketeers on his payroll?"

"He's implementing a ten-year plan which will make us the greatest inland city in the country, with things like new sewers and roads and hospitals and even a municipal auditorium."

"Like his Ready-Mix Concrete Company, which pays hundreds of workers to pave a little creek running through the Plaza from which he gets huge kickbacks. All his projects feed his machine and the companies he owns. Smart money knows he stuffs the ballot boxes. Last year, in our city election, he paid hundreds of derelicts to rush from precinct to precinct to cast votes for him and his men at 25 cents a vote. Ask Rabbi Mayerberg, the rabbi at your temple. Ask him about the alcohol, and gambling, and illegal activities in your so-called inland city. Pendergast got his infamous pal, John Lazia, to try and gun down the troublesome rabbi."

Bert turned away. "Tom is handing out Thanksgiving dinners to indigent kids, and I'm going to help."

"Not if you want to work here, you're not. You walk out that door, and you're done."

"Dad!" Leslie cried.

Without another word, Bert turned on his heel and left.

Lee went to his office and slammed the door.

The employees had all gone quiet. Everyone looked at Les.

He took a deep breath and soothingly said, "Okay, folks. Let's get back to work. This will all blow over." He went to speak with his father.

"It's a small matter of a few hundred dollars," he told his dad.

"You don't understand. Our company's reputation is at stake," Lee answered."

That night, Beth fed the children and sent them to bed. "What happened today," she asked. "You seem so upset."

Leslie lit a cigarette. "What started as a question turned into a war," he said as he told her in great detail about the appalling day's event.

When Anna heard what happened, she tried to intercede.

"Stay out of my business," Lee told her.

"We need to talk about this."

"No," Lee responded. "What's done is done."

Nell tried to smooth things over. "Remember Aardvark," she told him, recalling the dictionary she'd brought Lee when his father quit speaking to him. "Surely, you can be more forgiving."

"This is different, and it's not your affair."

"No need to break up the family over something so trivial," Nellie said. "Bert has the right to choose his own friends."

"Not if they're crooks," Lee said.

"He's your brother's son," she reminded him gently.

"Are you taking sides? Lee asked, staring hard.

"Yes, if it means getting you to listen."

"Then you are no longer my sister," Lee said.

On January 5, 1933, Beth's father, Morris Ripley, closed his dry goods establishment early, planning to spend the late afternoon reviewing the accounting books and ledgers. He had managed to keep the store open and semi-profitable since the stock market crashed, but it had been a hard few years. Money was in short supply. Poor and middle-class people held off buying necessary items until the last moment or eschewed their purchases completely. Morris had voted for Franklin Roosevelt, and now, with the President in power for almost four years, he expected business to improve.

Seated at his desk, enjoying his view of the sun's reddish glow on the snow-covered peaks, he felt an unusual throb in his chest. He groaned, rubbed the area around his left nipple, and inhaled deeply. To his relief, the discomfort seemed to disappear. Indigestion, Morris speculated.

He'd probably overindulged at Alfred and Dolly's annual New Year's Eve Party, where he, Rose, and friends had gone to ring in the New Year.

Wiping his brow, he returned to his chores. Without warning, another pain came, fierce and crushing. He gasped, tried to draw a frantic breath, and collapsed across his desk, scattering his paper accounts.

That's where Rose found him. The doctor confirmed Rose's worst suspicions. At fifty-eight, a heart attack had taken her dear Morris.

A doleful telegram brought Beth and Les rushing to Denver on the overnight train. "Oh, Mom," Beth said, encircling Rose in her arms. "How could this happen? Tears trickled down her mother's cheeks, and she wiped them away. Leslie called the rabbi who had married them four years ago and made funeral arrangements.

"I'm so sorry," Rabbi Ishakoff told her and the children, eyes downcast, sotto voce. "I knew Morris only slightly. He didn't come to Temple except on High Holydays, but I assume you will want to sit *shiva*. I can help with that," he said.

Rose sat silently.

"Well then, as to the funeral…"

"At the Temple and not too long," Rose said. "Morris wouldn't want a big to do."

"May I suggest a regular service, an opening prayer, the twenty-third psalm? Words of his life, his accomplishments and of those who mourn him, and a closing prayer."

Rose nodded. "But no Hebrew."

"Except the Sh'ma." The rabbi glanced at Leslie. "Would you want to say a few words?"

"No. I think you'll do fine. And, of course, you'll conduct the service at the cemetery."

"Of course," the rabbi concurred.

"You must come live with us," Beth said after Rose and Morris's friends and visitors stopped coming. Rose declined, knowing two strong women in a household would never work. "I've got plenty to keep me busy. Go home and take care of yourselves and your children," and she stoically saw them off on the next day's train.

After they'd gone, she returned to her empty house. Seated in Morris's chair, at last, anguished tears began to flow. "Oh God," she wailed to the silent walls. "Why did you let this happen?"

Then she went to her desk. There were notes to write and bills to pay. Morris usually deposited money in their joint account on the first of the month. Withdrawing the checkbook, she noted he'd died before transferring the money. The last entry had been on January 5, the day before he died, leaving a balance of ten dollars.

She calmed herself, washed her face, and went for a walk. Over the snow-covered rooftops of the bungalows in her West Highland neighborhood, she saw the Rocky Mountains dressed in winter white gowns reaching into the crystal sky. She breathed deeply, smelled the dry, earthy scent of the Colorado winter, and gathered her courage. She would stay in her house, but at all costs, she determined never to become a burden to her daughter, Beth, and son-in-law, Leslie. The time had come to make a plan.

First, Ripley Dry Goods Store would have to be sold. Though she found a buyer, times were hard, forcing her to sell for less than the store's actual worth. Using the money and the thousand-dollar insurance policy Morris had left, she bought a little bungalow, fixed it up, and rented it out. When that turned out well, she saved enough to buy another and then another.

Over the next few years and with careful planning, she earned enough money to care for herself with a little left over. The time had come to ask for help. Her oldest sister, Frankie Rosenblatt, who worked in a Detroit, Michigan bank, suggested now would be a good time to enter the stock market. Frankie sent names of books for Rose to read and advice for her to consider.

I can't afford to buy stocks, Rose thought. My sister has lost her mind. But she had to admit the idea excited her, and her lust for knowledge sent her to the library. She hung Frankie's advice over her kitchen sink, where she'd be sure to look at it every day:

Don't buy stocks with the money you will need soon.
Read everything you can get your hands on about stocks
and bonds.
Study the market.
Build for the future.
Diversify.
Invest for the long term, 30 or 40 years, and hope for a
10% increase.

During the day, she managed her growing real estate business. She found a handyman to make necessary repairs. Evenings she spent at the library studying. The day finally came when she felt confident enough to begin. Because of her real estate business, she already knew and had confidence in a brokerage firm owned by Grant Adolphus, a man of the highest prestige. She gave ten dollars to the distinguished-looking man with a business-like attitude and told him to buy twenty shares of Standard Oil of New Jersey at $0.51 for every $1.00 of book value and a dividend yield of 4.35%.

"Excellent first investment," Mr. Adolphus agreed. "May I suggest you consider Proctor and Gamble for your next purchase?"

Rose studied the stock market every day and chose her investments with care. Once a month, she'd stopped by Grant Adolphus's desk and buy a blue-chip stock—General Motors, Union Pacific, Gillette. As she grew more confident, she expanded her horizons. Pillsbury, she discovered, traded at $0.27 for every $1.00 of book value with a dividend yield of 10.67%, an 85% drop from its peak in 1929.

Daring to dream big, she could only imagine what her growing stock market account would be worth in thirty or forty years, but this she vowed. She would be financially secure.

Beth looked forward to taking the children to Denver each summer. She loved staying in the old-fashioned West Colfax bungalow and enjoyed being with her mother. Leslie came for a few days in late August. He'd hike with the children over rocky mountain trails, grassy meadows, and beneath aspen-covered peaks. Sometimes, the family picnicked by shallow streams and waded in the sparkling waters surrounded by the lovely, blooming, purple-berried chokecherry trees.

During one summer's visit, Beth charged Lee, then twelve, to care for his eight-year-old sister, Betty Lou. They played with the many children who lived in the old Denver neighborhood from morning till night.

It happened on August 10, 1936. Rose remembered the exact date because it appeared on the newspaper clipping she'd saved. She had gone into town to take care of business. Beth instructed Lee and Betty Lou to stay close to home and went off to the Brown Palace Hotel for lunch with friends. With no reason to hurry home, she went clothes shopping at the upscale Cherry Creek Stores. On her drive home, Beth heard the sound of distant sirens and thought she smelled smoke. Pulling up in front of her house, she saw Mr. Umberson, the cranky old man from next door, staring at his garage. "Damn kids," he croaked.

"What kids?" Beth asked.

"Yours and a bunch of others," the old man wheezed. "I never could catch 'em, and they keep coming back. Now I think they've set my garage on fire."

People had begun to gather. "Did someone call the fire department?" a woman asked.

"Look," a lady in the street said, pointing to a child in the second-story window. A wisp of smoke curled around the lad's head, then circled the contiguous telephone pole and gently made its way toward the azure sky.

Beth shouted, "Lee? Are you in there? Get out of there this minute and bring your sister with you."

A young man burst out of the crowd and ran to the open garage door, but a billowing blaze of flames and smoke drove him backward.

"Lee?" Beth cried.

By now, a crowd had gathered. Acrid odors filled the air. With smoke wafting over their heads, one child and then another clambered out the second-story window and climbed down the telephone pole.

"So that's how them rascals escaped," the old man said. "They been doing this all summer."

"Betty Lou?" Beth yelled.

Lee appeared at the window, flames licking behind him. Beth watched in terror as he helped six children out the window and onto the telephone pole. Then, at last, he and Betty Lou left the burning building. He climbed down, but Betty Lou, her legs too short to reach the indentations, had to slide. Now full of splinters, she bravely limped to her mother as fire devoured what was left of the building.

The clanging white firetruck finally arrived. Beth huddled with her children as she watched the men extinguish the remaining embers. A man in shirtsleeves took pictures. He snapped one of Lee and patted the boy on the head. "Brave lad," the photographer said. "What's his name?"

"Lee Ripley Lyon," Beth said proudly. People clapped as Lee took a bow.

With the fire out, folks drifted away. Poor Betty Lou lay on the bed squirming while Beth and Rose pulled splinters out of her arms and legs. "If you lie still, I'll give you a penny," her Oma Rose said.

"Now tell me, have you been in that building before?" Beth asked her children. She learned they had spent much of their summer in the clubhouse—the second story of the garage.

When the paper arrived the next morning, Lee's picture, and an article—**YOUNG HERO SAVES CHILDREN**—appeared on the front page. Though distraught at the children's behavior, Beth decided Betty Lou had suffered enough. "And how could I punish a hero?" she asked Leslie when he called.

"Don't worry," he said. "I'll take care of it when I get there." Two weeks later, he came for his annual visit, but instead of taking the whole family to the mountains, he took only Lee. He drove his son through the aspens to a low-hanging ridge. As they sat in the car, windows down, in an off-the-road overlook, Les lit a cigarette and said, "Tell me about your summer."

"I played with the neighborhood kids. I got saddled with Betty Lou," he said, sounding irritated, "but we fellas read <u>King of the Royal Mountain</u> comic books."

"In Mr. Umberson's garage," Les stated.

Lee glanced at his father, his expression wary. "Yes."

"You knew you were trespassing," Les said.

"We didn't mean to hurt anything. We lit a campfire on the concrete garage floor."

"And you burned the building down."

"I got everyone out," Lee said.

"By God's grace. In my book, you wouldn't have been there had you not broken the law. That greatly disappoints me.".

Choking back tears, Lee hid his face in his hands. "I'm sorry," he whispered, but Les knew how Lyon men punished their children. He did not speak to Lee for the rest of the day.

Mr. Umberson sued Rose for the loss of his garage. Leslie offered to reimburse the owner. The old fella died two months later, his property sold, and the garage unbuilt. It was the last summer Beth and the children spent with Rose in Denver. After 1935, Lee and Betty Lou went to camp in Wisconsin, away from Kansas City's heat and humidity and deadly outbreaks of crippling polio. Both Nabagamon for boys and Pinemere for girls were owned and run by non-orthodox Chicago Jews.

Chapter Thirty-Four
KANSAS CITY

1933-1937

M. LYON & CO. WOOL, FUR, AND HIDE managed to survive the depression years. With the family relationship permanently shattered, Bert found a willing partner and spitefully opened his own hide business across the street from M. Lyon and called it BERT LYON & CO. FURS – WOOLS – HIDES.

Leslie and Beth still saw Bert and Helen at social functions and at Oakwood, their country club, but they barely spoke, and everyone knew to seat them apart.

Les and Eric tried to make arrangements to visit one another, but their plans never worked out. Nevertheless, they kept corresponding.

Eric wrote,

> *Just a note to let you know I am here in Palestine caring for sick and wounded Jews and non-Jews. Sometimes, I work at Bikur Holim Hospital in Jerusalem. The impoverished Arabs are fighting the British for independence and their long-time enemies, us Jews, for stealing their land.*
>
> *Now, in addition to French, German, and English, I can speak Hebrew and Arabic fairly well.*
>
> *I leave next week for home.*

One Sunday afternoon in May Leslie and Jules Ginsberg, a lawyer like his father, Lester, sat at a gin rummy game table by a window in the Oakwood men's card room. Bert walked by and smiled at Jules but ignored Leslie. He joined three men who sat waiting with two decks of cards and a scorepad.

"What's going on? You and Bert have a fight?" Jules asked as a waitress came to take their order.

Leslie lit a Camel and shrugged. "We should be out there hitting balls instead of cooped up here waiting for our friends to arrive for gin rummy." He gazed out the window at the golf course. Off in the distance, players and caddies traversed the fairways. Vast rolling hills were interspersed with forests of trees and dots of close-cropped circular greens with flapping flags on poles. Without turning his head, he said, "Did you happen to notice Roosevelt's New Deal idea in this morning's *Journal Post?*"

"Which one? Jules said. "They all sound like alphabet soup to me."

Les laughed. "Like the CCC?" he said. "Stands for Civilian Conservation Corps. It looks like the President may have found a way to put young men back to work. They join this government program that pays them $30 a month to work and live in camps in national parks planting trees and building trails and bridges."

"What a waste of valuable manpower."

"Maybe not. They'll spend their time improving the land."

A fresh-faced young girl wearing the club's perky pink dress and white apron outfit brought their lunch orders, Oakwood's chicken and ham Special Club topped with black olives on toothpicks, surrounded by a mound of crispy golden French fries. "Looks good," Jules said as he picked up his sandwich.

"I'm going East tomorrow to meet with my hide broker, and I plan to make a stop in Washington. I've a friend at the Department of Agriculture. The CCC will be up to them."

Jules looked puzzled as he dipped a fry into the catsup. "Why are you interested?"

"I'm wondering what those boys will wear."

Leslie glanced over at his cousin, Bert, and then lowered his voice. "Those guys will come from poor families, no education, no means of support. Not like the crowd we run with. It will put money in their pockets and hopefully mine."

"So?" Jules frowned.

Roosevelt means to give them something to do. The men will need clothes to wear. I'm hoping he'll opt for uniforms made of wool, of course." He paused again, staring out the window at the summery green.

Jules's face lit up. With a peak at Bert, he nodded. "I see," he said. "Clever. Get there first."

"That's my hope."

"While you're in Washington, will you look into something for me?"

"What have you got in mind?"

"I have a client, Gilbert Hirschman, who could use a little help."

"I know Gilbert," Leslie interrupted. "A little bald fellow. Grain business. Right? Kind of stuffy. Still, I like him."

Jules smiled. "He has a friend, Alvin Kirshbaum, who lives in Berlin. Alvin writes that things are getting intolerable for Jews. Many of them have been forced to close their businesses and their stores. Alvin had been restricted from selling his products to non-Jews and has now been forced to quit earning a living altogether."

"Time for him to get out of there," Leslie said.

"The man's worried about his son, Hans. He's quite young. The Nazis have threatened to close the schools and force boys to join a Hitler Youth Organization. Alvin fears for his wife and child and wishes to leave the country, but he's having trouble getting a visa."

"Gilbert's trying to help, of course. He's contacted the American consul General in Stuttgart and sent money. So far, they've had no luck getting visas. Gilbert says thousands of Jews want to leave. With so little information, you have to wonder what's going on over there."

"If I get a chance, I'll look into it next week. I'll let you know." Les shielded his mouth with his hand. "And about the CCC," he whispered, "I'd appreciate it if you don't mention it."

Jules glanced at Bert and, with an understanding look, agreed.

The next morning, on the way to catch his train to New York City, he swung by the store to see his father. "Quick question," he said as he slipped into Lee's office. "How much wool can we get our hands on?"

"Who's it for?"

"The government," Leslie answered.

Lee looked up. "Let me know how much you need."

The train ride to Grand Central Station took all day and overnight. Leslie spent his time reading, eating passable dining car meals, and catching a good night's sleep in his private birth. Arriving in New York well-fed and rested, he disembarked and caught a cab to the Astor Hotel. He got a room, deposited his suitcase, and prepared for his appointment with Hendrick Schreiber at Mendel Schreiber's Wool, Fur, and Hide Brokerage Firm.

A finicky little man with thin, rimless glasses, he and his company acted as buyer and seller for Lyon goods in the United States and overseas. He and Leslie spent most of Tuesday afternoon and Wednesday going over the Lyon accounts and discussing the disposition and pricing of same. Hendrick then took Les to dinner at the Oyster Bar, where they consumed mounds of raw oysters washed down with delicious, ice-cold vodka. Thursday morning, Leslie left the Astor Hotel and caught a train to D.C. Upon arrival, he called his Harvard friend, Clyde Herman, at the Department of Agriculture and Interior. "When are you free?"

"I'm busy all day. Not a moment to spare," Clyde said. "We are all tied up trying to implement the president's new deals and getting people back to work."

"That's what I wanted to talk to you about," Leslie said, "I hear there's a new work conservation program. Maybe they need wool for uniforms."

"I've heard something about that, too, but it's not my department. Talk to Henry Wallace, and good luck with that," Clyde said. "The gentleman loves to travel, so he's hard to pin down. I gotta go now."

Leslie knew the chances of getting an appointment with the Secretary of Agriculture were nil, but he had to give it a try.

The offices hummed with activity. A secretary came from an inner office, her cheeks flushed, a pencil behind her ear. In a high voice, she said, "If you have an appointment, take a seat. Otherwise, come back tomorrow." Leslie found a chair. "If you're here to see Mr. Wallace, you're out of luck. He won't be in the office until next week." The pencil fell from behind her ear and clattered to the floor.

"Where is he?" Leslie asked, retrieving the pencil and handing it to her.

"We're never quite sure," she responded as she slipped back into the inner office, "but I think he's headed for the Midwest." She waved her pencil at him in a gesture of thanks and closed the door. He turned to leave and caught sight of the one person he'd hoped to evade. Bert. Leslie ducked out a side door. He raced down the stairs and hailed a cab. If he had any hope at all, he would need to secure enough wool to provide thousands of uniforms for the CCC. Even though he hadn't talked to Wallace yet, he sent a telegram to his father—BUY AS MUCH WOOL AS POSSIBLE. BIG ORDER IN THE OFFING.

He picked up his belongings and rushed to the station, but the train to Chicago had already left, and there wouldn't be another until later in the afternoon. Perhaps he could catch Wallace there. But when he arrived in Chicago, he found the secretary had moved on to St. Louis. With the weekend approaching, where Wallace would go next was anybody's guess. Maybe Des Moines, his hometown. Not sure, Leslie stepped to the counter and asked the agent for a ticket to Kansas City. "Going to the fair?" the salesman asked.

"Where is it?"

"In Topeka, about an hour from Kansas City."

Leslie pictured the animals, rides, and cotton candy and decided that's exactly where Secretary Wallace would go.

The agent nodded, his face breaking into a big grin. That'll be $5.50 to Kansas City in coach."

Sunday evening, Leslie joined the crowd of young men listening to the secretary tell the wonders of the CCC. Camping, hiking, working in the wilderness. They'd be fed and housed and paid $30 a month to build roads, repair bridges, and care for the national parks. Wallace painted such a glorious picture that Leslie himself found the job tempting. Following the speech, he bought a big paper cup full of lemonade, lit a cigarette, and waited in line to see the secretary. When his turn came, he handed the watery drink to Wallace and said, "I bet you could use this."

The secretary smiled gratefully and took the cup. "Thank you."

"I'm Leslie Lyon of M. Lyon and Company. My father and I can supply the U.S. Government with all the wool it will need for uniforms for the CCC."

Surrounded by boys and men asking questions, Wallace took a thirsty gulp of his lemonade. "Good. I have to make a decision. If you wait, I'd like to speak with you later."

"I'll be by the sheepmen's tent," Leslie said.

He visited with people he knew while waiting and wondered if Wallace would be a no-show. When the secretary finally appeared, Leslie could hardly contain himself. The thought of supplying wool to the government excited him. "I can easily supply the clips of three thousand sheep, enough wool to make ten thousand uniforms," he informed Mr. Wallace.

"Ten thousand?" the secretary cried with a harumph. "That's only the beginning. Did you see all those poor boys who came to hear me tonight? They are only a few of the jobless young men hurt by this cruel depression. The President wants me to put them all back to work. Think in terms of several *hundred* thousand men. Can you supply that much, and all must be grown on American soil?"

Leslie did some quick calculations. "Yes, sir. Lyons can provide all you need. We buy excellent quality wool from all over the Midwest— Kansas, Nebraska, Oklahoma, Iowa, as far west as Utah."

The secretary nodded and offered Les a cigarette. "We'll need pants, coats, caps, and blankets. The price will be negotiable annually for as long as the program lasts. And," he hesitated long enough to light his and Les's cigarettes, "I have to decide by tomorrow morning."

He reached into his pocket and withdrew his card. "I'm spending the night at the Muehlebach Hotel in Kansas City, but I plan on leaving before dawn. I'll need your bid before I go. Attach my card to your bid and leave it at the hotel desk this evening."

Leslie felt sure he could ship more than two hundred and fifty-five thousand pounds of wool from the Midwest alone. He already had a price in his head, but then he spotted his immediate competition, Bert, and his partner walking toward the secretary. The three men spoke, and Leslie saw the secretary nod in his direction. Then he handed Bert his card.

Leslie drove straight to his childhood home. He needed to consult with his dad before submitting his bid.

"How much are we talking about here?" Lee asked when his son arrived.

"Wallace estimates the government will buy over a million pounds of wool over the next few years. Have you bought any yet?"

"I've contacted each of our customers and put them on alert. 18¢ a pound is the going rate." Leslie asked, "Can we do better than that? I think Bert will be our competition, and he'll shave it as close as he can."

"He's a small operation with little capital. He can't go below 17¢ and make any money," Lee said.

"But he's not the only one to beat," Leslie reminded his father.

"Okay. Say 16¢? Let me ask you a question. Are you seeing Wallace in person?"

"I hadn't planned to. He gave me his card and said to leave my bid at the desk."

"That's exactly what your competition will do. I suggest you get up early and go buy the secretary his breakfast. But don't go below 15¢. It's our rock bottom."

Leslie did as he was told and by the end of Monday morning's breakfast, he and Wallace had a deal. M. Lyon & Co. would supply the necessary wool for uniforms to the government's CCC project.

Chapter Thirty-Five
KANSAS CITY

1937 '39

DECEMBER 31, 1937

Les and Beth celebrated with a New Year's Eve party at their house. Beth decorated the house with purple and white balloons and Happy New Year banners printed in gold. During the evening, Les remembered to ask Jules Ginsberg what happened to Gilbert Hirschman's friend, Alvin, in Berlin.

"A sad tale with no end," Jules responded. "First, a three-year wait for passports and visas. The Nazis are causing the Jews to suffer terrible reparations. Many are desperate to get out."

"Really? There's not much in the newspapers, and I hear little about this when I'm in Washington."

"I know, and it's strange," said Jules. "Gilbert finally contacted Harry Truman."

Les groaned. "He's Prendergast's friend. What good can he do?"

"Don't forget he's a senator now, so he may be able to help."

Moving closer to Jules, Les whispered, "From what I hear, there's a quota on Jews."

"That's just it. Truman has a Jewish friend, Eddie Jacobson. They used to own a haberdashery store together. That and Gilbert's prestige may be why he is willing to work on it. He thinks Cuba could be an option."

This discussion left Leslie feeling helpless and depressed. "I wish him luck. If there is anything I can do to help, don't hesitate to ask."

"In the meantime," he brightened, "It's New Year's Eve. We've some celebrating to do." He threw an arm around Jules's neck and steered him to the whiskey-laden eggnog and Neosho's delicious hams, briskets, raw and cooked vegetables. As they filled their plates, Anna came bearing one of her famous chocolate fudge pies topped with mounds of whipped cream. "Save room," Leslie told Jules. "You'll not regret it."

In March of '38, while lunching at Oakwood before their Sunday gin rummy game, Jules Ginsberg asked Leslie if he had ever heard of the American Jewish Committee.

"A little," he answered. "I hear they are antizionists but give aid to Jewish refugees."

"That's right. You said at the New Year's Eve party if there was anything you could do to help, just to ask, so I'm asking. Have you heard what's going on in Germany?"

"It's terrible, but you must admit, it's nothing new. Persecuting Jews has been happening for centuries. Once the Nazis realize they won't be receiving all the wealthy German Jewish money, it will stop, and things will get back to normal harassment."

"I hope you're right. Nevertheless, it's time for you to join us. You know most of the members, and we can use you and your money."

Leslie gave it some thought. "I feel no loyalty to Germany," he finally answered. "They treated my family badly, and my grandfather, bless him, had the courage to leave the old country a long time ago. Hitler and his Nazi party are Jew-hating riffraff. If you can use my money, sign me up."

On November 11, 1938, Leslie went to New York to see his broker, Hendrick Schreiber. On his desk lay a copy of *The New York Times* with a screaming headline.

JEWS ARE ORDERED TO

LEAVE MUNICH

Some Told They Must Get Out

of Germany Despite Fact

They Lack Passports

FINE SHOPS ARE WRECKED

Four Synagogues Set on Fire

in Frankfort on the Main

—Many Jews arrested

"Those damned Nazis," Hendrick sobbed. "They burned and destroyed thousands of Jewish homes, businesses, synagogues, schools, and even cemeteries."

"Thank God my grandfather left when he did," Les said as he read over his broker's shoulder.

During the coming days, he tried to find out more about the events, but they faded from the news. Though Leslie noted stories about the

Nazis murdering Soviet POWS, gypsies, and even people of Slavic descent, few articles singled out Jews. He wrote to Eric Herzl in Vienna.

> *Are you safe, my dear friend? Perhaps you and your wife, Trudi, should come to America. I have friends in Washington who may be able to arrange it.*

On Leslie's next train trip back east, he listened to President Roosevelt on the radio. The President condemned the actions of the Germans, though he didn't mention any names. Many were suffering badly. That, coupled with the investigations of the House Unamerican Activities Committee, gave Leslie confidence the government was paying attention, but he wished Congress would take more action.

He spent the day working with his broker in Hendrick's office, and by five o'clock, numb with numbers, he left and went to his hotel.

First, a drink in the Astor's Palm Garden and then a fine steak dinner at his favorite restaurant, Delmonico's. Tired from his long day conferring with his broker, he sat at the Italian bar, blue lights draped with vines and flowers hanging overhead, lit a cigarette, and ordered a scotch on the rocks. A young woman slipped in beside him. He noted her beauty as slender, blond, and well-outfitted. She smiled and said, "They must be busy tonight. I guess I'm being ignored."

Leslie returned her smile, gave the bartender a shout, and pointed sharply to her.

Sleeves rolled up and green vest buttoned, the barkeep came with an apology. "Sorry, ma'am. What can I get you?"

"What'll you have?" Leslie asked her.

"Please bring me a gin martini with two olives."

"Two olives," Leslie joked. "Is that called a double?"

"It's called dirty," she responded. "I see you're a Scotch man."

"Like my father before me," he responded, "or at least I think he would be if he drank. He's a teetotaler. I'm Leslie, by the way."

When the bartender returned with her drink, she raised it to Leslie. "Hello, kind sir," she said. "I'm Sally."

In late December '38, Jules and Leslie met for their Sunday gin rummy game. "Hear anything interesting in New York lately?" Jules asked.

"My broker is distraught over the German's treatment of Jews. He thinks the U.S. should take on the Nazis, but my friends in Washington don't agree. In fact, I hardly hear it mentioned."

"I'm not surprised. No one wants another war, and no one gives a damn about Jews."

"I hope we stay out of it," Leslie said. "It's not our fight. After all, Jews have been badly treated for centuries. It's one reason my ancestors left and came here. They hoped things would be better."

"There's still plenty of antisemitism floating around. You just don't hear about it as much as we used to."

As the waitress approached, Leslie said, "That reminds me. Have you heard any more about Gilbert's friend in Germany?"

"Yes. Good news and bad. Senator Truman got them visas to Cuba, but the United States still has a Jewish quota and won't let them in."

Lunch arrived, and as they ate, Jules said, "You missed the American Jewish Committee meeting last Thursday night. Some of our members suggested we try to help the Jews get out of Germany. We're looking for host countries, but not many are willing to take us. Great Britain says they will only take a few. Some of the refugees want to emigrate to Palestine."

Leslie shrugged. "Anywhere is probably better than where they are."

"Some Jews think of Palestine as a Jewish homeland. Members of the Jewish Federation are lobbying for an independent State of Israel."

Les held up his hands. "I am firmly against a Jewish State. Judaism is a religion, not a race. But I'm not against Jews immigrating to Palestine. My old college roommate is there." He reached into his pocket and took out an envelope. "I got this letter yesterday. Have a look," and Jules read,

May 1939
Dear Les,

*Trudi and I are in Palestine. The Nazis chased us out
of Vienna in November '38. We escaped to Istanbul and
hitched a ride on a leaky boat to Haifa. There are hundreds
more Jews who need to get out. We've joined the Haganah.
(Hebrew for defense) Your President Roosevelt needs to help.*

Eric

"God," Jules railed. "That's horrible. Your college roommate, you say? What's he do?"

"He's a doctor. Been going to Palestine for years to treat sick and wounded Jews and Arabs. Eric wants to stay in Palestine, but maybe there is something I can do to convince the United States to take more Jewish immigrants."

Les got in touch with his friend, Harvey Cohen, from Harvard. "Do you or your dad know anyone who can help ease restrictions on Jewish quotas?"

"If we did, don't you think we'd have already tried? Why don't you give James McDonald a call? "He's Chairman of Roosevelt's Advisory Committee on Political Refugees. I think you met him when he was a guest lecturer at Harvard on foreign affairs."

On his way to New York, Les stopped off in Washington and rang the office of the Chairman, where he scheduled an appointment for the following afternoon. McDonald, middle-aged, tall, and handsome with once blond hair going gray, greeted Les with a smile. "I remember you. You're the German Jewish kid who doesn't speak German. Have you learned any since we last met?"

Leslie laughed. "I can say, Gesundheit."

"To your health," the Chairman said. "Now, what can I do for you?"

"I understand a ship sailed from Germany with nine hundred Jews aboard, and because of U.S. immigration restrictions, we didn't accept any of them. Is that true?" Les asked.

"I was afraid that's why you came to see me," James McDonald said as he sat and motioned Leslie to a chair. "Congress promised me $10,000 to work with, but I never got any of it. I've talked to a lot of people, but no one is willing to help. I can't even find homes for the refugees already here."

The Chairman poured himself a glass of water from the pitcher on his desk, offered one to Leslie, and then continued, "However, all is not lost. The President appointed me to an advisory board regarding the Jewish situation, and Mrs. Roosevelt agreed to help. I hear she went to a Hadassah affair and denounced the Nazi party. I have it on good authority she has prodded her husband to do more."

"Well, that's good news," Leslie said.

"Don't expect too much. Many members of Congress oppose raising quotas of any kind, most especially on Jews. However, I hear that the House on Unamerican Activities Committee is investigating the Nazis. Sam Dickstein chairs it. He's a New York Jew. You might want to give him a call. A feisty chap, he is known for denouncing Communists and hating the Nazi party. He can be curt but open to discussions. If you have trouble getting in to see him, let me know."

Leslie thanked the Chairman. With high hopes, he made an appointment to see Congressman Dickstein. He then headed over to the Office of Agriculture, where he haggled the price of wool with Secretary Wallace. Following a contentious discussion, they reached an agreement. Les left to find the office of Chairman Dickstein.

"He's in a meeting right now," his secretary said, "but he'll be back soon. He's looking forward to speaking with someone from Kansas."

"Missouri," Les corrected.

"It's all the same to us here," she grinned. "Have a seat."

The wait lasted fifteen minutes, and then the door burst open, and a short, nattily dressed man of middling years came flying through.

"Your next appointment is here, sir," the secretary said, pointing to Les.

The Congressman removed his hat to reveal unruffled, gray-brown hair parted meticulously on the left side. He was small, five feet four or five, and perhaps a hundred and forty pounds. "You the person from Kansas City?" he asked.

"Yes, sir," Leslie answered. "Kansas City, Missouri. My name is Leslie Lyon. I'm a member of the American Jewish Committee in Kansas City. We're hoping you can offer us advice and help us get beleaguered Jews out of Germany."

"To tell the truth, I don't hear much about them. I agreed to see you because I wanted to know what a committee like yours does in a small town like Kansas City."

"We're not so small. There are well over three hundred thousand people in Kansas City at last count, two percent of whom are Jews."

"Still small by Eastern standards." Dickstein motioned him into his inner office. "What can I do for you? I haven't got all day."

"We are searching for ways to help get Jews out of Germany."

"I can tell you this. The Nazis are the most dangerous threat to our democracy that has ever existed. But our government wants to stay on friendly terms with them, so there is not much I can do. No one listens to me."

"Well, sir," Leslie responded. "The AJC wants to do whatever we can to support you. We can raise money and perhaps help get visas and passports to German Jews, but we've been told Congress has imposed strict quotas on Jewish refugees. My mission is to request your assistance."

Dickstein paced his office from closed door to desk piled high with papers. He talked at great length about the importance of Russia's security agency, the NKVD. Glowering with irritation, he finally said, "I absolutely must stay in touch with those people for the sake of United States security, but some of my colleagues think I'm in it for the money."

Feeling his request had missed the mark, Les drew a breath and tried again. "About the quotas," he ventured.

"I have identified one hundred spies who entered this country to spread propaganda about the Nazi regime, but I can tell you this, young man. My success in limiting German spies does not increase Jewish immigrant quotas to our country, though I intend to keep trying."

Leslie thanked the Congressman and ended the meeting, having gained little or nothing. He left Washington the next day and headed for New York to meet with his broker. On the train, he read *The New York Times*. President Roosevelt condemned the actions of the Germans and called Hugh Wilson, his ambassador to Berlin, home for consultation. That and the investigations into Nazi activities by the House on Unamerican Activities led by Congressman Samuel Dickstein gave Leslie slim hope. The government didn't seem to be paying enough attention to the happenings in Europe, but there was little a small businessman like himself could do.

He leaned back in his lounge chair with scotch and soda in hand and thought about Sally. She'd charmed him when they first met, and he saw her occasionally when he was in town. Maybe she could help him take his mind off this whole nasty matter. He'd give her a call.

Sally suggested they meet for drinks at the Astor, and she brought along an interesting friend, a correspondent for *The New York Times*. Fortyish, casually dressed, sharp-eyed, and quick-minded, he had only recently returned from the Soviet Union. Inevitably, the conversation turned to the war.

"I was traveling with the Red Army," the reporter said, "when I heard men talking about a place in the Soviet called Babi Yar. They said tens of thousands of Jews had been murdered there and thrown into a ravine."

"My God," Leslie groaned.

"I heard numerous stories mostly from the Soviets who were deemed unreliable sources," the correspondent continued, "but I figured this was a big enough story I ought to go see for myself. I managed to wangle my way to the northern edge of Kiev and traipse into that gully but saw only weeds and trash. I talked to a few people, but no one said anything about a mass murder." He shrugged. "There are lots of tales like that circulating around. A guy from Switzerland said he heard about Jewish bodies being made into soap."

"That's disgusting," Sally said. "Can we talk about something else?" And their conversation turned to the new show on Broadway called *OKLAHOMA*.

Chapter Thirty-Six
KANSAS CITY

1941-1945

On a warm September evening at the beginning of the school year, Beth, Leslie, and the children sat at the dining room table as Monica served dinner. Hired as the governess but now called the second girl, Monica cleaned, did sundry chores, and waitressed for the evening meal.

"Who won the game today?" Grandpa Lee asked thirteen-year-old Betty Lou, so petite her Wisconsin Jewish summer camp friends called her Peewee.

"We did, of course," she leaped to answer. "Satchel Paige was pitching." Betty Lou loved baseball as much as Grandpa Lee did. As soon as she'd turned eight, he'd begun taking her with him to the games at the Municipal Stadium. At 22nd and Brooklyn, it was in the heart of Negro Town. There, they watched the Monarchs, a team of all Negro players. He'd drive his highly polished '34 green La Salle, park it in his colored friend's driveway, and buy Betty Lou all the popcorn and hotdogs she could eat.

Monica came from the kitchen and placed a standing rib roast before Leslie. As he honed his knife, Beth asked Lee, now seventeen and a high school senior, "Did you have a good day?"

"Yeah."

"That's no way to answer your mother," Les said. "Look at her when you speak and tell her what you did today."

Lee came out of his stupor. "I'm taking English, Latin, speech, and trigonometry with Mr. Unterman. Everyone says he's hard, but I like him."

"Sounds interesting. And you, Betty Lou? "Where do you go this year?"

"I'm a freshman at Southwest and I want to be called Betty."

"Not Betty Lou?"

"No. Just Betty."

"That will take a bit of adjustment," her father said, "but if that's what you want, we'll try."

"I wanted to send her to Sunset Hill," Beth told Grandpa Lee, ignoring the name-change subject, "but Les insists his children attend public school.

"That's because I want them to know all kinds of people, not just rich ones."

"Southwest is fine," Betty said. "It's big, and I don't know a lot of people yet, but I've been invited to join Thalian."

Leslie sliced the juicy red meat and placed a portion on a plate he handed to Beth. She spooned on mashed potatoes and green beans and gave it to Monica. The second girl placed the plate before Grandpa Lee and returned to Beth's side.

"What's a Thalian?" Les asked.

"It's a literary society. There are two better ones, Sappho and Sesame, but they don't take Jews."

Grandpa Lee harumphed.

"Sappho and Sesame. It's Greek to me," Les said, laughing, "which reminds me, Dad. I've been meaning to ask. Did you see where Germany invaded Russia?"

"I read about it in the *Star* and about the ghettoization of hundreds of Polish Jews. Then, I heard conflicting stories on the radio. You don't know what to believe anymore."

Leslie pursed his lips. "There is no such word as ghettoization. You made that up." He and his father frequently argued over the spelling of a word.

"Of course there is. Betty Lou?"

It's Betty, now," she said as she jumped up and ran for the dictionary.

After dinner, Beth called one of her friends. "How does your daughter like Sunset," she asked Hazel.

"It's expensive," Janice answered, "but she's getting a good education. Why? Are you thinking of sending Betty Lou?"

"Maybe. Betty Lou told us that two literary societies at Southwest don't accept Jews. I've never heard of such a thing."

"Oh, Beth. You are so naïve," Janice said. "It's everywhere. Even Sunset Hill only takes two Jewish girls per class. We enrolled Marilyn way back in kindergarten. It's the same for the boys at Pembroke. Surely, you've noticed no Jews belong to the Kansas City Country Club."

"Country clubs have every right to ask who they want. But a public high school? That's different." Beth frowned deeply.

"There are twenty girls in Joan's freshman class. When there's a social event, the Jewish kids aren't invited."

"That must hurt their feelings. Why do you send Joan there?"

"Because they guarantee an excellent education, and she has a better chance of being accepted at Smith or Wellesley or Vassar. Her father and I are thinking of her future."

"But what of now?" Beth said. "It must be so hard."

"We have come up with a partial solution. The girls have put together a Jewish sorority. They've asked Emily to sponsor them."

"Emily Rothschild? But she has no children."

"No, but she's perfect for the job. A lovely woman, beautiful, and socially prominent. She understands the problem. She accepted, saying she thought it would be fun. When he's not at work, her husband Louis volunteers to take in hand the Jewish boys at Pembroke."

"Does Betty Lou know about this?" Beth asked.

Janice laughed. "I'm sure she does. She's *your* daughter, isn't she?"

Beth hung up the phone. She found Betty Lou in the sunroom listening to the ball game with Grandpa Lee, who was losing his hearing.

The radio was so loud Beth could hardly think. "Why didn't you tell me about the new sorority?" she asked loudly.

"I may not join," Betty answered.

"Why not?"

Betty motioned her mother into the quiet of the living room. "Because Dorry Epstein, my best friend at Southwest, wasn't invited."

"I play bridge with Dorry's mother. She's a lovely person. Can't you nominate Dorry?" she suggested.

Betty scowled. "I don't understand the whole Jewish thing. Why do people hate us?"

"Nobody hates you, honey. They just think you're different."

"My two best friends from Bryant, Caroline, and Lelia, got invited to Sappho. They ended up going to Sunset instead. Now they act like I'm invisible."

"Phil Rizzuto just hit a home run," Grandpa Lee yelled from the sunroom.

"Oh my gosh, I gotta go," Betty ran back to the ballgame.

Some weeks later, Beth asked about Dorry.

Betty shrugged.

"Did you do as I suggested?"

Mom," Betty cried. "I'm the youngest member of the sorority. No one listens to me." Tears sprang to her eyes. "It's too late now, anyway. Dorry and I are barely even friends anymore."

"Growing up is hard," Leslie said when Beth told him what happened. He closed their door and made ready for bed. "Betty Lou will figure it out." He chuckled. "I mean Betty," he said as he began to undress.

Beth shook her head and smiled.

"I heard good news and bad news today," he told her. "Which do you want to hear first?"

"Good and no bad."

"All right. First, the good." Les continued to disrobe. "Remember the family Gilbert Hirschman rescued from Germany? They've been in Cuba for the past two years. They finally made it to America, and Gilbert found them a place to live."

"Wonderful. We must invite them over." Beth went to her cherry dresser and began to withdraw a sheer silk nightie from her nightgown drawer.

Les shook his head.

"I'll see to it," Beth said, crawling naked between the sheets.

Though they usually slept in twin beds, Leslie slipped beside her and tenderly enfolded her in his arms. With gentle hands and soft lips, he made love to her while murmuring impassioned words of endearment.

"What's the bad news," she whispered.

"It can wait till tomorrow," he said.

The next morning, Les told Beth he needed to go to New York and would be gone for a few days, a common occurrence. With a sad face, Beth gave him a hug and kissed him goodbye. "Can I come?" Betty begged.

"Maybe next time," her father answered.

Patrick, the milkman, drove into the driveway. Neosha beckoned him in and poured him a cup of her strong coffee. Monica tended to Beth in the breakfast room with tea and freshly squeezed orange juice. The milkman left two bottles of milk in the ice box, the cream rising to the top, and one small bottle of coffee cream. Antonio's vegetable truck arrived. Beth went with Neosha to pick out the makings of the week's meals and plan the menus.

Tonight, Beth anticipated a peaceful dinner. Life was good and perfectly normal—until it wasn't.

Chapter Thirty-Seven
KANSAS CITY

1941-1945

"Where's Pearl Harbor?" Lee asked Eddie Rothman, his Harvard roommate who had just walked in the door.

"Hawaii, I think. Why do you ask?"

"Some guy on the radio announced the Japanese have attacked Pearl Harbor. You think it's a joke?"

"I don't know. Turn up the radio."

They heard the frantic voice of a broadcaster cry, "Japanese aircraft have bombed U.S. ships at Pearl Harbor, and we are hearing reports of attacks on Manilla in the Philippines."

"Sounds real to me," Eddie said.

Harvard students burst from their dorms, running into the yard, questioning each other, some crying in disbelief. Dorm proctors and Harvard officials tried to calm everyone down to no avail.

The next day, at 12:30 p.m., President Roosevelt came on the air. Students and professors crowded around radios to hear their President speak.

"Yesterday, December 7th, 1941, A date that will live in infamy..."

Thirty-three minutes after the President's speech, Congress declared war on Japan, and Lee sent his parent a telegram.

CAMBRIDGE MASS DEC 8, 1941

TONIGHT HISTORICAL - THOUGHT YOU MIGHT LIKE HEAR FROM ME - I'M FINE - NO DANGER HERE BUT CLAIM MIGHT BE A GERMAN DE-STROYER IN THE ATLANTIC - NEW YORK MAY BE BOMBED - EVERYONE EXCITED - MASS MEET-ING TONIGHT - DEAN SAID STAY AT COLLEGE - LETTER FOLLOWS.

LOVE LEE

A week later, he received a letter from his father that included the front page of the *Kansas City Star.* December 11, 1941, **U. S. MEETS WAR CHALLENGE OF ENTIRE AXIS** and a note that said, I agree with the dean. Stay in school. Love, Dad

December 20, 1941

Dear Mom, Dad, Grandpa, and Sis,

Well, we're at war. We all knew it was coming, but we didn't know when. We even thought we were all ready for it. But now that it is here, we don't know how to act and are rather upset.

War is really so incomprehensible. Firstly, it disrupts everyone's plans for the immediate future. Secondly, it kills, eventually, someone who knew someone who you know, and that brings it close to home. And so you realize that the war will change things, and you can't just go on living as you normally would.

The first of these things serves to excite a very personal hatred against the Japs, in this case, or us all, and so does the second. Everyone goes around saying, "Those goddamn dirty bastards of Japs," and that makes it war for sure. Mostly, you feel insulted that a puny island like that can have the nerve to insult our mighty eagle, and second, infuriated because they have succeeded to some extent in crippling us by their lightning-like strike when no one was really expecting it. Even then, it wasn't awfully real until you realized that American cities were blacked out to keep from being hit by Jap bombs, and we say, vengefully, "We'll kill those filthy Japs," and over the radio, they call the episode dastardly, like the villain in the old melodrama, (dastardly is like the radio word for damn rotten)

You read the papers and feel like saving them because they are history, and you are a part of it. And then, eventually, you burst out with such a condemnation of the invaders that you have to back it up with something, so you threaten to enlist. Sometimes, you really do. If so, it is to the tune of the Star Spangled Banner, and hats off. Someday, you fight. Was this why you enlisted? You wanted to kill some Jap, but you haven't even seen any, although you have seen plenty of dead Americans, your former pals.

Nooo! There is no use laboring under any false impressions. War is not glorious. You go because it is not perhaps your duty but your ideal. You are fighting to preserve a thing that you think will perhaps vanish without your aid. Then you say to yourself, "It is worth fighting for." And you think again of the Star-Spangled Banner, and of the Declaration of Independence, and of '76, and of the paintings of Washington, and Lincoln, and of the Bill of Rights, and of the Constitution, and then you can think again, "Is it worth fighting for?"

You're damn right it is.

Love,
Lee

Upon receipt of the letter, pride filled Les's heart.

"He'll make a fine soldier," Grandpa Lee declared, his eyes misting.

"He's only seventeen. He's not old enough to go to war," Beth said, sounding relieved.

"But he'll be eighteen in June," Betty said, eyes flashing.

August 1, 1942
Maxwell Airforce Base

Dear Folks,

We arrived here last night at Maxwell Air Force Base in Montgomery, Ala.

We are billeted at a hotel and were rousted out of our beds for our physicals bright and early this morning. They checked everything, and I do mean everything. The doc said if I plan to be a pilot, I have to lose twenty pounds.

I may starve to death, but I will do it.

Love,
Lee (Please tell Betty to write)

September 3, 1942
Maxwell Airforce Base

Dear Folks,

Sorry I haven't written. No time. They really keep us plenty busy. Last week, they gave each of us a thirty-caliber carbine rifle to take apart and put back together. Now we're learning to shoot, and I'm doing okay. Yesterday, the drill sergeant inspected mine. He found a spot on it and made me run 5 loops (that's a mile each) and do 50 pushups before putting a spit shine on my rifle. Everyone hates him.

Love,
Lee
PS: I've lost 15 pounds

October 12, 1942
Maxwell Airforce Base

Hi All,

Well, I made it out of basic training. I'm in flight school now. We do drills in the morning and spend the rest of the day in class studying mathematics, navigation, and the fundamentals of flight. And Morse code. Ugg!

We're supposed to be able to send and receive six words a minute. So far, all I know is diddy dum dum diddy, which they say is short for SOS.

More later.
Lee

January 23, 1943
Maxwell Airforce Base

Dear Folks,

Our hopes ran high this morning when we lined up to receive fight gear—helmets, goggles, and parachutes. Then we went to the flight line and met our flying instructors. Mine is a sergeant named Flannery. He led me to a two-seater biplane called a Stearman PT-13. The cockpits are open and tandem, one behind the other. He told me to get into the front, and he climbed into the rear. Next thing I knew, we were taxing down the runway and lifting off.

We circled the field a couple of times. Then he tapped me on the shoulder, threw his hands over his head, and pointed to the controls. Questioning, I pointed to me. He nodded. I grabbed the wheel, and suddenly, I was flying. WOW!

Lee

April 1, 1943
Maxwell Airforce Base

Dear Folks,

I flunked out of the Air Force and have been transferred to the artillery to learn how to shoot a cannon like Dad did.

!!!APRIL FOOL!!!

The truth is, I soloed today. I had made my second landing in the Stearman when Flannery unstrapped and got out of the aircraft. "She's all yours," he said. "Take her around a couple of times. "Surprised and a little scared, I nodded and taxied down the runway, gently lifting her nose into the air. I leveled her off at 5,000 feet and felt alone in the world, strangely, wildly free.

Smiling, I watched the world below float by as I made my turns and came in for a landing. That didn't go so well. I misjudged the distance and came down pretty hard. The plane bounced, but I kept a steady hand, and she settled and finally rolled to a stop. "Not bad," Flannery said. "Need to work on those landings."

Well, that's it for today.

Love,
Lee (Tell Betty I got her swell letter. Keep ☒em coming.)

Lee felt like he'd never finish the required sixty-five hours in the trainer, but he finally wrote he'd begun learning to fly B-25s. He didn't write how homesick he was or that sometimes he cried himself to sleep at night, trying to muffle the sound in his skinny pillow. He hoped those close to his bunk didn't know, but if they did, they didn't say anything. Maybe they cried, too.

One night, after lights out, a soldier slipped up to Lee in his top bunk and whispered, "What's the matter? Little Jew baby sad?"

"You son of a bitch," Lee cried, furious. He swiped at his tears as he leaped out of bed and started swinging.

His heckler laughed and backed away. "Little Jew baby's got his dander up."

Outraged, Lee clenched his fists and barreled into his opponent. A real fight ensued. Circled by a screaming bunch of fellow trainees, they went at it. Lee landed a right hook on the agitator's jaw that decked him.

"Are you really a Jew?" a fellow trainee asked.

"Yeah. So what?"

"So nothing. I just never met one before."

Nobody mentioned it again. Lee worked off his weeks' worth of detentions, but he'd found he'd earned a fighter's reputation and didn't cry into his pillow anymore.

Not long after, he went on a Saturday night leave. Even though he didn't drink, he went carousing with his buddies. They got him so drunk he had to be carried back to base. He didn't write home about that. Nor did he write home about a girl who 'put out', which he found enjoyable and educational until he tested positive for the clap and had to take the cure.

Some information was classified—theaters of operation and the planes they'd be flying. He didn't write about guys who washed out of flight school or got injured on takeoffs or landings, but he felt bad when Betty wrote that one of her friend's brothers had died flying his navy Grumman Hellcat into a seawall.

The torturous September Alabama heat had begun to lessen. From the air, yellow tips of corn stalks danced across the fields, and rows of cotton looked like real estates of snow. Only two weeks till graduation. Those who'd made it would get their wings and second lieutenant commissions. Then what?

At the Monday morning briefing following graduation, Lee received a pleasant surprise. He'd been assigned to a flight wing at an airfield near Sedalia, Missouri, for more training, this time on C-47 transport planes. At times, he got weekend leave and, grabbing a couple of his buddies, drove the sixty miles home for good food, good times, and good sleep.

Fifteen-year-old Betty became quite a nuisance. She insisted on accompanying the nineteen and twenty-year-old officers everywhere and taking them to her sorority parties if she could get them to go. She said she loved showing them off. They looked so spiffy in their handsome uniforms, gold bars gleaming, and silver wings shining on their chests.

But it all ended way too soon. Right before Christmas 1943, Lee's flight wing, a large formation of airplanes, received orders.

"Where you going?" Betty asked as he was leaving.

"Bowman Field, Kentucky," he said. "I've never been to Kentucky."

He and his friends received more flight training and did a lot of sitting around. "Just as I'm getting good at poker," he wrote Betty in June, "I've been told to report for orders, but I don't know where."

He soon found out. At the next briefing, he and the others sat together, waiting to receive their assignment. He chewed a hangnail as an anxious hum settled in the room. Finally, he heard his name. "Lyon," an officer called out.

"Here, sir." Lee stood.

"Co-pilot-C-47. Report to Macintyre in the rear."

A first lieutenant rose. Tall, blond, his visor cap placed carefully under his arm, he motioned for Lee to follow. "Glad to meetcha." He donned his hat. "Call me Mac. Guess we'll be seeing a lot of each other for a couple of days."

"Yes, sir. What's next?" Lee nervously asked.

"Get your stuff together. Our flight wing is scheduled to begin takeoffs tomorrow at 6 a.m."

"Where we headed?"

"Newfoundland. I'm told to expect a rocky trip. Storms all the way."

Stephenville Air Base was closed in with heavy, dark clouds and drizzle when they arrived over Newfoundland. Lee's heart beat a little faster when he checked the fuel gauge, "I guess those guys in the tower know we're running low."

"Let's hope so." Mac picked up the mike, pressed the button, and said, "801569 reporting."

"Welcome to beautiful Newfie, flight 801569," came the jolly reply. "Get in line and hold your position. We got a lot of youse guys to bring in."

They made wide circles around the field. Lee tried to stay calm, but his worries rose by the minute. Finally, he couldn't help himself. He said, "We should tell 'em we're getting close to empty."

"They know," Mac answered. "Calm down. We'll be all right."

To Lee's undying relief, they finally got clearance to land, and Mac took her in. He set her down nice and easy. "If the weather stays like this, it's going to be hard getting out," he said as they taxied where the ground crew directed. "Let's get the hell out of this contraption. I'm hungry enough to eat a moose." He unstrapped and headed toward the door.

Lee saw hundreds of aircraft gathered at Stephenville, along with numerous crews to man them. Everyone was waiting for the weather to clear so they could transport the planes to England and other destinations. For days, they sat around playing poker, sleeping, eating, socked in, bored, and antsy.

Finally, one evening, fifty C-47 pilots were called to a briefing. It was evening, and there appeared to be a slight break in the weather. They were given a heading and told to take off. Lee was paired with an older pilot, John Griswold, balding at age twenty-five. As they walked to their plane, Lee said, "Damn, it's freezing."

"Not good flying weather," John croaked and was seized with a fit of coughing.

"Looks like we've got a passenger," Lee said, pointing to a soldier coming toward them. "Do you know him?"

Griswold shook his head.

"Why don't you go find out while I do the preflight," Lee suggested and began the rigorous walk-around routine.

Lee knew that C-47s were often flown without navigators, but that night, a young, red-headed lieutenant named Sullivan came on board. "I'm the one that's supposed to get you where you're going," he said with a grin.

"Where's that?" Griswald asked as he settled in and cranked up the engines.

"The Azores," the young lieutenant said.

"Never heard of them."

"They're near Portugal," Sullivan said.

"How far is it?" Lee asked.

"About 2500 miles."

Griswold nodded to the air marshal, motioning them forward. "Okay, boys. Here we go." With engines roaring, twenty-five C-47s took off through the soupy night on the heading given to them at the briefing.

No long into the flight, Sullivan came forward. "I 'shot' the stars, Lieutenant," he said to Griswold. "It's really murky out there. I only got one crack at it, and I think we're headed in the wrong direction."

Surprise flashed across Griswold's face. "You've got to be mistaken. I'm dead on the heading they gave us."

"Like I say, I only got one shot, but I'm sure it was a good one," the young navigator said.

"Don't you guys usually take three or four 'shoots to verify a heading?" John Griswold asked, coughing up phlegm.

"Yes, but this cloud cover is too thick. I can't get through it."

"Are you sure you're right?" Lee asked.

"Absolutely," came the firm reply.

"I don't know," Griswold wheezed.

"Look, John," Lee said. "This guy's a navigator. I think we have to trust him."

Sullivan turned to head back to his seat. "You guys can argue it out and call me when you want the right heading."

"Wait a minute," Griswold muttered. "Okay, but you better be right." He put the plane on the new heading, and they flew on blind through the thick clouded blackness of night.

At four in the morning, Lee unstrapped, stood, and went to talk to the navigator. "We should be hearing a signal from the radio beacon on the Azores pretty soon, don't you think?"

Sullivan nodded, but as ordered, their radio remained silent.

Lee sat down and re-tightened his seatbelt.

Four-thirty came. Then, a quarter to five. Dawn broke, and still, they heard nothing.

And then, just as they emerged through the clouds, the Azores signaled, and Lee caught sight of their destination.

They landed safely, thanked the navigator, and each man reported for duty. Griswold went to the hospital with pneumonia. Sullivan got sent to England, and Lee wrote home he'd been reassigned, but he couldn't say where.

Later, they heard only three planes made it that fateful night. The rest flew on the incorrect heading until their gas ran out, and they crashed into the sea.

Chapter Thirty-Eight
DINJAN, INDIA

1943-1945

L agens Field on the island of Terceira in the Azores had two 6000-foot runways, one for incoming planes and the other most often used for outgoing aircraft. After a few days' rest, Lee received his assignment. He was to co-pilot a C-47 attached to the Third Combat Cargo Air Transport Command bound for India.

"I thought we were going to the European theater of war," Lee said.

"Nope," the officer said. "Dinjan Airbase in Northern India to fight the Japanese."

"Why India?" Lee asked.

"Roosevelt says China has huge petroleum and iron resources, which Japan wants and needs. They've been fighting for years and have hundreds of thousands of troops in China. Our job is to help China keep the Japs there."

"Huh? Why?"

"Because if the Japanese are busy fighting for oil in China, they won't have as many troops to deploy to the Pacific. Get it?"

"Yeah. I guess," Lee shrugged. "Clever." Lee's thoughts turned back to the problem of getting to Dinjan. "Do we get a map this time?" he asked, only half joking.

"Yes, and another navigator, too," the officer said.

Dinjan in the China, Burma, India Theater of War, known as the CBI, was a big, busy, noisy airbase. An army air force corporal named Yancy took Lee to his quarters. "Luxury at its finest," the corporal told him as he showed Lee to his basha, a tiny bamboo hut with a miserable-looking wood cot. "They tell me the monsoon season is about to begin. That means rain. Lots of it, I hear. We're supposed to put all these bashas on stilts, so be prepared. In the meantime, stow your gear, and I'll show you our nightclub." Yancy grinned.

"God. These living conditions are an abomination," Lee said.

"You got it, sir," the corporal agreed.

A few weeks later, with the monsoon season in full swing, temperatures and humidity soared. Lee wallowed in mud back and forth to work. Everything mildewed. C-rations and drinking water dosed with iodine became routine. Getting into the air was a joy, except when it wasn't.

The roar of aircraft landing and taking off never ceased. Lee flew supplies into Burma's rugged, roadless, low-lying jungles where six to eight hundred thousand Japanese fought poorly equipped, poorly trained Chinese. He felt sorry for the Chinese but prayed he and his crew would get back in one piece.

Overnight, Dinjan-based airmen refueled the planes, maintained them, and loaded the flyable ones with everything from gas to rice, medical equipment, and Kotex. Planes took off early in the A.M. and dropped supplies over steaming narrow jungle valleys flanked by soaring, snow-covered peaks.

Lee was assigned to a "'scarce drop" unit, so-called because few aircraft were made available to fly supplies to Burma. With poor navigational equipment, his wing tried to make it home before dark.

He made his first flight with an experienced pilot a year older than himself, twenty-two-year-old Lieutenant Robby Carter from Bridgeport, Connecticut. He'd been flying the Burma runs for three months.

They flew only a few hundred feet off the ground over a dense jungle of broadleaf mangroves and sprawling vines of Rangoon creepers.

"Makes it harder for the Jap fighter pilots to find us," Carter said. "And unfortunately, they are damn good at their job. There are times we fly so low we feel like we can reach out and touch the leaves of those pretty, white flowering teak trees," he told Lee. "Or maybe get shot by Japanese marksmen on the ground. With a little luck, we'll kick our cargo out and make it home."

"So we can load up and get sent out again," Lee said.

Carter kept his crew's spirits high with chatter and jokes but got serious when they approached the DZ—the drop zone. "Eyes on the ground," he commanded sternly. A silence fell over the "kickers," a sergeant and two corporals whose job was to get the goods out the door.

"There they are," a crew member yelled over the engine's roar.

"Got 'em," the pilot said, making a pass over the small clearing as the men booted food supplies, ammunition, and equipment out of the plane. Making slow, tight turns, Carter steadied the plane and brought it back over the DZ so the kickers could finish the job.

"That's it," the sergeant yelled, coming forward.

"Okay, Lieutenant Lyon," the young commander ordered. "Take her home."

"Who are those people on the ground?" Lee asked, pointing to half-naked men and women gathering goods.

"That's the Chinese army," the pilot said. "Sorry bunch, aren't they? But they're keeping those Japanese busy." He trained his eyes on the surrounding sky. "We were lucky today. No fighter planes found us."

Lee flew copilot for three more missions and then received orders to take one up on his own. He headed to the airstrip, where he collected his kickers, ran a check on his plane, and took off. It was 5:30 a.m.

Those treetop flights made him edgy. Each trip had its own challenges—enemy fire, fighter planes, weather, breakdowns. When the clouds closed in, navigation became difficult. Months of combat rattled his nerves. A respite would have been nice, but in the tea-growing area of the Assam region, there was no place to go. The nightclub Corporal Yancy had mentioned had a canteen where men bought cigarettes and other essentials. They could get a cup of coffee, but there was no place to relax with music or entertainment. Fly the mission, eat, sleep, and wade through months of monsoon mud to the next assignment. There was little time to make good friends.

While on a flight to north Burma, the left engine of Lee's C-47 caught fire. "Probably a lucky shot from a Japanese marksman," he told his crew.

"Maybe we should call in our location," said his nervous crew chief.

"Can't. We're on our own," Lee said calmly. "Radio silence. We'll find a way to get her home. Shut her down," he told his copilot, pointing to the burning engine. "Let's see if we can get some altitude."

Using his good engine, he took her up and trimmed the aircraft. "Okay, everyone. Pray."

With luck and good flying, they reached the Dinjan runway. A tire blew on landing, and they ended up in the ditch, but they'd made it home alive, for which Lee earned the rank of first lieutenant.

That night, he ate C-rations with a couple of guys who flew supplies over the Himalayas. The hump they called it laughingly comparing harrowing tales of barely missed tall peaks due to wind, ice, and blinding snow. "It's a bitch," one fellow said. "We lose a lot of pilots and planes flying over those godforsaken mountains."

One night, as the airmen performed round-the-clock operations, Lee slept fitfully in his basha, placed high on stilts out of the monsoon mud. He woke up shaking with chills and fever. His alarm went off at 4:30. Muscles aching, he crawled off the cot and put his feet into his muddy boots. Then came diarrhea, unrelenting and exhausting. Somehow, he made it through the muck to the airfield but collapsed before reaching his plane. He awoke in a clean bed with a raging headache and a pretty girl leaning over him, her hand on his head. "How you doin', soldier?"

He gasped, gripped with uncontrollable dysentery.

Embarrassed, he closed his eyes and groaned as they cleaned him up and started him on massive doses of quinine. The pretty nurse returned with iodized water, fresh bed linen, and more quinine.

"What's your name," he finally felt well enough to ask.

"Nochie. RN, Lieutenant US Air Force. And I already know yours, Lieutenant Lyon."

"How long have I been here?" he asked.

"A couple of days," she said. "It takes a while to get over malaria, but everyone seems to catch it, even the Japanese."

"I hope they die," Lee said, feeling awful. "I wish I could."

She smiled. "You'll feel better soon."

"Guess I should have taken the Atabrine they gave me when I first arrived, but everyone said not to bother."

"Atabrine is almost as bad as the disease," Nochie said. "Turns your skin a sallow yellow and gives you chills and fever. Almost no one takes it."

After the malaria subsided, Lee and Nochie continued as friends. If they managed to be off duty at the same time, they'd go to the canteen for a cup of coffee. He told her about the times the free-fall packages weighed so much it was a giant test just to get the plane off the ground or the day his cargo shifted due to some careless loader, causing him to almost crash. She wept as she mentioned the boy who died from wounds caused by Japanese fire and the kid who lost both of his legs. But mostly, they exchanged stories of home. She was from Chicago and engaged to be married.

As they sat smoking and drinking coffee one evening at the canteen, an army captain stood and turned up the radio loud. "Quiet! he yelled. "Everyone listen. Something big is happening. Winston Churchill is speaking."

"The German war is, therefore, at an end."

"What did he say? Someone yelled.

"Shut up and listen." The noise simmered down.

"Finally, almost the whole world was combined against the evildoers, who are now prostrate before us. Our gratitude to our splendid Allies..."

"Does this mean the war is over?" Nochie whispered.

"but let us not forget for a moment the toil and efforts that lie ahead. Japan, with all her treachery and greed, remains unsubdued."

"Not for us, I guess," Lee said.

Three months later, they heard atom bombs had been dropped on Hiroshima and Nagasaki. In September '45, the Japanese surrendered. Demobilization quickly began. The Air Force had their own way of doing it. In an awards ceremony right before leaving Dinjan, Lee received a Captain's commission, several air medals, and the Distinguished Flying Cross. Nochie could hardly wait to get back to Chicago and get married. She and Lee hugged and said goodbye.

Hardly able to wait to see his family, he decided it would be fun to surprise them.

It was after eleven at night when the doorbell rang. Startled and wary, Leslie Lyon tied his robe belt around his waist, hid his .38 revolver in his robe pocket, and went to answer the door. "It's Lee," he yelled, thrilled, and wrapped his arms around his son.

Grandpa Lee, in his white cotton nightshirt, rushed to the head of the steps, false teeth still in a glass of water on his bedside table, yelling a toothless version of "Lee's home."

Betty, pajamas flapping, jumped out of bed and ran down the stairs.

Meg grabbed her robe and breathed a deep sigh of relief. Finally, for her family, World War II had come to an end.

Chapter Thirty-Nine
KANSAS CITY

1945-1947

L es and Jules Ginsberg, now the legal counsel for the antizionist Ameri-can Jewish Committee, played golf at Oakwood Country Club on a sunny autumn Sunday. Walking from the sixth golf course green to the seventh lake hole tee, Les tossed his putter into his bag and said, "It's so hard to believe the numbers. The newspapers say the Nazis have murdered hundreds of thousands of Jews."

"My contacts say it's more like millions," Jules said. "What's shock-ing is to learn President Roosevelt was instrumental in forming the United Nations, but then they did nothing to condemn the actions of the Germans."

Standing in the shade of fall-colored red maples and golden elms, Les took his seven iron out of his bag and teed up his ball. Surrounded by drooping redbuds and dogwood, the deep lake, not much bigger than a pond, menaced Oakwood golfers. Landing in it gave them no hope of retrieving their ball.

"To tell the truth, we're all to blame," Les said. "We ignored the situation or weren't paying attention, but I am now." He took a mean cut at his ball.

"Good shot," Jules cheered, stepping onto the tee to take his turn. He watched with satisfaction as his ball flew over the lake and landed safely on the fairway.

The two men walked down the overgrown pathway leading to the lake, swinging their clubs to clear the tangle of vines. Their cleats clicked noisily on the wooden bridge that took them over the creek and onto the fairway. "Have you heard the AJC now supports immigration? Someone needs to deal with all the displaced Jews," Jules said, stepping off the bridge.

"I agree. I joined the American Jewish Committee because they support Jewish immigrants but not a Jewish State."

Jules stared after his friend, nodding heartily.

Les made monthly trips back east as the hide business gathered momentum. He often met with his broker and visited the Department of Agriculture to keep his finger on the pulse of the industry. By September of 1947, Henry Wallace had moved on to another job, and Les's Harvard buddy, Clyde Herman, had been appointed secretary. Divorced and at loose ends, he and his sometimes girlfriend, Vanna, joined Les and Sally for dinner. They made a compatible foursome, nothing serious but good company.

"Since the General Assembly appointed an ad hoc committee to study the Palestine problem, this city is buzzing," Clyde said. "There are so many Zionists in town calling on anyone they think has congressional influence. Even my office is beginning to look like a synagogue."

"That would be something to see," Vanna said. "You don't know what a synagogue looks like."

"Never you mind," Clyde answered. "The Zionists are arm-twisting everybody."

"What do they want?" Les asked.

"They want us to approve a Jewish State of Israel. I hear the committee is trying to divide Palestine—half Jewish, half Arab—and how they do it is anybody's guess. Know what I mean?"

Sally laughed and said, "I have no idea."

"Right now, the Arabs have all the highlands that supply water to Tel Aviv, but it looks like the committee will give Israel the Sea of Galilee and the Red Sea. One of the Zionists, Abraham Goldman, a farmer from upstate New York, dropped off a proposed map yesterday," Clyde said. "He's concerned that the Jews will be forced to take too much untillable land. To tell the truth, what he showed me looked like a checkerboard. Arabs get places where the most Arabs live, and Jews the same, even if they are right next door to each other. It sort of looked like both will have coastal access, though I can't be sure of that. Abe showed me a chunk of great farmland he says is slated for the Jews." Clyde burst out laughing. "That cracks me up," he said, snorting. "Jewish farmers."

Les thought a moment and then said, "Maybe Truman's friend, Eddie Jacobson, can influence the President."

Clyde sipped his drink. "I bet Jacobson's no friend anymore. The Jews are haunting the White House. I hear the Zionists are driving Truman nuts. They and the rest of us Jews have a lot of power. The Dems lost significant Jewish votes in the last election, and the President needs every single one of them to beat Tom Dewey in the upcoming presidential election. Losing the Jewish vote would sink him," Clyde said.

Leslie flew to New York for a meeting with Hendrick Schreiber. It had been a few years since Hendrick pounded his desk with tears in his eyes and asked Les, "What's wrong with you, American Jews? Does your self-absorption and indifference make you blind to the fate of those poor, suffering Jews in Europe?"

Many long discussions followed, but they'd found ways to work together and even become friends.

Light snow fell as Les's airplane took off, and dark clouds appeared outside his first-class window. "I'm afraid we're in for a little weather," the captain announced. "Stay buckled up, everyone. If you need help, the hostesses will assist you."

Les ordered a scotch and soda. He leaned back to enjoy the flight and thought about where to take Sally for dinner.

A copy of today's New York Times, November 29, 1947, sat on top of the glove compartment. The headline caught his eye.

U.N. Partitions Palestine, Allowing for Creation of Israel

Leslie read every word. The assembly voted for the Palestine Partition by a vote of 33 to 13. The article went on to say the Arabs, highly upset, walked out, but the work was hailed as great by Aranha as the session ended. The words began to blur as Les wondered who Aranha was.

Ordinarily, he loved flying, but on this trip, the weather turned turbulent. Upon arrival, he didn't feel well, so he took a cab straight to the Astor Hotel. He'd only had one drink on the plane, so his nausea couldn't be attributed to that.

His room was on the ninth floor, and his condition worsened as the elevator rose in starts and stops. He barely made it to the bathroom in time.

Les removed his suit coat, loosened his tie, kicked off his shoes, and staggered to bed, stomach cramps curling him into a fetal position. When the nausea lessened, he picked up the phone and spoke with the hotel operator. "Is there a doctor in the house?" he stammered.

"We have one nearby," the woman answered. "Shall I send for him, sir?"

"Yes, please. And hurry. Lyon's the name. I'm in room 918." Les hung up. He stripped off his clothes, head throbbing, and fell back on the pillow, eyes closed.

Then, remembering his date, he sat up and called Sally. "It's off for tonight. I'm sick as a dog," he told her. "I've called a doctor."

Her smooth voice calmed him. "I'm so sorry. Let me know what he says. I've picked up tickets to a show, but I'll come by later if you like."

"God, no. I don't want you to catch whatever this is."

"Okay. Feel better soon. We'll get together next time." She made a kissing sound and hung up.

The doctor, a slim man of indeterminate age, finally arrived. He asked Les a few questions and slipped a thermometer under Les's tongue. "Hum. Your temperature is a hundred and one." He placed his stethoscope on Les's chest and listened for a long time. "How long's this been going on?" he asked.

"Just today," Les croaked, coughing.

"I'm not sure what you've got, but I'm seeing a lot of it. There's a new drug called penicillin. Seems to take care of whatever it is. I can give you a shot in the butt. You should feel better in no time." He reached into his bag and withdrew a syringe and a little bottle.

As Les lowered his drawers, the doctor added, "But I think you may have another problem."

"What's that?" Les asked.

"When you get home, you should ask your doctor to take a look at your heart."

"My heart?" Les asked, alarmed. "What's wrong with it?"

"I think I hear something." The doctor pulled off his stethoscope and stuck it in his bag. "Do you smoke?"

Les nodded.

"You should quit. I've got to go. I've a long list of patients to see. I'm leaving you five days' worth of Tamiflu," the doctor said as he placed his stethoscope in his black bag and tossed the syringe and bottle into the wastebasket. "You can pay my bill at the desk."

Les swallowed two of the pills the doctor left, closed his eyes, and slept for the next twenty-four hours.

When he woke, the nausea and headache were gone. He took two more pills, but feeling better, he called Hendrick Schreiber and apologized for missing his appointment. "Any free time today?" Les asked.

"Come around four. First, we talk business, and then we have time for a celebration," he said.

Showered and shaved, Les dressed and went downstairs to the hotel restaurant, where he ordered a chicken sandwich. Promptly at four, a cab dropped him off at Mendel-Schreiber Brokers.

Hendrick didn't keep him waiting. He waved Les into his office and asked, "How you feel? I think mein wife has it, too."

They discussed the disposition of the hundreds of hides Lyon had to offer. "Ya, but I've got a good deal for you," Hendrick answered.

"And what about wool?" Les asked, happy to hear the government was still buying it for uniforms. The hard stuff came next, discussions about quantity, quality, and price, but after a couple of hours, they had the business part worked out.

"Now we go next door and get a drink," Hendrick said. "My Frau is recovering and not eating much, so probably made no dinner."

Seated comfortably at a table in Hogans Bar, Hendrick ordered a martini, but still cautious, Les went with a Coca-Cola. "When I first called, you said something about celebrating," he said.

Eyes sparkling and martini glass raised high, Hendrick said, "Ya. Here's to the United Nations and the new State of Israel." He reached forward and clinked Les's cola glass.

"I've been sick. What have I missed?" Les asked, remembering reading about this on the airplane newspaper.

"The United Nations partitioned Palestine, allowing for the creation of a State of Israel." Hendrick Schreiber straightened his back and leaned forward. "You've heard of David Ben-Gurion," he said.

"Yes. I've read about him in the papers," Les answered.

"He is leading the quest for a Jewish state," Schreiber said. "His real name was Gruen, but he changed it to Ben-Gurion, which in Hebrew means son of a lion cub. Do you know the story of Daniel and the lion's den?"

Les smiled. "My grandfather told me the story when I was only a boy. 'Do as Daniel did. Love God, pray to Him, and He'll take care of you.'"

Hendrick picked up a magazine lying on the bar. He pointed to the picture of a tough, stalwart-looking man of medium build in what looked like an army uniform. "Behold, Ben Gurion," he said, "a young lion fighting for the rights of Jews to live and pray to God in their own country—Israel."

"I've been thinking a lot about that," Leslie said. "I feel desperately sorry for the displaced Jews, but I'm still opposed to Zionism."

Schreiber looked startled. "Surely not. For two thousand years, Jews have wandered the earth with no place to call their own. The Bible says, 'God will bring you to the land your forefathers possessed, and you will take possession of it.' Don't you see? God promised the new country to the Jews.'"

"I read," Les said, "where Congress won't help without the Jews and the Arabs agreeing, and that's not likely to happen. For years, they've been killing each other. Ben Gurion is proposing a large-scale immigration of Jews to Israel. That sounds like Zionism to me." He paused and stared directly into Schreiber's eyes. "I'm Jewish. The United States is my country. My children and 500,000 other Jewish men and women fought and won a war for the right to be called Americans."

Hendrick shook his head. "Maybe you don't understand. Thousands of miserable, hungry Jewish people need a homeland."

"And I want to help all those people, but the word 'homeland' implies a race," Leslie said. "Africa-Black, Palestine-Muslim, Israel-Jew."

Hendrick pounded the bar. "No, no. You've got it all wrong. France-French, Poland-Poles, Canada-Canadians."

"My choice is America-Americans." Les thumped his fist on the bar.

"Israel-Israelis," Hendrick Schreiber countered. "Think about it."

"I shall," Les said, rising.

Chapter Forty
KANSAS CITY

1947-'48

On the plane home, Leslie picked up a *Time* magazine with a story about Oswaldo Aranha. The Brazilian President of the UN General Assembly had been influential in allowing many displaced Jews to obtain visas to Brazil. According to the article, for three days, he'd kept the UN vote at bay until, on November 29, 1947, the Partition Resolution passed, dividing Britian's mandate of Palestine into Arabian and Jewish states. David Ben Gurion and Menachem Begin (and maybe Eric) agreed to the creation of the State of Israel but not till May of 1948.

Arriving back at Municipal Airport in Kansas City, Leslie retrieved his car and drove across Hannibal Bridge. He glanced below at the Missouri River. As a young boy working at the Third and Delaware store, he had waded on those muddy banks, unaware of the dangerous currents. When he caught his daughter, Betty Lou, doing the same thing, he stopped bringing her to work with him.

Miss Evans—though married, he still called her Miss—looked up and smiled when he entered. "How's Dad?" Les asked.

"He's limping a little, but otherwise, fine and dandy. He'll be glad you're back."

Waving from the door, Les went to his office and called Beth on his phone. "I'll be home in time for dinner," he said.

"Good. Something nice has happened," she said. "I can tell you about it later."

"I have time. Tell me now."

"The neighbors next door came to call."

"What did they want?"

"They invited us to a party. Can you imagine? They've never done that before."

"A hopeful sign for Jews," he said, irascibly. "We can talk more about it later. Right now, I need to go say hello to Dad." He hung up the phone and went to his father's office.

After greeting each other, Lee motioned Les to a chair and asked, "So, what's going on in New York?" a copy of the day's newspaper in his hand.

"According to Schreiber, there's talk of a state of Israel."

"I've heard that, and I agree." Lee got up and shut his office door. "I've been reading about the situation in Europe. All those Jews confined to displaced persons camps. David Ben-Gurion is visiting there now. He hopes to find ways to get some of those Jews to Palestine."

"I feel sorry for the Jews in Europe, but Ben-Gurion is a Zionist. He wants a Jewish State."

"Those destitute people need someplace to go," Lee said.

"I believe the United States should take more than a paltry twelve thousand Jews," Les said.

"Are you sure you want that?" Lee asked. "They're not all Germans."

Shocked, Les stared at his father and whispered, "I know."

Lee cut the end off a fresh cigar and lit it. "Truman agrees. It's up to you and your antizionist friends to convince Ben Gurion that Jews and Arabs could live together. So far, it hasn't worked."

Les closed his eyes and slowly nodded. "Yes, you're right. We call it democracy."

Lee cleared his throat. "Speaking of which, have you noticed your Gentile acquaintances being nicer since the end of the war?"

Les nodded again. "We've been backyard friends with the Arnolds for years, but I've never even been in their house nor they in ours. Now, after all these years, Beth tells me they've invited us to a party. I think it's because they feel bad about the holocaust and the Jewish situation."

"Yes," Lee agreed, "but not too bad. My old friend Henry still hasn't invited me to join his country club. What about you?"

Les laughed. "No, but it's nice to make new friends."

"We need to get back to business. I left three big orders on your desk that need your attention."

"Okay," Les said as he got up to leave, "but what I said about Jews. I care most about Germans, but I care for them all. They are Jews and fellow human beings."

"I understand." His father smiled. "Now get the hell out of here."

On the way home that evening, Les mulled over his comment to his father. He worried that poor, Orthodox, Yiddish-speaking Jews of Eastern European descent would have no interest in assimilation. Would they destroy what American Jews had worked for generations to attain—full acceptance by non-Jewish Americans?

Focused on his thoughts, Leslie drove mindlessly south through Penn Valley Park. Surprised, he found himself off the beaten track. He parked near the bronze statue of a horse carrying a handsome bronze native warrior. The Sioux Indian scout shielded his eyes with his hand and stared north toward M. Lyon and Co. and the Missouri River. His people, too, had been shunned and segregated.

Farther on, Les drove by St. Luke's Hospital, where Jewish doctors weren't allowed to practice. Les and others were already raising money for a Jewish hospital where all qualified doctors, Gentiles and Jews, would be welcome.

A few blocks on brought him to the Plaza, a vast array of stores, businesses, and apartments built by the racist, xenophobic developer, Jesse Clyde Nichols. Nichols created a miraculous Spanish-themed village, a place of charm and beauty. Though conceived out of prejudices, the area provided joy and happiness for anyone who lived or shopped there. Many of Leslie's wealthy friends kept their mistresses living conveniently on the Plaza.

Les's heart lightened when he observed the white Raffaello Romanelli's marble statue of a little boy peeing into the mouth of a frog and the carvings of playful children and beautiful women. He smiled remembering the many customers he had taken to Putsches 210, his favorite restaurant, where the waiters knew him by name.

Turning south on Wornall Road, he saw the thirty-foot turret going up on Jack Henry's Men's Furnishing Store. The tower would show off next year's beautiful Plaza Christmas lights.

A few miles on, he drove up his driveway hill and into the garage of his 56th Street and Wornall home. An old bicycle hung on the wall reminding him of Lee, now twenty-three, and at Harvard studying economics.

Lee never spoke of the war, saying only that he'd flown supplies to the Chinese in China. Les understood that the bright, sensitive boy who'd gone off to war had seen and done unspeakable things. He'd come home a tough, serious-minded man. Back at Harvard now, he'd graduate next year and join his father in the family business.

Les pondered the life he'd inherited and the one he'd chosen. Grateful to his ancestors for choosing religious freedom, he nevertheless thought little of being Jewish though he let Beth drag him to High Holiday Services the fall of each year. He knew about Hanukkah, the rededication of the Jewish Temple in Jerusalem, but Lee and Betty would be home from college soon to help decorate the Christmas tree, open presents, and attend parties.

A tiny twitch on his left side made him remember he'd never told Beth what the doctor had said about stopping smoking and his heart. Stubbornly, he refused to believe smoking had anything to do with his heart. All Lyon men smoked.

Full of incongruity, he found himself grateful for each day. Sighing deeply, Leslie got out, walked across the floor, climbed the three wooden steps leading to the kitchen, and opened the door. There, for the first time in many months, he noticed the mezuzah he himself had nailed to the casing. Beth's father had given it to him to keep Beth safe. It had done that and much much more. Leslie touched it gently with his fingers and softly closed the door.

Chapter Forty-One

TEL AVIV

1948

7 APRIL 1948

Dear Les,

Happy graduation. Are you surprised I remember? I took you to the pricey Locke-Ober restaurant in Boston. We reveled in the crystal lighting and nude paintings, stuffed ourselves with elegant French food, and drank outrageously expensive wine. How I miss those carefree days.

I would love for you to come to Palestine to visit us, but not now. Since the United Nations approved creating two states, Jews who love the idea and Arabs who've always hated it have been killing each other. I'm busy trying to save enough lives so that when the time comes, each can occupy its own domain.

Trudi and I have been drafted into the Haganah (Jewish for army). I remember you defending us quota Jews at Harvard, so you know I'm a lover, not a fighter. I teach at the University and work in The Hadassah (which means Myrtle Tree) Rothschild University Hospital at Mt. Scopus (Lookout) outside of Jerusalem (City of Peace.) But the Arabs have blocked the road from Jerusalem, and supplies are running dangerously low. Right now, I am helping to organize a convoy of supplies and personnel to the hospital.

The British are supposed to protect us, but they are doing a lousy job. Their mandate expires on May 14 at Midnight. I'll be glad to see them leave. More on this later.

Eric

1 May 1948

Dear Eric,

Of course, I remember. How could I forget? You didn't have enough money to pay the bill, so I had to do it. Hard to believe we'll be fifty next year. How I'd love to see you. It sounds like this would be a good time for you and Trudi to get out of Palestine and come visit us in America. We could meet in Boston and go to our second most favorite place, the Oyster Bar, since Locke-Ober still serves only men. And this time, I won't mind treating.

The next part of this letter is hard for me to write. You know how I hate being wrong. But the death of 6 million Jews and hundreds of thousands of displaced persons with no place to go has convince me to agree with you. A homeland for Jews, is the right thing to do.

Stay safe, my friend.
Les

May 16, 1948

Dear Leslie,

Though time and distance have failed us, I feel like we've met. Eric has read all your letters to me and told me of your college adventures so I'm writing to tell you about him.

On the morning of April 13, Eric joined a convoy of three buses, three trucks, two ambulances, and a Haganah armored car. Doctors, nurses, and much-needed supplies were headed from their Jerusalem base to Hadassah Hospital on the outskirts of town. The only access is a small, narrow road through the deeply Arab neighborhood of Sheikh-Jarrah.

At 9:45 AM, Arab forces attacked the convoy. The Haganah suffered immediate losses. A road mine blew up their truck. Only one of its soldiers survived. He went for help but was killed before he could contact anyone. For seven hours, bullets and mortars fell on the convoy's trapped personnel who pleaded for aid. Though the British troops were only 200 yards away, they did nothing to help. They were told to let the Jews and the Arabs fight it out.

At 3:30 in the afternoon, the Arabs threw Molotov cocktails at two of the buses, setting them on fire. Those passengers still alive were incinerated. Any who tried to escape was killed by gunfire. The British finally stepped in and negotiated a peace with the Arabs at 7 PM. By then, only 28 Jews survived. 78 men and 23 women were dead or unidentifiable. Eric's body was never found. I prefer to think of him as one of the missing, forever healing this land he'd grown to love.

On May 14, 1948, the British withdrew before Midnight, and David Ben Gurion proclaimed Israel a state. President Truman, bless him, recognized the State of Israel eleven minutes later. Eric's vision came true, though at a terrible cost to us all.

Someday, you and Beth must come and visit. I will be in Tel Aviv waiting to show you Eric's dream.

Love,
Trudi

THE END

ACKNOWLEDGEMENTS

Eight years ago, my cousin, Senior United States District Judge Howard Sachs, and I had a conversation about our family history that sparked the writer in me. Based on true facts, *The Lyons Den*, which follows the lives of my immediate family, begins in 1847 with the birth of Morris Lion. I'm told burial sites for Lions can be found as far back as 1541 but that was too big a project for me. I've used my imagination to fill in the parts I could not verify.

Andy Barnett, who liked "the business" but wasn't in line to own it, got me started by piquing my interest in M. Lyon & Co. My father, Leslie, passed away, and my brother, Lee, and his son, Mike, who helped me with details, sold the company and became well-known artists. Covid was upon us, so travel and libraries were out. The prospects of research didn't look good, but I learned how to use the internet.

So many kind and generous people have helped me. Thanks first to Howard Sachs. He's been an invaluable resource. Also relatives Larry Burgheimer and Jonathon Lyon. Thanks to my son, Tom, a history buff, who encouraged me onward, and daughter, Lynn, who read every word more than once and helped with many revisions. Kudos to my patient husband who emboldened me before his untimely death, and Deborah Shouse, bless her, who struggled through most of my first attempts. Thanks to my writer's groups, the Homers and especially Sally Jadlow, and the Sedulous Writing Group, including Theresa Hupp, Jack Kline, Pemela Eglinski, Katie Arnett, Dane Zeller, excellent writers all, who have been critiquing my work every week or two for the past twelve years.

I'd be remiss if I didn't mention my bridge bunch who understood I could only play one day a week, friends who waited until after five to call, and grands and great-grandchildren who wondered if I'd ever finish this project.

Well, yes! I'm done. It has been a great adventure. My hope is that generations to come will know a little bit more about their ancestors and are able to separate truth from bits of fiction.

ABOUT THE AUTHOR

Beth Lyon Barnett (Betty), an award winning author, was born in Kansas City, Missouri. Her family lived just beyond the Plaza and Loose Park on 56h Street and Wornall Road. After graduating from Mills College, Oakland, CA., she returned to Kansas City where she was privy to all the rights and wrongs of her hometown. Beth married her high school sweetheart and together they raised their family. Beth became an X-ray technologist at Menorah Hospital and then a sales rep with CGR Medical Corporation, a division of Thomson CSF specializing in electronics. Back problems ended her career but allowed her to do what she'd always wanted to do—write. First came *Jazz Town*, a Thorp Menn semi-finalist, about prohibition and a little boy who became a famous band leader, then *Adams Needle*, set on a farm in the Missouri Ozarks where good and evil reside, followed by *Hitchhiker*, a Godly story of a girl with a serious disease, and finally, *This Borrowed Land*, a wild tale of oil wells and conservation.

Writing *The Lyons Den* has required years of research, but it has been a blast. Read all Beth's books on the Kindle, buy on Amazon or order at bookstores wherever available and visit her blog, http://www. BethLyonBarnett.com